"The always terrific Anne Gracie outdoes herself with *Bride by Mistake* . . . [with] great characters, a high-tension relationship, and a wonderfully satisfying ending. Not to be missed!"

—*New York Times* bestselling author Mary Jo Putney

"A fascinating twist on the girl-in-disguise plot . . . With its wildly romantic last chapter, this novel is a great antidote to the end of the summer."

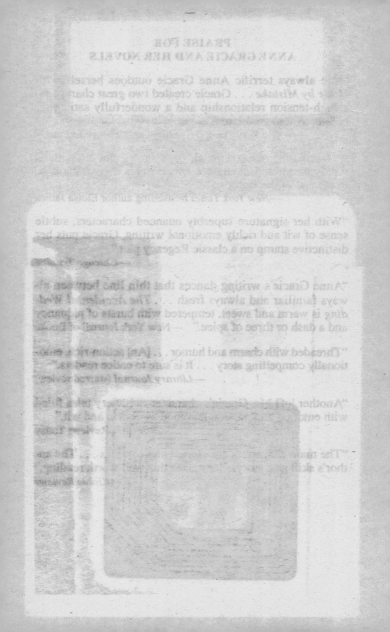

Marry
in
Scandal

ANNE GRACIE

JOVE
New York

A JOVE BOOK
Published by Berkley
An imprint of Penguin Random House LLC
375 Hudson Street, New York, New York 10014

Copyright © 2018 by Anne Gracie
Penguin Random House supports copyright. Copyright fuels creativity, encourages
diverse voices, promotes free speech, and creates a vibrant culture. Thank you for buying
an authorized edition of this book and for complying with copyright laws by not
reproducing, scanning, or distributing any part of it in any form without permission.
You are supporting writers and allowing Penguin Random House to continue to
publish books for every reader.

A JOVE BOOK and BERKLEY are registered trademarks and the B colophon
is a trademark of Penguin Random House LLC.

ISBN: 9780425283820

First Edition: April 2018

Printed in the United States of America
1   3   5   7   9   10   8   6   4   2

Cover design © Sarah Oberrender
Cover art © Judy York
Book design by Kristin del Rosario

*To all those doing battle with reading disabilities,
including the many I've taught over the years
in adult literacy classes.
Bet you never thought you'd have
a book dedicated to you, did you?*

Prologue

> "I can never be important to any one."
> "What is to prevent you?"
> "Everything—my situation—my foolishness
> and awkwardness."
> —JANE AUSTEN, *MANSFIELD PARK*

Ashendon Court, Oxfordshire, 1811

"WHAT DO YOU MEAN, THE CHILD IS UNTEACHABLE?" LILY Rutherford's father, Lord Ashendon, narrowed his cold gray eyes at the governess standing stiffly before him. He spoke quietly, but that silky tone was the prelude to a temper his children had learned to fear.

Lily stood by her father's desk, her back straight, her head high, biting down hard on her quivering lower lip. Showing fear in front of Papa was fatal. Rutherfords feared nothing.

Her sister, Rose, was the fearless kind of Rutherford— she waited just beyond the door, listening illicitly. Rose was supposed to be upstairs in the schoolroom, doing her lessons, but she'd whispered, "Don't worry, Lily, I'll protect you," when the summons came.

Miss Glass, the governess, stood quite calmly before Papa. She'd given her notice after just two weeks, weeks that for Lily had been almost worse than those when Mama was dying. A week of tests and tears and punishment. Then more tests. And more punishments. And more tears.

"I will not waste my time on a child who cannot even read. I have standards. And I won't take responsibility for this child's failure to learn."

Papa snorted. "Of course she can read. She's what, ten, isn't she?"

Eleven, nearly twelve, Lily thought, but she wasn't about to contradict him. Nobody contradicted Papa, especially when his temper was roused. Her hands were shaking. She hid them in the folds of her black dress. Black for mourning, black for Mama.

"My late wife taught both the girls. She never mentioned any problem with Lily."

Miss Glass gave a slight shrug. "I cannot help that. Lady Rose is well enough, skilled in all the ladylike arts, though she has a tendency to be careless with her embroidery and—"

Thump! Papa slammed a fist on his desk. "I don't care about embroidery, and we're not discussing Rose! It's Lily we're talking about."

"Lady Lily is illiterate." Miss Glass enunciated every syllable, almost with relish. *Il-lit-er-ate.* She'd made Lily copy it out a hundred times. Along with words like *ig-nor-ant*, *un-ed-u-cat-ed* and *un-lett-ered.*

Lily's insides shriveled.

All this time, Mama and Lily and Rose had kept her shameful inability a secret, hidden from Papa. But Mama was dead, and this tall, terrifying governess had come to take her place, this woman with her lists and tests, and her pale goatish eyes and the whippy little cane that she used on slow pupils—on Lily—the better to learn her lessons.

And now this, in front of Papa. A different kind of flaying, exposing Lily to her father, like a scientific specimen Lily had seen in a display once. Exposed, defenseless, mortified.

"Are you saying she is lazy?"

"She is obedient enough and strives to please, but she is unteachable. She cannot read, she cannot do simple sums, and she consistently mixes up her left from her right. As I said, Lady Lily is illiterate and nothing I have tried has made any difference."

"Illiterate? Nonsense! Come here, Lily!" Papa pulled Lily to him. He seized a book from his desk and opened it at random. "Read that." He waited.

Lily stared hard at the page, a lump lodged thick in her throat, searching for even one word she recognized. But as always, the letters seemed to slide under her gaze, like worms trying to rebury themselves.

"Well?" His impatience grated against her nerves.

She tried to swallow the lump and stared harder. But all that came was a single slow tear.

Papa, frowning, seized a pen and wrote something. "Read that, then."

Lily was shaking all over now. Tears blurred her vision, and she could barely see the word he had written. It was short, but still . . .

"C. A. T.—Cat!" her father yelled. "Read it!"

"Cat," Lily whispered. Her stomach was in knots. She thought she might throw up.

"And what's this?" He wrote something else, the letters bold and black and fierce-looking. "Read it, come on. It's not difficult, for God's sake! It's three blasted letters! *Three!*" Tears slid down Lily's cheeks.

"Stop it! Leave her alone!" Rose burst into the room.

"Stay out of this, Rose." His voice was mild. Rose was Papa's favorite.

"No, you're upsetting her."

"I'm upsetting her? She's damned well upsetting me. My own daughter—a Rutherford—unable to read the simplest words!"

"Lily tries the best she can. She can read a little, but standing over her and yelling only upsets her and makes it worse."

There was a long silence. "So it's true, then. Your sister cannot read. At ten years of age."

"She's nearly twelve," Rose said quietly. She put her arm around Lily. "You mustn't blame her. She tries so hard to learn, she's always tried."

There was a long silence. "Your mother knew about this and kept it from me?"

Rose nodded. "Mama said it wasn't Lily's fault. That it was God's plan for Lily."

"To make her *an imbecile*?"

"She's not an imbecile," Rose flashed. "Lily's not stupid, she just can't read."

"Is it her eyes?" He looked at Miss Glass. "Perhaps she needs spectacles."

"I've tested her sight," the governess said crisply. "She can see perfectly well. She just cannot read. Or do simple arithmetic, or tell her left from her right."

Slowly, deliberately, Papa pushed Lily away. He wasn't rough, but she felt a coldness coming from him. "A Rutherford, unable to read." He looked at Lily as if he'd never seen her before, as if she were no part of him. "Unteachable."

There was a long silence, then Papa said, "Take her upstairs, Rose."

Rose and Lily left, but Rose left the door slightly ajar. "Shh," she whispered. "I want to hear what they say."

They pressed themselves as close to the door as they dared. There was some low-voiced conversation that Lily didn't catch and then she heard Papa say, "I assumed she was normal. She can ride like a demon . . ."

They heard the clink of glass as he poured himself a drink. "What do I do with the girl now? No man will want a wife who can't read."

"Don't worry, you can live with me when I'm married," Rose whispered. Lily gave her a troubled look. She loved Rose, but . . .

"There are discreet institutions . . ." Miss Glass murmured.

Lily shivered. She didn't know what a *discreet institution* was, but it sounded horrid. She loved her home. She didn't want to be sent anywhere. They waited breathlessly for Papa's response.

"No," Papa said heavily. "I couldn't do that to her. She might be an embarrassment to the family but she's a good enough little soul."

An embarrassment to the family? Lily's throat closed.

Papa spoke again. "Now that their mother's gone, someone must take them on. I don't have time for children, let alone girls."

"No self-respecting governess would bother with a child

like that," Miss Glass said. "A good school might take her—illiterate or not, an earl's daughter would add luster to their reputation."

"What would be the point of that?"

"She might not be teachable, but they can train her to be a lady, at least."

There was another long silence as Papa considered that. "An excellent solution. I'll put them both in a school—I believe there are several in Bath, where my younger sister lives. She's a spinster and can keep an eye on them."

Lily's stomach cramped. They were both going to be sent away? Rose too? Because Lily couldn't read?

They heard the rustle of stiff bombazine as Miss Glass stood up. "If that is all, I'll take my leave of you now, my lord. I have my own arrangements to make."

The two girls hurried upstairs.

"I'm so sorry, Rose," Lily began as soon as they were out of earshot.

"Don't be," Rose said fiercely. "I'd rather be with you at some horrid school than stay here without you. Papa is a selfish pig. No time for girls indeed!"

"It's not you, it's me." Lily swallowed and forced the words out. "I don't think Papa loves me anymore."

Rose put her arms around her. "I'm sure deep down he does, darling. It was just a surprise to him, that's all. Papa likes to imagine that all Rutherfords are perfect."

But Lily knew better. The way Papa had looked at her, as if she was a, a *thing* . . .

As they entered the bedchamber she and Rose shared, her gaze flew to her bride-doll, Arabella, sitting on her bed. Arabella had funny eyes—she'd been dropped once and a piece of her carved wooden eye had broken. Mama had painted the eye in again but it hadn't quite worked. Arabella always looked a bit cross, but Lily loved her anyway.

An embarrassment to the family. No man will want a wife who can't read.

Half blinded by tears, Lily pulled off the elaborate, lacy dress Mama had made for Arabella, the little veil ringed with tiny beads to look like pearls. The veil ripped as she tugged it off. She threw the clothes on the floor and dumped Arabella naked on the shelf near the window. She was just a doll, a collection of cloth and painted wood, a stupid make-believe *thing*.

Lily and Rose went to bed early that night. Rose had tried to comfort Lily, but Lily was not to be comforted. Everything was horrid; they were going to be sent away from home, and it was all her fault.

She didn't sleep. Papa's words kept churning in her head, over and over.

A gleam of moonlight sliced through a gap in the curtains. The clock in the hall chimed two. Lily slipped out of bed. She picked Arabella up and carefully dressed her again.

She smoothed the doll's carved and painted hair. "Don't worry, Arabella," she whispered. "We *will* get married. Papa is wrong. Someone will love us, even if we're not perfect. I promise."

Chapter One

❧

Ah! there is nothing like staying at home
for real comfort.
—JANE AUSTEN, *EMMA*

London, 1818

"I HAVE SECURED A DUKE FOR THE OPERA TONIGHT," Agatha, Lady Salter announced with an air of triumph. Bone thin and immensely elegant, her steely silvery hair intricately coiled, piled high and bound into a kind of turban, she fingered her lorgnette with long fingers and eyed her three nieces with a critical gaze.

Lily Rutherford, Lady Salter's youngest niece, swallowed. She sat with her sister, Rose, on the *chaise longue* facing the old lady. George, technically a great-niece rather than a niece, lounged casually on the armrest of a nearby chair.

"Do dukes sing?" Rose idly twirled her fan. "I had no idea."

"Don't be facetious, Rose," Aunt Agatha snapped. "You know very well why I have arranged this opportunity—it's for you in particular." She added, "As well, he is bringing two friends, one of whom—"

She broke off, her eyes narrowed. Lily tensed as the old lady raised her lorgnette. It was a warm day and Lily's thighs were sticking together, but she didn't dare move. Aunt Agatha despised fidgeting.

But her gaze came to rest meaningfully on George, who

gave the elderly dowager a bland smile in return and stayed where she was, one leg swinging in an unladylike manner.

"George*iana*! Are you wearing *breeches* under that habit?"

George shrugged, entirely unrepentant. "We're just back from our morning ride."

The old lady closed her eyes in a heaven-help-me expression, muttered something under her breath, took a deep breath and continued, "As I said, the duke is bringing two of his friends, and one of them *might* be interested in you, Georgiana—though *not* if you sit like that! Or wear breeches. No gentleman of taste—"

"And one of them might be interested in Lily." Rose smiled warmly at her sister.

Aunt Agatha glanced at Lily. "Perhaps," she said dismissively. She raised her lorgnette and raked it critically over the person of her youngest niece.

Lily, knowing what was coming, sucked in her stomach and held her breath. But it did no good.

"I see you have failed to follow my advice about the diet that was so effective for Lord Byron, Lily. You're as fat as ever."

"Lily *isn't* fat," Rose flashed angrily. "She's lovely and rounded and cuddly. But not fat!"

"And besides, she *did* try that dreadful diet," George said. "For two whole weeks and it made her quite sick for no result. Potatoes drenched in vinegar? Ghastly."

"A small sacrifice for the sake of beauty," Aunt Agatha said with all the complacence of a woman who had never had to diet in her life.

"Lily is beautiful as she is." Rose squeezed her sister's hand comfortingly. "We *all* think so."

Aunt Agatha snorted.

"Better to be sweet-natured and cuddly than a nasty, well-dressed skeleton." George gave a meaningful glance at Aunt Agatha.

Lily tried not to squirm. She hated this, hated people quarreling over her, hated it when Aunt Agatha examined her through her horrid lorgnette—as she did every time she visited. Under that cold, merciless gaze, Lily always felt like a worm—a fat, unattractive, stupid worm. And she couldn't bear another evening of it.

"I'm sorry but I can't come to the opera tonight," she found herself saying. "I have a—a previous engagement."

There was a short, shocked silence. Rose and George blinked and tried to conceal their surprise.

Aunt Agatha's gaze, her eyes horribly enlarged through the lens of her weapon of choice, bored into Lily. "*What* did you say, gel?"

Lily swallowed but held her ground. "I said, I have a prior engagement." She pressed her lips together. She was hopeless at arguing; she always gave in eventually, so it was better to say nothing.

Aunt Agatha gripped her carved ebony stick in a bony grasp and stamped it on the floor. The floor being covered by a thick Turkish rug, the effect was rather lost. "Did you not understand me, you stupid gel? A duke and two of his friends have agreed to join our party at the opera. A *duke*! *And* two other eligible gentlemen. And you say you *can't come*? What nonsense! Of course you will come!"

Lily eased her fingers out of her sister's grasp. Now her hands were sweaty, as well as her thighs. She wiped them surreptitiously on her skirt and said with as much dignity as she could muster, "I was under the impression you had issued an invitation, Aunt Agatha, not an order."

Beside her, Rose gasped. It was usually Rose or George who answered Aunt Agatha back. Lily was supposed to be the meek, biddable one. But she wasn't going to be bullied, not this time. Aunt Agatha didn't really want her company tonight—she just hated being crossed.

In any case, Lily wasn't very fond of opera—she had no ear for music, she didn't understand it and she had a tendency to fall asleep. And the kind of men that Aunt Agatha always found to accompany them were, frankly, terrifying— cynical, world-weary and too sophisticated for words.

Aunt Agatha's mouth tightened. "Do you have *any* idea what it took to get this duke to agree to join myself and you three gels at the opera tonight? *And* to bring two of his Very Eligible Friends for you and Georgiana."

George, who loved music but hated being called Georgiana, said, "Blackmailed his mother, I suppose." If Lily hadn't been so tense, she might have smiled. It was probably true. Half the ton was terrified of Aunt Agatha; the other half was merely nervous. But dear George was frightened of nothing and nobody, certainly not Aunt Agatha.

Aunt Agatha stiffened and directed the Lorgnette of Doom at her great-niece. *"I beg your pardon!"*

"Apology accepted," George said provocatively and with mock innocence. "Isn't that what you usually do? Blackmail or bully them into doing what you want?" Apparently oblivious of Aunt Agatha's swelling outrage, George strolled over to the mantelpiece, lifted a posy of violets and inhaled the fragrance. "Gorgeous. Don't you adore violets? So small but so sweet. They used to grow wild at Willowbank Farm." Her old home.

Lily envied George's cool assurance. Despite her refusal to buckle under Aunt Agatha's insistence, Lily was shaking in her shoes. And trying desperately not to show it.

"How clever of you to secure a duke, Aunt Agatha," Rose said quickly. "Which duke would that be?" Oil over troubled waters. Not Rose's usual approach.

Aunt Agatha shot a last vitriolic glance at George and another at Lily, before turning to Rose. "At least *one* of you appreciates the trouble I go to, to ensure you gels make suitable marriages. The nobleman who will join us in my box tonight is . . . the Duke of Everingham." She waited as if expecting applause.

Lily said nothing. She'd never heard of the Duke of Everingham, but she knew what he would be like. Since the start of the season Aunt Agatha had been throwing eligible gentlemen at all three girls, and not one of them had looked twice at Lily. Not that Lily wanted them to.

Aunt Agatha had a taste for sophisticated, jaded, rakish gentlemen who invariably looked bored and uttered the kind of witticisms that always had some hidden meaning, a meaning that everyone except Lily seemed to get. She always felt hopelessly out of her depth with Aunt Agatha's "eligible gentlemen," and she was sure this duke and his friends would be just the same.

He was, of course, intended for Rose, the eldest of the three of them and the most beautiful. Aunt Agatha was determined that Rose, at least, would become a duchess. Whether Rose wanted it or not. Rose herself was indifferent to marriage and planned to put it off as long as she could. Not that Aunt Agatha knew that.

Lily didn't reply, George twirled the violets under her nose, inhaling the perfume with a blissful expression, so it was left to Rose, who had no ambition to become a duchess, to make a vaguely appreciative sound.

Aunt Agatha, irritated by their lack of understanding, explained, "Everybody is *desperate* for Everingham to attend their balls and routs. A hostess is *in alt* if he so much as condescends to accept an invitation—and even then there's no guarantee he will turn up. But his mother—to whom I am godmother, Georgiana, a woman who *values* my advice—has promised faithfully that he *will* come to the opera tonight, *and* join us in my box, *and* bring a couple of friends."

"How very delightful," Rose said brightly. "I do so admire a man who does what his mother tells him." There was a muffled snort from George, and Rose hastily added, "What a shame Lily has a prior engagement. But you set such store on correct behavior, Aunt Agatha, you would surely not wish her to renege on an invitation she has already accepted."

The old lady's lips thinned. Her expression showed that she thought nothing of the sort. In her view the opportunity of a duke trumped everything, and good manners depended wholly on the situation.

She directed a basilisk gaze at Lily. "What is this engagement you set so much store on keeping?"

"I'm going to a party with Emm and Cal."

Aunt Agatha's thinly plucked brows rose. "The Mainwaring rout?" She gave a contemptuous snort. "An insipid gathering of mediocre nobodies."

"Emm and Cal are going too," Lily pointed out. The Earl and Countess of Ashendon, her brother and his wife, were hardly nobodies, and as for being mediocre, well, Cal was magnificent—a war hero. And Emm was a darling—a darling who could parry Aunt Agatha's horrid stabs without turning a hair. Unfortunately Emm and Cal had gone out for a walk before Aunt Agatha had descended on them.

"Your brother and sister-in-law felt obligated to accept the invitation," Aunt Agatha corrected her. "Sir George was your brother's commanding officer at one time. But given Emmaline's interesting condition, they would have been able to make a token appearance and leave early. However if you attend, Emmaline will be *obliged* to stay longer." Her tone suggested that by staying late, the succession of the Earls of Ashendon would be endangered. And if Emm lost The Heir, Aunt Agatha would know whom to blame.

"I don't mind if we leave early."

Aunt Agatha sniffed. "Your sister and Georgiana, frivolous as they are, understand a golden opportunity when it is offered to them. *They* had no difficulty in writing to Lady Mainwaring to make their apologies for this evening. Why can you not do the same?" Her lip curled. "Apart from the obvious."

"That's not fair—" Rose began hotly.

Before another argument about her deficiencies could begin, Lily said, "Because I promised someone I'd meet her there. A girl I knew at school." Rose gave her a curious look, which Lily avoided. "She's new to London and I said I'd introduce her to some of our friends. I don't want to let her down."

It wasn't exactly true. She hadn't made a promise, but when Sylvia had asked whether she was going to the Mainwaring rout, she'd said she was. As an excuse to avoid an evening suffering the slings and arrows of Aunt Agatha's company, it would do.

Aunt Agatha's brow arched higher. "You would dismiss a *duke* and his friends for the sake of *some gel you knew at school*? Pfft! Who is this gel, and who are her people?"

"Nobody of any significance. You won't have heard of

her." Lily shot Rose a warning glance, a silent plea for her to say nothing.

Rose frowned but remained silent.

Aunt Agatha sniffed. "Why does that not surprise me? You have no ambition, do you, gel?"

"Not much," Lily admitted. "I just want to be happy."

"Pshaw! I suppose by that you mean you want to fall in love! Tawdry, sentimental middle-class nonsense! When will you gels *learn*? Marriage is for position, advantage and land." The old lady got to her feet. "Since you're determined to waste the opportunities I make for you, Lily, I wash my hands of you. Rose, Georgiana, my carriage will collect you at seven."

"WELL DONE, LILY. YOU WERE VERY BRAVE, STANDING UP to Aunt Agatha like that," Rose said as the girls trooped upstairs.

"Positively heroic," George agreed. "I thought the old tartar would burst when you said that about it being an invitation, not an order."

Lily gave a shaky laugh. "I was terrified."

"You didn't look it. You did well, young 'un." George opened the door to her bedchamber. "Hello, my darling boy. Were you waiting for me?" She ruffled the ears of Finn, the great shaggy wolfhound who'd bounded out to meet them.

"Young 'un?" Lily said in mock indignation. "You're only eleven days older than me."

George grinned. "And therefore I'm older and wiser. Aren't I, Finn? Yes, so much older and wiser." Finn squirmed with delight, his tail madly scything the air.

"Ah, but I'm your aunt. And *you*, therefore, owe *me* respect." Lily gave George a playful smack as she passed. She'd stood up to Aunt Agatha, and not only had she survived—she'd won. She bounced onto the bed.

Rose tugged on the bellpull. She'd arranged for tea and buns to be brought up after Aunt Agatha had left, and that was the signal. She sat on the bed, curled her legs around and said, "So, who is this school friend for whose sake you braved Death-by-Lorgnette?"

Lily grimaced. "It wasn't really about her," she admitted. "She was just an excuse. The truth is, I couldn't bear to spend another evening out with Aunt Agatha. The way she looks at me . . ."

Rose leaned forward and gave her a hug. "I know. It's horrid. Just ignore the old witch—you're not fat, you're curvy. Aunt Agatha is one of the thin Rutherfords! George and I take after her—physically, George, not in any other way, I'm glad to say—whereas you're like darling Aunt Dottie."

"Who never married," Lily reminded her. "Whereas Aunt Agatha married three times."

"I know. It's a mystery."

George snorted. "Yes, but all three of Aunt Agatha's husbands died on her—which I think is perfectly understandable. What else could you do once you found yourself married to a vitriolic dragon?"

They all laughed. "But why would they marry her in the first place?" Lily wondered.

"Probably too terrified to refuse."

There was a knock at the door, and George went to answer it. A maid brought in a tray with a pot of tea, three cups and a plate containing six iced fruit buns and two thin, dry wafers. George poured the tea, handed the cups around and placed the plate of buns on the bed between the two sisters. She took a bun and bit into it with a blissful expression.

Lily tried not to notice. She pushed the plate away and sipped her tea, no milk, no sugar. There were wafers if she wanted anything. She was ravenous, but the memory of Aunt Agatha's lorgnette stiffened her resolve.

Rose made an exasperated sound. "Oh, will you stop worrying about your shape, Lily. You're gorgeous the way you are. It won't make any difference to finding a husband, and starving yourself will only make you miserable!" She shoved the plate back. "Besides, as heiresses, none of us will have any difficulty finding a husband. We could be cross-eyed, snaggletoothed and hunchbacked and we'd *still* find men who'd marry us."

"Yes, for our money," Lily responded. "I don't want that sort of husband."

"I know, but we're not exactly hags," Rose continued. "Each one of us is perfectly adorable"—George snorted and Rose poked her tongue out at her—"so there's no hurry. We can take our time and choose from a delightful array of men."

"Not me," George said. "I never had a penny to spare before this year, and now I'm rich, why would I want to hand over my money to some man who can do what he likes with it—and me? Go back to being dependent on a man's sense of honor? No, thank you."

"Not all men are like your father," Lily said softly.

George shook her head. "Dogs and horses are much nicer and more trustworthy. I'd rather find a nice place in the country and live happily ever after with my money and my dogs. Like the Duchess of York, only with horses as well."

"Poor thing, such a shame she never had any children. I'm sure that's why she has all those dogs. Don't you want children, George?" Lily asked.

Lily herself wanted very much to marry. She wasn't ambitious, she didn't care about titles and she wasn't interested in the kind of sophisticated and intimidating gentlemen Aunt Agatha kept pushing at them. Lily just wanted to fall in love with a nice, comfortable gentleman, and be loved in return. And to have children.

George considered it. "I don't know. I've never had anything much to do with children. I'm probably better with puppies and foals." She picked up another bun and bit into it. Lily's stomach rumbled. She sipped her black, sugarless tea.

"So who is this school friend you're meeting at the Mainwaring party?" Rose asked.

Lily's stomach suddenly felt even more hollow. "Sylvia Gorrie."

Rose frowned. "Who's Sylvia Gorrie? I don't remember any Sylvia Gorrie from school."

"Gorrie is her married name. She used to be Sylvia Banty." Lily waited for the explosion. She wasn't disappointed.

"Sylvia Banty?" Rose stared. "That bitch?" She turned to George. "She was caught stealing—and from girls she had the gall to call her friends. She even stole Mama's locket from Lily—all Lily had of her!" She snorted. "I never liked Sylvia. Butter wouldn't melt in her mouth, the sneaky little cow!"

"That's a bit unfair, isn't it?" George said.

Rose blinked in surprise. "Do you know Sylvia too?"

George shook her head. "Never met her in my life. But I like cows. Lovely, gentle creatures. Beautiful eyes. Calling this Sylvia person a cow—or even a bitch, for that matter—isn't fair on cows. Or bitches. Dogs are some of my favorite people."

"Very well, call her a miserable little cockroach, then." Rose turned back to her sister. "Why on earth would you want to associate with Sylvia Ba—what's her name now? Gorrie?"

Lily nodded. "I ran into her at the park the other day and she apologized for the way she'd behaved. She told me she'd been very unhappy at school. So were we, at first, remember, Rose?"

"Yes, but we didn't steal from our friends."

Lily shrugged. "We've all done things when we were young that we later regret. And it was four years ago—a lot of water has passed under the bridge since then. We're older and wiser now—or we should be. She told me that after she left school—"

"She didn't *leave*, she was *expelled*."

"Yes, she left in disgrace, and because of it she never had a season. Her parents forced a hasty marriage on her, to a much older man when she was only sixteen. From what she's let slip, he's rather a cold and unkind person and she's very unhappy. She seemed very sincere, Rose, and very apologetic about the past. She's lonely and she doesn't know very many people in London. So I said I'd introduce her around a bit. Where's the harm in that?"

Rose shook her head. "You're too soft for your own good. She's a nasty little thief!"

Lily didn't agree. "People can change. Everyone should

have a chance to live down the mistakes of their past. Besides, the things she took were small and unimportant—she didn't know how precious Mama's locket was to me. She shouldn't be punished for it for the rest of her life."

Rose regarded her sister a moment, then sighed and turned to George. "Very well. Give my apologies to Aunt Agatha, George, and tell her—"

"What? What are you doing?" Lily asked.

"Going with you, of course. You don't think I'd leave you to face a deadly dull party *and* the dreary Sylvia Gorrie alone, do you? She might pinch your pearls while you're not looking."

"You're being ridiculous," Lily said firmly. "I don't need you or anyone to hold my hand. If anything, you need me to keep *you* from getting into mischief."

Rose laughed. "True enough. It's going to be a tedious night with Aunt Agatha and her duke. I might have to do something desperate—shoot a duke, perhaps. But seriously, Lily, are you sure you'll be all right on your own?"

Lily hugged her. "Perfectly sure. And I won't be on my own, I'll be with Emm and Cal and a hundred other people."

"I know. It's just . . ."

"It's just that you're my big sister and you've looked after me all my life. But I'm all grown up now."

"You're only eighteen."

"George is only eighteen too."

"Yes, but George has looked after herself all her life."

"Then perhaps it's time someone looked after George for a change," Lily said softly. "Now, stop worrying. I'll be perfectly all right. If anything, I should be worrying about you."

"Me?"

Lily laughed. "I know that look. You're up to mischief. You don't like opera any more than I do. So what is it? Are you meeting a man?"

"Yes, a duke. Have you forgotten Aunt Agatha's triumph already?"

"You know what I mean." In all the illicit adventures they'd had in Bath, Rose was the instigator, Lily the moderator. Rose was easily bored, and the restrictions of society life made her restless.

Rose's eyes danced. "What if I am?" She handed the last bun to Lily.

Lily looked down at the bun in her hand, soft, squidgy and delicious. She should put it back on the plate. Lemon icing. "Just be careful, Rose. We're not in Bath now, you know."

"And I thank God for it every day. Although I do miss dear Aunt Dottie."

"Me too." Lily tried not to inhale the rich, sweet, yeasty fragrance. She had to resist. Finn was eyeing the bun with the mournful air of a dog who hadn't been fed in weeks. "But you never know, you might even like this duke or one of his friends."

"Oh, I'm sure." Rose rolled her eyes. "How many dreary old dukes has Aunt Agatha thrown at me so far? I can't imagine where she digs them up from. I didn't know there were so many unmarried dukes in the country."

"I suspect she had the last one exhumed," George said.

Rose laughed. "Exactly. And if he isn't stodgy and ancient, he'll be the kind of bachelor that has a string of beautiful mistresses. He'll want a respectable young bride to bear him an heir, but he won't change his habits at all. He'll continue to keep a mistress or two, but expect his wife to be like Caesar's—beyond reproach."

"Men are horrid," George agreed.

"Cal doesn't have a mistress," Lily pointed out. Not all men were horrid, surely. She picked a little bit of icing off her bun.

"It's different for Cal," Rose said. "He and Emm are in love. Oh, for heaven's sake, Lily, stop drooling and eat that bun. Consider it breakfast." She picked up the wafers and tossed them to Finn, who gulped them down in two bites.

WHERE WAS SYLVIA? LILY SCANNED THE CROWDED BALLroom for the dozenth time. After braving Aunt Agatha's displeasure—well, it was as much for her own sake as for

Sylvia's—it looked as though Sylvia wasn't coming after all.

"Would you care for this dance, Lady Lily?" Mr. Frome, a pleasant middle-aged gentleman, bowed before her.

Lily glanced at Emm, who nodded her permission. As Mr. Frome led her onto the dance floor, she reflected that Sylvia or no, she was having a much nicer time than she would have had at the opera. She'd danced every dance, and although her partners were mostly older gentlemen, they were attentive and charmingly flirtatious, paying her extravagant compliments and telling her how pretty she looked—not that any of them were the slightest bit serious, but it was fun all the same.

Much better than sitting under the eye of a dragon and having to try to make conversation with dukes and their friends. How was Rose getting on, she wondered. George would have no interest in dukes—the opera was all about the music for her.

But Rose . . . Maybe Lily should have gone to the opera, instead of being selfish. Her sister was like a cork in a bottle, ready to pop unless she was able to escape the prim and proper social round from time to time. This assignation of Rose's . . . Lily hoped it wasn't anything foolish.

"Lily?"

Lily turned. "Oh, Sylvia, there you are. I'd almost given you up."

Sylvia grimaced. "I'm so sorry, Lily dear. It's my husband. He doesn't approve of frivolous social pursuits. I had to wait until he fell asleep."

"Oh, but . . ." Lily's gaze drifted to the smartly dressed young gentleman who stood at Sylvia's side.

Sylvia laughed. "Oh, good heavens, this isn't my husband. This is my cousin, Victor Nixon, who's visiting London from his home in Paris. Victor, this is my dear friend from school, Lily—oh, no, I must call you by your correct title now, must I not? We're schoolgirls no longer." Sylvia tittered girlishly. "Lady Lily Rutherford."

Mr. Nixon bowed low over Lily's hand. "Delighted to make your acquaintance, Lady Lily."

"Victor was kind enough to escort me here," Sylvia said. "My husband rarely ventures out. He's a complete stick in the mud. Now"—her gaze ran around the room—"who do we have here? I see the former Miss Westwood is here, playing the duenna, no doubt—she was a teacher at Miss Mallard's school," she explained to her cousin. "She married Lady Lily's half brother and has done very well for herself. From poor, plain spinster to Countess of Ashendon."

"Emm isn't plain—" Lily began indignantly, but Sylvia swept on.

"Oh, and there's the former Sally Destry, dancing with her husband, Lord Maldon. Who would have believed that such a spotty little creature would grow up to marry a handsome young lord? And is that—yes, it is—Jenny Ferris, as was! Heavens, hasn't she grown frightfully fat?"

"She's just had a baby," Lily murmured.

Sylvia snorted. "She's as big as a barn! You should recommend your dressmaker to her, Lily—I mean Lady Lily. That dress you're wearing is quite slimming."

Mr. Nixon glanced down at Lily. "I rather like a few extra curves in a woman," he murmured, his gaze delving down her neckline.

Lily felt herself flushing.

Sylvia laughed. "Behave yourself, cousin." She smiled at Lily. "I'm afraid Victor is a terrible flirt."

"I thought you said you knew nobody in London," Lily said. "You seem to know quite a few people after all."

Sylvia sobered. "Did I sound awful? I expect I did. Sorry, I'm just . . . frustrated. The former Mallard's girls in London have refused to recognize me. Just because I left school under something of a cloud, none of them can forget it." She linked her arm through Lily's. "You're the only one generous enough to overlook my youthful folly." She glanced around the room. "I suppose it's too much to expect Rose to be friendly. She slapped me once, over absolutely nothing."

"Rose does have a temper, but—"

"I don't see Rose here. I hope she's not indisposed."

"No, she's at the opera with our aunt."

"Damnation," Mr. Nixon exclaimed suddenly. "I've left something important in my carriage. If you ladies will excuse me, I'll go and fetch it."

"Bring us a drink when you come back, will you, Victor," Sylvia said. "It's horridly stuffy in here with all these candles burning, not to mention the hot and sweaty bodies."

"Will do." He hurried away.

He was back in ten minutes, bearing a couple of glasses of fruit punch. Lily drank hers thirstily. Mr. Nixon whispered something in Sylvia's ear. She frowned and glanced at Lily. "Are you sure?" she asked in a low voice.

He nodded.

"Tell her, then."

They both turned to Lily. "When I went outside," Mr. Nixon said, "there was a shabby young boy trying to gain admittance to the house. Of course, the butler refused him, but I happened to hear the boy say he had an urgent message for Lady Lily Rutherford."

"Urgent? For me?"

Mr. Nixon nodded. "I hope you don't mind, but I took the liberty—slipped him a shilling and promised him I'd deliver the message." He produced a folded scrap of paper. "He said it was an urgent message from your sister—Rose, is it?"

"Yes, Rose," Lily said distractedly. A note. Urgent from Rose. Oh, she'd *known* Rose was going to do something dreadful tonight. What on earth had happened? With shaking fingers she opened the note, and stared blankly at the contents. As usual the letters seemed to shift before her very eyes. She took a deep breath—it was always worse when anyone was watching; she felt so self-conscious and stupid—but this was Rose, and important so she had to make it out, she just had to. She stared harder, willing the words to become legible.

Sylvia and her cousin pressed closer. "Well?" said the cousin.

Lily swallowed, anxiety for Rose battling with shame. She had no idea what the note said. She glanced around, looking for Emm or Cal.

"Oh, for heaven's sake, how stupid!" Sylvia exclaimed.

Lily flinched, but before Sylvia could loudly reveal Lily's dreadful flaw to all around them, she said, "I forgot for a moment—Lady Lily can't read a word without her spectacles. Here, give it to me." With a wink at Lily, she plucked the note from Lily's nerveless grasp and quickly scanned the contents of the note.

Lily held her breath.

"It's from Rose. She says she's in trouble and needs your assistance. She's waiting in a carriage outside the house and says you're to go to her immediately."

"Of course," Lily said. She was feeling a little dizzy. "I'll just let Emm and Cal know." She scanned the room, but she couldn't see Cal or Emm anywhere.

Sylvia placed a hesitant hand on Lily's arm and said in a discreet tone, "Far be it from me to interfere, but she sent the note to *you*, Lily, not your brother or his wife. It sounds to me as if Rose doesn't want them to know."

"Oh, of course," Lily said, flustered. It would be just like Rose to do something reckless and try to hide it from Cal especially. Whatever had she done? Rose could be so hot-headed at times.

"I saw a golden-haired young lady sitting alone in a carriage outside," Mr. Nixon said. "Quite a beauty. Would that be your sister?"

"Yes, yes, it would." Lily bit her lip. Rose leaving the opera on her own didn't surprise her in the least. Her sister had always been a rule unto herself. She scanned the room anxiously. "But I must tell—"

"In the absence of your brother, I would be happy to escort you outside." Mr. Nixon offered his arm.

Sylvia nodded. "Go and see what Rose wants, and if you need your brother or his wife, you can come back in and fetch them. It'll only take a minute."

Lily hesitated. She shouldn't go outside with him, she knew. But he was Sylvia's cousin, not really a stranger. And her sister needed her.

Mr. Nixon proffered his arm again. Lily gave one last agonized look around the ballroom and nodded. "All right." She took his arm.

"Do you have a cloak?" Mr. Nixon said as they neared the exit.

"What?" Lily gave him a distracted glance.

"It's cold outside and your sister was shivering. I'll fetch it for you." He hurried toward the cloakroom.

Lily rushed out of the house and down the front steps. She stopped dead. In the street stood a long line of waiting carriages. Which one was Rose in? She hesitated and found herself swaying a little. The dizziness was getting worse. She should have eaten something at supper.

"Here." Mr. Nixon dropped her cloak over her bare shoulders. She shivered. He was right. It was cold outside. "Your sister's carriage is along here. Come." He led her around the corner, to where a lone carriage waited.

He opened the door. The interior was dark and gloomy. "Rose?" Lily peered inside. A shadowy figure was huddled in the far corner of the coach. "Is that you, Rose? Whatever is the matt—" Without warning she was pushed hard from behind. She fell half into the coach and before she knew it, her legs were seized and she was shoved bodily onto the floor of the coach.

Lily tried to scream but someone grabbed her chin in a rough grasp and stuffed a rag into her mouth. It almost choked her. A heavy cloth was bundled over her head. Someone caught her flailing arms and bound her tight. She couldn't see or move. A pair of heavy feet pressed her to the floor.

"Go!" Mr. Nixon shouted. With a jerk, the carriage moved off, its wheels rattling over the cobblestones.

Chapter Two

❧

There is nothing lost, that may be found, if sought.
—EDMUND SPENSER, *THE FAERIE QUEENE*

"YOU LOOK AS SICK AS A DOG," CAL TOLD HIS WIFE.

"Such a charming way with words you have," Emm said, smiling despite the nausea that had suddenly swamped her. Her current condition made her extra sensitive to smells, and the close atmosphere of the room, combined with the clashing scents of burning candle wax, strong perfumes and overheated bodies made her distinctly queasy.

Cal slid an arm around her. "Even pale green and drooping you're beautiful. But you need to be in bed, so we're leaving." He glanced around the room. "Where's Lily?" He frowned. "Wait here and I'll go and find her."

He settled Emm in a chair with a glass of water at hand and asked the Countess of Maldon, one of Emm's former students, to keep her company.

He looked in every room in the house, even sending a female acquaintance into the ladies' withdrawing room to look for Lily, but there was no sign of her.

"Maybe Sylvia will know," Emm suggested when he returned with no news. "I think she was talking with Lily before we stepped outside."

"Sylvia?"

"That woman over there. Help me up." Cal helped her to rise, and together they approached Sylvia.

"Oh, yes, she and I were talking," Sylvia said vaguely

after the initial pleasantries were concluded, "but that was some time ago. She received a note, a message from her sister, I think."

"From Rose?" Emm frowned. "What kind of message?"

Sylvia gave her a troubled look. "I couldn't say. But she did look a bit worried." She looked around uncertainly. "She might have stepped outside for a moment. It's quite stuffy in here, I'm sure you'll agree."

"Could she have gone into the garden?" Emm exchanged glances with Cal.

"I'll check," he said, and strode from the room.

"I must congratulate you on your marriage, Lady Ashendon," Sylvia said. "It seems such an age since we were all at Miss Mallard's. I see several of your former pupils are here. Little Sally Destry—a countess now! And you, now a member of the peerage, as well. Marriage changes things, doesn't it? It certainly changed my life."

But Emm wasn't listening. She was watching the exit to the garden. In a few minutes Cal appeared in the doorway and shook his head.

"Sylvia, are you sure she went into the garden?"

Sylvia looked surprised at the question. "No, I didn't see where she went. She was talking to my cousin, and frankly, I felt a little *de trop*, if you know what I mean."

"Your cousin?" Cal asked.

"Yes, Mr. Victor Nixon. He's visiting from France. He and Lily were flirting, so I thought I'd be tactful and was edging away, planning to take myself off, you understand. But then she got the message and she and Victor were talking about it, but I confess, I wasn't taking much notice. I'd seen someone I wanted to talk to, and well, this room is so stuffy and crowded, it's almost impossible to keep track of anyone, isn't it?"

"Where's your cousin now?" Cal snapped.

Sylvia shrugged. "In one of the card rooms, I expect. That's where he usually ends up. He's hopeless, but since my husband won't escort me anywhere, I have to make do with Victor."

"You don't think she's gone home without us?" Emm

said to Cal. "If she got a message from Rose and couldn't find us, she might have left on her own."

Cal's lips tightened. "It wouldn't be the first time she and Rose have gone gadding about on their own at night. Dammit, I thought all that nonsense was behind us."

"I thought it was too," Emm said. "Did you ask the butler? Or whoever's at the door?"

He shook her head. "Let's go." He gave a brusque nod to Sylvia, took Emm's arm and hurried toward the exit.

Inquiries from the butler revealed that Lady Lily had indeed left the Mainwaring house some twenty minutes earlier, along with a tall young gentleman who'd collected her cloak.

Cal sent a footman out to summon his carriage.

"I'm going to strangle Rose," Cal muttered as they waited for the carriage to arrive. "I thought she'd given up on her old tricks."

"I thought so too." Rose and her antics were the reason Cal had married Emm in the first place. "Even so, if there was some problem with Rose, I don't understand why Lily didn't come to tell us."

"Don't you?" Cal darted her a grim look. "Lily's very loyal. If Rose is up to some mischief, wild horses wouldn't drag it out of Lily."

Emm gave a rueful grimace. It was true. "So where do you think she's gone?"

Cal shrugged. "I'll take you home first, then—"

"Oh, no, I'm feeling much better now."

Cal snorted. "Says the woman who's as pale as paper and looking ready to cast up her accounts at any moment." He slipped his arm around her waist and said in a softened voice, "Home first for you, my love, to put your feet up and rest. And don't worry about my wretched sisters. I'll track them down soon enough." He glanced at her face and added, "And when I do find them, I'm going to throttle them for adding to your worries."

LILY LAY ON THE FLOOR OF THE CARRIAGE, GAGGED, bound up in a shroud of heavy cloth and unable to see a thing. She struggled to breathe. Waves of dizziness and a strange lethargy added to her fear and confusion. She tried to move her legs, but it was as if there were weights attached to them.

The cloth covering her was musty and stank of horses and mildew. A horse blanket? She pushed at it. "Keep still, you!" a man snarled. Not Mr. Nixon; his voice was rough and uneducated. Something pressed down on her neck—a foot? She froze, her heart hammering in her chest. She could barely breathe as it was. If he pressed any harder . . .

After a moment Mr. Nixon said, "Ease up. She's no use to me if you break her neck."

"I wasn't planning to."

"No, but a bump or pothole might jar your foot and then where would I be? With a useless body to dispose of. I didn't pay you for that."

A body? The flat indifference in the voices was terrifying. Lily's heart hammered harder.

The pressure on her neck eased. She lay still, struggling to breathe. Questions swirled uselessly in her brain. What did these terrible men want? It sounded like Sylvia's cousin, Mr. Nixon, was in charge. Was Sylvia part of this? Did she know what was happening to Lily or not? And who was the other man? Some rough hireling from the sound of things. Most pressing of all, why had they taken her? For what purpose?

And why was it so difficult to marshal her thoughts? Had she been hit on the head, that she was so dizzy and lethargic? She thought about her head. It wasn't sore—at least not in the way it would be if something had hit it.

Her mouth tasted sour and cobwebby. So much fabric had been jammed into her mouth that her jaw ached from being forced open for so long. Her tongue was wedged to the side, pressing painfully against a sharp tooth. Every jolt and bump and swerve of the carriage was painful.

What did they want with her? Were they planning to murder—no, he said a body was no use to him. What then? Ransom?

She recalled something her brother, Cal, had said to her and Rose a lifetime ago in Bath, when they'd sneaked out alone at night. Something about girls being kidnapped and sold into some kind of slavery. Yes, that was it. *White slavery—do you know what that means? Sold into a Turkish harem or a brothel in the seamiest foreign cities. And never seen again.*

A chill ran down her spine. Was that it? Would she disappear into some Turkish seraglio and never see her family again? Tears squeezed between her tightly closed eyes.

She couldn't give in to despair. She wouldn't. She had to fight this. Somehow. She swallowed convulsively, and immediately had to battle the instinct to gag.

Lily didn't know how long she lay there on the cold floor of the carriage, in a kind of stupor of helplessness and nausea, but eventually she realized the carriage was slowing. It stopped. Now what? She blinked hard, trying to breathe, to force herself to think. It was like wading through a heavy fog.

"How much of that stuff did you give her?"

Stuff? What stuff?

"A bit, just enough to keep her quiet. Any more and she'd have tasted it."

"Better give her another dose before I leave you, then."

She snatched a realization from the swirling bewilderment. The fruit punch at the party. It must have been drugged. No wonder she was so confused.

She could hear them moving in the carriage, shifting things, and then abruptly she was grabbed by the shoulders and jerked into a sitting position. The blanket was pulled off her face, and the wad of cloth dragged from her mouth. She swallowed, gasping deep gulps of air in relief, but before she could gather her wits, someone grabbed her hair and forced her head back, painfully.

A hand gripped her chin, hard, and the neck of a small bottle was thrust between her lips. She choked and spluttered as some nasty-tasting liquid was forced down her throat. She struggled with all the feeble strength left to her, but it did no good. The holder of the bottle—she couldn't see his face in the dark—simply jammed it painfully against her teeth, while the other one pulled harder on her hair, forcing her head back until she feared her neck might break.

"Careful, not too much now, a dead bride will do you no good at all."

A dead bride? A bride?

The vile bottle was removed and Lily, coughing and weak, found her wrists seized and bound. She tried to resist but it was like trying to swim in mud. The dizziness and lethargy were worse now.

"Good. Now, keep her doped up until you get to Scotland."

Scotland?

Hard hands replaced the gag, still damp from her own spittle, but this time tied around her mouth instead of being stuffed into it. Small mercies.

She lay on the carriage floor while Nixon paid the other man. Then she was scooped up and dumped roughly into something like . . . a box? A *coffin*? Panic threatened. She breathed deeply—as deeply as she could through the gag. *Stay calm, Lily. Not a coffin.* She would have seen a coffin. They were still in the carriage. *Think, Lily, think.*

It was some kind of container—no, a space under the seat. Yes, a space for storing cushions and rugs and extra luggage. And abducted women. As the realization came, a lid closed over her, turning the night from a terrifying thing of darkness and shadows into absolute pitch-blackness.

Slowly, grimly, through the swirling fog of the drug, she pieced it together. They were taking her to Scotland. As a bride.

"THERE'S NO USE INSISTING, CAL, I WILL NOT GO UPSTAIRS and sleep—not while Lily and Rose are missing! I couldn't sleep a wink, even if I wanted to."

"But—"

"Until you walk through the front door, with all three girls safe and sound—because if Rose and Lily are up to mischief, you can be sure that George will be involved too— I will wait downstairs. I'll be perfectly comfortable here in the front sitting room, on the *chaise longue* with my feet up. Now, stop fussing about me, my darling—go and find Lily!"

"Very well, but you will ring if you need—"

"Go! I'm feeling perfectly well now, just worried about Lily."

Cal briefly scrutinized her face, gave a brusque nod and turned to leave. He'd taken just two steps when the front door opened, and Rose and George entered, laughing.

"Aunt Agatha is in high dudgeon," Rose told them, her blue eyes dancing.

"High dudgeon? She's spitting fire and brimstone!" added George with a grin. "I always knew she was part dragon."

"Her precious duke never even turned up. She had to cancel supper— What is it?" The laughter died from Rose's eyes. She glanced from Emm to Cal and back. "What's the matter?"

"Where's Lily?" Cal demanded.

"What do you mean?" Rose asked. "She went to the party with you, didn't she?"

"She left the party early," Cal said grimly, "when she received a note from you."

Rose looked blank. "I never sent her a note."

"Rose," Cal growled, "this is no time for—"

She cut him off with an impatient gesture. "Don't be stupid, Cal. I would *never* send Lily a note. Why would I, when we all know Lily can't read?"

There was a sudden silence. "Oh, good God, we never thought . . ." Cal gave Emm an agonized look. Emm shook her head. In the worry and confusion, it hadn't occurred to her. Someone must have sent Lily a note purporting to come from her sister.

Rose sat down on a chair with a thump. "Are you saying Lily is missing?"

Cal nodded. "It seems so."

"How? What happened?"

"It's my fault." Emm felt wretched. She was meant to be guarding Lily, chaperoning her. Instead she'd failed her. "I was feeling ill, so we stepped outside—"

"Nonsense! It wasn't your fault," Cal said curtly. "We were only gone for a few minutes—ten at the most. We left her inside, in the home of our friends, surrounded by members of the ton, and talking to a friend, perfectly safe and happy."

"Cal decided to take me home, but when we went looking for Lily to bring her with us, we couldn't find her."

Cal stood abruptly. "I'm going back to the Mainwarings'. Somebody must have seen something. For all we know she's still there. She might have just stepped out for a few minutes for fresh air, like we did."

Emm shook her head. "Into the garden, perhaps, but not into the street. That butler said she'd gone into the street with a man."

"What man?" Rose demanded.

Cal gave her a searching look. "You don't know who he might be?"

"No, of course not."

"There's no man she fancies? No man who's been paying her attention lately?"

Rose stared at him. "Are you imagining she's eloped? That's ridiculous! Lily would never do such a thing. Besides, I'd know if she was planning anything like that."

"In any case," George said, "why would she run off to get married? If she wanted to marry someone you'd give her your blessing and start arranging for a wedding with all the trimmings, wouldn't you?"

Cal nodded slowly. "If the fellow was worthy of my little sister. But if he wasn't . . ."

"Has anyone asked for Lily's hand and been refused?" George asked.

"No."

"Well, then."

Cal said nothing. The look on his face was grim.

Emm looked up at her husband. "You're thinking she's been abducted, aren't you?"

He gave her a hard look. "She's an heiress. And I don't like the sound of that damned note." He bent and kissed Emm briefly. "I'm going back to the Mainwaring place, talk to the other servants and the Gorrie woman again. Someone must have seen something."

"I'll come with you," George said, but Cal shook his head.

"No, you and Rose stay and look after Emm. Besides,

Lily might come home any minute." He strode off, and in a few seconds they heard the front door slam.

"Pray she does," Emm murmured. An anxious silence descended.

How could Lily be abducted in the full view of half the ton? According to the butler, Lily had left the house willingly. Why? Because of the note?

And surely if she'd looked frightened or in distress someone would have noticed and stopped her. Surely?

Horrid possibilities churned in Emm's mind.

Rose frowned. "Cal said 'the Gorrie woman.' Did he mean Sylvia?"

Emm nodded. "She was talking to Lily when we went into the garden. It was Sylvia who told us about the message, but she was very vague about it. Apparently Lily was talking with Sylvia's cousin, but she didn't notice where they'd gone."

"Sylvia always was completely self-centered. Oh, I wish now I'd gone with Lily to the rout. I nearly did, but . . . That wretched duke of Aunt Agatha's. Oh, do stop pacing, George. It's very unsettling and it doesn't help."

"It helps me," George said. "I hate doing nothing. I'd rather be out searching for Lily."

"Me too, but where would we search? We can't just rush out into the streets and run around looking. We need a starting point," Rose pointed out. She sat on the end of the *chaise longue* and slipped her hand into Emm's. "You don't really think that she's been abducted, do you, Emm? Not our darling, softhearted Lily."

Emm gave her hand a comforting squeeze. "No, I'm sure it will be all right. It will just be some silly mix-up. Cal will no doubt arrive at the Mainwaring house and find Lily there, wondering where we've gone."

But from the look in their eyes, Rose and George believed that as little as Emm did.

THE MAINWARING ROUT WAS STILL IN FULL SWING, BUT Lily was nowhere to be found. Cal questioned the Mainwarings' servants again, and this time he found a footman who thought—though he wasn't sure—that the man Lily had left with had arrived earlier with a young woman dressed in blue. Lily had worn a dress that Emm had told him was in shades of peach. He decided that meant some kind of pink.

Cal then spoke to Lord and Lady Mainwaring, asking them, though without much hope, for discretion. For all he knew, Lily had just stepped out on some foolish escapade with a young man she fancied. It wasn't like her, but in his experience, young women were unpredictable. He hoped it was something as simple.

"Can you recall any of your guests who wore a blue gown, Lady Mainwaring?" It was the slenderest of leads, but it was all Cal had.

"Good heavens, Lord Ashendon, I'm sure I couldn't possibly remember such finicky little details, especially after everything I've had to organize today. My husband says I'm the veriest scatterbrain and I'm afraid it's quite true," Lady Mainwaring said with a little laugh. She gave her husband a fond look, then proceeded to list every woman who wore any shade of blue.

As she spoke, Cal noted the names, thinking that his friend Gil Radcliffe could use such a "scatterbrain" in his network of spies and informers.

"—and dear Libby Barker wore a pretty gown in sky-blue silk and blond lace. Such a nice girl. And I think that's all. Oh, no," she said on an afterthought, "I seem to recall that Mrs. Gorrie wore a rather commonplace blue dress with white trimming and—"

"Mrs. Gorrie?" Cal interrupted. "I don't suppose she's still here." He should have pressed her harder earlier, but at that point they weren't as worried about Lily.

"No, she left quite early, I think."

"Would you have her direction?"

Lady Mainwaring made a vague gesture. "Heavens, no, but I'm sure my butler will know it."

Cal went in search of the butler again, and got the addresses of every one of the women who'd worn blue that night. He started with Sylvia Gorrie.

The Gorries' butler stood firm. "I regret, my lord, that Mr. and Mrs. Gorrie are not receiving. Please return at a more convenient hour tomorrow."

"Nonsense. This is an urgent matter."

"My sincere regrets, my lord, but I cannot—"

"What's all the noise about, Barton?" an irritable female voice said from inside the house. "If my husband is woken there'll be hell to pay."

The butler turned and said in a hushed voice, "A Lord Ashendon is here, wishing to speak to you, madam."

"Ashendon? Good grief, whatever could he want? Oh, well, I'm still up, so you might as well show him in. But quietly, I beg of you."

Cal was shown into a sitting room. Sylvia Gorrie was standing in front of the fire, still wearing the dress he'd seen her in earlier, blue with white trim, though he'd taken no notice at the time. She was holding a note in her hand and as Cal entered she looked up with a petulant expression.

"Good evening, Lord Ashendon. Lord knows what you can want with me at this hour—nothing pleasant, I see from your expression—but it has become a night of nasty surprises"—she indicated the note in her hand—"so go ahead."

Cal didn't beat about the bush. "My sister Lily is missing."

She frowned. "Still? Didn't you find her earlier?"

"Obviously not. You said earlier she received a message."

"Yes, a note from her sister, Rose. Of course poor Lily can't read, so I read it out for her. I must say—"

"A footman said she left with a man—"

"Well, then—"

"A man who had arrived a short time earlier with you on his arm."

She frowned. "With *me*? Are you sure?"

He wasn't, of course, but he wasn't going to reveal how little he actually knew. "It was you, definitely. So who was the man?"

Sylvia glanced down at the note in her hand and said in a puzzled voice, "I came with my cousin, Victor Nixon. But he disappeared on me. I thought at first he was in one of the gaming rooms—he has an addiction to piquet, you know—but he wasn't, and then I realized he must have gone home with some tart—well, it wouldn't be the first time—leaving me to get home by myself. But when I got home I found this note—"

"Where does this Nixon fellow live?"

"Paris."

"Paris?"

She nodded. "He's lived there for the past five years. He has a house in the—oh, I forget where. Near some gardens. But when in London he stays with us, of course."

"Then where is he?"

"It's as I was trying to tell you!" Sylvia exclaimed crossly. She brandished the note. "He says he's gone back to Paris—in the middle of the night, and without so much as a thank-you or a by-your-leave! What sort of a house-guest is that, I ask you? My husband will be furious! Victor owes him money—they played cards the other night—oh, it isn't much, but my husband is the sort of man who counts every penny and—"

"May I see that note?" Without waiting for her permission, Cal plucked it from her grasp and read it.

Dear coz,

Sorry to have to push off home without notice. As you know, my circumstances have been rather dire of late, but thanks to your little introduction tonight, I have a plan to bring the dibs back in tune. When I see you next, I'll be a married man. Make my apologies to your husband.

Au revoir, Victor

Cal crushed the note in his hand, ignoring Sylvia's squeak of dismay. "What 'little introduction'?"

Sylvia made a petulant gesture. "How would I know? He's

been in London a week or more, and I've introduced him to dozens of people. He has no consideration at all, rushing off like that. My husband will blame me, of course, and—"

"He said 'tonight.' Did you introduce him to Lily tonight?"

"Of course. I introduced him to lots of peop—"

"Did you tell him Lily was an heiress?"

Sylvia gave him an irritated look. "I don't recall. I might have. Everyone at school knew that both Rose and Lily would inherit a fortune on marriage—some people have all the luck." She glanced up at his face and stepped back hurriedly. "What? Why are you looking at me like that? It's not a secret, is it?"

"No, it's not a damned secret! But it looks as though your damned cousin has gone off with my sister Lily."

Sylvia gasped, then clapped her hands. "You don't say! How romantic. Of course, Victor was always a charmer, but—"

"It's not in the least romantic," Cal snarled. "Lily wouldn't elope on the strength on one night's acquaintance. She has no need to elope at all. He must have abducted her."

Sylvia stared, then shook her head. "I don't believe it."

"I don't give a damn what you believe," Cal said as he strode from the room. "But I'm going to find your precious cousin, and if he's abducted my little sister, he's a dead man!"

"Don't slam the—" she shrieked.

Cal slammed the front door behind him. If it woke her husband, it would serve the fellow right for marrying such a silly and irritating woman. With a soon-to-be-dead cousin.

"How this Nixon fellow has convinced Lily to go with him is beyond me. I assume it has something to do with the supposed note from Rose," Cal said to Emm. He'd told her and the girls what he'd learned from Sylvia earlier and was now upstairs, changing out of his evening clothes into breeches, boots and greatcoat while his horse was being saddled.

"If the note said Rose was off to Paris, Lily might decide to follow her," Emm suggested. "She's always been the moderating influence even though Rose is her elder. And if this Nixon fellow offered to escort her . . ."

"If that's the case, we can put that down to her experience of Rose's earlier harebrained exploits. But it doesn't explain those blasted hints in the note Nixon left his cousin. Lily might think she's off to rescue Rose, but that bastard is planning to marry her, mark my words."

"It's not Rose's fault," Emm reminded him. "She didn't send that note, and she's been very well behaved since we came to London." Emm put her hand on her husband's arm. "Rose is already blaming herself for whatever has happened to Lily, even though she's innocent of any wrongdoing. She's extremely protective of Lily, you know that."

"I know." Cal picked up his pistols, checked them and slipped them into the pockets of his greatcoat. "And I'm not blaming Rose. I'm just worried for Lily. But with any luck I'll overtake them before they reach Dover."

Emm eyed the pistols with misgiving. "And if you don't?"

He shrugged. "I'll follow them to Paris."

"And if they're not in Paris? Before you spoke to Sylvia, you thought Lily was being taken to Gretna, didn't you?"

He nodded. "I know, but this cousin of the Gorrie woman has her, I'm sure. He was seen leaving with Lily, and the note he left for his cousin is utterly incriminating. It said he was going home—which is in Paris. In any case, I've made arrangements for a couple of men—Radcliffe's men—to head up the Great North Road, just in case. They have orders to search for a young woman and a young man traveling in that direction. They'll go all the way to Gretna and if Lily turns up there, they'll find her."

He took her hands in his. "Don't worry, my love. I know France well and my French is excellent. I'll find her and make sure nothing bad happens to her. Even if she has eloped for some reason, she won't be forced into a marriage she doesn't want—I know how you feel about that. You just take care of yourself and this little one." He placed his hand briefly on her stomach and kissed her. "I'll be back with Lily before you know it."

As she followed him downstairs, the clock in the hall

chimed one. Just over three hours since they'd first missed Lily. It seemed so much longer.

"How long does it take to get to Dover?" asked George from behind them. She'd changed out of her evening dress and was clad in breeches and boots. Her intention was obvious.

"You're not going," Cal told her.

"I am. I have to do something!"

"You can stay here and behave yourself," Cal snapped. "That goes for you too, Rose," he added, seeing Rose behind George on the stairs. "I'm not having any more of you going missing! Stay here and look after Emm." His horse was waiting in the street. He took the reins from the groom, swung lithely into the saddle and headed down the street. The sound of hooves echoed in the night.

Emm and the two girls watched until he'd disappeared. "I don't care, I'm going after them," George began.

"No, you need to stay here," Emm told her. "You heard Cal—how do you think he'd feel if any more of his beloved girls went missing? It flays him badly enough to have lost Lily."

George put up a stubborn chin. "Yes, but I'm not one of his 'beloved girls.' I'm just a duty to him. I'm not even a sister."

Emm slid an arm around the girl's slender waist and said gently, "You're not his sister, but you're not just a duty, either. Cal cares deeply about you—and not just because he feels ashamed at the family's neglect of you in the past. If you didn't enjoy clashing with him so much, you'd see what he really thinks of you."

George sighed. "That I'm a pest, a wild girl and trouble."

Emm laughed. "You can be at times, but even though he growls and snaps sometimes, never, *ever* doubt that Cal loves you. It's *because* he loves you that he growls."

George looked skeptical, and Emm said, "He also admires you, George—he's quite proud of his wild young niece, you know. He cares for you, and he loves you." She slid her other arm around Rose and added, "Both of you. *All* of you."

"Yes, but Lily is his favorite," Rose said.

"I don't care about that," George said. "I just need to *do* something."

"I know." Emm squeezed her affectionately. "But there's no point in us running around like chickens with their heads cut off searching for Lily when we have no idea where she's been taken. There is something we can do to help, though. It may not be dramatic or exciting, but we will have to be clever."

Rose narrowed her eyes. "How do you mean, clever?"

Chapter Three

Long is the way and hard,
that out of hell leads to up to light.
—JOHN MILTON, *PARADISE LOST*

"STOP THE COACH!"

In the darkness of her cramped prison, Lily stirred, willing the drugged haze to pass. She focused her dazed attention on the voices outside.

"What the—who the devil are you and what business do you have stopping my coach?"

"No need for alarm, sir. We're on official business."

"Indeed? What's the problem?"

"A young lady has been abducted. They're believed to be making for the border."

Rescue! They were looking for her. Lily tried to call out but all she could manage was a muffled moan. Nixon covered it with a coughing fit. He said in a loud voice, "A lady abducted, you say! How shocking! Whatever is the world coming to!"

Lily tried to bang on the walls of her prison, but the thick blanket they'd rolled her in impeded her movements and muffled any sound. The space under the seat was a tight fit. She couldn't even raise her arms enough to reach the gag.

She tried to call for help again, but with her throat so dry, her mouth so tightly gagged and her drugged, thick tongue barely able to move, all that came out was a whimper.

And from the sound of the conversation outside, the men didn't hear a thing.

"So you haven't come across a young lady in distress in your travels, sir?"

"No, and as you can see, gentlemen, there's only myself in this carriage," Nixon said. "No young women at all, sadly. I could do with one to while away this dreary journey to Carlisle."

One of the men laughed.

Lily tried again, calling out and banging her head against the roof of her prison but again, there was no reaction from the men outside.

"So you're not destined for Scotland, sir?"

"Heavens, no! Carlisle is quite far-flung enough for me. Best of luck in finding your young lady, gentlemen. The villain who abducted her deserves to be horsewhipped."

Hearing the men take their leave, Lily tried to call out one last desperate time, but a moment later the carriage lurched on its way, and she was once again left alone with her abductor.

Sick with fear and feeling desperately alone, she sank back. She was never going to get away from him. He was too clever, too plausible. He'd planned it all so carefully. Who would have thought of making a hollow space under the seat and keeping her captive there? And invisible.

Those men . . . if only she could have made them hear . . .

A few moments later the lid of the seat was raised and the smothering, dusty rug pulled off her face. She blinked as her eyes adjusted to a soft gray light. Morning? Already? She'd been here all night.

"Awake, are we?" Nixon's sneering face loomed over her. "I heard your feeble little squeaks. Lucky for me there's a filthy wind blowing down from the north and it drowned everything."

Hard fingers pulled at the knot of her gag, ripping at her hair uncaringly. He dragged the damp strip of fabric aside. Lily moved her aching jaw experimentally.

"I should have dosed you earlier," he said, and grabbed her hair, forcing her head back.

She glimpsed a blue bottle in his hand, and as he jammed it into her mouth, she retained just enough presence of mind to push her tongue into the bottle's opening. She pretended to swallow and struggle and cough, and only a trickle of the vile drug passed her lips.

"That'll do it." He released the painful grip on her hair, corked the bottle, retied the gag and pushed her down, back into the dark, airless space under the seat. "I'll wake you when we get to Gretna, darling. Sleep well."

He was laughing at her, laughing at her helplessness, her foolishness in falling for his trap in the first place.

How she hated him.

That note from Rose. She'd believed every word of it. But now she'd had time to think. Rose would never have written to her. Lily hadn't thought at all, just reacted. This mess she was in was all her own fault. Stupid, stupid, stupid!

She lay in the lightless gloom, berating herself, and fighting the effects of the drug. She'd ingested a smaller amount this time, but still, it was strong enough to keep her woozy and lethargic.

She would not give in to it. Somehow she must fight this thing. Sylvia's cousin would not get her, not get his horrid, cruel, greedy hands on her inheritance. She would rather die than marry him. And she didn't want to die.

Sylvia . . . Was she part of this? Would she do something so cruel? No. Why would she do such a thing to Lily? What had Lily ever done to her except try to be her friend?

THE JOURNEY SEEMED ENDLESS. THEY STOPPED AT INNS and posting houses to change horses, but Nixon never left her alone, never let anyone come near enough to hear her. He sat on the seat above her whistling and kicking his heels. Mr. Carefree.

The pressure on her bladder was becoming unbearable.

Without much hope of being heard, she did her best to call out again, but almost immediately the lid of her imprisonment was lifted. "What?" Nixon demanded.

She couldn't speak, so she tried to signal her desperation.

"Need to piss?"

She nodded.

He put the lid back down, and if she could have, she would have screamed. Surely he couldn't ignore her urgent need?

But a few moments later the coach pulled up and the lid was jerked open again.

He grabbed her arm and pulled her upright. "Come on, then, out you get."

Acting dizzier and more lethargic than she felt, Lily struggled to free herself of the heavy blanket and climb out of her imprisonment. It wasn't entirely an act—she was stiff and sore, aching from being squashed into the cramped space for who knew how many hours.

As she jumped down from the carriage her legs crumpled beneath her and she found herself sprawled in the mud. "Get up," Nixon said.

She struggled to stand, but her legs were so cramped from being in a confined space for so long, there was no feeling in them. He jerked her roughly to her feet, and she stifled a moan of pain as pins and needles—painful pins and needles—brought the return of sensation.

The wind blew sharp and strong over the moors. After the smothering airlessness of her confinement the bitter cold of it sliced through her, but Lily didn't care. Anything was better than being in that black hole. She inhaled deeply, breathing in energy and clarity as she took stock of her surroundings. Moorland as far as the eye could see, muddy and wet from recent rain. No buildings, no sign of life.

She glanced up at the coachman, who sat holding the reins, staring straight ahead, pointedly indifferent to her fate. No help there.

Nixon gave her a little shove. "Go on, then. What are you waiting for?"

She indicated her bound hands—she couldn't relieve herself without free hands to deal with her skirts. He hesitated, then untied her. "Don't think you can get away. There's nothing for miles."

She pulled the gag off and, rubbing the circulation back

into her hands, she staggered toward a small clump of grass, slipping and stumbling in the mud as she went.

The clump of grass didn't provide any privacy, and she was aware of him standing only a few yards away, openly watching her, enjoying her shame and embarrassment as she squatted to relieve herself.

Despite her fear, despite the drug and the freezing cold and her deep humiliation as she squatted in the open under the gaze of two horrid men, a warming surge of anger sparked deep within Lily. This man, this vile excuse for a man, was nothing to her—less than nothing. He was vulgar, greedy and cruel, but even though he had her trapped and in his power at the moment, she vowed he would not win.

She would not be a cowering frightened creature, a victim of his evil scheme. Die before she let him marry her? Never!

She would kill *him* before she let him take her as his wife.

"Finished?"

She straightened, feeling so much better than she had just a few moments before. The fear of lying, trapped, in a puddle of her own making had passed, and the bracing, moisture-laden wind had given her fresh hope and determination. And anger, she discovered, gave her strength.

She looked around. Even if she'd been steady on her feet, there was nowhere to run. The road was empty and there was no sign of people or any kind of habitation. She had no choice but to return to her captivity.

She made her way carefully back to the carriage to where Nixon was waiting. He grinned at her discomfort, at her disorientation and unsteady gait.

How she loathed him.

She wasn't even a person to him, she was a *thing*, a way to get money. He would happily ruin her life just to enrich himself.

He retied her wrists and replaced the gag, then helped her into the carriage. He lifted the lid and gestured for her to get in. It was fastened, she saw, with a small hook catch. If she could block that . . .

"Carriage coming, sir," the coachman called out.

Nixon swore. "Get in, blast you, woman." He shoved her roughly back into the space beneath the seat, and jammed the little blue bottle into her mouth. She managed to stop it again with her tongue, but not before a trickle of the vile liquid made it down her throat. He pushed her head down and closed the lid. An instant before it closed, Lily tried to slip a fold of cloth over the catch. But in her haste, she missed, and the lid closed tight above her.

As the lid closed over her once more, shutting her into that dark, cramped airless space, Lily fought the sensation of despair that threatened to swamp her.

For the second time, she'd managed to block the neck of the bottle with the tip of her tongue and keep from ingesting the amount of drug he intended. That was some kind of victory, she told herself, a kind of fighting back.

And next time he let her out to relieve herself, she'd try again to block the catch of the lid. She was better off than before, she told herself; now she had a plan.

Still, she'd absorbed enough of the drug to have to fight with every bit of willpower she had to keep from sliding into unconsciousness again.

If she didn't stay awake, she couldn't escape.

Time passed. She fought the drug with everything she could think of, mentally reciting poems and rhymes she'd learned over the years, reciting her times tables, counting backward, keeping her eyes wide open, staring into the dark, and scrunching up her toes and tightening and relaxing her muscles to keep her legs from falling asleep again as they had before.

She needed to keep her legs in full working order in case she got the chance to escape.

"ANY NEWS?" ROSE SAID BEFORE SHE WAS HARDLY IN the room. She and George had just returned from their morning ride. Emm had practically had to force them to go out as usual.

Emm shook her head. Rose flung herself onto the settee. "I *hate* this, hate going about pretending Lily is just sick in bed upstairs. I don't know why we have to go riding and pretending everything is all right. I need to *do* something!"

"I know, my dear," Emm said patiently. "But though it doesn't feel like it, you are doing exactly what needs to be done. It's the best—the *only*—way we can protect Lily at the moment—act as if nothing is the matter." They'd had this out before. The girls were desperate to take action of some sort, but there was nothing they could do except wait. And hope and pray that Cal would find Lily soon and bring her home safe and sound.

In the meantime they must all act as usual, so that nobody would suspect anything was wrong.

"But it's *unbearable*, having to make meaningless, polite conversation when *anything* could have happened to poor darling Lily!"

"I know. Mrs. Pinkley-Dutton commented today that Lily must be afraid of a little rain, missing two morning rides in a row—and I wanted to hit her!" George said.

"We can't protect Lily, but we can protect her reputation," Emm reminded them. The trouble was that neither Rose nor George cared much for their own reputations.

And women must wait. Whoever wrote that didn't know how very difficult waiting was. Action was so much easier.

LILY LAY HALF DOZING IN THE DARK, WAITING FOR HER next opportunity.

Twice more they had stopped to let her relieve herself, and each time, Lily pretended to be more affected by the drug than she was. The third time, as Lily was stuffed back into her prison, she managed to wedge a fold of her cloak between the catch and the hook.

She held her breath, waiting for him to jerk open the lid and pull away the cloth impeding the catch. But nothing happened. He hadn't noticed.

The coach set off again, swaying and jolting along the road. Eventually Lily worked up the courage to push ever so slightly against the roof of her prison. It lifted.

And again, Nixon noticed nothing. He was taking her helplessness for granted.

Despite the cruel bite of the gag, Lily smiled. She was still trapped in the dark, still bound and gagged, still battling the effects of the drug, but she was no longer locked in. She could push the lid up, and the knowledge gave her a fierce surge of hope.

She just had to wait for the next posting inn or some other chance to escape. The journey to Scotland took several days. An opportunity was bound to arise.

"I HAVE HEARD *A WHISPER*!" AUNT AGATHA ANNOUNCED. There was a short silence. She raised her lorgnette and examined each of them one by one, with unnerving thoroughness. "Well?"

Emm sent a warning glance to Rose and George. "What have you heard, Aunt Agatha? The ton is full of whispers."

"Where's the other gel?"

"Lily? She's indisposed," Emm said.

"With what?"

"A cold," said Rose.

"A sprained ankle," George said at the same time. She glanced at Rose and said, "A cold *and* a sprained ankle."

Aunt Agatha gave them both a withering look and rolled her eyes. "I thought as much. What is going on, Emmaline? And don't prevaricate, for as I said, I heard *a whisper*."

Emm sighed, accepting the inevitable. "Lily has gone missing. We think she's been abducted."

"Why did you not immediately inform me?" the old lady said crossly.

"We thought the fewer people who knew, the better."

Aunt Agatha snorted. "I am not *people*! I am *family*! And if one of my family gets herself into trouble—"

"Lily did *not* 'get herself into trouble,'" Rose snapped. "She was *abducted*! Through *no* fault of her own!"

Aunt Agatha gave her a thoughtful look and said in a surprisingly mild voice, "When did she disappear?"

"The same night that duke of yours didn't turn up at the opera," George said.

The old lady narrowed her eyes at George, but didn't rise to the bait. "And who, outside the family, knows she is missing?"

"Nobody. Cal has gone to France because that's where we think she's been taken. But he also sent some men to search for her on the Great North Road, in case his information was wrong. But they're men he's worked with before, in whose discretion he trusts."

"Sylvia knows Lily went missing," said Rose. "And the Mainwarings."

"But we've told them all Lily was just feeling ill and went home early without telling us," Emm said. "Lady Mainwaring was glad to hear it—sorry for Lily's indisposition, that is, but reassured that it was nothing more serious."

Aunt Agatha swiveled in her seat and directed the lorgnette at Rose. "And this Sylvia person you mentioned?"

"Sylvia Gorrie, a former school friend of the girls'," Emm explained.

"No friend of mine," Rose muttered.

"Cal thinks Sylvia's cousin abducted Lily," Emm continued. "He questioned Sylvia on the night Lily disappeared, but she knew nothing about it and seemed more upset that her cousin had left without notice and owed money to her husband. She did call here the next day to inquire after Lily, and I told her that Lily wasn't missing at all but had left the Mainwarings' because she'd been feeling ill."

"With a sprained cold," Aunt Agatha said acidly. "So nobody else knows?"

"No."

"What about the servants?"

Emm shook her head. "I don't believe they would talk, not about this." She'd spoken to them and had been assured of their discretion. Of course, what people said and what they did wasn't always the same.

"Well someone must know *something*, because, as I said, I heard *a whisper*."

"What exactly did you hear?"

The old lady made an impatient gesture. "Nothing solid, just the hint of a rumor about 'one of the Rutherford gels,' and the suggestion that she'd run off with a man."

"Lily would never—" Rose began.

"Pish tush, gel, we know that. But the whisper is out there and we need to do something about it." Leaning heavily on her silver-topped ebony cane, she rose to her feet. "Off you go, gels, and fetch your hats and coats. We're going for a drive."

"I don't want to go out," Rose said. "I want to stay in case there's news—"

"The best you can do for your sister is to appear in public as usual with nothing to worry about except that your sister has . . ." She thought for a minute. "The influenza, something serious, not a sprain or a cold. In fact, it would look better if you came to stay with me, Emmaline, to protect your child. And you gels will come as well, for fear of the infection. It will strengthen the story."

"It won't. I'd never leave my sister if she was ill," Rose declared.

"I'd stay too," George said. "I never catch colds or the flu—I'm as healthy as a horse."

Aunt Agatha closed her eyes briefly. "Such a vulgar metaphor, Georgiana. Health is a desirable state for a young lady, but when you invite people to compare you with an animal . . ." She gave a pained shudder.

Emm laid a calming hand on George's arm and said firmly, "Nobody is moving anywhere. I told Cal I'd wait here, and so I will—we all will. But fresh air and a public family outing in the park is an excellent idea, though perhaps the girls could accompany you on horseback—with their groom in attendance, of course." She gave both girls a speaking look.

Better for them not to be stuck in a barouche with their aunt. They were so tense and worried about Lily that Aunt Agatha's pronouncements, which rubbed them up the wrong way at the best of times, would today be like a flame to a tinderbox. She glanced at Rose. Or gunpowder.

"Now, Aunt Agatha, while the girls are changing into their habits, how about a nice cup of tea?"

LILY CAME AWAKE WITH A JERK. AGAINST ALL HER RESO-lution, she'd dozed off. Something had changed. What?

And then she realized. The carriage had stopped. Some-one shouted. She couldn't make out what, but a moment later Nixon shouted back. "In this weather? Damned if I will!"

She cautiously cracked the lid of her prison open a sliver.

Another shout. The coachman. She couldn't hear it all, but it sounded like he wanted Nixon to get out and push. The coach was stuck in mud. Nixon refused again, this time in even worse language.

The coachman's voice sounded suddenly loud and close. "Want to wait until help comes, do ya? With that special cargo of yours tucked away? Risk 'em finding her, will ya?" He must have climbed down.

There was a short silence. Lily held her breath. Nixon swore again, then ordered the driver to do the pushing, while he led the horses.

She heard the door close, then the voices came again, muffled, as if from a distance. Nixon and the driver were out of the coach. Now was her chance. Heart thudding, braced for the lid to be slammed back down on her, she raised it, inch by inch. And breathed again.

The carriage was empty. She scrambled out, then peered carefully out the window. She could hardly see a thing—it was raining—but from the shouts exchanged, it seemed Nixon was up ahead with the horses and the coachman was on the other side of the coach, stuffing bracken and gorse under one of the wheels.

Lily threw her cloak over her—thank goodness it was a dark color—stealthily unfastened the door, then leapt from the coach and ran into the low scraggly vegetation that stretched for miles on either side of the empty road. Her only hope was to lie down in it, go to ground like a hunted hare, and hope they wouldn't see her.

Half a dozen steps later she found herself falling helplessly, landing facedown with a hard *splat*. She lay, winded for a few moments, her lungs straining for air, her brain racing, trying to make sense of what happened.

She was in some kind of hole . . . no, it was a ditch, running parallel to the road. Her breath returned in a rush. Keeping her head well down, she lay in shallow, freezing, stagnant ditch water, gulping lungfuls of cold, bracing air, trying to marshal her drug-hazed wits.

Had she made any noise when she'd fallen? She couldn't remember, but a small scream or exclamation seemed likely. Had they noticed? Or had the gag muffled any noise she'd made? She peered cautiously over the lip of the ditch, through the meager cover of the vegetation that lined it.

In the driving rain she could barely make out the shape of the coach. She squinted through the gloom, hardly daring to breathe.

Nixon and the coachman continued shouting instructions—and abuse—back and forth. Lily breathed again. They hadn't noticed her escape. Yet.

With some difficulty, for her wrists were still bound, she pulled her cloak over her head. Thank goodness she'd worn it to the Mainwarings' rout instead of the cream silk and taffeta one. The dark blue velvet would at least hide her, if not keep her warm and dry—between the rain and the ditch water, she was drenched to the bone. And somehow, wet or not, the heavy weight of the velvet was comforting.

The Mainwarings' rout. It seemed an age ago. Was it only last night? Or the night before? She didn't know. The drug had stolen time.

Released from the tight constriction of her prison, she could raise her bound hands enough to scrape her gag off. Thankfully, she gulped in fresh, damp air. Her wrists were still bound tightly, but she could breathe and she could run.

Bending low Lily half crept, half crawled along the ditch, praying she wouldn't be noticed.

A loud shout almost stopped her heart. She froze, expecting any moment to be roughly seized and dragged back to the coach, but nothing happened. Eventually, unable to bear not knowing, she peeped over the side of the ditch.

Through the veil of rain, she saw Nixon climb back into the carriage and the driver take his seat and gather up the reins. The carriage moved slowly away. She watched breathlessly until it breasted a slight hill and disappeared.

She forced herself to wait—what if Nixon decided to lift the lid and check on her?—but after a few agonizing moments Lily decided she could delay no longer. She clambered out of the muddy ditch and began to run.

Chapter Four

❧

Her mind was all disorder.
The past, present, future, everything was terrible.
—JANE AUSTEN, *MANSFIELD PARK*

"WOMAN ON THE ROAD UP AHEAD, SIR," NED GALBRAITH'S coachman said through the communication hatch. "Looks like she's in some distress."

Ned glanced out the window. There was nothing for miles, no sign of habitation. "Alone?" It was not unheard of for women to feign distress as a trap for unwary travelers. They'd stop to help and the female's colleagues would emerge from hiding and rob them.

"No place to hide that I can see," Walton agreed. "A poor spot for an ambush, I reckon."

Ned sighed. "Very well, let's see what—"

"Another coach just came over the rise." Walton's voice rose with excitement. "Looks like they're trying to run her down—and bloody hell, sir, I think her hands are tied!"

Ned poked his head out the window. Sure enough a bedraggled-looking female was running unsteadily toward his coach, waving her arms frantically—and yes, they were bound at the wrist. Another carriage was bearing down on her, the driver whipping at his tired-looking horses.

She looked terrified.

Ned didn't wait; he swung down from his slowing carriage and ran toward the woman. At the same time a dark-haired man jumped from the other carriage and seized her in a rough grasp.

"Help!" she shrieked, struggling to pull herself free, but she was no match against his brutal strength.

The man growled something Ned didn't catch and dragged her back toward his carriage.

"What the devil is going on?" Ned picked up his pace.

"None of your damned business," the man shouted over his shoulder. "Go on your way."

"He's abduct—" Her captor jerked her hard and she nearly fell.

"My wife is not herself," the man began. "She's a drunken bedlamite."

"Not his wife." She fought him, clumsily, using her tied hands like a club. "Drugged. He drugged me!"

"Shut up!" The man hit her hard across the face, and she reeled, almost collapsing, just as Ned reached them.

He grabbed the man by the collar and jerked him back hard, twisting it so that the fellow almost choked. Releasing the woman, who fell to the ground, he turned on Ned with a savage snarl. "I told you—"

Ned punched him hard in the face. He didn't know whether these two were married or not, but whatever the circumstances, no woman deserved that kind of violence. He said so.

The fellow staggered back, blood spurting from his nose. "Listen, you bastard, I can treat her how I want. She's my wi—"

"I'm not his wife, sir, I prom—Mr. *Galbraith*? Oh, it *is* you! Oh, thank God!"

Ned started. She knew his name? Distracted, he glanced down at her but before he could make out her features under the smears of mud, a heavy blow knocked him sideways.

He staggered and turned. The fellow's coachman raised a cudgel to hit him again. Ned kicked out and caught him in the leg. He fell to one knee, just as his master attacked.

Ned punched him again, a blow to the gut, then another to the jaw that knocked him cold. The driver staggered to his feet and came at him. A pistol shot stopped the driver in his tracks.

Ned's coachman stepped forward. "I got two of these

beauties." He gestured with the pistols. "Make another move and you die."

"Thank you, Walton." Ned probably should have used a pistol in the first place, but truth to tell, he didn't mind a brawl on occasion. It reminded him who he was. He helped the girl to her feet. She was a mess, drenched and filthy, her face dirt-streaked—or was that a rising bruise?—and her clothes bedraggled and caked with mud.

He gave her face a searching glance. Nope. No idea who she was.

She gave him a shaky smile and clung to his arm, determined but wavering, as if unsteady on her feet or ready to swoon. She was soaked, shivering. The thought had crossed his mind initially that she was some country wench, taken up for a nasty kind of sport, but her sodden cloak was velvet, and the few words he'd heard her speak were unaccented, educated.

And she knew his name. "Who are you and how do you know my—" He broke off, thrusting her behind him as the man he'd felled lurched to his feet and came up swinging.

Ned hit him again, and he crumpled. Ned shoved him with his boot. "Take your master and go."

"The girl—"

"Stays with me."

The driver hesitated. The girl clutched Ned's coat. "Pass me the pistol, Walton," Ned said calmly. "These two were undoubtedly born to be hanged, but—"

"No need for that, sir." The driver backed away, his hands raised in placation. "I don't want no trouble. Just a hired driver, sir, nothing to do with me what he was plannin'." He hooked his master under the armpits and dragged him back to the carriage like a sheep about to be shorn. He bundled him inside, climbed up on top, turned the carriage around and drove away.

As the coach disappeared over the horizon, the girl sagged against Ned. "Thank God you came along when you did, Mr. Galbraith. If he'd caught me again . . ." She was shivering uncontrollably. Cold or reaction. No doubt a bit of both.

He pulled a knife from his boot and cut through her bindings. "Who are y—"

"Sorry," she gasped, and bent and retched, a thin stream of bile that just missed his boots.

When she finished he handed her his handkerchief. She wiped her mouth and handed it back. He received it gingerly, gave it a distasteful glance, then dropped it in the mud. "Let's get you into the carriage."

She took a few wobbly steps, then stumbled. "I'm sorry. The drug . . ." She reeled.

Ned scooped her into his arms and lifted her into the carriage. She was drenched right through. Her soaked clothing dampened his clothes. And she stank. Of dank mud and ditch water, of vomit and animal manure and God knew what else.

She slumped onto the seat and almost fell as the coach jerked into movement. She looked up wildly. "Where are we going?"

He'd been heading to Fountains Abbey, near Ripon, to a house party there. It wasn't far, but he certainly wasn't going to arrive at Fountains in the company of a damp and bedraggled damsel in distress. A sure route to scandal that would be.

No, he'd have to return her quickly and quietly to wherever she came from. "London?" he suggested, and she sighed in relief.

"Oh, thank goodness, yes, please. They'll be so worried about me."

He knocked on the roof, gave Walton their new destination, then turned back to the girl, intending to question her, but her shivering had worsened. And her stench was slowly filling the carriage. First things first. He had all the time in the world to ask her questions, but he was damned if he'd travel another mile with a half-frozen woman who stank like a midden.

"You can't travel in those wet clothes," he informed her. "You'll catch your death."

She looked down at the ruins of her dress, some light-colored thing partly revealed beneath the filthy cloak, and sighed. "I s-suppose so." Her teeth were chattering.

He lifted a small valise from an overhead rack and pulled one of his shirts from it. "Take off everything that is wet, and then put this on."

"Here? In the coach?" Beneath the mud and bruising a blush crept over her skin. She gave him a look in which innocence fought with awareness and strove for indignation. For a girl who'd just fought off an abductor, and who looked—and smelled—like she'd been dragged through a haystack and then rolled in a pigpen, it was almost seductive.

Which was ridiculous.

He said irritably, "Well, unless you expect me to stand outside in the rain while you change"—he gestured to the window to point out that rain was pelting down again—"yes, here in the coach."

And before she could suggest that she would prefer him to get soaked while she stripped off her odiferous attire, he grabbed a fur-lined traveling rug. "Here, I'll hold this up to protect your modesty. You can wear one of my shirts—I'm afraid I don't have any gowns with me—and then wrap yourself in this. We'll stop at the next town and get something more suitable for you."

"Very well." She unfastened her cloak and shrugged it off and handed it to him. He dropped it on the floor. And his mouth dried.

She was wearing a badly soiled evening gown, filthy now, but it was apparent to Ned that it had been both expensive and in the first stare of fashion. Wet, filmy layers of pinkish gauze clung to her like a second skin, almost transparent, outlining luscious curves. Her face and hands were muddy, but her breasts, enticingly displayed by the low-cut neckline, were creamy and lush.

With an effort he dragged his gaze to her face.

She gazed back at him, wide-eyed, her eyes as gray and liquid as a winter sea. Dark hair streamed down over her shoulders in dripping clumps, a mermaid come to call, wet, luscious and enticing. A pair of tight, berry-hard nipples thrust invitingly toward him.

He swallowed. It was just the cold. Nipples did that in the cold. But it took all his self-control to keep his gaze focused on her face.

"You'll have to help me. It's fastened down the back."

He put the rug aside and moved to the seat beside her. She turned and lifted the wet mass of her hair so he could undo her gown. He stared for a long moment at her pale, vulnerable nape, then set himself to the task at hand.

The dress was cunningly constructed of a series of overlapping layers that, sodden, clung to his fingers. He was well experienced at helping women out of their clothes, but he was damned if he could see how to unfasten this blasted dress.

"The hooks are very small, I'm afraid. Can you find them?"

He fished around and found a row of tiny hooks. Of course they would be tiny. He swore silently as he fumbled with each minute and impossible fastening, then became aware of the soft creamy flesh he was revealing beneath. Cold, damp flesh, he reminded himself. She was still shivering. He all but ripped the last dozen hooks from the dress, then removed himself to the opposite seat and raised the rug in front of him to block out the sight of her.

Behind the fur barrier she wriggled and rustled and sighed.

It was damnably erotic.

"What should I do with my dress? It's making the seat all wet and dirty."

"Throw it on the floor."

He heard a sigh. "It was a beautiful dress once," a sad little voice said from the other side of the fur blanket. A dirty pink bundle plopped wetly onto the floor between them. He scraped it into the corner with the toe of his boot.

He waited. The wriggling and rustling did not resume. His arms were getting tired. "Are you finished?"

"No." There was a pause, then, "Did you say I should take off everything that was wet?"

"Yes. Unless you want to catch an inflammation of the lungs."

"But . . . I'm soaked to the skin."

To the skin. He closed his eyes. He did not need this, the thought that this unknown, filthy and yet somehow appealing female was going to be naked, with nothing but a fur rug between them. He said in a hard voice, "Take it all off, then. Your virtue is safe with me."

"Oh, I know that, Mr. Galbraith." There was not a shred of doubt in her voice.

He was almost insulted. He had a reputation as a rake, dammit! Who the devil was this girl—who on the one hand seemed like a virtuous maiden, unless he misread her completely—and yet she would climb into a carriage with a perfect stranger and happily strip to the buff at his command.

Trusting him not to ravish her.

Though it seemed that to her, he was not a stranger. How *did* she know his name?

He pondered that conundrum as she wriggled and panted and tossed soggy white garments onto the pile on the floor, garments he preferred not to think about. First a petticoat, then a chemise, followed by stays, and oh, lord, there went the stockings. He waited for a pair of drawers to join the pile, but there were none.

Only three kinds of females didn't wear drawers: the sheltered, old-fashioned kind; women who couldn't afford them; and tarts.

He waited. The suspense was unbearable. "Are you finished?"

"Yes, but I'm still quite damp. Do you have anything I can dry myself with before I put your shirt on?"

Damn. He should have thought of that. "Hold the rug for a minute."

She took hold of it and lowered it to her chin. Her eyes were light gray, rimmed with long dark lashes, and gleamed in her dirty face like polished pewter. The pupils were huge and dark and looked slightly unfocused. The effects of the drug, he assumed.

"It's strange but I don't feel as cold without my wet clothes, even though—" She blushed and looked away.

Ned didn't need to complete the sentence. He was only too aware of her naked state. He fished in the valise, found a small towel, tossed it over to her side of the rug then took the rug back, raising it again to block out the sight of her.

"How do you know my name?"

"You're a friend of my brother's. We met at his wedding."

Ned frowned. He usually avoided weddings. They invariably sparked his grandfather to fresh attempts to match him up with some female he—Grandfather—considered suitable.

"You were his best man."

His best man? Ned almost dropped the rug. He'd only ever been one man's best man. "You're Cal Rutherford's sister?"

She grabbed the drooping rug from his nerveless grasp and tucked it around her naked body—she had not yet donned his shirt—not showing the slightest awareness of her appalling situation as she gave him a warm and trusting smile. "Yes, don't you remember me? I was one of the bridesmaids."

He stared at her—she'd wiped her face clean—and tried not to let his gaze drop to where the fur rug was nestling like an animal against lush, bountiful breasts. This was Cal Rutherford's sweet-faced little sister? Naked in his carriage—naked!—covered only by a rug? "You're . . . Lucy?"

Her smile dimmed slightly. "It's Lily. I'm Lily."

"Put the shirt on," Ned said gruffly. He wasn't up to taking the rug from her grasp, so he stood and turned his back. Cal Rutherford's little sister. Good God.

"Make sure you tuck the rug around you as well. The shirt isn't very warm. You don't want to catch a chill." He needed her to be wrapped in thick, opaque, shapeless layers—preferably dozens of them—and not just because of the possibility of a chill. She was a luscious little armful—too luscious for his peace of mind.

His friend's little sister. Not so little anymore.

Marriage bait.

"You can turn around now," she said after a moment.

He turned. She sat huddled on the seat like an orphan from the storm, her feet tucked under her, swathed to the chin in silky dark fur, the white edges of his shirt collar just showing beneath it. Her pale complexion, clean now and flawless—except for the deepening bruise on her cheekbone—glowed like a pearl in the shadowed interior of the carriage. Her mouth was full and lush, but her eyes were ringed beneath with heavy purple shadows. She looked exhausted.

How the hell had a sister of Cal Rutherford ended up in such a sordid mess?

He leaned forward and gently cupped her chin, tilting her face toward the light to examine the bruise. She sat quietly under his examination, blushing slightly. Her innocence, her open, trustful expression frustrated him. She had no business trusting strange men. Even if she knew—or thought she knew—who he was.

No one was who they seemed to be. No one. Not even him. Especially not him.

"Does it hurt?" he asked, then silently berated himself for a fool. Of course it hurt.

"Not very much."

He didn't believe her. That bastard hadn't held back with that backhander. A nasty blow from a ruthless villain. God help her if she'd ever married him.

Her gaze dropped to his knuckles, skinned and raw. "Your poor hands, are they—"

"No." He shoved them in his pockets and sat back. The movement drew his attention to the soggy pile of clothing on the floor. "Faugh, that stench!" He opened the carriage door and kicked the pile of sodden, muddy clothing out onto the road.

"My clothes!" she exclaimed. She peered out the window, then turned to him accusingly. "What did you do that for?"

"They were filthy."

"But that was my favorite dress."

"You can buy another one." She continued exuding silent

indignation, so he added bluntly, "Look, whatever muck you fell in stank like a midden. I'm not traveling all the way back to London with a stink like that in the carriage. We'll stop in the next town and get you a hot bath and something clean to wear."

"Oh." She glanced down at herself, sniffed cautiously, and blushed. He cursed himself silently for embarrassing her. She stank, but it wasn't her fault.

"Do you have anything to drink?" she asked. "I'm very thirsty."

He passed her a bottle. "Cold tea—a habit I picked up in the army. Never know when you might need it." She drank it all down, draining it dry. Thirsty indeed.

"Thank you. I needed that." She handed it back with a tremulous smile.

"So, I gather you weren't eloping with that bastard?"

That put the starch back in her spine. "No, of course I wasn't! He abducted me."

"How?"

She flushed slightly. "He tricked me." She fidgeted a little, tucking her toes more securely under the fur rug. "I was at the Mainwaring rout with Cal and Emm . . ."

She explained how she'd been enticed outside.

He frowned. "You didn't realize the note was a forgery? You didn't recognize your own sister's writing?"

She turned a dusky rose-pink and didn't meet his eyes. "No," she mumbled, but didn't explain. She'd probably had too much to drink, he decided.

She continued her story, explaining how she was shoved into a carriage and drugged—kept in a damned airless box like a coffin—and his anger grew.

She glossed over the part where she'd been let out to relieve herself, mentioning only that the pins and needles had made it hard to walk, and that the fresh air had made her more alert, but he could read between the lines at her complete mortification.

He wished now he'd beaten that bastard to a pulp and then dragged him and his damned coachman off to jail. If he'd realized at the time what he'd been dealing with . . .

"So his destination was Gretna Green and a forced marriage," he said when she'd finished. "An heiress, are you?"

She nodded. "Cal always warned us that men might want us for our money, but I never imagined . . . I didn't think . . ." Her face crumpled and the big gray eyes filled with tears. "I've made such a mess of things. Everyone will be so worried."

"Not your fault," he said heartily, hoping to head off the incipient waterworks. "In fact, dashed clever of you to have the presence of mind to stick your tongue in the neck of that bottle."

She looked up in surprise. "Clever?"

"Absolutely. You escaped from that villain all by yourself, didn't you?"

"Yes, but if you hadn't come along—"

"Don't even think about it. I did, and that's all that matters. We'll get you back home safe, don't worry, and nobody will know of your little adventure. And you won't be tricked by any plausible blackguard in future, will you?"

She bit her lip. "I hope not." It came out as a shamed whisper.

There was a long silence. He didn't know what to say. He knew nothing about this girl, apart from who her brother was. He wasn't used to the company of virtuous young women. He'd done his best to avoid respectable women since he'd sold out of the army.

He had no desire to marry, no desire to take on the responsibility for anyone's future except his own. It would be necessary one day, he accepted that—he owed it to Grandfather, and to the family name. The blasted title.

But not yet.

She gave a sudden, convulsive shudder, then glanced at him self-consciously. "Just thinking about what a lucky escape I've had."

He nodded.

"I can't imagine what it would be like to be forced to marry a man you don't know." Her words were a little slurred still and the pupils of her eyes were dark. The remnants of the drug.

"Mmm."

She added shyly, "I've always wanted to marry for love."

"Ah." He nodded, as if he had some idea of what she was talking about. Love? Marriage was about duty. And heirs. And responsibility.

Last year he'd almost married a woman he barely knew, the daughter of a friend of his grandfather. Only to please the old man, who he'd thought was on his last legs—the cunning old devil.

Ned hadn't particularly fancied the girl, but he was philosophical about marriage—no matter what way you looked at it, it was a lottery—and he would have gone through with it. He'd let Grandfather down enough in his life; might as well do this one thing to please the old man before he breathed his last.

Luckily once the girl got to know him better, she'd called it off. What had she called him? *A rake and a libertine, coldhearted, irreligious, unprincipled and irredeemable!*

Which was accurate enough. There was worse too, in his past, though she didn't know about that. Nobody knew, only himself. And the dead.

But Grandfather was still alive and kicking, which was the best outcome of all. If he loved anyone, it was his grandfather.

After a moment Lily glanced outside.

"Where are we, Mr. Galbraith? I have no idea how long I was shut in the darkness."

"Call me Ned. Or Edward." *Mr. Galbraith* from a girl only a handful of years younger than him made him feel like his father, even if his father was dead. For most of his adult life he'd been Lieutenant, or Captain or Major Galbraith. Or simply Galbraith to his peers. He glanced out the window. "We were a few miles before Boroughbridge when we met up."

She shook her head, clearly having no idea where Boroughbridge was.

"A dozen or so miles from Harrogate."

She gasped. "Harrogate? Harrogate in *Yorkshire*?"

He nodded.

"Then I've been missing for—how long? What day is it? I've lost all track of time."

He told her.

"Thursday afternoon?" she whispered incredulously. "It can't be. The Mainwaring rout was on Tuesday night." He watched as the truth sank into her. "Two nights away . . ."

They traveled along in silence after that. Ned was relieved when she finally closed her eyes. Pools of misty gray, fringed by thick, sooty lashes.

Cal Rutherford should have set a guard on her. She was a walking temptation to any man, and not just because she was an heiress. She was positively delectable—and too damned trusting for her own good.

Look how she was preparing to go to sleep, right there in front of him. A man she barely knew.

For all she knew he could have the morals of a tomcat— as bad as or even worse than the fellow who'd abducted her. She'd just admitted she was an heiress. Just because he was her brother's friend didn't necessarily mean he could be trusted with women. Or heiresses.

Of course he'd cut off his right arm before he harmed her—he did have some shreds of honor left—but she wasn't to know that.

The coach swayed as it took a bend and she tilted dangerously, her eyes still closed. Lord, if she wasn't careful she'd fall right off the seat. He swapped seats to sit beside her, and pulled her gently upright again.

Those long, dark eyelashes fluttered; she murmured something he didn't catch and snuggled up against him. He looked down at her. Her head rested against his arm, her wet hair dampening his sleeve. He didn't usually encourage—or even allow—women to cuddle up to him. He wasn't the cuddling sort.

Blasted drug.

She muttered something unintelligible, and moved restlessly. The rug slipped to her waist. He swallowed—that shirt was too damned thin for words.

"Lily."

She didn't stir. He tried again, louder, and tried to push

her into a more upright position, but she was deep asleep. He reached across her to tug the rug back up to decency again, and she sighed and snuggled into his inadvertent embrace, her warm, soft curves pressed against him, her unbruised cheek cuddled against his shirtfront.

He regarded her helplessly. She lay against him, more or less in his embrace, relaxed and wholly trustful. His arm hovered a moment over her, then he sighed and wrapped it carefully around her—only to support her, he told himself. The road was bad. There were bumps and potholes. She could fall.

She slept on in his arms.

The bruise on her cheekbone was deepening. Lavender shadows darkened the delicate skin beneath her eyes. Tiny curls sprang from the mass of her damp hair as it dried. She must have worn it up in an elaborate twist the night she was abducted, for though it was wet and bedraggled, it was still partly pinned up. He could see a few pins glinting in the light.

Carefully he eased them out, one at a time, trying not to disturb her. Finally he had them all. He gently sifted his fingers through her soft, damp hair, loosening the tangles and spreading it out to help it dry. Dark curls twined about his fingers.

A damp lock of hair fell across her mouth. He carefully lifted it away and smoothed it back behind her ear. A small, dainty ear, with a tiny hole in the lobe. Had she lost an earring?

Cal Rutherford's little sister. Courage obviously ran in the family. She'd been drugged, abducted, imprisoned for hours at a time in a cramped, airless compartment under a seat, subjected to lord only knew what indignities and humiliations. She was bruised, cold, wet and filthy—he'd forced her to strip in his presence and had thrown away her ruined clothes. Most females he knew would be hysterical by this stage.

Instead she'd curled up against him, practically naked but trustful as a kitten, and gone to sleep in his arms. The remnant effect of the drugs. At least he hoped it was.

Her brother had made a practical marriage in order to protect his sisters. He'd be beside himself now, poor fellow, not knowing what had happened to Lily. Brothers needed to take care of their sisters.

Ned was grateful he had no younger sisters to take care of—or brothers, for that matter. He'd proved long ago that he couldn't be relied on to take care of anyone. He stared bleakly out the window at the shifting scenery, the weight of warm, soft woman heavy against his chest. It was raining again, a soft gray mist.

She twisted restlessly. The rug slipped, pulling the shirt awry and revealing the curve of a creamy breast and a bare, vulnerable shoulder. There were bruises on her body as well as her cheek. He dragged his gaze off her, tugged the shirt up, tucked the rug in more securely and resigned himself to the inevitable: The trip to London was going to be torture.

The carriage rattled onward. They stopped for a change of horses, but Lily didn't stir. Her sleep might be heavy but it wasn't restful. Her body twitched and wriggled, and the expressions that passed across her face . . . Whatever dreams she might be having, they weren't pleasant.

He should have killed the villain who'd done this to her.

He couldn't return her to her brother in this sorry state. It wouldn't be fair either to her or to Cal. A handful of lines from his school days came to him: *Sleep that knits up the raveled sleave of care, The death of each day's life, sore labor's bath, Balm of hurt minds, great nature's second course, Chief nourisher in life's feast.*

His initial plan had been to drive on through the night and most of the next day—getting her back to London in the shortest possible time. She needed sleep, but not in a rattling jolting carriage. Proper sleep, in a bed that didn't bounce with every pothole. And any journey to London would be interrupted every twenty miles or so when they stopped to change horses.

He wanted to relieve her of her ordeal, not add to it.

She needed calm and uninterrupted sleep, and time to let the drug pass from her system. Food. And a bath. He would restore her to her family with her dignity intact, not half naked, bruised, dirty and dazed.

He reached up with his free hand and rapped on the roof. "Find a suitable small town," he said when Walton opened the hatch. "We need an inn, but nothing fashionable. The lady needs a bed, a bath, food and clothing. And all with the utmost discretion, Walton. Nobody is to know who she is."

He hoped to hell that her family had kept her missing status a secret. No one must learn she was not still in London, safe in her own home in the care of her brother.

Because if they did, God help her.

Chapter Five

Seldom, very seldom, does complete truth belong
to any human disclosure; seldom can it happen that
something is not a little disguised, or a little mistaken.
—JANE AUSTEN, *EMMA*

AUNT AGATHA WAS IN HER ELEMENT IN HYDE PARK, TAK-
ing various cronies and acquaintances up in her barouche
for a turn around the park, and complaining to them of the
foolish stubbornness of her niece by marriage and her
charges, Rose and Georgiana—indicated by an irritable
wave of a hand as the two young girls rode behind and
sometimes beside the carriage.

Emm heard the first part after Aunt Agatha had set her
down to walk—exercise being good for a breeding
mother—as the carriage moved slowly off. "The youngest
gel, Lily, is stricken with what the doctor believes is the
vilest case of the influenza, but will Emmaline or the gels
consent to reside with me until all danger of infection
passes? Pshaw! They will not!"

Emm hid a smile. Aunt Agatha's cronies would be used
to complaints about ungrateful and intractable relatives.
Much more convincing than her showing concern for a
niece she'd never had much time for.

From time to time the girls broke away to tell Emm what
their aunt was saying. "You should hear her, Emm," Rose
said, half entertained, half indignant. "She's telling everyone how furious she is with you for refusing to move in
with her because of Lily's supposed illness! Apparently

you're risking the health of the Rutherford heir with your stubborn foolishness—as if she has a direct connection to God and knows what sex the baby will be."

"Oh, I hope she's a boy," Emm said. "Aunt Agatha wouldn't forgive her if she wasn't, poor little thing."

"She's mad at us too," George added. "We're disrespectful of our elders and recalcitrant and—what were the other words she used, Rose?"

"Intractable, undisciplined and unmanageable," Rose said with relish. "And we are, as far as she's concerned. I don't think that part was an act."

"In my day gels had more respect for the wisdom of their elders . . ." George said in a surprisingly good imitation of the old lady.

Inspired by the old lady's vehemence, they were determined to spread the news of Lily's illness far and wide, and it took all Emm's powers of persuasion to convince them not to mention Lily at all, unless anyone asked. They rode off, a little disappointed to have learned that discretion really was the better part of valor—at least this time around.

They looked stunning on horseback, one so fair and the other so dark and both such elegant horsewomen. How she wished they were a threesome, though.

Oh, Lily . . . It was impossible not to worry, even though Emm knew it did no good.

The barouche passed at a sedate trot. A drift of conversation reached Emm. "Ashendon? Oh, *he's* in no danger of infection. He's off seeing to some estate business in the country. Men are *never* there when you need them."

The old lady was very convincing. Each time the barouche passed, Aunt Agatha's passengers would turn their heads and direct reproachful looks at Emm. She sat on a bench, trying to look guilty but defiant, crushed, and at the same time foolhardy, stubborn and recalcitrant.

And keep a straight face.

She shouldn't have found anything to laugh about with Lily still missing and the situation looking grimmer every hour she was gone, but the truth was it was a relief to have anything to smile about, even if her amusement had to be hidden.

"Lady Ashendon, Lady Ashendon!"

Emm turned to see who was speaking, just as Sylvia rushed up to her. "I just heard that Lily has been stricken with the influenza! So she's back, then? You found her? Oh, what a relief! I was so certain she'd eloped with my horrid cousin—what? What have I said?"

"Keep your voice down, Sylvia," Emm snapped.

Sylvia looked bewildered. "But why? Lily didn't elope after all, did she? Everyone is saying she's been taken ill and that's why nobody's seen her in the last few days."

"Yes, she's ill, with the influenza," Emm said in a firm, clear voice, hoping any ears pricked in their direction could hear. "I don't know where you heard anything to the contrary, but—"

"People were saying that one of the Rutherford girls had eloped," Sylvia explained. "Well, I knew it must be Lily because Lord Ashendon came to my home in the middle of the night searching for her—oops! Is that meant to be a secret?"

"No, but we don't want to spread untruths, do we?" Emm, well aware of several members of the ton standing nearby, forced herself to sound calm and unworried. "Lily left the Mainwaring party without telling us because she was feeling ill. Of course Cal, being very protective of his sisters, became worried—he has a tendency to overreact. But as it turned out the poor girl was coming down with the influenza and was a little feverish and confused."

"Oh, is *that* what happened? I'm so sorry I got the wrong end of the stick! But don't worry, I'll let everyone know the truth. Give poor Lily my love and tell her I'll visit as soon as the infection has passed."

Sylvia hurried away, leaving Emm staring after her. She casually glanced around to see if anyone had been close enough to hear. Several elegant ladies glanced quickly away and moved closer together, murmuring quietly. One word drifted to Emm's ears: Eloped?

Emm borrowed a word from Cal's vocabulary. Damn!

* * *

DUSK WAS FALLING WHEN THE CARRIAGE ENTERED A sleepy little village a few miles off the main road. Ned looked out the window. Walton had chosen well. It was neither so small a village that they would stand out and be memorable nor a large enough town to attract members of the ton who might recognize them.

They stopped outside an ancient inn, crooked with age, but otherwise as neat as a pin, with mullioned windows polished to gleaming, a well-swept courtyard and several half-casks filled with flowers on either side of the entrance. There were no fashionable traveling coaches in the street outside, no phaetons or curricles—only a rustic wagon or two and an ancient-looking dogcart. Perfect.

"Wake up, Lady Lily," he said, raising her gently. He had no intention of letting her realize she'd slept sprawled across him, her head snuggled against his chest, her breasts pressed against him. Testing his self-control to the maximum.

She stirred and abruptly came awake with a jerk, flailing out with her fists. One of them caught him in the eye. "Ouch!" He caught the other fist in his hand. "Gently now. You're safe."

Her eyes flew open and for a moment she stared blankly at him. Then the tension drained abruptly from her. "Oh. It's you. Sorry, I thought you were—"

"I know. But you're safe now." He released her hand and picked up the rug from the floor. He tucked it back around her, trying not to notice—unsuccessfully, even with a watering eye—exactly how thin and inadequate his shirt was on her.

Her gaze flew to his eye. "Oh, dear. Did I do that?"

"It's nothing."

"No it's not, it's all red. Let me—"

He pushed away her hands. "It's all right. I've had worse." He hated being fussed over. "We're here. I'll go ahead and make the arrangements. I want you to wait in the carriage until—"

She glanced outside, frowning. "Where are we?"

He shrugged. "Some village. There's an inn here where we can pass the night in relative comfort." More comfortable than trying to sleep with a luscious, far-too-trusting siren draped across his lap.

"An inn?" She gave him a wary look and pulled the rug closer around her. "I don't want to stay at an inn. I thought you were taking me straight home."

Ned wanted to roll his eyes. *Now* she got suspicious. He was simultaneously pleased at the evidence that she did, in fact, have a cautionary bone in her body, albeit a slow one, and irritated that after all this, she should be suspicious of him.

He'd been practically a saint for the last few hours, letting her sleep while snugged up against him, keeping her decently covered, for the most part—she was a restless sleeper. And resolutely ignoring the raging appetites she stirred in his body.

"I am taking you home, but it'll be dark soon, so we'll stop for the night here."

She bit her lip. "It's just that they will be frantic with worry."

"Your brother will be on your trail as we speak. He's not the sort to sit back waiting to hear—and if I know Cal, he'll have a team of men out looking for you as well."

She gave him a troubled look. "I think some men came looking for me when we were on the road. I tried to call out, but I was gagged and under the seat and the drug made it difficult to think, and"—she sighed—"they didn't hear me."

His jaw tightened. That swine should be rotting in jail, or better still dangling at the end of a rope.

"I'll send your family a note by messenger; don't worry, it'll get to London faster than a coach and four. There's no need to travel through the night. Your abductor might have done so, but it's dangerous, especially when there's no moon, and I have more consideration for my coachman and the horses." And for his passenger. She was worn to the bone. She needed food and sleep and care before undertaking another long, uncomfortable journey.

Besides, even if they drove hell-for-leather, stopping

only to change horses, it would still take all night and part of the next day to get to London.

He hoped to hell Cal had managed to keep the whole affair under wraps, come up with some story to explain her absence. As long as he had—and Cal was no fool—and as long as he could get her back to London with no one else the wiser, the consequences to her would be limited to a nasty experience and a few bruises.

"Besides, we need to get you some proper clothes"— he quirked a brow—"unless, of course, you *want* to arrive in London naked but for a man's shirt and a fur traveling rug."

She gave a halfhearted little laugh. "No, of course not."

"Good. Then wait here while I make the arrangements."

Lily waited in the carriage, the rug wrapped tightly around her. Guilt wrapped her even tighter. The sleep had helped, but the drug still lingered like glue in her veins, making her limbs heavy and uncertain.

Her thoughts, however, were becoming clearer by the minute.

Everyone at home would be so worried about her. Rose and Emm and George would be frantic, and Cal—Cal would be out somewhere on the road from London, out in the cold and rain, worried sick, looking for her.

Mr. Galbraith—Edward—had had to turn back from wherever he was going and make the long journey back to London. And deal with a muddy, miserable, droopy creature who couldn't even stay awake! She was entirely dependent on him.

She wasn't even a friend of his. He might know Cal, but he hadn't recognized Lily at all.

All this trouble and anxiety and inconvenience was her fault. Oh, Mr. Nixon might be the villain responsible, but deep down Lily knew she was to blame. If she'd had her wits about her . . . If she hadn't been fretting about Rose doing something reckless . . .

But the fact was, Rose would *never* have sent her a note.

You didn't realize the note was a forgery? You didn't recognize your own sister's writing?

She hadn't been able to bring herself to explain to him about her dreadful inability. As it was, he only thought her careless. Or maybe stupid. Which she was, but in a much worse way than he'd imagined.

She'd hoped that once she left school she'd be able to hide her weakness from everyone. Now . . .

She burrowed deeper into the rug. The trouble was, she wanted him to like her.

Though why on earth would he like a girl who'd dragged him into such a mess, who'd spoiled his plans and forced him to make the long, uncomfortable journey back to London, a girl who—she sniffed at herself cautiously—still smelled faintly of mud and vomit and animal dung . . .

The carriage door opened, jerking her from her gloomy reverie, and he stood there, looking handsome and serious, his brow a little wrinkled but the rest of him elegant and immaculate. The contrast between them couldn't have been more depressing.

"I've told the landlady you're my sister and that you had an accident on the road. Your luggage—because, for reasons known only to yourself, you traveled only with bandboxes—was ruined when you and your carriage went off the road and into a river."

Lily blinked.

"I was following behind in my own carriage," he continued. "I am a bad-tempered fellow and female chatter annoys me, so we travel in separate carriages." He gave her a wry look. "It was the best I could come up with on the spur of the moment."

He held out his hand. "Luckily this inn, small as it is, has a bedchamber with a sitting room attached. It's very small, but clean and adequate. How are you feeling? Can you stand?"

"Yes, of course." She stood on legs that felt as if they'd been stuffed with sawdust and started cautiously down the carriage steps, then squeaked in surprise as he swept her off her feet and held her against his broad, firm chest.

"Oh, but you don't need—"

"Has to be this way," he said gruffly. "Don't want the *hoi polloi* gawking at your bare legs and feet, do we? Besides, the cobbles are wet and cold and dirty." He carried her toward the inn, where a plump, motherly-looking woman waited with a concerned expression, holding the door open for them. "The landlady, Mrs. Baines," he said in her ear. "Oh, and your maid broke her leg in the accident. We had to leave her behind in the care of a local physician."

Lily barely heard him. She'd never been carried by a man in her life. Not since she was a small child and Cal carried her about on his shoulders. She held her breath, desperately wishing she were slimmer, lighter, daintier.

He strode into the inn and mounted the stairs rapidly, seemingly indifferent to her weight. He wasn't even breathing heavily. The inn was small, the floors and ceilings crooked with age, and Mr. Galb—Edward—had to bend his head to get through the doors. At the top of the stairs, a door stood ajar. He pushed it open with his boot, carried her in and deposited her gently on a rag rug.

The sitting room was small, furnished with a worn settee, an overstuffed armchair and a small table with two wooden chairs. Though an open door Lily could see an even smaller room containing a large bed with a spotless white counterpane and a plain oaken wardrobe. Everything was worn and a little shabby, but it all looked and smelled very clean.

A sturdy young woman was crouched before the sitting room fireplace, blowing hot coals into life with fresh kindling and a pair of bellows. At their entrance she jumped to her feet and bobbed an awkward curtsey.

Mrs. Baines, who'd followed them up the stairs, said, "My daughter, Betty, sir, she'll take fine care of your sister." Turning to the girl she said, "Didst tha fetch them clothes for the young lady?"

"Not yet, Ma, I was getting the fire—"

"Well, run along and fetch 'em, then." The girl hurried away. Her mother turned back to her guests. "Dinner will be ready in half an hour, sir—enough time for the young lady to take a bath and—Oh, here are the lads now."

Two hefty young men—her sons by their resemblance to her and Betty—had appeared in the doorway, carrying large cans of gently steaming water. A younger boy followed, half hidden beneath a tin hip bath carried on his back, like a snail. Under one arm he carried a smart leather valise, which Mr. Galbraith took delivery of.

Under their mother's direction the lads placed the bath in front of the merrily blazing fire and filled it with water, while she fussed around fetching towels and a pot of soft, strong-smelling homemade soap.

Lily stood huddled in the rug, feeling useless and very self-conscious as the young men glanced surreptitiously at her, noting her bare feet and calves.

"Stop gawking at the poor young lady!" their mother snapped. "Ha'n't she endured enough already without a pair of great useless lummoxes staring at her as if they'd never seen a foot before! Now, get along downstairs wi' you—there's work a-plenty for idle hands yet!" Her sons left sheepishly.

Betty arrived a moment later with an armful of clothing, which she took through to the bedchamber and dumped on the bed.

"The girl will assist you at your bath and in all other ways," Mr. Galbraith told Lily. "Consider her your personal maid for the time being—I've arranged it with her mother."

He glanced at Mrs. Baines, who was in consultation with her daughter, and handed Lily a small hinged tin that he'd taken from his valise. "You might find this more to your taste. Now, take your time and be sure to send for more hot water if you need it. And when you're ready for dinner to be brought up, let the girl know. We shall dine up here, in private." He gave her a searching look. "Is there anything else you need?"

Lily shook her head. "Thank you, no. You're very— you're *all* very kind," she amended for the sake of her audience, recollecting that he was supposed to be her brother and brothers were expected to be kind. Truth to tell, she was feeling a little overwhelmed.

The door closed briskly behind him and Mrs. Baines, and the room was suddenly quiet. Recalling the small hinged tin he'd given her, Lily opened it. It contained a cake of soap. She sniffed it cautiously and smiled. It smelled delicious, of clean, slightly exotic masculinity and somehow, of safety and warmth. Much nicer than Mrs. Baines's homemade soap.

"Dost tha—I mean do you need a hand getting undressed, miss?" Betty said tentatively.

Lily, recalled to her senses, gave an embarrassed half laugh. "Not exactly," she said, and dropped the rug. It pooled around her feet.

Betty gasped. "Oh, my lordy lord! A man's shirt? Is that all? Ma said you'd lost all your clothes in the accident but— not even a shift!"

Lily grimaced uncomfortably, not knowing how to explain her scandalous lack of even basic underclothing. Before, in the carriage, when she was wet and half frozen, still dazed by the drug—and dizzy with relief to have escaped—it had seemed perfectly natural to strip down to her skin, dry off and then put on the only dry garment available.

At the time the feel of the finely woven fabric against her skin and the scent of clean linen with a hint of starch had been oddly comforting. Now, under Betty's horrified gaze, she inwardly cringed.

Betty glanced at the smears of dried mud still clinging to Lily's skin and the bruise on her cheek and her voice softened. "It musta been a terrible accident, miss. Hop into the bath now, before the water gets cold. You'll feel better after a hot bath and some clean clothes and one of Ma's good dinners."

She tugged the shirt off over Lily's head and stepped back. Lily stepped into the bath and sank gratefully into the steaming water. It was bliss.

Lily wet a washcloth and picked up the soap Mr. Galbraith had given her. A hint of sandalwood, the tang of lemon, the warm fragrance of cinnamon. Clean, spicy, exotic. Essence of Edward Galbraith.

She scrubbed herself first from top to toe with the rough-textured washcloth, determined to remove all trace of her noxious adventure, then knelt in the bath and lathered herself dreamily with Edward's delicious soap. The scent surrounded her, like balm to her bruised spirits.

Betty bustled about, draping towels over a stand in front of the fire and chattering happily. "Ma's the best cook in the village, so we'll soon have you feeling fine and dandy. Better'n your poor maid, I'll be bound."

Lily blinked. "My maid?"

"Broke her leg in the accident, Ma said."

Lily recalled the story Edward had told the landlady. "Oh, yes. It was terrible, poor girl."

Betty gave her a critical look. "Washing your hair, eh? Then you'll want some of Ma's special rinse. Puts a nice shine on your hair, it does, and smells lovely." She leaned forward and sniffed. "Though not as nice as that soap."

"Thank you, but there's no need—"

She broke off as Betty poked her head around the door and shouted, "Jimmy, fetch us up some of Ma's hair rinse! She'll know which one the young lady needs."

A few moments later a small hand poked a corked bottle through to Betty. "Here you are, miss, Ma's special rinse. Famous in the village she is for her rinses."

Full of misgivings about the greenish-yellow contents of the bottle, Lily resolved to find some tactful way of refusing the offer. She soaped her hair, then stood to let Betty rinse off the suds from her hair and body with a pail of clean, hot water. She bent over, wrung out her hair and put her hand out. "Pass me a towel if you please, Betty."

"Not yet, miss. There's Ma's rinse to go, remember?"

"Oh, but I don't think—"

Betty emptied the bottle over Lily's bent head, patting it thoroughly through the wet hair with enthusiasm. The liquid was cold and bracing and made Lily's scalp tingle. While Betty fetched a towel from in front of the fire, Lily sniffed her dripping hair cautiously. "Is that *berries* I can smell?"

"That's right, miss. Ma uses blackberry leaves for this one. Nice, isn't it? Funny color, I know, but it smells like a breath of summer. Once your hair's dry you won't hardly be able to smell it, though, but your hair will be nice and shiny."

Wrapping herself in towels that were threadbare but clean and beautifully warm from the fire, Lily stepped out of the bath and dried herself in front of the fire, then turned to try on the clothes that Betty had fetched. What if they didn't fit? Betty was a strong and vigorous country girl, and the only thing plump about her was her bosom. Lily would be mortified if the clothes were too small.

The chemise and petticoat were loose and shapeless garments. Lily sucked in her stomach as Betty fastened a corset around her and laced it firmly. Then she tossed the dress over Lily's head and tugged it down. "It's me favorite go-to-church dress, but Ma insisted you have the best, you being gentry and all." Made of vivid red linsey-woolsey, it was embellished with cream satin bows, pulled in with a drawstring under the bosom and flared out at the hips.

"There you are, miss, it's perfect on you. Pretty as a picture, you are."

There was no long looking glass in the inn, so Lily had to take her word for it. The dress was a little snug in the bosom, the design was far from fashionable and she'd never worn such a bright color. Again she mourned the beautiful dress Miss Chance had made for her, with the elegant layers of gauze that skimmed her curves lightly and made her feel . . . beautiful.

But there was no going back. Her poor dress lay abandoned in muddy ignominy, miles back, somewhere beside the road. She would have to face Edward Galbraith feeling—and no doubt looking—like a colorful cushion, tied in the middle.

Betty was watching her with an expectant expression.

Lily gave her a warm smile. "Thank you, Betty. It's a very pretty dress, and it's very generous of you to lend it to me." She slipped her feet into the slippers Betty had brought. They were a bit too big, but that was better than too small. She folded the thick woolen stockings so they doubled over her foot and put the slippers back on. That was better.

Betty gave a brisk nod of satisfaction, then stuck her head out the door and let out a piercing whistle. "That's to let the lads know to come and fetch away that water. Then I reckon you'll be ready for your dinner, won't you, miss?"

Lily was about to respond when her stomach did it for

her, rumbling noisily. Betty laughed. "I reckon you are, and all. You keep drying your hair by the fire, miss, and I'll let everyone know you're ready for your dinner."

NED SAT ON A BENCH IN THE STONE-FLAGGED TAPROOM, sipping the landlord's very decent dark ale. He'd written a note to Cal Rutherford but, not knowing the messenger, had taken the precaution of writing, if not in code, then in a manner Cal would understand. After their wartime experiences, such discretion was second nature to both of them. It might not be wartime, but the potential for scandal was real. If it reached Cal, he'd be reassured, but if the note fell into the wrong hands it would appear innocuous, and no harm done.

He'd share the unsavory details with Rutherford later; no need to distress him or his family any more than necessary. The girl was safe and would be home late tomorrow night, God and the state of the roads willing. That was all they needed to know.

He spoke to Baines, the landlord, who produced what he claimed was a reliable man to deliver the message to London. Hoping the fellow was indeed reliable, he handed over the letter and enough money to cover the cost of hiring horses to enable him to ride through the night. He promised him a handsome sum on delivery and told him the receiver would pay him a bonus if he delivered it by the morning. He'd added a postscript to Cal to that effect.

It was all he could do. Even if the messenger proved feckless, or irresponsible, knowing he'd sent a message would at least relieve some of the worry in Lily's mind. In any case, barring any unforeseen circumstances, she'd be back in the bosom of her family by tomorrow night.

He was sipping his ale when a light, affected voice came from behind. "Excuse the interruption, my good fellow, but I would ask a small fav—good gad, it's Galbraith, isn't it?" the man exclaimed as Ned turned. "Last fellow I expected to see in this poky little place."

Swearing silently, Ned inclined his head. "Elphingstone." What the hell was Cyril Elphingstone, of all people, doing in this little out-of-the-way town?

The veriest Pink of the Ton, Elphingstone was dressed in dove-gray skintight breeches, gleaming gold-tasseled boots that Ned would swear had never met a horse, a high collar with a neckcloth arranged in such a complicated knot he could barely turn his head and a lavishly embroidered pink satin waistcoat. His red-brown hair—surely not its natural color—was elaborately curled and pomaded. He stood out in the smoke-stained little country taproom like a flamingo in a foundry.

Without being invited, he seated himself at Ned's table. He snapped his fingers in the air, which caused a liveried minion to scurry forward with a glass of port. "Carriage problems too, eh, Galbraith? My demmed chaise cracked a wheel and the blasted wheelwright says he can't fix it until tomorrow." He leaned forward confidingly. "Understand you've secured the only bedchamber in the house. Don't suppose you'd let an old pal share?"

"No," Ned said with uncompromising bluntness. Elphingstone was not and never had been an old pal, nor even a friend of any sort. He was, however, one of the biggest gossips in the ton, and right now Ned wished him at the farthest end of the country.

"Dash it all, you can't expect me to sleep"—Elphingstone gestured distastefully around the taproom—"down here among the rabble and riffraff."

Ned drained his tankard and stood. "Frankly, Elphingstone, I don't care where you sleep."

"I meant, of course, on a trundle bed. Surely—"

"No."

"What about the sitting room? I gather you've reserved that too."

"No. You'll have to look elsewhere."

Ned turned to leave, just as the young maidservant bounced in, saying, "Your sister is ready for her dinner now, sir. I've let Ma know and the boys will be bringing it up to your room in a minute."

"Your 'sister,' eh?" Elphingstone quirked a salacious eyebrow.

Ned swore under his breath. Elphingstone knew perfectly well he had no sister, no other siblings at all.

Elphingstone chuckled and said with a leer, "Now I know why you're so reluctant to share—and I don't blame you. Cozy armful, is she?"

Ned's fingers curled into a fist. He shoved it in his pocket. "Nothing of the sort," he said in a bored voice. "I'm escorting a young relative—well, more of a ward—to London, that's all."

"And sharing her bed, eh?"

There was a sudden cold silence. His gaze bored into Elphingstone until the man dropped his eyes, flushing.

"I don't care for your insinuations, Elphingstone." His voice was soft, icy.

The leer slid from the dandy's face. "Meant nothing by it, dear fellow. Nothing at all."

Ned paused a long moment as if considering the man's apology. Elphingstone swallowed convulsively.

"Take care what that idle tongue of yours suggests. The young lady's maid will sleep on a trundle in her bedchamber. I shall sleep elsewhere. Not that it is any business of yours."

Ned mounted the stairs, swearing under his breath. He'd been planning to sleep on the settee in the adjoining room—purely for her protection and with the door firmly closed between them—but now with Elphingstone sniffing around, he'd have to make other arrangements.

He was doing his best to ensure that there were no further repercussions from Lily's abduction, but if the dandy got the slightest whiff of her identity, she—no, *they* were done for.

Chapter Six

> "The pleasantness of an employment does not
> always evince its propriety."
> —JANE AUSTEN, *SENSE AND SENSIBILITY*

EDWARD—EVERY INCH OF HER SKIN SMELLED OF HIS SOAP
and she couldn't think of him as Mr. Galbraith anymore—
entered just as Mrs. Baines and Betty were setting out the
dinner on the table in the private sitting room.

He gave her one swift, all-encompassing glance, gave a
brusque nod, and moved to the window. He stood there,
gazing out across the night-dark moors in silence.

By his position, he was waiting for the women to finish
bustling around, but she could tell by his grim expression
that something had disturbed him earlier.

It took her back to the first time she'd ever seen him, at her
brother's wedding. She'd found him rather intimidating back
then, so tall and handsome and elegant and sophisticated—
the kind of man she just knew she'd never be able to talk to
without making a complete fool of herself.

But she'd watched him, nevertheless, unable to take her
eyes off him. The wedding reception had been held at her
former school—Miss Mallard's, where Emm had been a
teacher—and all the girls—all the females there, in fact,
old or young, married or not—had made such a fuss of him.

He'd been perfectly charming. The rumors were that he
was a dangerous rake who'd recently been jilted. Or had
jilted some poor girl—the stories were contradictory, but

the girls at Miss Mallard's didn't care which it was, they just loved flirting with a handsome man. The hint of danger that lurked about him only added to their enjoyment.

He'd handled their attentions with lazy indifference, those winter-green eyes of his glinting with subtle amusement. She couldn't hear what he said, but it seemed to her that every time he opened his mouth all the girls giggled and sighed and fluttered their eyelashes.

Of course the schoolgirls at Miss Mallard's rarely met any men, except at church and they were mostly ancient, bald or toothless, so any halfway decent-looking man was guaranteed to have girls twittering around him. A man like Edward Galbraith, lean, dark and crisply elegant, with a hard, clean-shaven jaw, a bold nose that was not quite straight, and a firm, masculine mouth—well, any female would be dazzled.

Even if she didn't have the courage to talk to him herself.

He'd flirted easily with any female drawn to his orbit, which was most of them, Miss Mallard included. But somehow, Lily thought, it wasn't in any way . . . personal. It was as if he'd been presented with a kitten, petted it absently so it purred happily, and then set it down, all without noticing or caring which kitten he had. Or what happened to it afterward.

As if women were all the same to him: old, young, pretty, plain.

But once, just for a few moments, when he thought himself alone and unobserved, she'd seen him gazing out over the company with the bleakest expression. She remembered thinking then that he had the saddest eyes she'd ever seen.

Then someone said something that drew him back into the present, and it was like a blind coming down—the bleakness vanished as if it had never been, and he was the sophisticated rake again.

Had he been jilted? Was he heartbroken? Something had to account for that desolate expression.

She studied him now as he stared out into the darkness. The last dying light had faded and the moon was hidden behind clouds. She couldn't quite read his expression; she could only see his stern, unsmiling profile, but his body looked tense, his jaw clenched tight.

"There now." Mrs. Baines stood back and surveyed the preparations with satisfaction. "There's faggots to start with—"

"Faggots?" As far as Lily knew a faggot was a bundle of wood, not round meaty balls in some kind of gravy.

"Savory ducks, then, some people call 'em," Mrs. Baines said.

Lily looked closer. "They don't look like ducks to me."

"Of course not, young miss—they're made of pig's liver, pork and bread crumbs," she said, as if Lily were showing appalling ignorance.

"What's that spiderwebby stuff they're wrapped in?"

Mrs. Baines laughed heartily. "Pig's caul, of course. Ah, you Londoners . . ." She shook her head.

"Famous for her faggots, Ma is," Betty said proudly.

Mrs. Baines smoothed her apron modestly. "Best in all Yorkshire, I've been told, though I don't know about that."

Edward turned away from the window and Lily was glad to see the bleak expression was gone from his eyes. There might even be a faint glimmer of amusement, though in the lamplight she couldn't be certain.

"I'm sure they'll be delicious, Mrs. Baines," he said.

Beaming up at him, Mrs. Baines waved him to the table. "Now, sir, sit yourself down and make a start on 'em while they're hot. You got to eat, keep up your strength, fine big lad like yoursel'. I'll away back to the kitchen, and Betty and one of the boys will bring the rest up in a few minutes."

Lily hid a smile as he held a chair for her to be seated. With his lean, rangy build, Edward was apparently the kind of man that women enjoyed feeding. Her brother, Cal, was the same. Nobody was suggesting Lily needed to keep up her strength, even though— Heavens! It must be *days* since she'd eaten.

She hadn't felt at all like eating before. The drug had made her feel so queasy. But now—her stomach rumbled again—she was ravenous.

Betty was back in a twinkling with the rest of the meal, assisted by her little brother Jimmy. She placed all the dishes on the table and directed Jimmy to bring a couple of jugs over. "There's Pa's best ale for you, sir—he said to tell you sorry, but we don't carry table wines, no call for 'em around here, see. And Ma thought the young lady might like a bit of barley water?" She gave Lily a worried look.

Lily nodded. "Perfect, thank you, Betty." When she was a little girl, Nurse used to give her barley water when she'd been sick, and now it was just what she felt like.

Betty gave a relieved grin and wiped her hands down her apron. "Right, then, if there's owt else you want, just call down the stairs."

The door closed behind her and a sudden silence fell as Lily and Edward were left alone.

After a moment he said, "I sent a message to your brother. He'll receive it tomorrow, in the morning if the messenger makes good time."

"Thank you. He—well, all of them must be so worried."

"We've done the best we can." His gaze skimmed her. "That bath has done you good. You look quite fetching in that dress, and the color suits you. You'll feel even better once you've eaten, I'm sure."

Lily agreed. She surveyed the table. It was a veritable feast. As well as the faggots there was mutton pie, the crust light and golden and smelling heavenly. It was served with mashed potatoes, carrots glazed with butter and a little grated nutmeg, and a dish of stewed greens. Also on the table was thick, crusty fresh baked bread, butter and honey.

He filled her glass with the barley water, picked up the jug of ale and waved at her to start. "No need to wait. A good ale takes a while to pour, so you go ahead."

She said a quick grace under her breath then buttered a slice of bread. It was fresh and smelled delicious. She bit into it and chewed slowly. Bliss.

"Will you try one of the faggots? They're an old Yorkshire country dish, very good."

"I'll try a bit," she said cautiously. "You seem to know a little about this part of the world. Are you from Yorkshire?"

He cut a slice off one of the faggots and placed it on her plate. "Gravy?"

"Just a little, please." She took a cautious bite. "Oh, it's very tasty."

He placed the rest of the meatball on her plate, then cut her a generous slice of the pie. Tender chunks of meat and rich gravy spilled from the flaky golden crust. He passed her the dish of greens, the carrots and the potatoes, ensuring she'd been served before filling his own plate.

"That was wonderful," she said when she'd cleaned her plate. She leaned back with a happy sigh. "I hadn't realized I was so hungry."

"Long time since you ate, I expect." He polished off the rest of the pie and buttered a fourth slice of bread. He'd eaten nearly three times as much as she had and yet somehow, he still looked as lean and hungry as a wolf.

She took a deep breath. "Mr. Galbraith, would you lend me some money, please?" She'd made her decision while she was taking her bath. And before that, while she was lying trussed like a goose in the cavity under Mr. Nixon's seat, she'd vowed to become more independent.

He looked up frowning. "Money? What for?"

"To pay for a coach ticket back to London."

He returned his attention to his dinner. "You're not returning to London on the mail coach." He said it as if she had no choice, no say in the matter.

"Yes," she said firmly. "I am." She'd already experienced the worst coach trip she could imagine. The Royal Mail could not be so difficult. People traveled on it all the time. "I'll take Betty with me, if that makes you feel better. I'm sure her mother would allow it if we paid her well enough, and Betty and I would chaperone each other. It would be quite respectable. As long as you will lend me the money for the ticket. Naturally my brother will repay you."

"Well, he won't, because I'm not lending you a penny." He snorted as if the very idea of her traveling on the Mail were ridiculous. "I'm returning you to your brother's care and that's the end of it." He sounded quite cross, as if she'd offended him in some way.

But she was not a package to be delivered. "Mr. Galbraith—Edward, I'm extremely grateful to you for rescuing me and taking such good care of me while I was . . . indisposed, but I'm in a much better case now, and there is truly no need to put yourself out for me."

"I'm not."

She gave a frustrated sigh. "If I were a total stranger, would you change your plans and turn back to London in order to return me to my family?"

He barely even considered her question. "But you're not a stranger, you're Cal Rutherford's sister and I owe it to our friendship to protect you, just as I would expect him to protect my sister in a similar situation."

"Do you have a sister?" she asked, momentarily distracted by the idea of him with sisters. On the few occasions she'd seen him, she'd gained the impression he was very alone.

"No. No siblings at all," he added, anticipating her next question.

"Sad for your parents."

"They're both dead," he said indifferently.

"Mine are too, but I have Cal and Emm and Rose and George. And the aunts," she said on a soft surge of emotion. She'd always taken family for granted.

There was a short silence. The fire crackled. Outside in the distance an owl hooted.

She straightened her spine and returned to the matter under dispute. "Whatever you think my brother might expect, I can see no reason why your plans should be ruined simply because I landed myself and my mess in your lap."

"My plans weren't ruined."

"But you were traveling north for some reason, I presume."

He shrugged. "A house party. Nothing important."

"But your friends will be disappointed when you don't show up, won't they?"

He gave her a flat look. "They're not my friends."

"They're not? Then why would you—?" She broke off. "I'm sorry, it's none of my business."

A knock sounded on the door and the innkeeper's daughter entered with a covered dish, followed by her brother carefully carrying a jug. "Gooseberry pudding with custard," she announced. "Put it there, Jimmy—careful, it's hot."

Ned was not displeased to have their conversation interrupted. The house party he'd planned to attend was nothing special, just something to do, a way of passing the time.

And how lame was that? Was this what his life had come to, finding the least disagreeable way to pass the time?

He brooded over that insight as the girl bustled about, swiftly clearing the table and passing the dirty dishes to her brother to stack onto a tray.

The people he'd expected to see at the house party? He wouldn't miss any of them. He doubted they'd miss him, either.

Several of the women invited had given him subtle but unmistakable indications that he'd be welcome in their bed, but he was under no illusions as to the significance of that. If he didn't turn up they'd find another willing man. There would be no shortage of substitutes.

The thought left a sour taste in his mouth. Was his life really so meaningless? He lifted his tankard and drank the last of the landlord's good dark ale.

"Shall I bring you up some more ale, sir?" the girl asked. Ned shook his head, and she and her brother swept from the room. The gooseberry pudding sat on the table in front of him, golden and luscious, steaming softly. Lily was staring at it, as if half mesmerized.

"A little pudding?" he asked her.

"I shouldn't . . . But it looks and smells so delicious . . . Perhaps just a taste." He cut two generous portions of the pudding, poured custard over each, and passed the smaller bowl to her.

"I take it we are agreed that you will return to London with me, and no further argument." It wasn't a question.

She sighed. "I suppose so. Though I don't like to cause you so much tr—"

"Nonsense." He cut her off brusquely. "It will be my pleasure to escort you." And to his surprise he realized it was true. He would much rather spend sixteen uncomfortable hours in a coach with Lily Rutherford—half drugged or not—than spend a week in the bed of one of the jaded ladies of the house party.

Only because he owed her a duty of care, for the sake of her brother, he told himself. His honor—what was left of it—required it.

She finished her pudding with every evidence of enjoyment and sighed as she set down her spoon. "Now I really am full. I think perhaps I'd like to go for a walk, just a short walk to stretch my legs."

"Not tonight, you won't."

She glanced at the window. "But it's stopped raining."

"I don't care about the weather." His voice was grim. "You're not leaving this room until I say so."

Her eyes widened, and Ned cursed himself for a fool. Of course, given her recent experience, she'd put the worst interpretation on his words. He hastened to explain. "Nothing to worry about, just that you can't go wandering around the inn or the village. If you are to emerge from this mess without damage to your reputation, nobody must learn you were ever missing from your brother's care. Nobody must see you—I mean nobody from our world, nobody who might recognize you."

Her face fell. "I know. But surely in this little out-of-the-way place—

He shook his head. "There's a fellow downstairs who's a notorious society gossip. He's an irritating little tick, but he's seen everywhere—you might even know him. Cyril Elphingstone?"

"Elphingstone . . ." A soft crease formed between her brows. "Is he a slender, nattily dressed man with a pointy nose and extraordinary chestnut-colored hair?"

"That's him in a nutshell. That's if chestnut is a sort of reddish-brown."

"It is. He's a friend—well, an acquaintance—of my Aunt Agatha. I don't like him very much. He always has some story to tell that's often rather nasty underneath. My sister, Rose, calls him 'the gnat.'"

"Very apt. The thing is, when we were downstairs earlier, he overheard the girl refer to you as my sister. He knows perfectly well I haven't got a sister."

"Oh."

He nodded. "That long nose of his was twitching with curiosity. He did his best to discover who you were, but I put him off."

"What did you tell him?"

"Just that I was escorting a young relative to London, and of course, he doesn't believe that, either."

"Why not? Does he know all your relatives, then?"

Ned opened his mouth to explain, then shook his head. There was nothing to be gained by telling her that no one in their right mind would entrust a beautiful young woman to a man of his reputation. Not that he'd ever been accused of trifling with innocents. In fact, he avoided them like the plague. He preferred women of experience, women who knew what they wanted—his body, not his name.

"It's Elphingstone's nature to be suspicious," he said. "Anything for a good story, I suspect, so don't step outside this door unless I tell you it's safe."

Her mouth drooped. "I suppose you're right, it's just that—I know discretion is important, but—" She shook her head. "No, I'm being silly, wanting to go for a walk. I can walk with my sisters when we get home again." Her lower lip wobbled. She bit on it and turned her head away so he wouldn't see.

And suddenly Ned realized. She'd spent most of the last two days locked in a tiny, dark, airless compartment, bound and gagged, unable to move. She'd told him how she couldn't lift her arms, not even to adjust the gag, how it had felt like she was locked in a coffin, and how she'd done her best to keep sensation alive in her feet. And how painful the pins and needles had been when she was finally able to walk again.

Of course she wanted to go outside and stretch the muscles that had been cramped for so long. And to breathe in the fresh air, and to loosen the tension he could see still gripped her body, despite the rest and the bath and the food.

Instead Ned had confined her to a poky little room, and all because of an irritating little busybody. She didn't deserve that.

"Wait here," he told her, and left the room.

Lily was surprised at his abrupt exit, but then she was finding Edward Galbraith surprising in a number of ways. She'd believed him the sort of desperately sophisticated gentleman that Aunt Agatha favored, spouting witty and urbane persiflage of the sort that often went right over Lily's head, the kind of man who would flirt charmingly with Rose and George, who were beautiful, and would look right through Lily, who wasn't.

Edward hadn't looked right through her, but neither had he flirted. He'd been brusque and bossy, remote and sometimes curt, and yet, underneath it all, he'd been . . . kind. Protective. Considerate.

He was, she decided, a puzzle.

A yawn surprised her. She ought to prepare for bed. She laid out the thick flannel nightgown Betty had lent her, but before she could undo a button or a lace, there was a brisk knock at the door and he was back, a heavy brown cloak draped over his arm and a pair of sturdy lace-up leather shoes dangling from his fingers.

"You'll need proper shoes, not slippers, if we're going to take a walk," he said, giving them to her. "Two steps outside and those slippers will be soaked through."

"But I thought—"

"There's a way out the back. Elphingstone's in the taproom at the front. The girl—Betty, is it?—will keep watch for him. If you still want to go for a walk, that is."

She did. She swiftly donned the shoes—Betty's again—doubling the woolen stockings under her feet and tying the laces firmly so that the slightly-too-big shoes were snug and comfortable. She fastened the cloak and tugged the deep hood up to ensure her face was well hidden. Despite its heavily practical fabric and color, a jaunty little gold silk tassel was fastened to the tip of the hood. The small touch of frivolity made Lily smile.

Ten minutes later she and Edward were walking along a narrow path that led between the houses behind the inn and up toward the hills that overlooked the village. The night was dark, with fitful glimpses of moonlight showing between the scudding clouds. They passed the last few houses in the village, warm and cozy-looking, their lamplit windows gleaming golden squares defying the night.

They trudged along the path, skirting a dense thicket of trees, making for the top of the hill silhouetted against the night sky. He'd adjusted his long-legged gait to hers. There was something so special in walking along in the night, side by side, alone and yet together.

"This is lovely," she murmured.

"Lovely? It's dam—dashed cold. Are you warm enough?"

"Perfectly warm, thank you. This cloak is very thick." Her face was actually quite cold and her hands were chilled, but she didn't mind. Betty hadn't provided gloves and Lily hadn't thought of them until they were well away from the inn. She'd been wearing long white evening gloves when she'd been abducted. What had happened to them? She had no idea. Not that satin evening gloves would be at all warm.

Besides, cold hands didn't matter a jot compared with the exhilaration of tramping along in the darkness, breathing in the moist, crisp air, putting the horrid events of the last two days behind her. The bath, the meal and now the cold, brisk air acted like a purge, making her feel clean and whole and herself again, scouring away the memory of the sourness, the fear, the shameful helplessness.

She'd survived; she was free. Nobody could force her to marry. She belonged to herself again. And to her family.

"Whoops!" she exclaimed lightly as she skidded in a patch of mud.

"Here, take my arm." Without waiting for her agreement, he tucked her arm into the crook of his. Warmth flowed into her chilled fingers.

"When do you think we'll get back to London?" she asked.

"Depends on the state of the roads and the availability of horses, and assuming we encounter no obstacles or problems on the way, it'll take most of the day and part of the night—sixteen or seventeen hours at least. I'd prefer to drive through in one day." He gave her a sidelong glance. "If you can bear it, that is."

"Of course I can. I'd rather be home than spend another day on the road." After the nightmare trip with Mr. Nixon, she could bear anything. "But it's a long day. Can your coachman manage that kind of journey?"

"He can. He's driven a lot longer and in much worse conditions. And I pay him well."

"So what time in the morning shall we lea—eek!" She broke off with a shriek as something huge and winged swooped out of the darkness straight at her. She felt the whoosh of air against her face, caught a glimpse of talons poised to attack, and ducked, just as something caught on the hood of her cloak. The tug almost overbalanced her and she would have fallen had not Edward grabbed her and pulled her hard against him.

"Wh-what—?"

"An owl." He made no move to release her, his arms wrapped firmly around her. "Did it hurt you?"

"N-no, it just gave me a fright." She gathered her wits. "When I saw those talons coming at me . . ." She shivered.

"But it didn't touch you," he soothed, his voice deep and reassuring.

For a moment she simply gave herself over to the comfort of his embrace, leaning against him, her cheek pressed against his chest, his arms firm and solid around her. She took a few deep breaths, breathing in the familiar scent of him, of soap and sandalwood and starch. And safety.

Then, remembering her resolution to be more independent, she straightened and stepped back. "But why—I mean, owls don't normally attack people, do they?" His embrace loosened, but he didn't quite release her.

He ran his hand up her spine and cupped the back of her head, exploring briefly. "I think you'll find that little gold tassel was the target." His hand was warm.

"The tassel?" She felt the tip of the hood. Sure enough, the tassel was gone. "I was attacked for *a tassel*?"

His mouth quirked. "It was a *gold* tassel, after all. Your owl clearly has expensive tastes."

She stared up at him a moment, then laughter bubbled up from somewhere. An owl with expensive tastes. How perfectly ridiculous.

Ned held her while she laughed, her body soft against him, her laughter a little high, a little out of control. More than was warranted by a mild joke and a small fright with an owl.

She hadn't cried at all over her abduction ordeal, but now . . . This laughter was a release. He held her close in the darkness, just for comfort and support, he told himself, even as he breathed in the scent of her, the spicy tang of his own soap wrapped around the sweet, warm fragrance of woman, a combination he found quite . . . irresistible.

A hunger stirred in him, deep, long denied. He fought it. This wasn't for him. *She* wasn't for him. Innocent, vulnerable, sweet—no.

Her laughter ended on a hiccup, and she rested her cheek briefly against his chest before pushing herself gently out of his embrace. "Sorry, I got a bit carried away there. I must be more tired than I realized." Wiping under her eyes with her bare fingers, she glanced apologetically up at him, and her hood fell back just as a beam of fugitive moonlight bathed her satin-pale face.

Her hair was pulled back in a knot, but tiny dark curls clustered like feathers around her forehead and ears. The bruise shadowed her cheekbone, like a stain on a pearl. Her eyes were wide and fathomless, her mouth lush and damp and sweetly curved.

Ned couldn't take his eyes off her, couldn't breathe.

A single tear glittered unnoticed on her cheek. He reached out a finger to collect it and caught himself up in mid-gesture. Gloves. He pulled them off and stuffed them in his pocket. She watched him, frowning slightly.

"I'm perfectly all right," she began.

He cupped her cheek—her skin was like cold silk—and with his thumb smoothed the tear away.

"Edward?" she said hesitantly, but she didn't move, didn't push him away, just stood there, with her cheek cradled in his hand and her eyes dark pools of mystery in the moonlight.

The clouds buried the moon again and they were standing in darkness with the scent of spring-damp earth all around them. His awareness filled with her, still and somehow breathless and expectant. Her skin warmed under his touch.

He couldn't stop himself. He bent and kissed her, softly, a bare whisper of skin against skin. A tremor of heat. A wisp of sensation.

She shivered but didn't move away. He tried to read her expression in the moonless dark but could see nothing. She sighed, and her breath warmed him.

He kissed her again, and with a soft murmur her lips quivered, then parted. She leaned into him and he tasted innocence and luscious heat and sweet, intoxicating acceptance.

She returned his kisses, eagerly, a little clumsily, pressing her softness against him, loosing a ravening hunger deep within him. He pulled her hard against him, deepening the kiss, inflamed by the taste of her, the feeling of her in his arms.

She slid her hands up his chest, along his jaw, and her fingers were cold, so cold, and her mouth so sweet and warm and giving. He was all heat and hunger, filled with an aching, ravenous longing that . . . that frightened him.

It brought him to his senses. This was wrong. She was Cal Rutherford's sister and he—he was not fit for an innocent girl's embrace.

He released her, pushed her away, not gracefully, staggering back as if in recoil.

"E-Edward? What's the matt—"

"No." His voice was harsh, repelling. "This is wrong. A mistake."

"But—"

"No. Forget it ever happened." He wiped his mouth roughly with his sleeve as if to remove all trace of her—as if anything could—she was in his blood now. But the moonlight—the damned interfering moonlight—caught his gesture, lit it clearly, and he saw the ripple of pain pass across her face as if he'd slapped her.

He reached out to her in an involuntary gesture, but she'd turned away and missed it—and that was a good thing, he told himself. He had to remain strong. He clenched his fists, fighting for some semblance of the sangfroid he was known for, breathing deeply and calming slowly as the cold air scoured him.

Never had a few simple kisses thrown him so far off balance. Never had any woman, let alone a young vir— No. Pursue that thought to its natural conclusion and court madness.

Away in the woods a fox screamed, lustful and forlorn. Ned knew how the wretched beast felt.

After a long moment, Lily turned. "Shall we continue on our way, or is it time to return to the inn? I know we need to make an early start." Her smooth, low-voiced question, so very composed-sounding and mundane, surprised Ned.

Was she as calm as she seemed, or was she doing her best to hide the same sort of turmoil that raged inside him? Her breathing was audible and slightly ragged but otherwise there was no sign of agitation in her voice or face or body—not that he could see, not in this damned elusive moonlight. Had she felt what he— No! He forced himself to take another step back. It didn't matter what she felt.

It. Could. Not. Be.

She was a romantic, gentle young lady—even her recent ordeal, nasty and terrifying as it must have been, hadn't dimmed her sweetness or her seemingly natural optimism. While he—he might not have reached his thirtieth year yet, but compared to her he was a hundred years old.

He took a deep breath. If she could take a couple of kisses in her stride, so could he.

A couple of kisses. It felt like so much more.

"Time to go back," he said. It came out gruff and abrupt, but he couldn't help that.

She put up her hood, pale fingers arranging dark fabric,

and he remembered how cold those fingers had been against his skin.

"Put these on." He shoved his gloves at her.

"I don't need—"

"Put the damned things on, your hands are freezing." His gloves were leather and lined with fur. He couldn't believe he hadn't noticed she wore no gloves, and had no pockets in which to warm her hands. And that she hadn't mentioned it.

Did this girl not know how to complain and demand she be looked after? Every other woman he knew had it down to an art form.

She gave an infinitesimal shrug, took his gloves and slid her hands into them. They were, of course, much too big, but at least they would be warm. "Now"—he was about to offer his arm, but thought better of it; he didn't need the contact—"after you." He gestured, and she stepped before him onto the narrow path.

They walked in silence, the sounds of their footsteps and the faint scuttles and far-off cries of wild creatures of the night all that accompanied them. And thoughts, tumbling, nagging, roiling . . .

Suddenly she stopped, turned to face him and said, "Was it me?"

For a moment he didn't understand. "What?"

Her face was pale and intent in the moonlight. "Why you stopped. Did I do it wrong?"

He closed his eyes. Christ! He swallowed. "No. You didn't do anything wrong."

She waited for him to explain further, but he couldn't bring himself to say another word. And if she stood there much longer, looking up at him with those big fathomless eyes, biting down on those soft lips, he wouldn't be responsible for his actions.

"It's late. Keep moving." It sounded harsh, but it was for the best. Her best.

Some expression quivered in her face, too fleeting for him to grasp, then she turned and resumed the walk. The path was wider now, a worn dirt track. Going downhill she skidded a little in the mud, and he leapt forward and seized her arm, preventing her from falling.

"Hold on to me," he told her. It was an order.

She gave him a look he couldn't read, then slipped her gloved hand into the crook of his arm. A knot deep within him eased.

Chapter Seven

Lady you bereft me of all words,
Only my blood speaks to you in my veins,
And there is such confusion in my powers.
—WILLIAM SHAKESPEARE, *THE MERCHANT OF VENICE*

THEY WALKED IN SILENCE. LILY DIDN'T FEEL THE SLIGHT-est bit cold, and it had nothing to do with his gloves or her hand tucked into the crook of his arm. Her whole body was alive and zinging. She darted a sideways glance at the stern profile of the tall man striding along beside her. What was he thinking? Why had he stopped kissing her, just when it was getting so . . . delicious?

Questions clattered in her brain like a tree full of star-lings at dusk. Did he not want to kiss her? Had she thrown herself at him? She thought back over the events of the night. She might have. She hadn't meant to.

An owl with expensive tastes. It wasn't even that funny, but she hadn't just laughed at Edward's little joke, she'd ended up clinging to him, laughing like a madwoman. And crying at the same time. So embarrassing. Who'd want to kiss a madwoman?

But he had. And then, *This is wrong. A mistake.* In such a harsh voice.

A mistake for whom? For him? Or for her? So frustrat-ing when people—men—made announcements and then refused to explain them.

That first brush of his mouth over hers, so light and tender—his lips were cold from the chilly night—had given her no warning of what was to come. Heat had blossomed wherever they'd touched, that . . . streak, like hot wire spiraling through her whole body.

She hadn't known it could be like that. Intoxicating, addictive. She'd wanted more, hungered for another taste of him, even now, after he'd pushed her away.

This is wrong.

Lily's cheeks burned. It hadn't felt the slightest bit wrong to her. It was lovely. Her mouth was still tingling. She could have gone on kissing him for hours.

Instead he'd broken off the kiss and pushed her away. Like offering a feast to a starving beggar, then snatching it away after one taste. Not that she was a beggar. She hadn't even known she was starving for his kiss until she'd tasted him.

Did I do it wrong? What had possessed her to blurt that out? Stupid, not to mention embarrassing. And of course he wouldn't tell her the truth. He was a gentleman, invariably polite!

But she really wanted to know. *Had* she been clumsy? Lacking? It was her first kiss, after all.

She'd thought she knew what to expect of kissing—the girls at school used to discuss it endlessly. To some it was all roses and clouds and soft music—utter bliss—but to others it was awkward, disconcerting and unsavory—all wetness, teeth-and-tongues and bumping noses.

Kissing Edward was nothing like that. It was . . . like hot spiced wine, and . . . fire—oh, there were no words, only feelings. She hugged them to herself. His kiss had called to something deep within her, something almost . . . animal. A little bit frightening. And irresistibly exciting.

She'd reacted instinctively, opening her mouth to him, pressing herself against him, seeking more. Had she been too forward? Ladies weren't supposed to encourage liberties from men. Was that it? Had her behavior disgusted him?

On the other hand, could his opinion of her get any lower? She'd met him in the most sordid manner: frantic, dizzy from drugs, wet and stinking. Then she'd thrown up in front of him, narrowly missing his boots. Then she'd stunk his carriage out so badly that he'd made her strip—

and she had! Stripped right in front of him, down to her birthday suit, with only a rug between them! And after he'd tossed her clothes out onto the road, she'd fallen asleep all over him, wearing nothing but his shirt and a rug. Probably drooling on him as well.

And now she'd thrown herself at him, all because of an owl.

No, poor owl, she couldn't blame him. It was Lily, all Lily. Because she liked Mr. Edward Galbraith a little too much.

Smoke from hearth fires hung in the air. They were nearing the village and Lily was no further enlightened. If she wanted an answer—and she did—there was only one way to find out. She'd already embarrassed herself with this man in every way possible; she had nothing else to lose.

"Explain to me, if you please. Why was it 'a mistake'?"

He started, as if she'd poked him with a pin, and dropped his arm. "What? I told you—"

"Yes, but you didn't explain. We kissed. Why is that so wrong?"

He cast a glance at the sky, took a deep breath and said, as if it should be perfectly obvious, "What's wrong is who we are, you and I, our circumstances."

"What circumstances?" Vomiting, stinking, stripping naked and drooling all over him jumped to mind. She braced herself.

He gestured. "You, me, alone, out here in the middle of the night."

"It's not that late. And nobody knows."

"That's not the point. I'm supposed to be protecting you."

Ah, so he was being honorable, as she'd suspected. "You have protected me. You saved me from Mr. Nixon. You looked after me. And tonight you stopped me from slipping in the mud, and you saved me from an owl." She paused a moment, then added softly, "A kiss doesn't hurt anyone, does it?"

He scanned the skies again as if searching for the right words, then said in a hard voice, "Look, it means nothing.

It was a moment of passing lust, that's all. Ephemeral. Temporary. Men have a tendency to take advantage of whatever woman is available, and that's what I did. And given who we are, it was a mistake."

"I see." If his kiss had been prompted by lust, it meant she didn't disgust him. That cheered her up. "So if we were different people?"

"We're not. I'm not for you, and you're not for me."

She nodded as if she understood and accepted his words, which she didn't. It was some kind of obscure masculine reasoning, and she could see she wasn't going to get any proper explanation out of him.

At least she understood—sort of—why he'd kissed her in the first place. It was why he'd stopped that bothered her now.

"You're sure I didn't make a mull of it, the kissing, I mean? I need to know, because it was my first-ever kiss." She felt him tense and something prompted her to add, "And if someone kisses me in the future, I would like to get it right."

She wasn't sure, but she thought she heard a muffled groan. "You didn't make a mull of anything. You were— It was—" He shook his head. "It was just a moment of passing lust."

"I see. Like a passing owl."

He blinked at the analogy, then shook his head in exasperation. "No, not like a passing owl! This conversation is becoming ridiculous. Just—just put the whole thing behind you and forget all about it."

Lily thought about that for a moment, then said, "I don't think I can."

He frowned. "Did you not hear a word I said?"

She gave him a warm smile. "I did. Every word you said." And a few he hadn't. "But if you think I can forget my first-ever kiss, you're sorely mistaken." She took his arm again and they resumed walking.

After a moment she added, "And I'm sorry if you didn't enjoy it because I thought it was . . . lovely."

A kiss doesn't hurt anyone, does it?

He checked that the coast was clear and hurried her up the stairs.

Did I do it wrong?

Lord preserve him from luscious innocents with big wide eyes and questions that buzzed in his brain. It—*she* was the last thing he needed—or wanted.

If you think I can forget my first-ever kiss, you're sorely mistaken.

He whisked her into the tiny sitting room and closed the door firmly behind them. Now what? He found himself staring at her mouth, rosy and moist. Was it slightly swollen from— No. He dragged his gaze off her.

"Time for bed." Her cheeks flushed a delicate wild-rose pink and he added hastily, "I mean, of course, to *sleep.*" The flush was from the walk in the cold air, he told himself.

She gave him a shy smile.

"Not yet, surely. It's still quite early and the walk has woken me up." He looked away. He did not need to see her smile, did not need to look into those wide gray eyes. *I'm sorry if you didn't enjoy it because I thought it was lovely.*

"After all, I've spent most of the last two days and nights sleeping."

He seized on the excuse. "Yes, but it wasn't a natural sleep. Your body needs to recover from your ordeal, and after a bath and a good meal—and that walk—sleep is what you most need. You have a long journey ahead of you tomorrow." He added briskly, "The landlord's daughter will be up in a short while. I've arranged for her to sleep on a trundle in your bedchamber."

"Betty? Why? For propriety?"

"Yes. I daresay she'll be grateful for an early night too."

"Thank you, you're very thoughtful." Her eyes were shining.

She was making him out to be some kind of hero, dammit, and he wasn't. He'd arranged the girl to sleep in her room for his own protection as much as hers. So that nobody could be compromised.

"I'm sorry to be putting you to such trouble."

"Not at all," he said gruffly. "None of it was your fault.

Don't worry, I'll do everything in my power to ensure you aren't harmed by this." He glanced at the darkening bruise, and without thinking he cupped her cheek gently.

She gazed up at him, her eyes wide, her skin warm silk beneath his fingers. Her breath was soft on his wrist. He swallowed, unable to look away. The scent of her enticed him unbearably, the scent of her body overlaid with his own fragrance. It was a delicious taunt, a challenge, a possession that would never take place.

That bruise against her pale skin was an obscenity. He heard himself say, "No one shall ever hurt you again." It sounded like a vow.

Her eyes shimmered with emotion, her lips parted and, in an impulse he refused to examine, he drew her closer and kissed her.

Her mouth opened beneath his: eager, ardent, generous. The sweet-spicy taste of her spilled through him, addictive, feeding a hunger he didn't know he had. She gripped his shoulders, pulling him closer as she pressed herself against him.

A voracious hunger burned in him, and he took what she offered.

A knock sounded behind him. "Are you in there, miss? It's me, Betty, and me mum." With an effort Ned mustered the remaining shreds of his self-control. He dragged his mouth from hers, steadied her, then turned and opened the door.

Betty and her mother entered, bearing bedding and night-clothes. They bustled about, making up the trundle bed.

Ned stood back, watching the women snapping and smoothing sheets, the view from the window—unrelieved darkness, there was nothing to see—anything but Lily.

She'd seated herself in the chair by the hearth and remained there, gazing into the fire as if fascinated. He couldn't see her face, couldn't tell what she was thinking.

He forced himself to breathe slow, deep breaths as he fought to regain a semblance of cool indifference. He told himself repeatedly that he was glad they'd been interrupted.

His body knew it for a lie.

What had possessed him, kissing her again? He'd spent the last part of the walk distancing himself from that first imprudent and inappropriate kiss, making it clear to both of them that it meant nothing.

And then to kiss her again. Madness. But her words had eaten at him. *It was my first-ever kiss. Did I do it wrong?*

He couldn't leave her thinking that, could he? An ungentlemanly thing to do.

He snorted. So gentlemanly to kiss her half senseless. He glanced across at her. She hadn't moved, hadn't lifted her gaze from the dancing flames and glowing coals.

The truth was she kissed like an angel. A very earthy, sensual angel, ardent but untutored. A combination of eagerness and innocence that simply . . . unraveled him.

Blame the first time on the moon, the night, even the blasted owl—a moment out of time—but to do it a second time? What had he been thinking?

The truth was there'd been no thinking at all. Only reacting. What was he—a green boy to be unable to resist the innocent offerings of an unwitting siren? For siren she was, to him, at least.

But Lily Rutherford was not for him. He was standing in for her brother, that was all.

The women finished their arrangements. Mrs. Baines left first, adjuring Betty not to keep the young lady awake half the night with her chatter.

"I'm so glad you wanted me in here with you, miss," Betty confided when her mother had gone. "Pa went and rented out my bed to a gentleman downstairs—I think he must be a lord or summat, I never seen a man dressed so fine and fancy in me life. I thought I was going to haveta put Jimmy out of his bed and him sleep on a mat on the floor until Ma told me your brother wanted me to sleep in here with you, for your reputation." She threw Ned a sunny smile. "Pa's in the doghouse but Ma's right pleased with you, sir."

The news didn't please Ned at all. He'd decided to sleep on a bench in the taproom like Elphingstone, and keep an eye on the fellow. Lord knew where he would be lurking now. Ned didn't trust him an inch.

He glanced at Lily, but there was nothing to be said now, not with Betty there—and that was a good thing, he told himself. He took his leave, saying, "I'll bid you good night, then. Sleep well, ladies"—Betty giggled at the idea of being a lady—"and lock this door."

He waited outside until he heard the lock click. As he turned, he glimpsed a long nose and a well-pomaded curl of reddish-brown hair slide into the shadows along the hallway. Elphingstone, sniffing around.

With a sigh Ned seated himself ruefully on the stairs. It was going to be a long, uncomfortable night.

The landlady was still on the landing. She eyed him curiously. "Sir?"

"Would you bring me a blanket, please?"

"A blanket, sir?" She took in what he meant and her eyes widened. "You're going to sleep here? On the stairs?"

He gave her a cool look as if to say, *Why not?* It was not for her to question his actions. If he took a fancy to sleep on the stairs, that was his own business.

But her brow cleared and she gave him a warm, motherly smile. "I did wonder before whether the lass really was your sister—well, arriving with no luggage, and the state of her!—but I can see now you truly are her brother, sir, taking such good care to protect her from all possible harm. I'll bring you up a blanket and a pillow too, sir—and a nice hot toddy."

She bustled off, leaving Ned muttering irritably under his breath. Of course the inmates of the inn would speculate about the state of his "sister" arriving in an almost-naked state and with no luggage. He'd bet his last penny Elphingstone would have wormed that out of them already.

The landlady returned and, under her motherly eye, Ned wrapped himself in the blanket, smiling until she left him alone. How the devil had he landed himself in this fix? Lily Rutherford's future was no business of his. She still dreamed of marrying for love, still thought that escaping from her abductor was all that mattered. And that she was safe now.

Safe! She was in almost as much danger of a forced marriage now as she'd been with that swine, Nixon.

He should have found her a safe place and left her there—with some respectable matron. Or in a convent, surrounded by nuns.

Ned sipped the hot toddy gloomily. Where was a nunnery when you needed one?

He could see exactly where this affair was leading and could see no way out of it. The last thing he wanted was responsibility for a helpless virgin, but what choice did he have? He couldn't have left her in the state in which he'd found her: half frozen, filthy and still dazed from whatever drug she'd been given.

Stripping her of her wet clothes had been the only possible thing to do.

He hadn't known she would be . . . delectable, even in her filthy state. Not that it mattered whether she was beautiful—her being female and unmarried was the problem. And him being an eligible bachelor.

Even if he had taken her to the home of a respectable matron—there were one or two living in the district, friends of his grandfather—then what? Respectable matrons gossiped with the best of them. The story would have inevitably spread and the scandal would have ruined her anyway.

It was a damnable mess, and his only hope of getting out of it without causing a major scandal was to get her back to London without anyone knowing.

It could be done. He'd managed several covert assignments in his army days. He'd smuggled people across borders and spirited them out of palaces and prisons. Getting Lady Lily Rutherford back into her home without incident or repercussions should be—would be—quite straightforward.

He pulled the blanket tighter and tried to sleep.

"YOU CAN BLOW THE CANDLE OUT NOW, THANK YOU, Betty," Lily said. Betty snuffed the candle and the room settled into darkness, the only light coming from the fire in the little sitting room; they'd left the door open for the warmth, though it wasn't really cold. It was cozy, lying snug in bed, watching the glow of the coals.

After a few minutes, Betty said quietly, "He isn't really your brother, is he, miss?"

Lily hesitated a moment. "No, but don't tell anyone."

"I won't. Ma don't think so, either, but she likes that he got me to sleep in here with you. Shows he's a proper gent, she says."

Lily smiled to herself. "He is."

They lay in the darkness, the only sound the occasional crackle and hiss of the fire, and below them the murmur of men drinking in the taproom.

"He kissed you, didn't he?" Betty said. "Just before Ma and me came in."

"Yes."

"I thought so. What was it like, if you don't mind me askin'?"

Lily didn't mind. Betty was no real substitute for her sister, Rose, but Lily was bursting to tell someone. She tried to think of how to describe the glorious sensation of kissing Edward, but before she could say anything, Betty added, "I been kissed a couple of times—not that I wanted it. The first time it was Hec, the stableboy—he just grabbed me one day, without no warning—and he's ugly, miss, and old—forty or more—and his teeth are all black and broken. Ugh! It was horrible. I had to knee him in the you-know-whats to get away."

"The you-know-whats?"

Betty explained the process with relish, and Lily recalled that Cal had once told her and Rose about a man's most vulnerable place and how they could defend themselves if necessary. It seemed an age ago. In all the panic of her abduction, she'd forgotten.

"The second time," Betty continued, "it was a feller who was just passing through, on his way to—I forget where. I sort of let him, coz I wanted to know what it felt like, and he was clean and youngish, with nice teeth and good clothes. And he was passing through, so it wouldn't get all around the village and damage me good name."

"And how was it?"

Betty snorted. "I reckon he'd had a bit too much of me Pa's ale, coz it was all sloppy and mushy. Like kissing, oh, I dunno, a big warm snail. Ugh!" She laughed and Lily laughed with her.

There was a short silence, then a soft question came out of the darkness. "So what was it like for you tonight, miss— when Mr. Galbraith kissed you?"

"Bliss." Lily sighed with happy remembrance. "Simply glorious."

"Did he put his tongue in your mouth? I heard they do that, sometimes."

Lily felt herself blush in the darkness. "Yes."

There was a short silence. "Wasn't it horrible?"

"Not at all. It was . . . wonderful."

Betty considered that. "I wonder if I could get your Mr. Galbraith to kiss me—just so's I know what it's supposed to be like."

Lily was shocked at the surge of jealousy that spiked through her. She said stiffly, "I think it's only good with the right man."

"I don't s'pose he'd want to anyway, would he? Not after he's kissed a lady like you." Betty sighed gustily. "Trouble is, I've got a few fellers wanting to court me—the inn makes good money, and Pa's made it known that when I marry I'll come with a goodly sum—me marriage portion, I mean. And I like two of them fine, but not in any special way."

"Have you thought of kissing each of them and comparing?" Lily suggested.

"Yes, but it's risky, miss. I dunno what it's like for ladies from London, but around here you let a feller kiss you and next thing the vicar is calling the banns. Or else your reputation is shot."

"I see." Lily pondered that. It wasn't all that different in London, not for unmarried girls of good family. But kissing Edward was her secret, her very special, precious secret. Nobody in London need ever know.

A yawn surprised her. "We'd better get some sleep. It's going to be a long journey tomorrow. Night, Betty."

"Night, miss."

Lily snuggled deeper into the bed, closed her eyes and relived every sensation of the kiss. Kisses.

He wanted her. She could feel it. It wasn't just someone paying her an empty compliment. Edward *desired* her.

She'd been attracted to him from the first. Like all the other girls who'd flocked around him at Cal's wedding reception, she'd been drawn to him, like a moth to a flame. She'd hung back, knowing a man like Edward Galbraith was completely out of her league.

But tonight he'd kissed her. On two separate, glorious occasions.

Oh, he'd claimed it was merely a case of passing lust—and maybe it was—but inside she was still tingling. And she was dazed. Dazzled. Delighted. She didn't want to sleep, she wanted to dance and sing and twirl madly around. And kiss him again.

Edward Galbraith had kissed her, ordinary little Lily Rutherford.

Twice.

But even as she thrilled to the memory, guilt pierced her. She had no business kissing a man under a fitful moon, while her family was at home, frantic with worry.

"ANY NEWS?" EMM CAME TO A STANDSTILL AS SHE AND Cal asked the same question simultaneously—and realized in the same instant what the answer must be. Cal had just arrived home. It was almost midnight, but Emm, though tired, had been putting off going to bed. Just in case . . .

"They didn't go to France," Cal said wearily, pulling off his soaked greatcoat and gloves and dropping them on a nearby chair. "Not from Dover, at least. Storms in the channel prevented anyone crossing for the previous two days. All the ships were still tied up. I checked every one of them, and every hotel and inn—as well as inquiring at every post inn on the way; there was no sign of either of—" He broke off as he took in his surroundings. Under the spatters of mud, his face paled. "What the devil are all these flowers for? Emm?"

Emm hurried forward and hugged her husband tightly. "Hush, it's not what you're thinking. We put it about that Lily has the influenza, and the flowers are from her well-wishers. We've also been inundated with fruit."

He kissed her, a kiss full of rough desperation, then wrapped his arms around her and held her close for a long moment, rocking slightly. His weariness, his despondency were palpable. "Don't worry, I'll find her." He released her, smoothed a curl back off her face, and gave her a rueful smile. "Sorry, I've made that pretty piece of nonsense you're wearing all wet and muddy."

As if she cared about the state of her dressing gown. Her husband was worn to the bone. He'd ridden from London to Dover and back, and from the wrung-out look of him he hadn't had a wink of sleep in days.

"It will be Gretna, then." He passed a hand over his stubbled jaw. "I just need a change of clothes and something to eat and I'll be off." He was swaying with exhaustion.

"You'll do nothing of the sort," Emm said firmly. "You're going to have a hot bath, then a hot meal, then sleep." She tugged on the bellpull.

"I don't need—"

Burton, the butler, arrived, still in his day clothes and neat as a pin. He picked up the discarded clothing, saying, "You rang, m'lady?"

"A hot bath and a hot meal for his lordship, please, Burton."

The butler bowed. "At once, m'lady."

"I'll take the bath and the meal, but I can't wait around—" Cal began when Burton had gone.

"How long is it since you slept?"

He shrugged. His beautiful gray eyes were bloodshot, with dark rings beneath. She said softly, "The night before the Mainwaring rout, was it not?"

He said nothing, but his expression confirmed it. Through cracked lips he said, "Do you think I can sleep while some bastard has my little sister in his power?"

"Do you think you can search for her effectively without sleeping?" she countered. "You told me once that a person who gets insufficient sleep does not think clearly. They make mistakes. Remember? We were talking about the war." She gently rubbed his rough-stubbled cheek with her palm. "Be rational, my darling. Sleep tonight, and make clearer decisions in the morning."

He hesitated, and she added, "If Gretna is the villain's destination, the men you sent to search for her on the road will be there. They might even have found Lily by now."

"But they might not, and—"

"Did you not tell them that if they failed to find her on the road, one of them was to remain at Gretna and watch for her until further notice while the other one returned with whatever news they had?"

"Yes, but—"

There was only one way to deal with such heroic stubbornness. "Very well, if you don't go to bed and get some sleep, then I won't, either."

He gave her a shocked look. "But you *must*!" His gaze dropped to her burgeoning middle. "You need to sleep for the baby's sake."

She shrugged. "I couldn't possibly sleep knowing you were riding off into the night, worn to the bone and not having slept for the last three nights. Besides, you know I sleep better when you're in bed with me."

There was a long silence. "Stooping to blackmail, love?"

She smiled. "You give me no choice. Besides, you know I'm right. You'll do better after a sleep."

He pulled her into his arms. "I'm going to muddy up this frivolous garment again."

She held him tight and lifted her face to receive his kisses. "I'll be taking it off soon anyway."

Chapter Eight

> But far more numerous was the herd of such,
> Who think too little, and who talk too much.
> —JOHN DRYDEN, "ABSALOM AND ACHITOPHEL."

NED PASSED A COLD, UNCOMFORTABLE NIGHT ON THE stairs, sleeping fitfully and waking often. When he did sleep he was disturbed by dreams of owls and kisses and fur rugs that kept slipping off pale, silken skin, which didn't help. Then at some ungodly hour, after he'd finally drifted off, Elphingstone tripped over him.

"What the hell—?"

"Sorry, sorry, sorry, needed to visit the privy and can't find the poky blasted cubbyhole where they put me," the man babbled, backing away. "Didn't see you there in the dark, Galbraith."

A likely story. The fellow's curiosity was legend. Perhaps Ned should have let Elphingstone think he was traveling with his mistress, instead of whetting the man's curiosity with a mystery. But if he had discovered Lily's identity then, she would have been ruined for certain. This way, there was at least a chance.

For the rest of the night Ned dozed on and off, but he rose at dawn with a plan in mind. He went in search of hot water, shaved and made his ablutions, then went to find Mrs. Baines. Big, bluff and hearty though the landlord was, Ned had earlier decided that Mrs. Baines was the true general in that family. He explained his scheme to her.

The good lady took a little convincing, but he offered

her a handsome payment and she finally agreed to his proposal. That achieved, he went upstairs and found Lily and Betty already awake and dressed. He explained his plan to them. Betty went in to strip the beds.

In the morning light the bruise on Lily's cheekbone was dark and livid against her creamy skin, and there were faint lilac shadows beneath her eyes. But her eyes were clear and bright and lovely, with no shadow of a drug in them and for that he was thankful.

"How did you sleep?" he asked her while Betty bustled about in the next room.

"Surprisingly well, thank you."

"No nightmares or other problems sleeping?" It would be perfectly understandable if she did suffer a reaction to her ordeal.

She shook her head. "No, it's odd. I thought I might have bad dreams or wake up with night terrors of some sort, but I didn't."

"Perhaps the drug helped blot it from your mind."

She considered the suggestion. "You know, that might be it. Thinking back, it's almost as if that part of the journey—the part when I was shut in that horrid box—it's almost as if *that* were the dream. The nightmare. The bit that's clearest in my mind is when I was out of the coach, in the cold air, hiding in the ditch, running away from Mr. Nixon, and . . . and . . ."

"And fighting him off very bravely," he finished for her. Not to mention being hit across the face by the filthy brute.

She blushed at his praise. "You're the one that fought him. But, if the drug has helped me forget it, and allows me to sleep through the night without nightmares, well, that's something to be grateful for, isn't it?"

"It is indeed." Again he was impressed by her quiet courage. Most ladies of his acquaintance would be milking the situation for all it was worth, not trying to shrug it off. "Now, breakfast will be here in a few minutes. You're clear on what to do when you go downstairs?"

She nodded, and Betty, coming back into the room, added, "Yep. I'm goin' to enjoy this."

As he went downstairs he ran into Elphingstone. As he expected. He'd swear the fellow was usually the type to snore the morning away, but this morning he was up bright and early in order to sniff out the mystery.

"Morning, Elphingstone. Sleep well?"

"Not in the least. I passed a very disturbed night," he snapped. "I'm sure there were fleas in my bed!" Either his valet had not yet attended him—which seemed unlikely—or he was displeased with his master: Elphingstone's hair had lost a good deal of its puff and was distinctly lopsided.

"Join me for breakfast in the taproom?"

Elphingstone hesitated, and glanced up to the landing outside Lily's room, but Ned left him no choice. "I'll order for us both. Meet you in the taproom in five minutes."

Ned ordered breakfast for two and, while he was at it, quietly informed Mrs. Baines that Elphingstone was a notorious London gossip, out to make trouble for himself and his sister. He told her he planned to smuggle Lily out of the inn as soon as possible after breakfast.

"A nasty gossip, is he? I thought as much," Mrs. Baines said in a voice that boded no good for Elphingstone. "Driven us all mad, he has, with his finicking ways and fussing about this and that—nothing is ever good enough for Lord Fancypants. Well, who asked him to stop here, I ask you?"

Ned added fuel to her already smoldering fire. "He told me there were fleas in his bed."

"Fleas!" Mrs. Baines's already impressive bosom swelled mightily. "How dare he! I'll give him fleas! Don't you worry, sir, I'll make sure he stays well away from your sister. Fleas indeed!" She marched away.

After a large and sustaining breakfast, Ned sent for his carriage to be brought around. "Leaving, eh?" Elphingstone said.

"Yes, you'll be able to rent the room tonight."

Elphingstone snorted. "Not if I can help it. Demmed wheelwright ought to have my carriage ready by now. Sent my man around to check." He remained loitering in the hotel entryway, feigning interest in a collection of horse brasses displayed on a wall and peeping curiously up the stairs from time to time.

Waiting for Ned's "young relative" to appear, no doubt.

A few moments later a female figure, enveloped in a faded blue cloak, appeared at the top of the stairs, peered out from beneath the capacious hood as if to check that the coast was clear and then hurried downstairs.

Elphingstone sprang forward. "Let me help you, my dear. My name is Elphing— Oh!" he exclaimed as Betty pulled back the hood.

She grinned. "Mornin', sir, I hope I'll be gettin' my bed back tonight."

"Yes, yes," he muttered crossly. "Get along with you, girl." He returned to demonstrate further fascination with the horse brasses and ignored Betty as she collected a large knotted bundle from her mother and went outside.

A moment later another cloaked and hooded figure tiptoed cautiously downstairs.

Again Elphingstone sprang forward. "May I assist you, my dear?" He seized an arm.

The hood fell back and Betty's younger brother Jimmy glared up at Elphingstone. "I ain't nobody's dear, and certainly not yourn." He wrenched his arm from Elphingstone's grasp and stepped away. "That basket for me, Ma?" he said, and collected a large covered basket from his mother.

"Very considerate of you to be so helpful toward the inn's staff, Elphingstone," Ned commented casually. "Though I'm not sure the landlord will take to you roughing up his son. Or his daughter, for that matter."

"I wasn't—I—oh, forget it," Elphingstone muttered, just as another young woman came down the stairs, half buried beneath a large bundle of laundry.

"Want me to strip your bed, sir?" she asked Elphingstone as she passed. Her soft Yorkshire burr was muffled by the load she carried.

"No, no, get along with you," he snapped, stepping back ostentatiously to let her pass.

"I'll be off now," Ned told him after the young woman had disappeared. "Good luck with getting your wheel fixed."

"Eh, what?" Elphingstone glanced around. "But where's your—" He broke off, realizing he'd been tricked, and hurried to the entrance to try for a glimpse of Ned's elusive companion.

Mrs. Baines stepped into the breach, blocking his exit. "Now, my fine gentleman, what's this I hear about *fleas*? I'll have you know there's never been a flea yet in my inn, and by all accounts you have a reputation for spreading nasty rumors, so . . ."

As Ned swung lithely into the carriage, he heard the sound of raised voices, a grim female one and a light male voice babbling in protest. He grinned. "Your mother is a redoubtable woman," he told Betty.

"I dunno what that means, sir, but she ain't one to be crossed, right enough. Serve him right for spreading nasty rumors. Me bed's as clean as a whistle—all the beds are— and I changed his sheets meself." She added with a grin. "The wheelwright he's waitin' on is me uncle Billy—Ma's brother—so Lord Fleabit'll be lucky to get his wheel fixed anytime this week."

They all laughed. He glanced at Lily. "That wasn't a bad Yorkshire accent you did before. I was almost fooled myself."

She smiled. "Betty coached me."

He suddenly realized there was one passenger less in the carriage. "Where's your brother, Betty? I promised your mother—"

"Jimmy's up on top—mad about horses, he is. Wants to drive a coach when he grows up. Mr. Walton said it was all right by him as long as it was all right by you." She bounced excitedly on the seat, almost dislodging the large covered wickerwork basket beside her. "London, eh? Jimmy and me are that excited. We never been farther than Leeds. I want to thank you, sir, for takin' us up. Ma said you need me to chaperone Miss Lily, and Jimmy is comin' to look after me."

"Yes, and I promised your mother I'd put you on the coach back home myself."

"But not before you've seen the sights of London, eh, Betty?" A tiny smile hovered on Lily's mouth. He couldn't look away. "Until this year, I'd never been to London, either, so I've promised to show Betty and her brother all the famous places and sights she's heard about. Only not—" She glanced at Betty, her eyes dancing.

"Turns out the streets ain't paved with gold, after all," Betty said in disgust.

Ned smiled faintly at Betty's naïveté. She'd never been twenty miles past her village, and travelers at the inn had filled her ears with some very tall tales about the nation's capital. He leaned back in the corner of the coach and let the female chatter wash over him.

They had a grueling journey ahead of them. Normally he wouldn't attempt to cover that distance in one day, but the longer Lily was away from home, the more likely it was that the story would get out.

He pretended to be gazing out the window, but at a certain angle he could see the pale shadow of Lily's reflection in the glass. He couldn't take his eyes off her.

He was glad he'd arranged for Betty to come in the carriage. Being alone in the carriage with Lily would have been . . . unbearable.

She would fall asleep eventually—it was a hellishly long journey to make in a day—and if they'd been alone, he would have been obliged to hold her again, to prevent her from falling. He'd have to feel her softness against him, smell the fragrance of her hair and body.

At least she was fully dressed this time. He wasn't sure whether he was grateful for that or not.

He watched her face in the glass, fascinated by the changing of her expressions, and the sweetness of her. Anyone would think she really was interested in a tavern maid's conversation.

He'd hired Betty to ensure that everything would be drearily and safely proper and respectable. *Everything* meaning himself.

What had he been thinking of, kissing Lily last night? And why could he not put the memory of those kisses out of his head?

He'd kissed scores of women, slept with dozens and

moved on from them all without regret. Why was this one girl so impossible to dismiss? He was aware of every movement she made, every shift in position. His ear was attuned to the timbre of her voice. And whenever she moistened her lips it was as if he could still taste her.

Fifteen more hours to London.

It occurred to him suddenly that the girls had fallen silent. He focused on Lily's reflection in the glass and found her staring back at him, or at least his reflection. Or was she staring through his reflection, and beyond to the passing scenery? He couldn't tell.

She cocked her head and gave him—or the window—a little smile. Did she know he'd been watching her?

He gazed thoughtfully out the window a moment longer, pretending fascination with a flock of sheep, then turned away from the window. "Ah, the bucolic pastoral life. So"—he glanced from one to the other—"run out of things to talk about? It's going to be a very long journey. I have some things here to help while away the hours." He opened a small compartment set into the framework of the carriage.

Lily leaned forward eagerly. "My father's carriage—my brother's now—has a similar compartment with all sorts of entertainment—card games, puzzles, backgammon and draughts."

Betty frowned. "Don't the pieces slip off the board with all this bumping around?"

"No, they're specially made for traveling," she explained. "They come in a little wooden box that opens out flat with hinges to form the board. All the pieces have little pegs, and they slot into tiny holes in the board so they don't slip or fall off when the carriage hits a pothole or bump. Cal's set has chess pieces too, from India I think, carved in ivory and ebony. It's beautiful, but I don't play chess."

"I have something similar," Ned said. "But since I was planning for a solo journey, I left the games at home. I think you'll enjoy these, though." He pulled out a small stack of books.

To his surprise, Lily made no attempt to examine the titles. She sat there with a frozen half smile, saying nothing.

Her expression gave him a sudden, unwelcome thought. He glanced at her companion. "Can you read, Betty?"

"Course I can," Betty said scornfully. "Went to the school in the village for three years, didn't I?" She examined the books eagerly. "Got any scary stories?"

That was all right then. For a moment he thought he'd embarrassed the girl, but of course an innkeeper's daughter would have some schooling. He selected a small gray volume and handed it to Betty. "Try this—Mr. Lewis's *The Monk*. It'll curdle your blood." Betty seized it gleefully and curled up with it in the corner of the carriage.

He selected a book bound in pretty blue leather and offered it to Lily. "This one might appeal to you. It's called *Persuasion*, by the author of *Pride and Prejudice*, who I know all the ladies love. By all accounts it is—"

"No!" The word almost burst out of her.

He frowned. *What the—?*

"Sorry, but no thank you." She avoided his gaze, her color a little heightened.

"Already read it? Then what about—"

"No! I—er, I cannot—" She took a deep breath and seemed about to say something, but then she hesitated, slumped a little and said in a defeated-sounding voice, "I get sick if I try to read in a moving carriage." She sounded almost ashamed, but plenty of people suffered from travel sickness in a carriage.

"Never mind, I used to have an aunt with the same problem," he said easily. "I'm sorry now I didn't bring any games or puzzles."

There was a short silence, and then he added, "Have you actually read *Persuasion*?"

"No," she said stiffly.

"Then what if I read it aloud to you?"

She blinked. "Aloud? You'd read it aloud—for me?"

He nodded. "It would be my pleasure. I never get carriage-sick, and I'd quite like to read this. So how about it?"

"That would be lovely, thank you." She gave him a brilliant smile.

He opened the book and began to read: "'Sir Walter Elliot, of Kellynch Hall, in Somersetshire, was a man who, for his own amusement, never took up any book but the Baronetage . . .'"

As he read, his voice deep and clear, even over the rattle and creak of the carriage and the sound of the horses' hooves, Lily's panic slowly subsided.

Can you read, Betty? Of course, ask the innkeeper's daughter that. Don't bother asking the earl's daughter—no question that *she* could read.

I get sick if I try to read in a moving carriage. It was perfectly true—except that she felt sick whenever anyone asked her to read.

When was she ever going to get over this, the fear of people discovering that at the age of eighteen Lady Lily Rutherford still barely could read? And not at all if anyone was watching her.

It was a disgrace, her greatest shame. And she had no excuse for it. There was nothing at all wrong with her eyesight. She could see perfectly well to embroider, to knit, to pluck a stray hair from her eyebrows. It was stupidity, that was all. There could be no other answer. She didn't *feel* stupid, but the evidence to the contrary was overwhelming.

And to admit to Edward Galbraith that she was so stupid as to not even be able to read—she simply couldn't bring herself to do it. That look would come into his eyes, the look she dreaded but was so horridly familiar with, the look first of incredulity, then scorn—or worse, of barely disguised pity.

And then they treated her as if she were really stupid and couldn't understand the simplest things. If Edward ever started to talk to her like that, she couldn't bear it.

He read on, his voice deep and almost mesmeric, carrying effortlessly over the rattle of the carriage and the sounds of the horses. "'His two other children were of very inferior value. Mary had acquired a little artificial importance by becoming Mrs. Charles Musgrove; but Anne, with an elegance of mind and sweetness of character, which must have placed her high with any people of real understanding, was nobody with either father or sister; her word had no weight, her convenience was always to give way—she was only Anne.'"

Like Papa, who valued Rose for her beauty and spirit, and had seemed to love Lily equally—until he'd learned, after Mama had died, that Lily, who was almost twelve at the time, still could not read.

Papa had called her *an imbecile*.

And so he'd sent them both—punishing Rose as well for Lily's inadequacies—away from everything they knew, from everything they loved, to an exclusive school in Bath.

And promptly forgot about them.

She had lost her father's love when she was almost twelve.

An imbecile . . . An embarrassment to the family

Lily forced the lump in her throat away. There was no use dwelling on the painful recollections of the past. Old hurts might not heal, but they eventually faded. She had to believe that.

She settled back against the deeply padded leather seat and listened to Edward's voice. She could listen to him all day. Only Rose and Mama had ever taken the trouble to read books aloud to Lily.

Besides, she wanted to hear what happened to this Anne Elliot, whose father so unkindly disdained her.

"I'll take it, Burton." Emm took the tray containing her husband's breakfast and quietly closed the door. It was almost noon. Cal would be furious. He'd asked to be woken at dawn, but he'd been so exhausted that he'd fallen asleep the moment he hit the bed, and she couldn't bring herself to wake him. Until now.

She drew back the curtains and light flooded their bedchamber. Cal stirred, pried open bleary eyes, stared at the weak spring sunshine and sat bolt upright. "What time is it?"

"Nearly noon. The coffee's hot, so don't spill it," she said calmly, and placed the tray on his lap, effectively preventing him from leaping out of bed, at least not without spilling hot coffee everywhere. Wifely tactics.

"*Noon*? I left instructions to be woken at dawn!"

"I know. I countermanded them. Eat your breakfast. You need to eat."

"Dammit, Emm, I have to—"

"A strange little note arrived a short while ago."

"*Note*? What note? Is it ransom?"

"No. It seems to be from Mr. Galbraith."

"*Galbraith*? Ned Galbraith? What's it say?"

"It was addressed to you, but I opened it anyway." He put out his hand for it, but she held it back. "I'll read it to you while you eat."

She waited until, with a long-suffering expression, he shoved a forkful of eggs into his mouth. Then she read the note aloud: "'Found your missing package in good condition. Will return it to you at earliest convenience—Friday night or early Saturday morning. E. Galbraith.'" She looked at Cal. "Well?"

He held out his hand and she gave the note to him. He glanced at the signature, then slumped back against the pillows. "She's safe! Galbraith's got her."

"Thank God!" Emm plopped down on the bed beside him. Coffee slopped over, dripping onto the tray, but they neither noticed nor cared. "I thought that's what the note must mean, but I couldn't be sure."

Rose and George burst in. "Is it true? Lily's been found? She's safe?" Clearly they'd been listening at the door.

Cal nodded. "Yes, she's safe. My friend Galbraith has her. He's bringing her home."

There was an outburst of relief—laughter and tears and hugging—and when it was all settled, and the coffee well and truly spilled—Rose plonked herself on the end of the bed. "We thought that's what the note must mean, but why would he call Lily a 'package'? Why send such a peculiar message?"

George nodded. "Yes, why not just say Lily's safe and he's bringing her home?" Her dog, Finn, had followed her in. He sidled up to Cal's side of the bed and sat down, looking mournful and underfed.

"It was something we learned to do during the war—send messages that on the surface appeared innocuous, but that the person receiving them would understand." Cal passed a piece of toast to the dog. "When did the note arrive?"

"About half an hour ago," Emm told him. "It was brought by a young man, dirty, unshaven and mud-spattered, so I wasn't sure what to think, especially as he claimed he was to be paid five pounds." She turned the note over and showed him the postscript. "But then I realized he looked much the same as you did when you got home last night. He's in the kitchen now, being fed, if you want to question him."

"We already have," George said. "He doesn't know anything about Lily, just that this note was sent by a man who arrived at the inn he drinks at, with a girl he claimed was his sister." She and Rose exchanged glances.

"He said the girl arrived wearing nothing but a fur rug," Rose said.

"What?" Cal stiffened. Coffee went everywhere and the plate with his half-eaten breakfast slipped to the floor. He took no notice. "What do you mean, 'nothing but a fur rug'?"

Rose shrugged. "That's what he said. And before you go and try to shake more out of him, he said he hadn't seen her himself, but that's what he'd heard."

Cal swore under his breath. Emm slipped her hand on his shoulder. "People can get things muddled," she said quietly. "There's no point worrying about it now. We'll see Lily and Galbraith tonight, God willing, or tomorrow, and then we'll find out what really happened." She gave the girls a look. "Thank you, girls. George, if your dog has finished with Cal's breakfast, you can take him outside."

Relieved, but subdued, the two girls left.

Cal's gaze burned into Emm. *"Naked but for a fur rug?"* He groaned.

"Stop imagining the worst. Your friend Galbraith said she was safe—just remember that." She slipped her arms around him and lay beside him, her head on his chest. "All we can do now is wait."

Chapter Nine

✑

"You men have none of you any hearts."
"If we have not hearts, we have eyes;
and they give us torment enough."
—JANE AUSTEN, *NORTHANGER ABBEY*

AFTER A WHILE THE JOURNEY TOOK ON A RHYTHM. Edward read, chapter after chapter, seeming never to tire of it. Betty soon put her book aside and became engrossed in *Persuasion*.

Whenever they stopped to change horses, they hastened into the inn to relieve themselves or simply to stretch their legs. And though Lily tried to persuade Edward to take a break—for the sake of his voice, not because she wasn't enjoying the story—he did for a short while, and then picked up the book and resumed the story.

She suspected he was enjoying it as much as she was.

When he wasn't reading aloud, when they were all sitting watching the scenery pass by, every time she glanced at him—and for some reason her gaze kept being drawn to him—he was watching her.

Oh, he seemed to be looking at the scenery, but she could see he was really looking at her in the reflection of his window.

It should have made her uncomfortable—and it did make her feel a little warm and sort of tingly and self-conscious—but somehow she didn't mind.

And once he started reading again and not watching her, she was free to watch him. He really was the most beautiful man.

Every stop was as short as they could make it—they wanted to reach London as soon as possible. They didn't even stop for luncheon—the large basket Betty's mother had given them proved to contain a veritable feast. There was cold chicken, salad, an egg-and-bacon pie, bread and butter, a rich fruitcake that Betty insisted be eaten with slices of cheese that her mother had provided, and apples that should also be eaten with the cheese.

The meal was washed down with something Betty called scrumpy, which was a kind of cider that her father made, though there was a bottle of ale for Edward. There was a large wrapped packet of food for Jimmy and Mr. Walton, but they only got a bottle of cold tea to wash their meal down because as Betty informed them, "Ma always says, 'Men what drives coaches shouldn't go a-drinking.'"

The scrumpy was delicious but rather strong, and after the meal Lily became quite sleepy. Seeing her yawns, Edward put the book aside and produced rugs, and she and Betty snuggled into them and soon nodded off.

She woke at one point and noticed that he too was dozing, his chin sunk onto his neckcloth, crushing its elegant folds. His long, booted legs were crossed and stretched out before him and his arms were folded.

He looked younger in sleep. Younger and somehow vulnerable.

He must have been aware of her regard, for he opened his eyes and looked straight at her. She smiled, their gaze held a long moment, then he shifted and sat up. He stretched and said quietly, "I don't know about that scrumpy, but the ale packed quite a punch."

She nodded. "The scrumpy did too."

He glanced at the sky. "Late afternoon. If our luck continues, we'll have you home again before midnight." He gave an endearing crooked half smile and added, "Like Cinderella."

She gestured to her borrowed clothing. "Not quite like Cinderella, but yes. Thank you. I'm very grateful for all you've d—"

He cut her off with a gesture, as if he didn't want her gratitude. "Shall I continue reading the story?"

She glanced at the still-sleeping Betty and shook her head. "Let's wait until she wakes. Despite her stated preference for a gory tale, I think she's enjoying this as much as I am."

The light inside the carriage dimmed as they entered a forest. Lily gazed out the window, watching the play of light and shade through the leaves and the tracery of branches. "Forests are magical places, don't you think? When I was little Rose and I weren't allowed to play in the woods near our house, so naturally there was nothing we wanted to do more."

"Naturally."

"Our nurse tried to frighten us with tales like 'The Babes in the Wood,' and she also told us the most terrifying stories of elves and pixies stealing us away." She laughed softly. "Of course that made us want to go and play there even more." She tilted her head and looked at him. "I suppose being a boy, you were allowed to go wherever you wanted."

"Guilty as charged, though only after I went to live with my grandfather, when I was six."

Her smile died. "Oh. What happened?"

"Nothing terrible, don't worry. I was born in London and spent my earliest years there, and until I went to Grandfather's the only garden I knew was bound by black iron railings and a locked gate. And woe betide any child rash enough to pick a flower or climb a tree."

She wrinkled her nose. "That's mean. Children need to play. So what happened when you were six?"

"I had weak lungs as a child, and each winter I fell ill—coughs and cold and terrible breathing problems. The winter I was six, I was coughing my lungs up as usual when Grandfather arrived on an unexpected visit. He took one look at me, declared that no child should be raised in a filthy city and swept me away to Shields—the family seat in the country—insisting that 'fresh country air would make the boy well again.' It did too. I lived with Grandfather from then on, leaving only to go away to school."

She gave him a troubled look. "Your parents didn't come with you?"

"No, they both preferred living in London. Mother was an acknowledged beauty and adored the social whirl, as did my father. I saw them each Christmas, of course."

"Of course," Lily murmured, wondering how any mother could just give her small son away like that. "And at your grandfather's home—Shields, was it?—was there a forest nearby to explore?"

A reminiscent half smile appeared on his face. "There was indeed. Grandfather gave me free run of the place— the stables, the forest, the village—as long as I told someone where I was going, and took my dog with me."

"Your dog?"

"Nipper. A terrier, the cleverest little dog you've ever seen. We went everywhere together." He was silent for a while.

"So you were happy at your grandfather's?"

"Oh, yes. It was heaven to a small boy whose greatest adventures to that point had been standing on a chair and gazing out the attic window, imagining himself climbing out and exploring the endless sea of rooftops and chimneys, mysterious lands half hidden in the swirling smog." He gave a self-deprecating grimace. "I was a foolish, dreamy child."

"Not foolish at all," she said softly. "What is life without dreams?"

There was a short silence, then she prompted him further—she was so enjoying this brief glimpse into his past. "And so at your grandfather's you had the whole estate and your very own forest to explore?"

"Not just explore, but to *command*. I was Robin Hood."

She chuckled. "And did you have a band of merry men to lead?"

And there, suddenly, was that bleak look. "I did—then," he said quietly, and turned his face away. He picked up a book—not the one he'd been reading to her—and began to leaf through it, a clear signal that the conversation was over.

What had she said? They'd been talking about Robin Hood and his merry men, and childhood games. Where was the harm in that? But he obviously didn't want to talk about it.

And before Lily could think of a way to get him talking again, a large pothole jolted Betty awake and ended their intimate conversation. But not Lily's thoughts about it.

Everyone changed between the time they were small to the adults they became, but the contrast between the dreamy little boy who imagined rooftop lands, and the happy child exploring the world with his dog, and playing Robin Hood with his friends in the woods—how had he become this man with a reputation for keeping people at a distance? A coldhearted rake? That wasn't the man who'd rescued her, and protected her, the man who'd kissed her under a moonless sky and the next day read to her for hours on end so she wouldn't be bored on a long trip.

At the next stop to change horses, when they all clambered stiffly out of the carriage to use the convenience, Lily's thoughts were still miles away as she wended her way through the busy inn. A loud, self-important voice broke through her reverie. "Lady Ampleforth requires—"

Lily didn't wait to hear what Lady Ampleforth required; she dived through a nearby door, dragging Betty with her. And found herself in a private parlor where a plump, elderly lady sat by the fire. She was dressed in shades of puce and wore a purple-and-gold turban. At Lily's gasp, she peered toward the doorway, then groped for and began to raise a lorgnette.

"Oh, heavens!" Lily whirled around and pushed Betty back out.

"What was that all about?" Betty said as they hurried to the conveniences out the back.

"That old lady, she knows me." Worse, she knew Aunt Agatha.

"So?"

"She mustn't see me."

"She did see you."

"No, she's very shortsighted, so she saw me, but I don't think she recognized me. She didn't have her lorgnette up in time."

She pushed Betty in front of her. "Have a look, will you? See if she's anywhere to be seen."

Betty peered through the door. "Hang on, she's talking to someone. Let's go around the other way." They crept around the outside of the inn, then made a mad dash to the carriage and practically fell inside, laughing in relief.

Inside the inn, Ned was arranging for hot coffee laced with brandy for his coachman, and sweetened tea for the ladies and the small boy, when he felt an imperious tap on his shoulder. He turned and his heart sank.

"Young Galbraith, what is the meaning of this?" A short, stout old lady stood regarding him with a grim expression. "That, if I am not mistaken, was Lady Lily Rutherford I saw just now—and she's just climbed into a vehicle that my coachman tells me belongs to you."

Ned swore silently. In as bored a voice as he could manage, he said, "It's not what you think, Lady Ampleforth."

She snorted. "You have no idea what I think, young man. So explain."

He gave a careless shrug and explained in his best sophisticated-rake drawl, "It's simple. I encountered Lady Lily and her maid a few miles back, in some distress after a carriage accident. Naturally I stopped to render assistance and, realizing who she was—her brother is a friend of mine, you know—I offered her a lift back to London. It's a dreary chore, of course, but there it is. Nothing else a gentleman could do."

She raised a well-plucked eyebrow. "Is that so?"

"It is," he said firmly. "I trust you're satisfied that there's nothing more to it than that. Gossip—especially when misplaced—is such a bore, don't you find?"

She drew herself up to her full five foot one and gave him a militant look. "I quite agree. I abhor gossip, especially when misplaced. Convey my respects to your grandfather. I trust he's in good health."

"I shall, thank you, and he is. Good afternoon, Lady Ampleforth." He bowed to the old lady, collected the flasks of tea and coffee and left, cursing silently.

"We had a narrow escape," Lily informed him as he

climbed into the coach again. "There was an old lady in the inn who knows my aunt Agatha."

"Lady Ampleforth? Yes, I spoke to her." He knocked on the roof to signal Walton to resume the journey. The coach moved off with a jerk.

Lily looked aghast. "You *know* her?"

"She knows my grandfather. All that generation seem to know each other."

She groaned. "I know. She and Aunt Agatha made their come-out the same year, and have been at daggers drawn ever since."

"Really?" He decided not to tell her that Lady Ampleforth had recognized her. It would only worry her, and if Lady Ampleforth was as discreet as she claimed there would be no problem. "The good news is she's traveling in the opposite direction, leaving London rather than going there, so you won't encounter her when you get home."

"Home," Lily echoed quietly. "How long now till we reach London, do you think?"

He did a quick calculation. "About seven hours. Shall I continue reading?" She nodded, and he resumed the story.

EDWARD FINISHED READING *PERSUASION* JUST AS THE LIGHT was starting to fade. Lily was glad of the happy ending—she liked Anne and thought she deserved to be happy with her captain—but there was a growing hollow feeling inside her—and it wasn't hunger.

They hadn't stopped for dinner; there was enough food left over in Mrs. Baines's basket to keep them all satisfied. Not that Lily ate much. The closer they got to London, the more nervous she became.

Three hours to London.

At the last change of horses, Walton, the coachman, had lit the carriage lamps. Not many people traveled at night; it was too dangerous. But Edward was determined to get Lily home as soon as possible, and she could only be grateful.

She was desperate to see her family.

Walton had also sent young Jimmy down—much against

the boy's will—to travel the last few hours inside the coach. How could Walton stand it? Lily wondered. Sixteen hours driving a coach—she was exhausted just from traveling, and she'd taken a nap or two along the way. But when she raised it with Edward, he'd shrugged and said he'd offered to hire Walton an assistant driver and he'd refused.

After Jimmy joined them, they played guessing games and memory games, and told a few stories, but everyone was tired, and soon Betty and her brother curled up in a corner of the coach and slept.

Lily wished she could sleep too. Edward had said he hoped they'd get to Mayfair before midnight. She was exhausted, but nervous energy kept her awake.

THE COACH PULLED UP OUTSIDE ASHENDON HOUSE JUST before midnight. In the faint light of the gas lamps in the street outside, the occupants of the coach stretched, and straightened themselves. Ned was a little surprised. He'd expected Lily to be out of the coach in a flash, up the stairs and into the arms of her family. Instead she was tidying her hair and tugging her borrowed dress into place, as if she were nervous or something.

Walton let down the steps and opened the carriage door. Lily took a deep breath. "I don't know how to thank you for everything you've done."

"Then don't. It was my pleasure." Ned didn't want her gratitude. He climbed out to hand her down, and at the same moment the front door of Ashendon House opened and Cal and his wife came rushing out. Lily practically fell out of the carriage into their arms.

Hugging, kissing, laughing, weeping, they walked slowly back into the house. Ned gave Walton an enormous tip, gave him the next two days free and sent him off with the horses and carriage for a well-earned rest.

"Coming in?" Cal stood at the front door, waiting. It was less an invitation than an order.

Inside the house pandemonium reigned. As Ned entered, two young women dressed in bedgowns and loosely fastened dressing gowns came flying down the stairs in bare feet, shrieking. They embraced Lily repeatedly, hurling questions at her so fast they would have been impossible to answer, even if they hadn't all been laughing and weeping and hugging and exclaiming in dismay over Lily's bruised face.

A little overwhelmed by the outburst of female emotions, Ned was relieved when Lady Ashendon finally said, "Come along up to bed, girls. It's late, we're all tired and poor Lily looks completely worn out. Your questions will keep. Plenty of time in the morning to hear what happened." She made arrangements for one of the maids to provide beds for Betty and Jimmy and whatever else they needed, and ushered the three girls upstairs.

The girls hurried ahead in a tight clump, still talking. Just before Lady Ashendon reached the first landing, she glanced back at Ned and said, "I'm sorry, Mr. Galbraith, you must think us complete savages—we are all at sixes and sevens in the joy of Lily's homecoming—but let me say how truly grateful we are to you for returning our darling Lily to us."

Ned bowed. He hated being thanked.

Lady Ashendon added, "You will call tomorrow, I hope?" Again it wasn't quite an invitation.

He glanced up, saw Lily looking down at him and heard himself say, "Of course, Lady Ashendon."

The ladies disappeared, their voices died away and silence fell. Ned turned to take his leave. "I'll be off then, Cal. I'm—"

"Step into the sitting room a moment, Galbraith, if you please." Cal seemed a bit stiff. Ned wanted to find his own bed, but assuming Cal had questions he wanted to ask without the ladies present, he entered the sitting room. A cozy fire was burning and he crossed the room to warm himself in front of it. "So, Cal, you have questions for me, I presume?"

"The messenger who brought your note—"

"Oh, you got it. Good. No problem about paying him the extra, I hope. He must have ridden through the night." For a man whose sister had just been returned safe and sound, Cal seemed very tense.

Cal dismissed the matter of the money with a curt gesture. He didn't offer Ned a seat; he just stood with his legs braced apart, eyeing him with a grim expression.

"The messenger told me when you carried my sister into that godforsaken village inn, she was naked but for a fur rug."

"Not naked—under the rug, she was wearing one of my shirts."

Cal's fists clenched. "Why was she virtually naked? Did that bastard—?"

"No, that was my doing. I made her strip—"

"*Your* doing?" Cal took two steps and grabbed Ned by the throat. "You stripped my baby sister naked, and—"

Ned broke his hold and pushed him away. "Calm down, you fool, it's not what you think. She stripped herself." Some demon of provocation made him add, "And if you haven't noticed, she's no longer a baby."

"You bastard." Cal threw a punch.

Ned blocked it and shoved Cal backward. "Oh, don't be such a fool! She was soaked to the skin and half frozen, so what would you have me do? Let her catch her death of pneumonia? Besides, she stank to high heaven."

Cal said belligerently, "My sister does not stink!"

"She does when she's fallen in a ditch full of God knows what. She was covered in mud and stank like a pigsty."

There was a short silence. Cal's fists remained bunched, the red light of battle in his eye fainter but still present. Ned, who'd kept a rein on his temper until now, felt it slipping. Much could be forgiven a man still on edge because his sister had been abducted and he hadn't yet heard the full story, but Cal ought to know better.

"Dammit, Cal, what kind of a man do you think I am? Do you honestly believe I would debauch *any* vulnerable innocent, let alone my friend's younger sister? I might have a reputation as a rake, but I've *never* dallied with innocents of any kind—and you know it!" He glared at his friend. "You mule-headed fool! Why the hell would I bring Lily home—let alone hire a chaperone for her—if I'd debauched her?"

"*What* chaperone?"

"Betty, the innkeeper's daughter—short young female, freckles, blue dress. Your wife just arranged for one of your maids to find beds for her and her brother."

"Oh, her."

"Yes, her! Why do you think I brought a couple of young rustics with me? To show them the sights of London?" He snorted. "I also hired Betty to sleep on a trundle bed in Lily's bedchamber at the inn while I slept on the stairs outside the door—and blasted uncomfortable it was too, you ungrateful sod!"

There was a short, fraught silence. Cal's fists slowly unclenched. Tension visibly drained from him. He waved Ned to a seat and said wearily, "I'm sorry, Galbraith—I do know you're a man of honor. It's just that—"

"You've been beside yourself with anxiety," Ned said. "I understand. She's a sweet girl, your sister." He dropped into a comfortable overstuffed armchair. "I'll forgive you your stiff-necked, ill-conceived, downright insulting suspicions if you pour me a large—a very large—brandy. The last few days have been hell."

"Believe me, I know it." Cal unstoppered the decanter on the sideboard, poured two large cognacs and gave one to Ned. "So tell me—was it Nixon?"

"It was. Tricked her into going outside at a party and shoved her into his coach. Drugged her too." He told Cal as much as he knew about Lily's abduction and eventual escape, leaving out the more sordid details—they were for her to share if she wanted.

"She rescued herself, you know," he finished. "Escaped, despite the drug, and hid in a filthy ditch until he'd gone. Bastard was trying to run her down in his carriage when I came along. Matter of luck that I was there to stop him." Ned sipped his cognac and stared into the flames. "Brave girl, your sister. You should be proud of her."

"I am." Cal frowned into his glass a moment. "I'm stunned by what you've told me. It's hard to believe that my little Lily was so . . . resourceful. I've always thought of her as a bit helpless."

Ned thought of what Lily had told him, how she'd worked to keep the feeling in her feet alive so she could run, how she'd blocked the mouth of the bottle with her tongue to prevent being drugged further, how she'd caught the fabric of her cloak in the catch of the lock. And afterward, she'd never once fallen into hysterics or had a fit of the vapors—as she would have been quite entitled to do. Helpless? Cal might love his sister, but he didn't know her very well. "Quite an ordeal that filthy swine put her through. She seems to have weathered it remarkably well, but as you and I know, sometimes these things can hit you later when the danger and the drama have passed."

Cal nodded. "I know. I'll warn Emm. She and the girls will take good care of Lily."

They sipped the fine French cognac and listened to the fire crackle and hiss.

"You really slept across her door, like a faithful hound?" Cal said after a few minutes.

"Wipe that smile off your face or I might be tempted to give you that punch after all," Ned said lazily. "It was for her protection. And"—he took another sip of cognac—"because Elphingstone was sniffing around."

Cal sat up. "Elphingstone! That little—"

"It's all right. He knew something was up—I'd told the innkeeper she was my sister, but of course Elphingstone knows I don't have a sister. But he never saw Lily's face and we never used her name."

"I notice you don't use her title."

Ned gave him a hard look. "I dropped it for the sake of discretion." He held out his glass for Cal to refill. "The only person who might cause us problems is Lady Ampleforth—she saw us when we stopped to change horses, and put two and two together."

"Blast! That old harridan is my aunt's greatest rival."

"Rival?" Ned was momentarily distracted. "For what?"

Cal gave him a wry look. "Dominance of the ton."

Ned snorted. "At any rate she was heading away from London—going home to Herefordshire, I assume—so I doubt she'll cause any trouble." He sipped his cognac. "You managed to stifle any gossip at this end, I presume."

"We've put it about that Lily is in bed with the influenza."

"Good move. So we've handled it, then, and her life can go on as before." He finished his cognac and rose. "I'll be off, then."

Cal rose and held out his hand. "I can't thank you enough, Galbraith."

"Nonsense. Anyone would have done the same. Pleasure to be of service to Lady Lily." They shook hands.

Cal opened the front door. "I suppose you'll be heading back up to that house party now."

Ned shook his head. "No, gone off the idea. Think I'll stay in town for a bit, see what's to do." He paused on the front step. "I take it you'll be hunting for that swine, Nixon."

"I will."

"I'd like to help."

Cal shook his head. "I appreciate the offer, but you've done enough. It's for me, as head of Lily's family, to seek justice for my sister. Good night." He stepped inside and closed the door.

It was a clear dismissal—and fair enough, Ned told himself. He wasn't family. He had no right to be involved in whatever justice—or revenge—Cal was planning. He'd done what he could—helped the girl and returned her to the bosom of her family—and that was that. End of story.

Ned walked to his lodgings. It wasn't far and the night was fine. Lily was safe in her own bed and all was right with her world again. He was free to go back to his own life.

So why did he feel so unaccountably flat?

Chapter Ten

❧

I know that's a secret, for it's whispered everywhere.
—WILLIAM CONGREVE, *LOVE FOR LOVE*

LILY STAYED INSIDE FOR THE NEXT FEW DAYS, WAITING impatiently for her bruise to fade. It was lovely to be home with her family again, but for some reason she felt restless and unsettled, and a bit bored.

It hadn't helped that Edward—she had to address him as Mr. Galbraith now that they were back in society—hadn't called. She hadn't seen him since the night he'd brought her home. He'd sent her flowers—a small, exquisite bunch of primroses and violets—with a note saying he hoped she was recovering from her indisposition.

Indisposition? Emm's view, when she read the note to Lily, was that he was being discreet, that he was maintaining the story they'd spread about Lily having the influenza.

Still, it was quite impersonal, coming from a man in whose arms she'd slept, dressed only in his shirt and wrapped in a soft fur rug, a man who'd kissed her on a cold and cloudy night.

Why hadn't he visited?

She missed him.

Her family didn't seem to think his absence in the least bit odd, even though Emm had specifically invited him to call the next day. They thought he had better things to do, and that such neglect was to be expected of a man of his reputation. He was almost never seen in polite company.

They were grateful to him, of course, but as Rose said, "Any gentleman would do the same if they came across a lady in distress." Lily didn't agree, but after several days she was forced to concede that his absence spoke for itself.

Her only outing had been to show Betty and her brother, Jimmy, some of the sights of London. She'd talked Emm into letting her go out, heavily veiled, accompanied by one of the maids and a footman, plainly dressed.

Rose and George had wanted to go too, arguing that fashionable people wouldn't be likely to be at the kind of places that Betty yearned to see, but Emm had pointed out that unveiled, they'd be recognized, and that three heavily veiled women would draw more attention than otherwise.

She'd also, with a shudder, firmly vetoed George's suggestion that she and Rose could go dressed as men.

Those surreptitious excursions with Betty had been the highlight of Lily's week, and Betty's gleeful enjoyment of her visit had enlivened Lily's dampened spirits. But Betty and her brother had been put on the mail coach back to Yorkshire, laden with parcels—Rose and George had taken Betty shopping for new clothes to replace the ones she'd lent Lily—food for the journey and souvenirs of their visit to the capital. Now Lily was feeling a little bit low.

Aunt Agatha insisted the others go out and about on their usual pursuits, where they were to casually mention— but only if asked about Lily's health—that it wasn't the influenza at all, but a severe cold, that Lily was recuperating nicely and should emerge from the sickroom quite soon.

Callers came and were thanked for their concern but told that "Lady Lily is still indisposed." Well-wishers sent her notes and flowers, fruit and small gifts—quite a few of which were books. Burton read her the notes and took back a verbal message from the invalid.

With all this kind attention, it was completely unreasonable for her to feel lonely and a bit lost, Lily told herself. She'd survived a nasty experience and should be grateful to be safe and well in the bosom of her family. She was thankful, of course she was, but she was also fed up with waiting for the horrid bruise to disappear and allow her out. All she did was sit around, knit or sew and those occupations were horridly conducive to *thinking*.

All Lily seemed to be able to think about these days was Edward Galbraith and what he might be doing. And thinking. And it was pointless wondering. His actions—or lack of them—showed what he was thinking: not about Lily.

He hadn't called once or sent anything apart from those flowers. She'd pressed some of them between the pages of a book. The best use she had for a book.

But there was no use brooding about him. To him she was just a parcel he'd had to deliver—Rose and George had told her about the note he'd sent Cal.

As for the kisses that haunted her dreams? He was a rake, after all. He probably had that effect on all the women he kissed.

She needed to forget about Edward Galbraith. She needed activity, entertainment, distraction.

So when Sylvia Gorrie came calling, Lily hurried to the looking glass, decided a dusting of rice powder would sufficiently conceal the fading bruise and asked Burton to show Sylvia up.

Cal and Emm had assured her that Sylvia had known nothing about her cousin's plans, but Lily wanted to talk to Sylvia herself, in private, just to be sure.

"Mrs. Arthur Gorrie," Burton announced, and Sylvia hurried in, talking nineteen to the dozen.

"Oh, you're out of bed already! I've brought you some candied licorice root. It's supposed to be marvelous for colds—I had the impression—but no matter, you seem to be almost recovered. No red nose, I see—it's the worst part of a cold, I think, that scabby redness from all the disgusting blowing and sneezing. But you are looking pale." Lily waved her to a seat, and Sylvia sat, saying, "I'm so very relieved to see you, dear Lily. I was so worried."

"It was just a cold," Lily began.

"I don't mean that—though I'm glad you're recovering; no, I meant—I suppose you heard about your brother bursting into my house in the wee small hours, demanding I produce Cousin Victor. He planted such horrid suspicions in my mind about you and my cousin—he actually believed you two had eloped—well, how ridiculous, when you had barely exchanged more than half a dozen words. But such things weigh on one's mind, you know. And Victor *had* disappeared—and so had you."

"Yes, I—"

"Oh, I know, you took ill and ended up in the wrong bed—Rose's, was it not?—and confused everyone. I was never more relieved when I ran into Miss Wes—Lady Ashendon in the park the next day and she told me you were ill—not that I was pleased you were ill, of course, but I was so relieved to find that you hadn't run off with my cousin."

"As a matter of fact—"

"You must think it strange of me to feel such doubts about my cousin—"

"Actually—"

"But I don't really know him that well. He only came to England recently and when we became reacquainted—well, there was I with my stick-in-the-mud husband, and here was this charming and personable new cousin. I cannot tell you how delightful it was to have a handsome young relative to squire me around the parties that Arthur—that's Mr. Gorrie, my husband—refuses to attend."

"Yes, but—"

"My husband is furious with me, because Victor owed him money, but it seems he's disappeared off the face of the earth, and I can't say I'm sorry. Some embarrassing things have come to light since he left, and—oh, I forgot, I brought you some ice cream from Gunters—nothing is as soothing for a sore throat as a delicious creamy ice, don't you think?—although your voice doesn't sound too bad. When I had the influenza my throat was so hideously painful, I sounded like a rusty saw!" She laughed. "Your butler should be bringing it up shortly—well, what perfect timing. Here he is now," she finished as Burton entered with a tray containing two bowls of creamy ices. "I hope you don't mind if I join you. I do adore ice cream but my husband thinks it a frivolous indulgence."

Lily, who had been about to confront Sylvia and inform

her that her cousin was every bit as big a villain as Cal had suspected—and more—subsided.

She examined Sylvia's face as she handed Lily a bowl of ice cream and dug happily in herself. There was no shadow of guilt or even self-consciousness in her eyes. Surely if she'd known or suspected anything about the abduction, it would show.

In any case, why would Sylvia conspire with her cousin to commit such a dreadful act? There was no benefit to her in it that Lily could see.

Lily didn't particularly like Sylvia, but she'd never been unkind to her. Quite the contrary.

No, she decided as she ate her ice cream. Sylvia had been deceived by her cousin, just as Lily had.

SEVERAL DAYS LATER, AUNT AGATHA STRIPPED OFF HER gloves and directed an accusing look at Lily, who had been summoned with the rest of the family—the female members. Cal was out. "The rumors are proliferating! They should be abating by now—you sent out those thank-you notes, did you, gel?"

"Yes, of course." Lily hadn't written them herself, of course; Rose had written them for her—a note for everyone who'd sent something to Lily; George had addressed them and Lily had sealed them.

"And we've told quite a few people that it was only a severe cold, not the influenza as first feared," Rose said.

"I included Lily in my acceptance for us all at the Peplowe Ball next week," Emm said. "The bruising will have faded completely by then, and everyone will see that she hasn't eloped and is her usual sweet self."

"Show me." Aunt Agatha raised her lorgnette with an imperious gesture, and Lily presented the offending cheek for her scrutiny. The old lady gave a grudging nod, then glared around the room, a tigress deprived of prey. "Then why are the rumors getting worse?"

Emm frowned. "Why, what are people saying?"

"A muddle of two stories—one that Lily ran off with a

Mr. Nixon on the night of the Mainwaring rout—to Gretna or Paris, the versions differ. The other—and far more serious in my view—is that she eloped with Galbraith, who seduced her, then dumped her."

"But he didn't!" Lily exclaimed indignantly.

"Be quiet, gel! You are ruined! Whether he seduced you or not is immaterial."

"How can the truth be immaterial?" Lily began.

The old lady snorted. "And there you show your youth and ignorance, gel. It's what society *believes* that counts."

"That stinks," George said.

Aunt Agatha gave her a pained look. "Must you use such a vulgar expression, Georgiana? And refrain from commenting on what you don't understand. A gel raised in a barnyard can have no idea of how polite society operates."

George bristled, and Emm intervened before an argument could start, saying, "Why do you say the second rumor is more serious, Aunt Agatha? I would have thought both stories were equally damaging to Lily's reputation."

"It is the *source* of the rumor that matters, Emmaline. The elopement story is being circulated by an inferior class of people—people on the fringe of the ton—aspirants, mushrooms, hangers-on." She made a distasteful gesture, as if dusting cobwebs off her fingers. "The Galbraith seduction-and-abandonment story is, however, on the lips of *la crème de la crème*—my own circle, in other words—the highest in the land." She eyed them accusingly. "And that is *far* more damaging."

"Who is spreading it?" Rose demanded.

"I have not yet tracked the rumor to its source. Nobody is willing to repeat it to my face."

"But it's not fair!" Lily was almost in tears. "Mr. Galbraith *rescued* me. He was a true gentleman in every way."

Aunt Agatha raised her lorgnette. "What does that have to do with anything?"

"Well, his reputation will be ruined too. And it's not fair."

"Pfft! Don't be so naïve!" Aunt Agatha said. "His reputation may be a little tarnished, but it will do him no harm in the long run. A rakish reputation is *expected* of a young man, and one who is handsome and also rich—well, society will forgive a few peccadilloes soon enough."

"Peccadilloes?" George began. "That's outrageous. If he did seduce Lily and dump—"

"But *he didn't*!" Lily almost shouted.

Aunt Agatha sighed. "You really are simple, aren't you, gel? Have you understood nothing I've said so far?"

"I understand," Lily began. "But why can't we track down the source of the rumor and tell them to stop telling lies?"

Aunt Agatha rolled her eyes. "As well try to hold back the Thames with your hands. No, you foolish child, there is only one way out of this; we must announce your betrothal."

Lily's jaw dropped. "Betrothal? Who to?"

"To *whom*, child—have you no grammar? To Galbraith, of course, who else?"

There was a short, shocked silence, then a cacophony of objections. "That's ridiculous. Lily barely knows the man," Emm said.

"Lily is innocent! Why should she be punished by being forced into a loveless marriage—" Rose began.

"Nor should her rescuer," George added.

"—simply because an evil man abducted her?" Rose finished.

"A man forced into an unwanted marriage is bound to resent his wife, whether she does the forcing or not," George said. Her parents had been forced into marriage. It had been disastrous for all concerned.

Aunt Agatha gave what in a less dignified person might have been called a shrug. "Life isn't fair. But it's nonsense to suggest anyone is being punished. Galbraith is a good match. He'll inherit his grandfather's title in a few years, and the estate is extensive."

"She doesn't need to marry for money or a title," George argued. "She already has a title, and when she turns one-and-twenty, she'll inherit a fortune—we all will."

"Which makes her an excellent match for Galbraith," the old lady said.

"But Lily has always—always!—wanted to marry for love!" Rose declared.

Aunt Agatha snorted. "Love? Pah! Love and marriage have nothing to do with each other."

"It does in this family," Emm said.

Aunt Agatha stabbed her lorgnette in Emm's direction. "You made a marriage of convenience to my nephew—don't try to deny it, Emmaline. And you must admit it has worked out very well."

"It has," Emm agreed, "because Cal and I fell in love. And I want the girls—all of them—to have that opportunity. I took a chance when I agreed to marry Cal. I never expected to love or be loved—only by any children I might be blessed with." She placed a hand on her swelling belly. "I was long past my first youth, alone in the world—or thought I was—poor, and unlikely to be courted ever again. I expected to remain a spinster for the rest of my life—until Cal made his proposition."

"And it turned out very well," Aunt Agatha said irritably.

"Yes, but it could have been otherwise. We were lucky." Emm caught Lily's hand and squeezed it fondly. "Lily is young—just eighteen—with her whole life ahead of her. She has a loving family, financial security, and a growing circle of admirers—just look at all the flowers she's been sent. I won't allow her to be forced into marriage just to satisfy the sensibilities of a bunch of old gossips spreading false rumors."

"Well said, Emm," Rose declared. George clapped.

Aunt Agatha, unimpressed, curled her lip. "Those admirers will soon fade away once it's known she's soiled goods."

"But *I'm not*!" Lily said indignantly.

Aunt Agatha sniffed. "In the eyes of the world, you are. Gossip is like acid; it eats away at the truth. Face it, child, if Galbraith doesn't marry you, you are ruined."

"If you say she is ruined one more time, I—I shall scream!" Emm declared.

Aunt Agatha directed a baleful glance at her. "Vulgar displays of emotion will not help the situation, Emmaline."

Emm glared at her. "I'm not so sure about that."

For a long moment, nobody said a word. Then George

spoke up. "You haven't said much, Lily. It's all very well for everyone to be telling you what to do, but what do *you* want?"

Lily's thoughts were in such turmoil she couldn't think of a single thing to say. Marry Edward Galbraith? Whether he wanted to or not? She looked at George and shook her head.

"Lily's wants have nothing to do with it," Aunt Agatha snapped. "The Rutherford name has been besmirched, and marriage to Galbraith is the only solution. She won't be the first bride who's found a husband thus—it is the way of the world."

"And what if Mr. Galbraith doesn't *want* to marry me?" Lily said.

Aunt Agatha snorted. "If we left it up to what men wanted, there would be precious few legitimate children born into the world." Rose gave a choked cough. Aunt Agatha gave her a withering look and added severely, "We know what they want, but it rarely includes marriage. Mr. Galbraith will get what Mr. Galbraith deserves—a virtuous, well-bred wife of good family who, God willing, will give him the heir his family requires."

It made Lily sound like a particularly large and indigestible pill.

"Whatever Mr. Galbraith deserves, this is about Lily, and I won't allow her to be forced into a marriage she does not want." Emm gave Lily a comforting smile. "She has just escaped that fate."

Aunt Agatha stamped her ebony cane. "Bah! It's not your decision to be made, Emmaline! Your husband is the head of this family—or has the whole world been turned upside-down and women wear the breeches? Don't say a word, Georgiana! Ashendon will understand there is no choice. He will speak to Galbraith—he might be a rake, but he is also a gentleman—and they will make the only honorable choice. You'd best start preparing for a wedding."

"We'll see about that," Emm murmured.

"PREPARE FOR A WEDDING INDEED—WHAT NONSENSE!" Rose said later that evening as the girls were dressing to go out. "How dare she try to force you into a marriage with a man like that."

"A man like what?" Lily asked quietly.

Rose gave her a surprised look. "Galbraith—he's just like those men you say you cannot bear, the ones Aunt Agatha keeps producing for us: cold, clever, sophisticated and bored to death with everything. Horrid!"

"Mr. Galbraith isn't like that really," Lily said. "He's much nicer than any of them."

"Nice?" Rose was incredulous.

"Yes, he's kind and nice and—"

"Are we talking about the same man? Galbraith—tall, dark, and with the coldest eyes you've ever seen. Like frost on green glass."

"He's not cold, he's just . . ." Lily groped for the right word.

"I hope you're not going to tell me he's shy," Rose said, and she and George laughed.

"No, he's not shy," Lily said with dignity. "He's reserved. I know he seems cold, but underneath, he's . . . different."

"How so?"

"I can't explain, but he's more than he appears to be."

Rose gave a snort worthy of her aunt. "Everyone is more than they appear to be."

George cocked her head curiously. "Are you saying you might be willing to marry this man after all?"

Lily shrugged. "I'm not sure. In any case, he hasn't asked." Yet. She was all a-flutter about the possibility. She wanted him to ask her, of course she did, but not if she was to be forced on him, like a bitter pill.

Though pills could be sweetened . . .

"But he's shown not the slightest bit of interest in you. If he did propose, it would only be out of duty."

Lily bit her lip. "Cal and Emm weren't in love when they got married."

Rose eyed her narrowly. "You're not in love with Galbraith, are you, Lily?"

"No, of course not," she lied. She wasn't sure if she was in love or not. She was, to put it simply, in turmoil.

Rose gave her a long, thoughtful look. "I hope it'll never happen, Lily darling, but if you gave your heart to that piece of granite, I fear he'd break it."

NED GALBRAITH HAD HEARD THE RUMORS HIMSELF. AT first there were just the odd few sly, suggestive hints, then one or two of his friends taxed him openly with it. He denied all knowledge of it and went in search of Elphingstone.

As luck would have it, he encountered the fellow as he was leaving his lodgings. Ned pushed him back indoors. "What the devil do you mean by spreading rumors about me and Lady Lily Rutherford?"

Elphingstone's eyes almost popped. "So it *was* Lady Lily at the inn, after all? Fellows at the club said you'd run off with her but changed your mind after sampling the goods—awkk!"

Ned grabbed him by his exquisitely arranged neckcloth and shook him like a rat. "Speak of her with respect—or not at all—if you want to live to see another day." He dropped Elphingstone back on his feet.

Elphingstone, his composure as ruffled as a cat dipped in water, smoothed out his rumpled clothing and fiddled with his crushed cravat, muttering, "It's ruined, quite ruined." Seeing Ned's expression he said pettishly, "No need for violence—it wasn't I who linked your name with Lady Lily's. I never saw the face of the lady you were with at that wretched inn, so how could I? I'm just repeating the *on-dit* around town. The tale was already out there, entries made in the betting book at White's before I even arrived in London—which was yesterday. That demmed village wheelwright took a week! A week to mend a simple wheel! A week at that dreadful inn!" He shuddered.

Ned still itched to strangle the man, but his story added up. If Elphingstone had only just arrived in town the day before, the rumors couldn't have spread as far as they had. Bets in the betting book at White's—damn, that was serious.

"Very well. But if I hear you've been adding to any of the gossip . . ."

Elphingstone gave him a shocked look. "Gossip? *Moi*? Perish the thought!"

Elphingstone was still spouting faux indignation when Ned left. Deep in thought—who the hell had spread the scandal?—he walked along Piccadilly, heading for White's—he wanted to check that damned betting book—when he almost bumped into a lady coming out of Hatchards bookshop.

"Watch where you're walking, young Galbraith!"

Startled, he looked up and came to an abrupt halt. "Lady Ampleforth? You're in London?"

She gave him a dry look. "A singularly foolish observation."

"I thought you were on your way to Hereford."

"Changed my mind, didn't I? Now, if you've quite finished blocking my way . . ."

He stepped back. She handed her parcels to a waiting footman and prepared to enter her carriage.

And it hit him. He lunged forward and stopped her. "There's a scurrilous story circulating among the ton, linking my name with that of Lady Lily Rutherford."

"Is there really?" Her look of mock innocence confirmed his theory.

He frowned. "You told me you abhorred gossip!"

Lady Ampleforth gave him a smug look. "Oh, I do." She looked like the cat that ate the cream.

"But you're the source of that gossip!" He was certain now—it could be no one else.

"Nonsense! It's not gossip when you speak the truth. I saw you and the Rutherford gel with my own eyes, traveling together."

He gritted his teeth. "I explained that."

She gave a scornful huff.

"*And* she had a chaperone with her."

Another huff delivered her opinion of Betty's value as a chaperone. "If you're finished talking nonsense, I wish to enter my carriage."

He didn't budge. "Why? Why would you do this? Lady Lily is a sweet young girl who's never harmed a soul in her life."

"No doubt she is," she said carelessly. "I doubt I've ever spoken to the gel."

"Then why would you try to ruin her reputation."

"Try?" There was a world of meaning in the way she said it.

Ned narrowed his eyes. "You mean you *wanted* to ruin her?"

She shrugged. "It's nothing to do with the gel herself. She merely gave me the opportunity."

"I don't understand."

"She is Aggie Rutherford's—Lady Salter she is now— niece. Aggie Rutherford! She holds herself so high—always has, ever since she was a gel—looking down on the rest of us and thinking she's soooo perfect!" She gave a self-satisfied smile. "And now we have a scandal involving her precious family—and, oh, how the mighty are fallen. I trust *dear* Aggie is squirming as much as I hoped she would." She pushed past him and climbed into her barouche.

Shocked by the vitriol in her voice, Ned watched her fussily arrange herself. To ruin Lily for the sake of some ancient feud with Lily's aunt . . .

"You vicious old trout! If you were a man . . ."

She laughed. "Words, words, words. Sticks and stones, they used to tell me." She smiled. "But words can hurt after all, can't they, young Galbraith? Coachman, drive on."

Fuming, Ned watched her drive off. He'd never taken much notice of the old lady before, but she'd always seemed pleasant enough. Did his grandfather know she was such a spiteful old cat? If not, he'd enlighten the old man when next he came to London.

He continued on to White's, where he greeted a couple of friends and acquaintances with the appearance of cool insouciance. He chatted of this and that, and then, aware of the covert interest of several members, he wandered over to the betting book and scanned it in a casual manner.

There were the entries Elphingstone had mentioned, linking his name and Lily's—Mr. E.G. and Lady L.—with bets made on a variety of possible outcomes. He swore under his breath.

He left White's and went straight to Jackson's Boxing Saloon, where he burned off some of his rage and frustration in a couple of fast and furious bouts. All the time his fists were flying, his thoughts were turning over and over, looking for a way out—for both of them.

He was all wrong for her. She was all wrong for him.

He thought of the whispers, the sly looks, the cunning innuendoes she would face; he recalled the smugness of that malicious, gossiping old bat, and the entries in the betting book. The reputation of an innocent young girl, so easily and carelessly ruined.

If it were anyone else but Lily . . .

Why couldn't the woman he'd rescued and accidentally compromised be older, plainer, more experienced, more self-reliant; the kind of woman he'd taken as a mistress from time to time. The sort of woman who wanted nothing more from him than his body, and occasionally his company. And usually his money.

Lily would want . . . so much more. The kinds of things he didn't have in him to give.

He wasn't opposed to marriage. He'd gotten almost as far as the altar last year with a woman who was all the things he required in a wife—she didn't even like him much.

But Lily. Lily dreamed of love. He could see the swirling echoes of those dreams in her eyes whenever she looked up at him.

His fault, for kissing her. For rescuing her.

Lord knew what kind of man she imagined him to be. All he knew was that he wasn't that man, could never be that man.

Oh, he presented well enough from the outside, and he had a name and position and wealth enough to keep a wife in comfort and style. But inside . . . inside he was a husk of a man, unfit to marry any sweet and dreamy young woman.

But they were trapped in a scandal not of their own making, and Ned had been born and raised a gentleman; he had no option but to offer marriage.

He left Jackson's and returned to his lodgings, where he bathed, shaved and changed his clothes. Time to call on Cal Rutherford.

Chapter Eleven

❧

Oh, Lizzy! do anything rather than
marry without affection.
—JANE AUSTEN, *PRIDE AND PREJUDICE*

NED REACHED ASHENDON HOUSE, ADJUSTED HIS NECK-
cloth, which had become unaccountably tight, took a deep
breath and rang the front doorbell.

The butler informed him Lord Ashendon was at home,
and ushered Ned into the front sitting room where Cal was
reading the *Morning Post*. Ned didn't waste time in social
chitchat. The moment the door closed behind the butler, he
said, "Rumors are rife about your sister and me."

"I know. Drink?" Cal folded the paper and set it aside.

"No, thank you. She's on the verge of social ruin."

"So my aunt, Lady Salter, tells us."

"Then you know why I've come."

Cal waved him to a seat. "Suppose you tell me."

Wasn't it obvious? "To make an offer for your sister, of
course." Ned made no attempt to sit. He was too wound up.
He took a position in front of the fireplace.

Cal steepled his fingers together and regarded Ned
thoughtfully. "It's very decent of you, of course, but I'm not
convinced marriage to you is the answer."

Ned stiffened. Having nerved himself to bite the bullet,
to do the honorable thing despite all his doubts and misgivings, it was a shock to hear his offer treated so casually. It
was one thing for him to worry that he wasn't the man for
Lily; it was quite another for her brother to imply the same.

"Why not? In some circles I'm held to be quite a good match."

"In some circles, yes. In others you're regarded as a rake and something of a cold fish."

A reputation he'd deliberately cultivated, which had now come back to bite him. "And which is your view?"

Cal shrugged "It's not about me. As far as I'm concerned you're a good friend and were a fine soldier. But my little sister is something else. She's . . . special."

Did Cal think he didn't know that? "Do you doubt I'd take care of her?"

"Materially, physically, I'm sure you will. But Lily has a tender heart. Even apart from your rakish tendencies, it wasn't so long ago you were preparing to marry a woman you barely even liked."

"That was different."

"Was it? Then it was your grandfather forcing your hand. Now it's society. Not much different from where I'm sitting."

"Dammit, Cal, Lady Lily is nothing like—like that other girl."

"Forgotten her name already, have you?" Cal was too damn acute. "And what was it you said to me back then? *'All cats are gray in the dark'*?"

It had been a stupid thing to say back then, a bit of bravado from an unwilling bridegroom, but Ned wouldn't admit it. He shrugged. "Yes, but you don't like cats. I do." Another stupid thing to say, and he could see Cal was getting annoyed. So was he.

"Lily is different. She's soft, and vulnerable. Dreamy. I don't want her hurt."

"And you think I'd hurt her?"

Cal met his gaze coolly. "Not deliberately."

"So what would you have me do? Walk away and let her face the slings and arrows of the ton alone? Damned if I will." Ned's hands were turning into fists. He shoved them into his pockets.

The ton was abuzz with rumors, and the wagers in the

betting book at White's only underlined them. Marriage was the obvious, the only way out. What the hell was Cal thinking to treat his offer so lightly? All very well for him to talk of protecting Lily; by the looks of things he was preparing to throw her to the lions.

Cal ran a hand over his jaw and said ruefully, "I don't know what to do, and that's the hell of it. If it were up to me . . . You're a good fellow, and you mean well, I know, but the women of my family are unanimous in opposing Lily's marriage to you. The exception being Aunt Agatha, who simply wants the gossip silenced and would happily marry Lily to a troll, as long as he was well born and rich."

Unanimous in opposing the marriage? Did that include Lily?

"You've discussed it already, when I haven't even proposed?"

Cal gave a sardonic half smile. "Where Aunt Agatha is concerned I'm not sure your views even come into it. She informed Lily yesterday that she had no alternative but to marry you."

Ned tensed. "And what did Lily say?"

"Not much. But the others made their views very clear. They are determined to prevent Lily from being forced into marriage with a man she hardly knows. And does not love."

It was exactly what he'd been thinking himself, so why should Cal's words annoy him so much? But they did. "Women are ruled by emotion. It's your decision as head of the family, is it not?"

Cal snorted. "There speaks the carefree—and ignorant— bachelor. On such things my wife and the girls have very strong opinions—and I can see their point. My own marriage was quite unpromising at the start, but . . . Well, suffice it to say that having found unexpected felicity in marriage, I want the same for my sister." He rose. "I'll let you make her your offer, and then, depending on her answer, the family will decide how to handle this mess." He moved toward the door but before he reached it, it opened and Lady Ashendon entered.

"Oh, I'm sorry, my dear, I didn't realize you were en-gaged," she said coolly. Ned took leave to doubt that. He was quite certain she knew exactly what had been going on.

"Mr. Galbraith, how do you do? So good of you to call on us. I was expecting you last week." There was a hint of reproof in her voice; this was not the warm and grateful woman he'd encountered when he'd brought Lily home.

Cal gave her a significant look. "Mr. Galbraith has come to pay a call on Lily."

"Of course. Please be seated." She arranged herself on the sofa and patted the seat beside her. Cal took it. She angled a cool glance at Ned and, recollecting she'd been a schoolmistress, he sat on a chair opposite.

"You have come to make Lily an offer." It wasn't a question.

"I have."

She nodded. "We have been considering the possibility—and our choices."

He raised a brow. "Indeed." As far as he was concerned there wasn't a choice.

"I've already—" Cal began. She slid her hand into her husband's and he didn't finish his sentence.

"There is no need for you and Lily to be forced into a marriage, Mr. Galbraith. The scandal was none of your making, and you are both innocent of any wrongdoing."

Ned watched as Cal stroked his thumb back and forth over his wife's hand. A small, barely noticeable movement—neither of them even seemed aware of the quiet caress; it was something they both took for granted—and yet watching it, watching them, caused a strange hollowness in Ned's chest.

She continued, "Indeed, you behaved quite heroically in saving her from an appalling fate, and we very much appre-ciate your honorable motives in being prepared to offer marriage to her." Her smile warmed. "But there is no need for such a sacrifice."

"Sacrifice?"

"On both your parts. If no scandal had arisen, would you be here now, preparing to make my sister-in-law an offer?"

"No, but—"

"Exactly. A scandal is temporary, but marriage is for a lifetime. We are Lily's family and we will ride this scandal out together. To be sure there will be some initial unpleasantness, but that will eventually fade. Lily is an earl's daughter with a handsome fortune. There will be gentlemen a-plenty willing to overlook a whiff of scandal for the sake of marriage with a titled heiress. So there's no need for you to concern yourself any further."

It was a clear dismissal, and he should have been relieved. Instead he was angry. This was the second time members of the Rutherford family had told him that Lily was none of his business, that he should take himself off and forget about it, about her.

But *they* were the ones who had let her be abducted in the first place. He was the one who'd saved her and brought her home. And he was not to be dismissed with a pat on the head, like a schoolboy returning a stray puppy.

"How?" he asked. Lady Ashendon paused in the middle of rising, and Ned repeated his question, "How do you intend to ride out the scandal? What exactly are your plans?"

She settled back on the sofa. "Since the rumors are contradictory, and there were no actual witnesses, we shall simply ignore it and go on as usual. Eventually some other scandal will occur and the ton's attention will move on."

"And in the meantime, Lily must simply endure being gossiped about until it dies down? Not acceptable." He folded his arms. "Besides, there was a witness, one that the ton will not doubt. Lady Ampleforth saw us traveling together."

Cal swore. His wife glanced at him. "Lady Ampleforth?"

"Aunt Agatha's greatest rival."

"I confronted her earlier," Ned said. "She has seized on it as a way of paying your aunt back for some ancient insult and is, quite gleefully, doing her best to keep the rumor alive. Short of a bullet, you won't shut her up." He rose to his feet. "So enough of this nonsense. Perhaps you would allow me to speak to Lily now." Lady Ashendon opened her mouth to speak and he held up a hand. "I don't need you to tell me I'm not worthy of her—believe me, I know it—but

I can and will protect her from a scandal she does not deserve."

"And after that?" Lady Ashendon asked. "When you are husband and wife?"

"After that . . ." He wasn't prepared to give false assurances. He swallowed. "After that I shall support her as any man does his wife."

There was a short silence as everyone in the room considered the inadequacy of that statement. Lady Ashendon spoke first. "And what if she refuses you?"

"It is her right. I won't try to force her. But whether her answer is yea or nay, know this—I won't walk away and leave her to face the scandal alone."

Lady Ashendon regarded him thoughtfully for a long moment. Then she gave a brisk nod. "Very well, Mr. Galbraith, Lily will be down in a moment." She put her hand out and Cal helped her to rise. As she did, her dress pulled briefly tight across her belly.

She was in the family way, Ned saw. Probably why Cal allowed his wife so much license.

As Cal opened the door for her, Ned thought of something. "Cal, before you go—"

Cal turned.

"Any news of Nixon?"

Cal shook his head. "But I'll get him, don't you worry." The door closed quietly behind him.

NED PACED BACK AND FORTH IN FRONT OF THE FIREPLACE. For the second time in his life he was about to offer marriage. He wished now that he'd accepted that drink from Cal. He was ridiculously nervous.

He went over in his mind the words he would use to make the offer. He wanted her to be clear what he was offering—no false promises, no raising of impossible and unlikely expectations.

A girl who'd always wanted to marry for love. A dreamer. And himself a cold, hard cynic.

Love was an ephemeral thing, impossible to pin down, impossible to promise.

Lily was a girl who treasured illusions, about life, about love. About him.

Dangerous things, illusions.

He swallowed. He would have to shatter her expectations immediately, before her illusions about him could grow any further. Small illusions, nipped early in the bud, would be much less painful for a girl who dreamed.

He was determined that if she accepted him—and her sister-in-law had planted doubts in him now, that she might refuse, and if so—no, he would not consider that possibility. If she accepted him, she needed to understand that the marriage was for purely practical reasons—a marriage of convenience—to stop scandal, to protect her reputation. And for an heir.

After the wedding, they would continue on in the same vein—in a practical marriage. He would take good care of her and support her in the manner to which she was accustomed, and that would be that.

Footsteps sounded on the floor outside and he turned to face the door. She entered, dressed in a soft yellow dress. Her hair was clustered in artless curls held back from her face by a band of yellow gauze. A breath of spring.

"Mr. Galbraith." A delicate flush rose in her cheeks.

"Lady Lily." He scanned her face. No sign of bruises or sleepless nights. "You're looking very well." She looked lovely, but . . . expectations.

He waited, leashing his impatience while she seated herself, smoothed out her dress and then folded her hands in her lap like an obedient schoolgirl. "Did your brother explain why I've asked to speak to you?"

Her blush deepened. She nodded.

"Good. Now, before we get to that, that question, there are a few things I need to make clear to you. There are—"

She tilted her head to look up at him. "Will you not be seated? It feels a little odd, you standing while I'm sitting."

He sat on a stiff little chair opposite her. His palms were

damp. "There are several things I want to make clear before I, er, put the question to you."

"Go ahead."

"This marriage, if you agree to it, will be an arrangement, a marriage for practical reasons—you understand?"

"A convenient marriage?"

"Yes." He was relieved she understood. "I'm sorry."

"Sorry? For what?"

"That you won't be able to do as you've always wanted— that there isn't time for you to meet a suitable young man, be courted and fall in love." There. He'd said it.

"Because of the scandal."

"Yes. You and I know there is no basis for the gossip, but it is the way of the world. A woman's reputation is based on what others think and say she did, not what she actually did."

"A man's reputation too."

"Eh?" Jolted from his train of thought, he blinked. "Oh, yes, I suppose so."

"They're saying you seduced and took advantage of me, but I know you are a man of honor and would never—"

He interrupted, saying in a hard voice, "They're saying that because they know I've seduced many women in the past."

"Oh."

Illusion number one shattered. "It is why I am called a rake by some. You know what a rake is?"

"A man who can't be trusted with an unmarried girl."

"Exactly." He wasn't going to muddy the water by telling her he never dallied with innocents. Better she have no romantic expectations of him before—if—she agreed to marry him. "That house party I was going to when we first met—"

"We first met at Cal and Emm's wedding," she said, correcting him.

"When I ran into you on the road then—do you know what happens at those parties?" Without waiting for her to reply, he explained what sort of a party it was, that several married women had already invited him to share their bed and that he probably would have accepted. He needed to strip her of any illusions she might cherish about him in that area.

She was a little pale when he finished, but all she said was, "It doesn't sound as though you like that sort of party very much."

"I don't."

"Then why do you go to them?"

He shrugged. He didn't have an answer that wasn't desperately cynical. "The point is, you don't know me at all."

"I know more than you think. I know that you knew Cal at school, that you went to war also, and that you are a war hero like him and—"

"A *hero*? On the contrary." His voice was harsh. "I'll spare you the details, but—"

She lifted her head. "You were mentioned in dispatches several times."

"How the h—how do you know that?"

She smiled. "When Cal was away at war, my sister, Rose, used to read the war news aloud—to Aunt Dottie and me. And Aunt Dottie remembered that you were a friend of Cal's, so naturally after that we noticed whenever your name was mentioned."

"I see. Well, those reports aren't to be relied on."

A crease formed between her delicately arched brows. "Why not?"

"Brave deeds—and dark ones too, for that matter— happen everywhere in war, at all levels. An illiterate foot soldier might perform the most heroic deed you've ever seen, but should a duke's nephew rattle a saber or take part in a charge, it will be him who's mentioned in dispatches, not the illiterate." And that would deal with her tendency to hero worship.

"I see." Her eyes were dark and troubled. "Why are you telling me all these things to your discredit?"

"Because if you accept me, you need to know what kind of man you'll be marrying. I won't lie to you, Lily; I'm no bargain. All I can promise you is a home, security for your lifetime and"—he swallowed—"any children of my body. But that is all." He hoped she understood.

The blush bloomed again, but she considered his words in silence for a few moments. Then, "And your offer of marriage is only because of the scandal?"

"Yes. I thought I made that clear at the beginning." Final illusions crushed. He felt like a brute, but it had to be done for her own good. "So, Lady Lily Rutherford, would you do me the honor of becoming my wife?"

She was quiet for a few minutes, then looked up. "If I do marry you, will you promise not to lie to me?"

He hesitated a moment but could see no harm in that. He might be less than she deserved, but he intended to do right by her. "I promise."

"And will you be a faithful husband?" When he did not immediately answer, she added quietly, "It is a consideration when one is marrying a rake, you see. Given such things as house parties."

"And if I say no, that I intend to continue my rakish ways?"

"Then I would have to refuse your very kind offer."

"Even though you'd be ruined in the eyes of the world?"

She nodded. She seemed quite certain, quite unruffled by the prospect. She was either courageous or naïve. He decided on the latter. She had no idea of what she might be facing.

He gave her a frustrated look. "Very well then, I promise you that once we are married I will be faithful to you and only you." It was not a hard thing to promise. Any man lucky enough to have Lily Rutherford in his bed would be a fool to stray.

She eyed him thoughtfully and the crease between her brows deepened.

"What are you thinking?" he asked after the silence had stretched to an unbearable point.

"I'm thinking you might come to regret that promise—both of them," she admitted.

He shrugged. "What's life without regrets?"

She considered that a moment, then shook her head briskly. "No, I was wrong to ask you. I give you back both your promises."

Was that a refusal? "But—"

"Honesty and fidelity cannot be forced. Unless they are freely given they have no value. Society, my aunt Agatha and my brother might have forced your hand to this marriage, but it's up to us to make it work."

He frowned. "You mean we should go into it without expectations?" It was exactly what he'd wanted from her; if she expected nothing of him, he couldn't disappoint her. So why did the prospect now make him feel so unsettled?

"It's not exactly how I'd put it, but yes, if you will accept that I will do my best to be a good wife to you and you will—" She waited, giving him an expectant look.

"Try to be a good husband." And try not to disappoint her too much.

"Then God bless us both."

God help us, Ned thought. And then he realized the implications of what she'd said. "Does that mean—?"

"Yes, Mr. Galbraith, I will marry you."

LEAVING EDWARD AND CAL TO DISCUSS SETTLEMENTS, Lily walked slowly upstairs, dawdling in order to put off the moment when she would have to tell Rose and Emm and George that she'd accepted him. Against all their advice. And wishes.

She was betrothed to Mr. Galbraith—to Edward. She should have been *in alt*, or over the moon, or any one of the usual states newly betrothed girls were supposed to feel. Instead she felt . . . She didn't know what she felt.

It had been a very businesslike proposal. He hadn't even kissed her. Perhaps that was why she felt a little flat. She had to admit she'd been expecting a kiss, at least. And looking forward to it.

Why had he tried so hard to paint himself in such an unfavorable light? Was he trying to put her off, or was he simply trying to be honest with her? It was impossible to know.

He'd admitted that his reason for proposing was the scandal—well, that was no surprise. Before Lily had gone in to receive his offer, Emm had told her that she'd tried to talk Mr. Galbraith out of proposing, just as she'd tried to convince Lily not to marry him.

But he'd chosen to propose. And Lily had chosen to accept.

Was it only his sense of honor that had prompted him to offer marriage to her? Or did he have some other reason, one he hadn't mentioned?

Lily had. She hadn't admitted it to anyone except Rose yet: She wanted Edward Galbraith. More than wanted, she loved him.

At least she thought she did. Rose said it wasn't love, that she was confusing love with the gratitude she felt for her rescuer, and Lily did feel grateful. But when Edward had kissed her in the dark woods and held her in his arms, it wasn't gratitude she felt.

When she'd told Rose and George about the kiss, Rose's view was that Lily was too inexperienced to tell. Galbraith was a rake; it stood to reason he would know how to kiss. What Lily needed, Rose said, was to be kissed by a lot of other men. Then she'd know what value to put on Mr. Galbraith's kisses.

Except Lily didn't want to kiss a lot of other men. She only wanted one man to kiss—Edward.

George had said that Lily didn't need to kiss anyone else, that any man who shared his kisses around like Mr. Galbraith was reputed to do wasn't worth having.

There was sense in their opinions, both of them. But Lily wanted Edward with a desperate yearning. She thought of him constantly, and even dreamed of him. Was that love? She didn't know.

Emm had suggested Lily was perhaps a little infatuated—which was understandable given the dreadful situation he'd rescued her from. It was also understandable, Emm said, that she was attracted to him; he was an attractive man and could be quite charming—when he wanted to be.

But he was so much older than Lily—nearly twenty-eight to Lily's eighteen—and so much more experienced.

Perhaps Lily could look around a little more. The ton was full of charming and eligible young men.

That made sense too, but Lily didn't want to look around.

She felt certain—almost—that she loved Edward, but was she *in love* with him? Didn't there need to be two who loved to be *in* love? Both of you, loving each other?

It was hard to know. He hadn't hinted at any feelings. He'd said things like, *I'm no catch, you deserve better, I'm no hero, I am a rake*—all very clear messages warning her off admiring him in any way.

But the more he tried to make her dislike him, the more she wanted to hug him. He was so much more wonderful than he thought he was.

Was she doing the right thing in marrying him? She didn't know.

Was she doing the wrong thing? She hoped not.

All she was sure of was that if she'd refused his proposal today, she probably wouldn't see him again, and that she couldn't bear.

Something had begun, in that trip back from Yorkshire, and every instinct she had was to nurture it. She felt certain—as certain as a girl full of doubts could—that this was what she had to do. She loved Edward and would do her very best to make him the best wife she could be. And she would hope and pray that he would become the loving kind of husband she'd always dreamed of.

He might be marrying in scandal, but she would marry in hope.

She reached the landing, turned the corner, and found Rose and George sitting at the top of the stairs, waiting for her.

"Well? Did you send him on his way?" Rose demanded.

"He's downstairs, talking to Cal."

Rose's eyes narrowed. "What about?" When Lily didn't respond, Rose made a dismayed exclamation. "You accepted him, didn't you? Oh, Lily!"

"I want him, Rose," Lily said quietly.

"I know you *think* you do, but . . . Oh, Lily, I just wish . . ."

"I suppose I must wish you happy, then," George said. She didn't sound very confident or in the least bit joyous, but Lily hugged and thanked her anyway.

Then Rose hugged Lily tightly, saying, "I'm sorry, I know I shouldn't be so— I just want you to be happy, Lily." Her eyes were bright with unshed tears.

"I'm going to be happy, Rose, just you wait and see." Lily's eyes were teary too. "He's a wonderful man, really he is. You just don't know him yet."

"I gather you've accepted Mr. Galbraith's proposal." Emm emerged from the sitting room at the top of the stairs. She held out her arms to Lily. "I hope this marriage brings you all the happiness you deserve, my dear." Emm was as full of doubt as the others; she was just better at hiding it.

Lily and she embraced, then Emm said, "Well, then, we'd better go downstairs and congratulate the happy groom. Cal will want to make a toast." She began the descent downstairs. George, Lily and Rose followed.

Congratulate the happy groom? At the moment Edward was probably more of a resolute groom. But he would be happy, eventually. Lily was determined to make it so.

Halfway down the stairs, Rose paused and gave her a sudden sharp look. "Did you tell him about—?"

"No. I'll tell him later."

"But don't you think you ought to—?"

"Later, Rose."

She didn't want to talk about it, not now—and if she was honest with herself, not ever. Edward had made a clean breast of his faults. That was admirable—assuming he'd meant it as a way of starting fresh and not a way of putting her off.

She hadn't done the same. She knew she should have told him about her reading difficulties. He'd have to know eventually. But she didn't want to see that expression in his eyes when she admitted her problem, the look she'd received from all but a few people. Even from Papa. Especially from Papa.

Did they think she didn't *want* to be like everyone else, to be able to read ladies' magazines, or lose herself between the pages of a novel, or to write letters and exchange convivial little notes? And not to have to ask—always ask—someone else to read or write for her?

So no, she wasn't going to tell him. Not yet, at any rate.

Chapter Twelve

❧

You must be the best judge of your own happiness.
—JANE AUSTEN, *EMMA*

"I BELIEVE I MUST WISH YOU HAPPY, MR. GALBRAITH."
Lady Ashendon came forward. She didn't sound in the least
joyful, more resigned. "Lily is a girl very dear to my heart.
You will take the very best of care of her, won't you?"

It wasn't so much a wish as an order, Ned decided. With
a clear, if restrained, assurance that should he fail, Lady
Ashendon would have something to say about it. A teacher's tactic, but she wasn't bluffing.

He bowed over her hand. "I will, Lady Ashendon."

Lily's sister, Rose, glided toward him, hands held out.
She was taller than Lily, slender and graceful, a golden-
haired beauty with ice-blue eyes and a smile that dazzled,
even as it chilled. No doubt the ton fawned over her. They
could keep this ice queen; give him Lily's warmth and luscious femininity any day.

"So you are to become my brother-in-law, Mr. Galbraith."
She stood on tiptoe as if to give him a pretty sisterly kiss and,
in a voice only he could hear, murmured, "Hurt my sister in
any way, Galbraith, and you'll be sorry you were ever born."
She pressed a dry, cold pair of lips to his cheek, stabbed him
with a glittering look and stepped back, smiling.

Thank God she wasn't the one Nixon stole. He might
have had to marry her.

The other girl, Lady Georgiana—curious that she was Lily's niece and yet was the elder—came forward with a loose-limbed, almost boyish stride that was oddly attractive. She held out her hand to him and murmured with a sweet smile, "Lily is a darling and if you don't treat her right, Mr. Galbraith, I'll gut you with a rusty blade."

He blinked, more amused than menaced by the melodramatic threat. Misinterpreting his expression, she gave a brisk, satisfied nod.

What a family of women. Such ladylike ferocity in defense of their sister. He found it rather charming, if a little insulting.

It was excellent that Lily had such a protective family, but really, did they expect him to beat Lily, or starve her? When he was in this position because he'd gone out of his way to protect her? They certainly had the lowest expectations of him. But perhaps his reputation bothered them.

His own fault, he supposed. Since selling out of the army after Waterloo and returning to civilian life, he'd taken pains to cultivate a rakish reputation and to avoid fashionable society. He had had no desire to be hunted by matchmaking mamas, and being in line for a title, a fortune and a handsome estate, he had had no doubt he would be hunted.

A movement at the door caught his eye. It was the biggest dog he'd ever seen, tall and gray and shaggy. He slunk in—if a dog that size could be said to slink—edged up behind Lady Georgiana and eyed Ned with an enigmatic expression. Lady Georgiana's dog, he presumed. Would she set it on him?

Ned liked dogs. He snapped his fingers and the dog padded forward. He sniffed Ned's outstretched fingers, then sat down with an expression that was a clear invitation to pat.

"Finn," Lady Georgiana said crossly. The dog thumped a lazy tail but didn't move. Ned had found the perfect spot needing scratching—just behind the ears.

Lady Georgiana gave Ned a narrow look, but it seemed to him that her glower had lightened somewhat.

"Ah, Mr. Galbraith!" A thin, immaculately dressed elderly lady stood in the doorway. Lady Salter, Lily's aunt. Ned braced himself for another ladylike death threat.

She raised her lorgnette, made a comprehensive sweep of the room with it, then said, "Well, is it to be a wedding—or from the faces you're all wearing, a funeral?" She turned to Cal. "The gel has done the sensible thing, I hope?"

Cal said, "Lily and Mr. Galbraith are betrothed."

"Excellent." She swept toward Ned like an angular, full-rigged galleon. "Mr. Galbraith, let me be the first to welcome you into the family. I am delighted, simply delighted that you have agreed to rescue my foolish niece from the consequences of her imprudence. I hope the gel will strive to be worthy of the honor you do her."

The atmosphere in the room bristled with silent indignation.

"It is Lady Lily who does me the honor," Ned responded coolly. "And I've already been given a most memorable welcome by the other members of her family. And if you will forgive me for correcting you on one or two points—"

Lady Salter raised her lorgnette with ominous significance.

Ned continued, "Lady Lily was not in the least imprudent; she is totally without blame and has shown nothing but grace and courage in dealing with a scandal not of her making."

Lady Salter boot-button eyes snapped with irritation. "Nonsense, she—"

"In fact, if there is any blame to be assigned, it must go to your old friend, Lady Ampleforth, who has been most assiduous—"

Her bosom swelled. "Henrietta Ampleforth is *no* friend of mine—"

"Yet you must accept your fair share of blame for Lily's predicament. It was to punish *you* that Lady Ampleforth attempted to blacken Lily's good name." He took Lily's hand and kissed it lightly. "But I hold no grudge against the two of you—"

"Against *me*?" Lady Salter drew herself up, a praying mantis in high dudgeon. "It has nothing to do with—"

"It is Lady Lily's forgiveness you must ask."

"What? Ask *Lily's* forgiveness?" She spat out the words like chips of glass.

"She is a generous-hearted girl. I'm sure you need not fear her disapproval," Ned finished smoothly. Leaving Lady Salter sputtering with indignation, he turned to Lily. "Now, my dear, do you favor a long engagement or a short one?"

"Long," said Lily's relatives in a chorus.

"Short," Lily said with a smile. Her eyes were shining. "The shorter, the better. How long does a special license take?"

"No special license!" Lady Salter rallied. "A quick marriage is what's required, but not a *hasty* one. Ashendon, you will arrange for the banns to be called at St. George's, Hanover Square. And send a notice of the betrothal to the *Morning Post* and the *Chronicle*. That should stop the gossip, or at least turn it into more acceptable channels. Lady Ampleforth"—she directed a waspish glare at Ned—"you may leave to me."

Ned took his leave a short time later, feeling quite as though he'd escaped from the lion's den. What a formidable pack of women. Thank God he'd ended up with Lily. She was the pick of the bunch.

Three and a half weeks and she'd be his wife. A married man; he couldn't quite imagine it.

He'd been more or less alone since his first weeks in the army. Since that first battle. Surrounded by men, but essentially alone. A few friends, but not the kind of friends he'd had before.

And since he'd returned to civilian life, he hadn't been close to any women, either. A few liaisons here and there, but again, no one close. An escort to the theater or to parties, a dance partner, a bedmate, but no intimacy other than physical. It was an arrangement that had suited him well.

The question was, could he achieve the same kind of balance in his marriage?

* * *

"I MUST SAY, LILY, MR. GALBRAITH WAS QUITE IMPRESSIVE in there." Rose linked arms with Lily as they climbed the stairs together.

"He was wonderful, wasn't he?" Lily could hardly stop smiling. She was betrothed to Mr. Galbraith. To Edward.

"Anyone who can stand up to Aunt Agatha so coolly can't be all bad."

"He's not bad at all. I keep telling you, Rose—"

"Finn liked him," George commented from behind. "But then Finn likes anyone who knows exactly where to scratch."

"Just because he's not intimidated by Aunt Agatha and knows how to pat a dog doesn't mean he's the right husband for Lily."

"The decision is made. I'm betrothed to Mr. Galbraith and that's that," Lily said firmly.

"It's not over until you're married," Rose muttered.

"It's not over until his ring is on her finger and she wakes up in his bed in the morning," George said. "That's what my granddad made sure of when he forced my father to marry my mother." She shook her head. "Forcing people is bad. My father didn't want to be married—he left my mother soon afterward and it fair broke her heart. So much misery, and all to make sure I was legitimate. And so that Mama wasn't ostracized as a fallen woman." She gave Lily a somber look. "But I don't blame you, Lily. Being a fallen woman . . ." She shivered. "I knew one once, nice girl she was too, from a good family. She ended up drowning herself rather than face a daily shunning from all those who used to be her friends."

"George!" Rose interrupted. "You're supposed to be reassuring Lily that she doesn't have to marry Mr. Galbraith, not frightening her with grim tales."

"No, I'm not," George retorted. "It's not up to me who Lily does or does not marry. It's her life and her decision."

"And yet according to you the alternative is daily shunning—not that that would happen. If anyone dared to shun my sister, I . . . I'd slap them. Or worse," Rose said fiercely.

"Nobody will need to slap anyone," Lily said. "George is right, Rose. It's my decision, and whatever the consequences, I'll deal with them. Myself."

There was a short silence.

"You've changed," George said. "Somehow, you're . . . tougher."

Lily glanced at Rose and saw that her sister agreed. "Being abducted and drugged and locked under a seat for several days, well, it makes one think. All my life people have looked after me, but when it comes to the crunch—to the big things in life—you're essentially on your own. I used to worry more about what people thought of me, but now I realize how futile that is. People will think what they want to think, regardless. I did nothing wrong, and I still ended up in a mess."

Rose pounced. "So you do admit it's a mess. Then you don't have to marry—"

"It's done, Rose. Like it or not, my reputation is ruined. Stop worrying about me and consider the implications for yourselves. Remember how Emm used to tell us what one of us did reflected on the others?"

Rose gave her a worried look. "I hope you're not marrying for my sake. It's not worth it."

"Doesn't matter to me what people think." George fondled Finn's ears. "I don't plan on getting married anyway."

Lily glanced at Rose, but she said nothing more. Rose never talked about her marriage prospects these days. When they were girls at school she used to talk about it constantly—they both did, dreaming of whom they might marry. Now it was Aunt Agatha who harped continually on about Rose's marriage prospects. Rose rarely spoke of it at all.

Lily slipped an arm around her sister's waist. "I'm not getting married for your sake, Rose. I'm marrying Mr. Galbraith for my own reasons. So stop fretting and be happy for me."

Rose sighed. "I'll try." But she didn't sound very confident.

* * *

THREE AND A HALF WEEKS TO THE WEDDING DIDN'T LEAVE
much time to order a new dress and make all the arrangements, but when the three girls and Emm arrived at the
House of Chance, Daisy Chance, the owner, laughed at
their anxiety and assured them she'd make something special in plenty of time.

"I'm thinkin' lace, Lady Lily, over creamy satin—
white'll make you look sallow, but cream will make your
skin glow like a pearl. Short puffed sleeves and a satin band
here." She gestured with her hands. "What do you think?"

"It sounds lovely." Every dress Miss Chance had made
her made Lily feel beautiful, and she trusted this would be
the same.

The dressmaker eyed her shrewdly. "I reckon you've lost
a bit of weight, Lady Lily. If you'd care to step into the fitting room, I'll measure you up again." She drew back the
green velvet curtains and escorted Lily to the fitting rooms
at the back of the shop.

She bustled about, taking Lily's measurements and
making small talk, which Lily responded to absently. It was
so uncomfortable, preparing for a wedding that none of her
family was happy about. It should have been a joyous occasion, but instead, everyone was pretending.

Rose and George had conceded that Edward wasn't
quite as bad as they thought; yes, he'd defended her against
Aunt Agatha—they did like that. But they knew he wasn't
in love—he'd made no pretense that he was—and they
were upset that Lily would never get her happy ending.
They were still certain she was infatuated with an imaginary version of Mr. Galbraith.

She couldn't help what they thought. She would marry
him, and then love would grow, and they would see what a
wonderful, kind, protective husband he would be.

"You all right there, Lady Lily?" Miss Chance asked.
"Something on your mind?"

"Oh, no, I was just—just thinking about a book I read
recently," she lied. She couldn't possibly share her doubts

and worries with Miss Chance, be she ever so nice and friendly.

"What was it called? Lift your arms, please—yes, that's right."

"*Persuasion*, by—"

"By the author of *Pride and Prejudice*."

"Yes, have you read it too?"

Miss Chance wrote some measurements in a little book. "Not yet. We've started it, but we're only into the first couple of chapters. How's that Sir Walter—don't he love himself? Mind you, I have one or two clients just like him. It's what I like about her characters—they're just like people you know."

They chatted about the book for a few minutes, then Lily said, "You said, 'We've started it.' Who is 'we'—if you don't mind me asking?"

"It's a group—a literary society I go to, run by me—by a lady I know. Several ladies take it in turn to read the books aloud, and the rest of us sit and listen and then talk about them in the interval—nothing too learned, though. It's all just for fun. I take me embroidery sometimes."

"That sounds wonderful," Lily exclaimed. "I love having books read to me."

"Me too," Miss Chance said. "Well, that's you done, Lady Lily." She wound up her tape measure and closed the little book with Lily's measurements in it. "You've lost a bit of weight, as I thought, but I'll leave a good bit of seam in, in case you put it back on in the next few weeks. Now, don't you fret, it will be ready in plenty of time. Now, what about nightclothes? Come through here and I'll show you me honeymoon specials."

She ushered Lily and the others through to another little room, an Aladdin's cave of nightgowns and negligees in the softest, flimsiest silks and satins and gauzes, trimmed with lace and ribbons; they were the prettiest—and the most improper—garments Lily had ever seen.

"Oh, my, these are so beautiful," she breathed. The thought of wearing one of these delicious nightgowns on her wedding night, and Edward's eyes when he saw her in it, was at once exciting and nerve-racking.

"I wore one of Miss Chance's beautiful nightgowns on my wedding night," Emm said quietly. All three girls looked at her, and she blushed. "It was a wedding gift from one of my former pupils." She stroked one of the silky nightgowns reminiscently, and the three girls exchanged glances and tried not to giggle.

"So how many will you want, Lady Lily?"

"Five," said Emm. She caught Lily's surprised look and said, "My own convenient marriage started with one of these lovely nightgowns. Let us give yours the best chance we can."

"And wiv a gorgeous Chance nightgown, how can you lose?" Miss Chance finished with a grin.

NED PAUSED IN FRONT OF THE BOW STREET OFFICE. HE'D been going to hire a runner to track down Nixon. More than a week since he'd returned Lily to her family, and Cal still had no news of the swine.

Be damned to Cal's stance that Lily was his own concern. Cal hadn't seen the state of her when he'd found her on the road. Cal hadn't seen Nixon give her a vicious backhander across the face. Cal hadn't held her while she struggled against the filthy drug Nixon had forced down her throat.

As Lily's betrothed, Ned now had the right to act on her behalf.

But on the very steps of the Bow Street office, he realized that a runner wasn't the answer. If Nixon was apprehended by an officer of the law, the matter would have to go to court. Lily's name would be splashed across the newspapers and the gossip would be worse than ever. She'd endured enough of that. He would act privately on the matter.

He turned away and headed to the Apocalypse Club, where former and current military officers gathered to relax. London was full of former soldiers with not enough to do. He'd surely be able to find some reliable men who would track down Nixon for a handsome fee.

And after they'd caught him? He'd work out what to do later.

As he passed through Covent Garden he noticed a man and a young woman beside a flower stall. The sweet fragrance of the flowers drifted to him, even over the general odor of London. As he watched, the man picked out a bunch of creamy little flowers and handed them to the girl. Blushing with pleasure, she raised the bouquet to her face and inhaled the fragrance. The man paid and the couple walked off, arm in arm, their happiness visible to the world.

A courting couple . . .

Ned watched them go, then continued on to the Apocalypse Club. From the minute he walked in, the comments started, half joking, from friends and acquaintances alike, all variations on the theme of him being caught in parson's mousetrap. It was all meant in good humor, he was sure, but it irritated him, all the same.

The inference was that he had no choice, that he'd been trapped, forced into marriage, which, while it was true, was also rather insulting to his own independence. It was also, by implication, particularly unflattering to Lady Lily, though no one was foolish enough to mention her by name.

He endured the jokes and banter with apparent equanimity, conducted his business briskly, found the names and addresses of several men who'd be glad of a little paid employment and left the club in a bad mood.

It wasn't the first time he'd been irritated by the jovial commiseration of his fellows; he was widely perceived as the victim in all this.

Which made Lily the villain. She was the one blamed, the one seen to benefit most by the marriage, the one who was trapping him.

The thought left a sour taste in his mouth. On impulse, he walked back to the Covent Garden flower seller and bought a posy of the same sweetly fragranced little flowers that the courting couple had bought. He had them tied with a blue ribbon and made arrangements for them to be delivered to Lily's address with a brief note.

He needed to make a more public show of courting her.

Then it wouldn't look to the outside world quite like the scandal-forced arrangement it was. A man had his pride.

Passing Hatchards bookshop, he recalled how much Lily had enjoyed the book he'd read to her in the carriage. He went in and ordered a volume of poetry to be delivered to her as well. Girls liked poetry, and the bookseller assured him anything by Lord Byron would delight a young lady. He added a short note to go with it and was about to seal it when an idea occurred to him. He opened the note, scrawled a postscript, then sealed it shut.

He left the bookshop in a much happier frame of mind. The appearance of a courtship, that was what he needed.

"A PARCEL FOR YOU, LADY LILY." BURTON, THE BUTLER, presented it on a silver tray.

Lily seized the small oblong packet and unwrapped it eagerly. "It's a book," she said in surprise. "Who would send me a book?"

"There's a note," Rose pointed out.

Lily broke the note open, stared at it for a long frustrating moment, then passed it to Rose, who read it aloud. "'To Lady Lily, with my sincere regards, Edward Galbraith.' And there's a postscript." She squinted at it. "His writing is atrocious, but I think he's asking to escort you to Almack's on Wednesday."

"Almack's? But Galbraith never goes to Almack's," George said. "He's famous for it."

"Well, that's what it says." Rose pursed her lips and contemplated the note thoughtfully. "I wonder if he knows he must have a voucher to be admitted."

"I'm sure he does," Lily said. "Everybody knows it." Emm had been granted vouchers for them all since the start of the season.

"Then there's the question of whether the patronesses will approve him or not."

"But surely they will," Lily said. It would be terrible if they didn't.

Rose shrugged. "He is a rake, after all. And they might wish to punish him for his refusal to attend in the past."

"They'll approve him," George said cynically. "He's young, handsome, well born and about to be tamed by marriage. They'll want him as an object lesson, like a butterfly displayed on a pin."

"Don't be so horrid, George." Lily retrieved the note, folded it carefully and tucked it away. "Write a reply for me, will you, Rose?"

"An acceptance, I presume." Rose fetched her writing desk and took out a small sheet of hot-pressed notepaper. She began to write.

George picked up the book, a very pretty volume bound in red leather. "Poetry and notes. You're going to have to tell him soon, you know."

Lily sighed. "I know. And I will. But not yet." He'd sent her flowers—a sweet-smelling posy—and now a book. He was making an effort to court her. She couldn't bear to expose herself to his judgment just yet.

"Girls, I've had a curious invitation." Emm entered the room, holding a note in her hand. "Do any of you know a Lady Davenham? Beatrice, Lady Davenham?"

They shook their heads.

"She's invited us—all of us, by name—to the next meeting of her literary society."

The girls exchanged blank looks. Lily thought of the book-reading group that Miss Chance had mentioned, but it was highly unlikely that a Cockney dressmaker, however wonderful her designs, would attend a literary society run by a titled lady of the ton.

Emm tapped the note against her fingers. "Well, shall we accept? The next meeting is tomorrow afternoon. None of you have any particular engagements, do you?"

They didn't, so Emm penned a swift acceptance and sent it off, along with Lily's note to Mr. Galbraith. Lily watched with a frown. How was she going to manage without Emm or Rose on hand? Handling a few invitations and notes was nothing to running a household.

Her stomach clenched. She was going to have to tell him soon.

LADY DAVENHAM'S LITERARY SOCIETY MEETING WAS HELD in her large home on Berkeley Square. Arriving shortly before the time indicated, the Rutherford ladies were escorted by a burly footman to a large room on the first floor. Chairs had been set out in semicircular rows around a small raised platform. A number of people had already arrived and were chatting in groups. Emm and the girls were pleased to find a number of friends and acquaintances among them.

They were introduced to Lady Beatrice, a vivacious elderly lady with surprisingly vivid red hair beneath a striped turban bristling with ostrich feathers. "Delighted to meet you at last, Lady Ashendon, and these are your pretty charges, eh?" She smiled at the three girls as they were introduced. "Such lovely gels—I hope you'll come often to my literary society. I adore the company of young people."

She glanced at Emm's waist. "I see you're increasing, Lady Ashendon—indelicate of me to mention it, I know, but I have no patience with such mealymouthedness—why should women hide away a swollen womb as if it's an embarrassment? Pshaw! It's a triumph, my dear, a female triumph! And I'm delighted for you." She sighed happily and patted Emm's hand. "I can vouch for the joy of having a baby in the house. I was never blessed with children, not until I got me some nieces, and now I have a little great-niece living here with me, and she's the delight of my autumn days."

"Thank you, Lady Davenham—"

"Call me Lady Beatrice, my dear, everyone does. So much better than being the *Dowager* Lady Davenham"—she pulled a face that made the girls giggle—"and besides, my papa was an earl, so I was born with the title, just as your girls were.

"Now, which of you is Lady Lily—ah, yes, of course." She raised her lorgnette and Lily braced herself, but the old lady simply beamed at her. "I've heard you're the first to be fired off—Galbraith, ain't it?—a fine, handsome boy. Takes after his grandfather. I hope you'll be very happy, my dear, very happy indeed. Now here is Featherby, to tell me we're about to start. Off you go and find a seat. My niece Abby's reading today and you won't want to miss a word."

Looking around for somewhere to sit, Lily was surprised to see her dressmaker, Miss Chance, sitting in a seat nearest the wall. A basket of silk threads sat at her feet. The chair next to her was vacant.

She hurried over. "Good afternoon, Miss Chance. Is anyone sitting here? May I sit with you?"

"Course you can, Lady Lily." Miss Chance patted the seat. "But best call me Mrs. Flynn in this company. They know both me names of course, but when I'm here, I'm here as Lady Bea's niece, not the dressmaker."

"You're Lady Beatrice's niece too?"

"Sort of. Wrong side of the blanket, but the old lady don't care. Now, shush. Abby's about to start."

As Lily sat, a gong sounded, and the murmur of voices died away. Into the hush, a stylish young matron said, "This is where we ended last time: 'Once, too, he spoke to Anne. She had left the instrument on the dancing being over, and he had sat down to try to make out an air which he wished to give the Miss Musgroves an idea of. Unintentionally she returned to that part of the room; he saw her, and, instantly rising, said, with studied politeness—"

"'I beg your pardon, madam, this is your seat;" and though she immediately drew back with a decided negative, he was not to be induced to sit down again.

"'Anne did not wish for more of such looks and speeches. His cold politeness, his ceremonious grace, were worse than anything.'" The young woman looked up and smiled at her audience. "And now, on to chapter nine . . ."

A sigh of anticipation rippled through the room. Lily caught Rose's eye and smiled. What a delightful way to spend a few hours. To think she'd been nervous about attending a literary society.

Lady Beatrice's niece Abby read beautifully, in a well-modulated voice that made the story come alive, but as Lily sat and listened, she was back in a carriage, listening to the same story read in a deep, entrancingly masculine voice . . .

What if she, like poor Anne Elliot, had been persuaded into refusing Edward's offer? Would she now be feeling as awkward, as unwanted and miserable, as Anne?

No, her case was different. Anne Elliot and Captain Wentworth had once been in love. Lily's situation was vastly different. If she'd been Anne, loved by a fine man and with a vain and selfish father and a sister who disdained her, nothing could have persuaded her to refuse Captain Wentworth, or whatever rank he'd been then.

Even with a man who had made it quite clear that he didn't love her, Lily had gone against the advice of her family—and they loved her and cared about her happiness.

Was it foolishness or faith? She wished she knew.

At the end of the chapter, there was a short break while another young woman took Abby's place. A hum of conversation rose as people discussed the story so far. Lily barely noticed; she was still thinking about Edward.

Miss Chance leaned across to her and murmured, "Don't take no notice of them, Lady Lily."

Startled from her reverie, Lily turned an inquiring face toward her. "Who?"

"Them—those two behind you." Miss Chance jerked her chin. "Don't listen to a thing they're saying."

Naturally that made Lily focus all her attention on the low but vehement exchange occurring in the seats behind her. Sentence fragments drifted to her over the hum of general conversation.

". . . such a fine man . . . a plump little dab of a girl. If it had been her sister, now I might understand it . . ."

"But my dear, didn't you know? Galbraith was trapped into offering for her . . ."

Lily stiffened.

"No other explanation for it—you must have heard the rumors."

"As if a man like Galbraith would be interested in a plump little ingenue with no conversation . . ."

"A shame . . ."

"Don't listen to 'em." Miss Chance tugged Lily's arm and explained in a low voice. "Mrs. Plunkett—she's the one with the hat like an upside-down coal scuttle— No, don't look, you don't want her to know she's upset you—"

"She hasn't." Lily squared her shoulders. What did the opinion of strangers matter when even her own sisters opposed her marriage? In any case, she ought to be inured to gossip and hard words by now. At school some of the girls had called her "the dummy" because she couldn't read. She'd learned to hide the hurt their words had caused. She'd do the same now.

Besides, if the price of marriage to Edward was to be ritually humiliated, it was a price she'd gladly pay.

"Oh? Right, then, good for you. Anyway it's all sour grapes. Mrs. Plunkett has been wanting your Mr. Galbraith for her daughter for ages."

Lily liked the sound of "your Mr. Galbraith." Not that he was yet.

"And the other one—well, you know what they say: 'Hell hath no fury'—and no, don't turn around! Look at them later when the tea comes around."

It took all of Lily's willpower not to turn and stare at the woman who'd tried to seduce Galbraith and been rejected. The reading recommended but Lily barely heard a word.

The incident, brief as it was, had brought one fact home to her: She was marrying a rake. How many other women would she come across in society who knew Edward better than she did?

Chapter Thirteen

Told herself likewise not to hope.
But it was too late. Hope had already entered.
—JANE AUSTEN, *SENSE AND SENSIBILITY*

WEDNESDAY EVENING CAME, AND EDWARD PRESENTED himself at Ashendon House, immaculately attired in a black coat, black knee breeches, and white silk stockings, a chapeau bras tucked under his arm.

He looked, Lily thought, magnificent. "Did you get a voucher?" she blurted. She'd worried about it all night. It would be mortifying if he was turned away.

He smiled. "Of course. Did you doubt me?"

She heaved a sigh of relief.

"You look beautiful," he told her, and she flushed with pleasure.

"So do you."

He laughed. "Men, my dear, are never beautiful."

Lily disagreed, but she wasn't going to argue. "Thank you for the flowers, and the book of poetry."

"Did you like it? I'm told that young ladies cannot get enough of Lord Byron."

"Oh, yes, he's wonderful." Lily had learned a couple of verses by heart—she might not be able to read, but she had a good memory—in case she needed to have a conversation about the book, but just then Rose and George came downstairs followed almost immediately afterward by Emm and Cal.

There were two carriages to transport them to King

Street; Cal and Emm and George rode in the first, and Edward, Lily and Rose in the second. "Playing gooseberry," Rose murmured to her sister with a grin.

But nothing could dim Lily's pleasure in the evening. They were admitted without hesitation and the gasps, the small silence and then the buzz of conversation that followed Lily's entrance on Edward's arm was everything any hurriedly betrothed girl could wish for.

Edward had broken his own rule; more, he had brought her to Almack's of his own accord. And everyone knew it.

"I won't be staying to the end," he told her. "They have this ridiculous rule that I can only dance with you twice, so I'll be leaving after that—you don't mind, do you?"

Lily didn't. It would only underline the reason he had come—for her.

He led her out for the first dance, a cotillion, which he performed with surprising confidence and grace. Somehow, Lily hadn't ever imagined him as a dancer, but it was obvious he'd spent many hours on dance floors in the past. She tried not to wonder with whom.

After the cotillion, he danced in turn with Emm, then Rose, then George—and even with Aunt Agatha. Then, for his second dance with Lily, he chose a waltz.

She stepped onto the dance floor, initially aware of the envious eyes on her, but the music started and soon she was aware only of Edward, his strength, his dark masculinity, and the masterful way he twirled her around. She was floating on air. Never had she imagined a dance could feel like this.

She was flushed and breathless when the dance finally finished, and not just because of the dancing. Edward led her to a seat. "May I fetch you something to drink?"

"That would be lovely. Ratafia, please."

He returned shortly with a glass of ratafia and as he handed it to her, he pulled a face. "Abominable refreshments they serve here. Not a decent drop of wine to be had!"

She laughed. "Almack's is famous for it, didn't you know?"

"I'd heard. Didn't believe it." They sat companionably side by side, watching the dancers, as she sipped her drink.

"Why did you decide to break your rule about Almack's?" she asked him.

"Rule? It wasn't a rule—I just never wanted to set foot in the place."

"What changed your mind?"

"I decided we needed the appearance of a courtship."

"The *appearance* of a courtship?"

"Yes, to stop the nonsense being bruited about that you trapped me into marriage. Once people see me appearing to court you, they'll think otherwise."

"Oh. I see." Lily sipped her ratafia. It tasted more bitter than usual. Not a real courtship, but the appearance of one. He wasn't doing it for her, but for them—the anonymous gossips who had nothing better to do than try to ruin other people's lives.

"Was that why you sent me flowers? And the book of poems?" She felt foolish now, having treasured them.

"Yes." He frowned and looked down at her. "And because I thought you'd like them, of course."

"Oh, I do. Thank you for your consideration."

"Are you all right?"

She forced a quick half smile. "Perfectly all right, thank you."

"Good. You won't mind if I slip out now?"

"No, no, not at all. Thank you for coming." She just wanted him gone, so she could be alone with her thoughts. And her disappointment. She'd thought he was changing the habit of a lifetime for her sake. Instead it was all for appearance.

As was their betrothal. And her forthcoming marriage. She had to remember that.

His plan made sense. But she didn't want a facsimile of a courtship—she wanted a real one.

He stood, then hesitated, frowning down at her. "Are you sure you're all right?"

"Yes, of course." She gave him a bright smile.

He took his leave then and Lily joined Emm, who was looking a bit tired. "I think I'll go home shortly," Emm told her. "Aunt Agatha has said she'll look after you and the others and bring you home afterward."

"I'll come with you," Lily told her. "I'm getting a headache."

THE DAYS FLEW PAST, FILLED WITH SHOPPING, SOCIAL engagements—the season didn't stop simply because Lily was getting married—and twice a week, the literary society, which they all enjoyed as much for the new friends they were making there as for the stories.

And there were dress fittings—Lily's dress was going to be the most beautiful dress she'd ever worn. She was even losing weight—Miss Chance had been forced to take some of the seams in. Lily was delighted.

Everywhere she went, people offered their congratulations on her forthcoming marriage, and as Emm had predicted, talk of her wedding began to eclipse the last remnants of rumor. All they needed now, George pointed out, was a nice juicy scandal involving someone else.

Every day something arrived from Mr. Galbraith, mounting evidence of the appearance of courtship, she told herself. And every second day he took her out in public, always with George or Rose, making the point: Forced marriage or not, he was courting Lady Lily Rutherford.

He even took Aunt Dottie out driving with them one day—she'd arrived from Bath a week before the wedding. "Well done, my dear," she murmured to Lily after he handed them down from his phaeton. "He'll do very nicely."

Today's gift was a small painted box. Lily lifted the lid, and tinkling notes filled the air.

"I suppose he's trying," Rose said in a grudging tone. Lily had told Rose and George what Edward had told her at Almack's.

"I think it's lovely." Imitation courtship or not, Lily couldn't help but be touched by the gifts and the effort he was making. She'd arranged them around her bedchamber. Flowers, a puzzle, boxes of sweets, and a small china owl—

that was her favorite. It was the most personal thing, recalling a moment only he and she knew the significance of. The night he'd kissed her.

She still relived those kisses every night, in the dark, in the privacy of her bed. She knew it was probably foolish, but she couldn't help herself.

Three days before the wedding, Emm sought her out for a private chat. "I thought you might have one or two questions about being married," she said when they were alone. Blushing, Lily admitted she did.

Emm then explained to her exactly what would happen on the wedding night, and answered all of Lily's questions about it. She'd given it a great deal of thought since, unable really to imagine how, physically, it was possible. But Emm had assured her that though it might be a little uncomfortable at first, with practice it would get better, and could even lead to a feeling of bliss.

Lily thought of the way Edward had kissed her. That was bliss. "Is it better than kissing?" she asked.

"Oh, yes." Emm blushed rosily. It made Lily eager to find out for herself.

Emm also gave Lily some more general advice about being married, explaining that it had taken her and Cal a while, a lot of patience and a good deal of compromise before they even began to be happy together. "We had quite a few quarrels at the beginning. Your brother is, as you know, terribly pigheaded, and I, well, I must admit I'm rather stubborn too."

They both laughed.

"And don't expect Mr. Galbraith to understand how you're feeling—men usually need to have things explained to them."

Lily soaked up all the advice, feeling rather proud that Emm was talking to her woman to woman, instead of to the baby of the family. Emm had been her teacher once, but now they were like sisters.

"You know I have reservations about this marriage of yours, Lily dearest, but there is a time to let doubts go. I wish you all the best with it. There will be difficulties and misunderstandings—I don't believe it's possible to have a marriage without them. But if you care for your husband—and I think you do—you must be prepared to work, and to change some of your ideas and beliefs, in order to achieve happiness." She laughed. "Don't look so worried, my dear; I have every faith in you, and in your common sense and tenacity. A happy marriage is a creation of two individuals, not an arrangement brokered by two families. Make up your mind to be happy, and work to make it so."

It was good, if daunting, advice. And it was starting to come home to Lily that spending a few days with Edward in a carriage and a few hours here and there under the scrutiny of society was a long way from being married to him.

What did she really know of him, after all? People had so many different sides to them. Would he feel, as those ladies at the literary society had said, trapped into marriage by her? She looked at Emm. "And if I can't make it so?"

"Then you must take your happiness where you find it, in friendship, in family and—with God's blessing—with your children. When I married your brother, I expected my whole happiness to reside in the friendship of you girls, and in any children I might have." She laid her hand on her belly and gave Lily a misty smile. "I expected a thimbleful of happiness, and instead I found an ocean. I wish the same for you, my dearest girl."

Lily came away from their talk full of thought, and resolving that she would do her utmost to make her marriage a happy one. Thinking about Edward, recalling their kisses, and reflecting that the marriage bed was supposed to bring even greater bliss, she was determined to achieve if not an ocean, at least a lake of happiness. Even a pond.

TWO DAYS BEFORE THE WEDDING, AUNT AGATHA announced she was taking Lily for a drive in the park—alone. "Why me?" Lily muttered as she put on her smartest pelisse. "She just tries to peck me to pieces."

"Not anymore." Rose handed her her gloves and bonnet. "As far as she's concerned, you agreed to marry Galbraith in the teeth of opposition from the rest of us, which makes you her current pet. It won't last, so enjoy it while you can."

"She probably wants to horrify you with gory tales of the wedding night," George said with a grin. In a very creditable imitation of Aunt Agatha's precise tones, she said, "Men are animals, gel, so close your eyes, open your legs and conceive a son. Then the nasty business and your duty as a wife is done. I highly recommend the state of widowhood."

Lily was still laughing as she went downstairs. As Aunt Agatha's elegant barouche drew away from the house, the old lady said, "We shall talk once we get to the park."

They sat side by side in silence as the carriage wended its way through the busy London traffic. The minute the carriage passed through the gates of Hyde Park, Aunt Agatha turned to her. "I'll come straight to the point. I assume Emmaline has explained your duties on your wedding night?"

Blushing, Lily said that Emm had.

"It is an unpleasantness we must all endure, and the best I can say of it is that it is quickly over. Galbraith should know his business, at least." Aunt Agatha gave her a sideways glance and sniffed. "I suppose Emmaline filled your head with nonsense about love—and quite forgot to instruct you in all the other duties—"

"It wasn't nonsen—"

"Don't be pert, gel—it is unbecoming. I have been married three times; you must concede that I know rather more about the institution than a sister-in-law who has not yet reached her first anniversary—there is Lady Bridlington on our right; bow to her as we pass."

"Yes, Aunt Agatha." Lily bowed, hoping it was to the right lady. The barouche continued on its way.

"The kind of marriage you are about to undertake, between a gentleman and a lady of the ton, has a number of unspoken but nevertheless important rules. Your first duty is, of course, to provide your husband with heirs, and a comfortable domestic situation. And not to shame or embarrass him in any way. And while we are on that subject, do not expect your husband to live in your pocket, as your

brother, Ashendon, does with Emmaline. It is unfashionable and quite unseemly."

"I don't agr—"

"Be quiet, gel, and listen— Good afternoon, Lady
Hunter, such delightful weather, I do agree— Public displays of affection such as those your brother and sister-
in-law indulge in are quite unacceptable in persons of our
order. Anything of that sort is to be reserved wholly for the
marriage bed, and even then, it is better off ignored."

"But Cal and Emm—"

"Pfft! Your brother spent most of his life at war—a totally
uncivilized environment—and Emmaline, though a good
enough woman in her way, was, after all, only a teacher—"

"Her father is a baronet."

"Exactly—not even a member of the peerage! Now will
you listen and stop interrupting! You are a daughter of an
earl, and your standards should be higher. There is that
Miss Peel waving at us. Daughter of a mushroom! Such
appalling manners. Ignore her."

Lily sent a shy smile to Miss Peel as the barouche swept
past. Aunt Agatha continued, "Do not be forever hanging
on Galbraith's arm, wanting him to escort you thither and
yon. Nothing bores a husband quicker than an overly dependent wife. You must make your own life and he will
continue on with his—a husband's life changes very little
with marriage; a wife's changes completely. Ah, there is the
Duchess of Dinstable. A charming gel. Bow."

Lily bowed to the pretty young duchess, and the stream
of instruction continued.

"You are responsible for your husband's domestic
comfort—run your household well, be strict with your servants and plan your meals entirely around his likes and
dislikes. Don't bother him over breakfast. Nothing irritates
a man more than female chatter in the morning. Better still,
take your breakfast separately." She gave Lily a critical
sideways glance. "In fact, a gel of your build would do well
to skip breakfast entirely."

Lily had no intention of obeying that one. She adored

her hot chocolate and pastries for breakfast. Or a boiled egg followed by toast and honey. Or bacon and—

"Are you listening to me, gel?"

"Yes, Aunt Agatha."

"Never contradict your husband or openly disagree with him. He will frequently be wrongheaded and in error—it is a male failing—but never point it out to him. Appear to accept his view and quietly do as you think best."

The instructions kept coming. Lily let them flow over her. Aunt Agatha's seemed a rather grim and joyless view of marriage. And yet she'd married three times.

"Finally, when you discover your husband has a mistress, you will—"

"A *mistress*?"

The old lady made an airy gesture. "Pish tush, don't sound so horrified. All men have them. The male sex is incapable of fidelity, but that's of little importance. Now, at some stage, when Galbraith inherits the title, he will take his seat in Parliament and in that case . . ." A flow of instructions followed. Lily took little notice.

Why was male fidelity—or infidelity—of such little importance? Men expected women to be faithful, so why could women not expect the same? She thought about Edward and those house parties he attended. Would he honor his marriage vows, or break them as Aunt Agatha seemed to expect?

"That covers the basics," Aunt Agatha finished. "Do you have any questions?"

Lily did. "You've covered all the things I need to do to make my husband happy. What should he do for me?"

Aunt Agatha turned to her in amazement. "What a foolish question! He marries you, of course. And thus he provides you with his name, a home, a position in society and an allowance for the rest of your life. What more could a gel like you possibly want?"

A good deal more than that, Lily thought.

THE FOLLOWING DAY AN UNEXPECTED VISITOR CALLED ON Lily. He was a stranger, but the moment Lily set eyes on the tall, spare, white-haired old gentleman whom Emm was about to usher into the drawing room, she knew who he must be. She hurried down the stairs to greet him.

"You must be Edward's grandfather, Lord Galbraith. The likeness is unmistakable." To see the elegant old gentleman was to know how Edward would look in forty or fifty years. "How do you do, sir? I'm delighted to meet you." Her gaze wandered past him, to where Burton was just closing the front door. "Edward isn't with you?"

"No, he doesn't know I'm here. The silly fellow thought you'd be too busy making last-minute bridal arrangements to deal with callers, but I'm afraid I couldn't wait to meet my granddaughter-to-be. Tell me I'm a nuisance and I'll go away at once." He smiled down at her, knowing perfectly well she couldn't tell him any such thing.

Lily laughed. "Of course you're not. Besides, there's really not all that much to arrange. My dress is ready, my trousseau is packed and I would much rather spend time getting to know you than anything."

"Then may an old man request the pleasure of your company for a drive through the park? It's such a glorious day, it's a shame to waste it by staying inside." He glanced at Emm, who nodded her permission.

"Thank you," Lily said. "I'll run and fetch my pelisse— won't be a moment." She hurried upstairs, a little nervous at being alone with Edward's only relative. She didn't know very much about him but could tell from the way Edward had spoken of him once or twice that he was fond of his grandfather. She wanted so much for him to like her.

By the time she returned he'd been joined by Rose and George. He turned to her as she arrived. "These charming young ladies have been telling me you all ride in the park each morning."

"Most mornings," Lily agreed. "Not when it's wet."

"I'm delighted to hear it. Not enough young ladies ride these days. My dear wife was an excellent rider, and I myself still enjoy the hunt. When you come down to Shields, we'll take you on some fine rides. It's the best way—I think the only way—to explore it." Shields was the family estate.

"Shall you and my boy come to Shields on your honeymoon?" He sounded a little hesitant, a little hopeful.

"I'm not sure where exactly Edward's planned for us to go—he mentioned somewhere called Tremayne Park?" She didn't really mind where it was; to be truthful, she hadn't thought past the wedding night. The whole question of it had been giving her some sleepless hours.

"Oh, I see. Quite a distance from Shields, then." The old man sounded a little downhearted. Then he smiled at her. "Shall we go? This weather cannot last." He bowed to Emm and the two girls, assured them he was very much looking forward to seeing them at the wedding on the morrow and offered Lily his arm.

A smart landau waited outside, pulled by a pair of matched bays. A liveried driver doffed his hat to Lily. Lord Galbraith waved away the groom who was waiting to assist them, helping Lily into the landau himself. He climbed in after her, fairly spry for a man of his age.

As soon as they were settled, he signaled the driver to move on.

"Now then, Lily—you don't mind if I call you Lily, do you?—tell me how you and my grandson met."

She told him how she'd met Edward first, at her brother's wedding and liked the look of him then. Lord Galbraith smiled, nodded and waited. Lily hesitated, not knowing whether she should tell him the story of her abduction. They'd all worked so hard to keep it secret.

"I understand he was able to help you when you got into difficulties recently," the old man said gently. "Of course, if you don't wish to talk about it . . ."

"No, it's quite all right." Relieved not to have to prevaricate, she explained how bravely Edward had driven off her abductor and rescued her, and how he'd turned back from his house party in order to take care of her.

When she'd finished, the old man said delicately, "I understand this is a somewhat hasty marriage. My grandson didn't—"

"No!" She was distressed that he could even suspect such a thing. "He was—he *is*—the soul of honor." She explained in great detail how he'd looked after her, and ended by reiterating how noble, brave, heroic and kind Edward had been.

When she'd finished there was a short silence. Then he took her hand in his. "You love my grandson, don't you?"

Lily nodded, unable to speak.

"Thank God, thank God," He pulled out a large handkerchief and blew fiercely into it. "Forgive an old man's foolishness, my dear. It is just that"—he wiped his eyes and blew again—"I've waited so long for my boy to find the right woman; I even tried to force his hand once, and that would have been a disaster."

"Please, don't say anything to him about what I just told you," Lily said anxiously. "It isn't that kind of marriage. He, he doesn't love me and I would hate to embarrass him with . . . unwanted declarations."

"Every marriage is unique, my dear. Don't let anyone tell you what yours is—no matter what the original motivation." He squeezed her hand sympathetically. "But it's a rocky path you walk. My grandson is a hard nut to crack these days."

"These days?"

He nodded. "He came to me as a young 'un, six or seven years old. A quiet little chap I thought him, sickly and undersized." He gave a reminiscent smile. "Well, that soon changed. I let him run wild at Shields—and he thrived on it."

"He told me he used to play at being Robin Hood with his merry men in the forest behind the house."

"Did he now, did he indeed?" He eyed her thoughtfully. "I'll take that as a promising sign. From all I can make out he never talks of the past."

"That's really all he told me," she said apologetically.

The old man sighed. "He left home when he was not quite eighteen, an openhearted, mischievous boy, a little wild, to be sure, but good-hearted . . ."

"He's still good-hearted."

He patted her hand absently. "I don't know what happened to change him—well, I do, of course—war is full of horrors, and whatever he faced over there, fighting against Boney's forces, when he came home—well, came back to

England—there was nothing left of that wild, merry boy of mine."

"He didn't tell you what his war was like?"

"Not a word. He never came home again."

"I don't understand."

Lord Galbraith turned to look her full in the face. "He hasn't set foot on Shields land since he left to follow the drum."

"You mean he hasn't visited you? Not since he was eighteen?" Lily was horrified. She'd been certain Edward loved his grandfather.

"Don't look at me like that—there's been no split between us that I know of. He writes to me regularly—he always has, since he went away to school. He's an excellent correspondent, as long as you don't want to know anything personal. But if I want to see him I have to come to London, or meet him in Bath, as we did once. Never at Shields."

Lily didn't know what to say. There was a world of hurt and bewilderment in the old man's eyes. "He fought very bravely in the war," she offered hesitantly.

"Oh, yes, mentioned in dispatches a number of times—not that he'll ever speak of it." He glanced at her. "His commanding officer—General Aldenworth—once congratulated me on my grandson's bravery, then added that it was his considered opinion that the reason for my boy's acts of heroism was that he didn't much care whether he lived or died. Cut deep, that did." Lord Galbraith gave a heavy sigh. "I think the fellow might have been right."

They were passing a marketplace. Lily gazed out over the colorful stalls, seeing nothing. Could that be true, that Edward didn't care whether he lived or died? And if it had been true during wartime, surely it wouldn't be true now, when everyone was at peace and he was back, safe in England.

Then again, there was that bleak look she'd noticed several times, when he thought himself unobserved and his thoughts were miles away . . .

But he'd never gone home again. Why?

"Gracious me, what am I doing, sharing such gloomy thoughts with my grandson's lovely bride-to-be on the eve of her wedding? Forgive an old man's maundering, my dear. Let us talk of merrier things. Is everything arranged for tomorrow—oh, and I almost forgot. I have a little something for you." He fished in a pocket and came out with a rather worn box. "It's a pearl set that belonged to my dear wife— necklace, bracelet and the other thingummy. She wore them on our wedding day—of course I've had 'em all cleaned and restrung for you—just a trifle really—there are much grander jewels waiting for you at Shields, if you ever get there—entailed of course, but if you'd prefer—"

"These are beautiful, Lord Galbraith. I couldn't wish for anything nicer," Lily assured him. "My wedding dress is cream satin and lace, and these pearls will be perfect. And they will mean so much more to me because they're . . . they're family pearls. And they come"—she hesitated a little before saying it—"with love."

"They do indeed. Thank you, my dear. You've made an old man very happy." His gray-green eyes, so like his grandson's, were bright with unshed tears. "Be patient with that young man of mine, won't you? And if he doesn't treat you right, then you just come to me. I'll soon sort him out." They both laughed, though it was a little forced.

"Now then, it's a glorious day—how about we stop off at Gunters for an ice? It's been a long time since I've had the opportunity to treat a pretty girl. I hope you're as fond of ices as I am."

An ice, Lily agreed, would be perfect. On impulse she slipped her arm through Lord Galbraith's. "I'm so glad we've been able to talk like this before the wedding, Lord Galbraith."

"So am I, my dear, so am I. And perhaps one day you could call me Grandpapa."

After a delicious brown-bread ice followed by a cup of tea, Lord Galbraith took her home. The next time she saw him would be at her wedding.

Lily found Aunt Dottie waiting for her when she got in. "Did you have a nice outing, my dear?"

"Yes, lovely. Lord Galbraith was very kind. Did you want something, Aunt Dottie?"

"Just a quick word with you about tomorrow."

"Yes, of course, Aunt Dottie. Shall we go into the sitting room?" Lily resigned herself to yet another long list of advice-for-a-new-bride. It was ironic, as Aunt Dottie had never been married.

"Oh, heavens no, it won't take that long. Weddings get so busy, I was worried I wouldn't have time to talk to you in private, and what I have to say is so important, I wanted to have your full attention."

Lily smiled. Aunt Dottie was such a sweetheart. "You have it now."

The plump little snowy-haired woman took Lily's hands in hers. "It's just this: I know everyone's been telling you what to think and what to do. All I want you to do is to trust your own instincts, my love. Don't let anyone tell you what you feel. Listen only to your heart." She gazed earnestly up at Lily. "And remember this—love is never wrong. Never. Will you promise to remember?"

"I will, dearest Aunt Dottie." Lily hugged her aunt and kissed her on the cheek. "My very favorite aunt." Aunt Dottie had taken the place of a mother after Mama had died and Rose and Lily had been sent away to school.

Aunt Dottie chuckled. "Not a great deal of competition, is there? Aggie's got bossier and more critical than ever. But I don't let her worry me, and you shouldn't, either. She means well, I'm sure."

Chapter Fourteen

❧

Know your own happiness. Want for nothing but
patience—or give it a more fascinating name:
Call it hope.
—JANE AUSTEN, *SENSE AND SENSIBILITY*

THE NIGHT BEFORE HER WEDDING, LILY SLEPT BARELY A
wink. The echoes of all the advice she'd been given circled
in her mind: *It may be a little uncomfortable at first . . .
never contradict your husband . . . a feeling of bliss . . . skip
breakfast entirely . . . take your happiness where you find
it . . . with practice it would get better . . . nothing bores a
husband quicker than an overly dependent wife . . . bliss . . .*

It seemed as though she'd only just fallen asleep when
George was there, pulling back the curtains, saying, "Wake
up, sleepyhead. Time to be up."

"Go away, George. It's my wedding day. I'm sleeping in."

"No, you're not," George said briskly. "If you lie here
thinking about what is to come, you'll just wait and
worry—I know you! So get up. We're going to the park."

"I don't want to ride out. Besides, it looks wet." The sky
outside was leaden with the promise of rain.

"A tiny hint of drizzle won't hurt you. Now, come on,
you need to get your blood moving so you'll be a fresh and
glowing bride." George reached for the bedcovers and ruth-
lessly pulled them back.

There was no resisting George in this mood, and besides
she was right. There really wasn't a lot for Lily to do to get
ready for her wedding. A bath, do her hair, and get dressed.
Everything else was in other hands.

Lily rose, put on her habit, and hurried downstairs to where Kirk, their Scottish groom, was waiting with the horses. He tossed each of them into their saddles, and they rode off.

It was cold and the rain came down in fitful spatters, but Lily was glad in the end that she'd come riding. It would be the last morning the three of them would ride out together as unmarried girls. They reached Hyde Park and found it virtually deserted because of the miserable weather, so George immediately took advantage of the lack of witnesses to urge them into a race.

She won it, of course, by a half length, but by the time they'd circled the park and reached the designated end-of-race tree they were breathless and laughing. "Aren't you glad you came now?" George said.

Lily's blood was singing in her veins. She felt marvelous.

"Oh, no! We've got to get out of here." Rose was looking over Lily's shoulder. "No, don't look," she exclaimed as Lily started to turn. "It's Galbraith and his grandfather—I said don't look! It's bad luck for the groom to see the bride before the wedding."

Without hesitation George pulled off her coat and slung it over Lily's head.

"Ow, George, what are you—"

"He can't see you now. Give me your reins." George took the reins from Lily's hands and, laughing, they rode quickly home, making a large detour around the park to avoid her husband-to-be, while Lily tried to explain between giggles and through the muffling layers of coat that it was the *dress* he wasn't supposed to see, not the *bride*.

Once home, Lily found her bridal gown laid out ready on her bed, a hot bath steaming gently, and Emm and Aunt Dottie waiting anxiously. "Hurry along, girls," Emm said. "Only two hours before the wedding."

"HE'S INSIDE, WAITING AT THE ALTAR." GEORGE HAD PEEPED into the church when they'd arrived. Rose and Emm gave the last tweaks to Lily's dress, an exquisite confection of lace over cream satin—Miss Chance had outdone herself—and a coronet of silk flowers, which anchored a lace veil. One last adjustment of the veil, and Emm went inside.

Lily was trembling like a leaf.

Aunt Dottie took Lily's white-gloved hands in hers and squeezed them affectionately. "Stop worrying, darling girl—I have one of my *feelings* about this marriage; it's all going to work out beautifully. Now, go in there, marry that handsome man and remember what I told you." Then she too went inside the church.

"What did she tell you?" Rose asked.

"I can't remember," Lily lied. *Love is never wrong.* How did Aunt Dottie know she loved Edward?

"You can still escape," Rose told her. "You don't have to do this, Lily."

Yes, she did.

Lily took a deep breath and stepped inside the church. It smelled of wood polish, brass cleaner and flowers. There was a dramatic musical chord from the organ and a rustling in the congregation as people stood and heads turned; a sea of faces, a mixed blur of goodwill and curiosity.

All Lily saw was Edward, waiting at the end of the aisle, tall and solemn and so darkly handsome it made her want to weep.

"Go on then if you must," Rose murmured from behind her. And Lily began the walk down the aisle.

"Dearly beloved . . ."

She'd taken off her gloves for the ceremony. His hand was warm. Hers felt frozen. She was shaking worse than ever. He kept hold of her hand and rubbed his thumb over it in a soothing rhythm, back and forth. Slow, steady, reassuring. She glanced up at him, saw him watching her and managed a small smile.

"Who giveth this woman to be married to this man?"

Cal stepped forward. Her big brother. "I do."

"Wilt thou have this man to thy wedded husband . . ."

Her throat felt dry, but she managed to say, "I will."

Her hand was shaking so badly he found it difficult to slip the ring onto her finger—for a moment there she'd thought he might drop it, but he gripped it firmly, and then it slipped on, still warm from his body, and fitting perfectly.

And then he spoke in that deep voice of his that somehow shivered through to her bones. "With this ring I thee wed, with my body I thee worship and with all my worldly goods I thee endow . . ."

With my body . . . She swallowed, and thought of what Emm had told her: *bliss.* Or what Aunt Agatha had said: *an unpleasantness we must all endure.*

Tonight she would find out for herself.

". . . I pronounce that they be man and wife . . ."

There, it was done. She was a married woman. The rest of the service that followed—the prayers, a short sermon and communion—passed over Lily in somewhat of a haze. But the shock of having to sign the register jerked her out of it.

"Sign your name, my dear," the vicar told her, indicating a heavy, bound book.

Lily stared blankly at the page, the words doing their usual slippery thing, resisting her comprehension. She stood staring down at it in silent panic. Where to write her name? Was she going to have to confess here and, now, on her wedding day, in front of her new groom and in the sight of God and His minister that she was a defective creature who could not read?

"Just here," the vicar said kindly, and placed his finger on the place where she was to sign. She seized the pen, dipped it into the ink, and quickly wrote her name. Or should she have signed it as Lily Galbraith?

She stared down at her signature, frozen with dread. Would she have to sign again? How did you spell Galbraith? Why hadn't she thought of that? She knew girls did that, wrote out their married name—or the name of the man they hoped to marry—over and over. But she hadn't.

"That's right, my dear." The minister reached across her to blot the ink and Lily jumped. He smiled. "Wedding nerves. Most ladies suffer from them. Never mind, Mrs. Galbraith, it's all over now."

Mrs. Galbraith. She was married.

* * *

LILY ATE VERY LITTLE AT HER WEDDING BREAKFAST. SHE was too tense. But because others kept urging her to eat, she nibbled on an almond biscuit, had a spoonful of some creamy chicken dish, and ate the corner of a small pastry and a few early-season strawberries, soaked in sugar syrup, because they were still a little tart.

It wasn't a particularly large gathering, but it seemed every single person there wanted to speak to her, to give her advice or make jests about marriage—some rather too warm to spare Lily's blushes—and what with all the merriment and the champagne for the toasts, her head was soon spinning. They cut the cake and drank the final toast. Then it was time for Lily to go upstairs and change into a traveling costume.

Edward had arranged for them to stay at a country house belonging to a friend of his, a short distance from Brighton, which meant a journey of five or six hours. Lily had never seen the sea and was excited by the prospect.

It was raining outside, so most people crowded into the entry hall to bid the bride and groom farewell and good luck, and only Cal, Emm, Rose, George and Lord Galbraith ventured outside to make the final farewell. A last round of hugs, kisses, good wishes and a few tears, and Lily turned to climb into the traveling chaise.

Aunt Dottie suddenly rushed out, oblivious of the damp, and hugged Lily convulsively. "It's all going to be splendid, darling girl, trust me." She glanced at Edward, standing tall and solemn, holding up an umbrella to protect his bride, and added, "And remember what I said."

Edward handed Lily into the carriage, signaled his driver and they pulled away, to a chorus of shouts and well-wishes. Lily leaned out the window, waving, until the carriage had turned a corner and they were all out of sight.

"Well, that's done," he said when she resumed her seat. "Went off rather well, I thought."

"Yes." Lily smiled. Ridiculously, she could think of nothing to say. She felt suddenly shy, couldn't even meet his eyes.

Edward tucked a fur rug around her. He pulled out a book. "Shall I read to you?"

"Not just now, thank you. I'm a little tired."

"I'm not surprised. Being abducted and married, all in one morning."

"Abducted?"

He put the book away, and pulled out a different one. "Wasn't that you I saw in the park this morning, with your sister and niece, being abducted with a bag over your head?"

She laughed. "It was a coat, not a bag—but you're quite, quite mistaken, sir. According to my sister, it's very bad luck for a groom to see his bride before a wedding—she's wrong, of course—but in case she's not, whoever they were abducting, it couldn't possibly have been me."

"Of course not," he agreed instantly. "I didn't see a thing. Peculiar habits your relatives have. I think my grandfather might have seen something, but grandfathers don't count, do they?"

"Not a bit. He's very nice, your grandfather. We had a lovely talk yesterday, and he took me for an ice at Gunters."

"Yes, he's a good old stick. He's very pleased about this wedding. He's been trying to marry me off for ages. Even tried to hoax me with a deathbed wish, once, but fortunately it didn't come off." He glanced at her and added, "He seems very taken with you; was singing your praises to me, even over and above his natural predisposition to like any respectable lady who could get me to the altar."

Lily wasn't sure whether to feel flattered or not. She didn't much like being referred to as a "respectable lady"— even if she was. As for getting *him* to the altar, a little reminder was required there. "Yes, Aunt Agatha feels much the same about you—delighted with anyone who'd be willing to marry me. Silly, really, when we've both been trapped into this."

Edward frowned, seemed about to say something, then picked up his book, opened it to a page he'd marked with a bit of paper and started to read.

Lily would have liked to hear more about his grandfa- ther's earlier attempt to get Edward married, but he'd signaled the end of that conversation by becoming absorbed in his book, and she didn't like to interrupt.

The carriage threaded its way through the London traffic. Lily watched the passing scenery—she hadn't lived in London very long, and there was always something to see—but in no time at all they were out in the countryside.

She kicked off her shoes, tucked her feet up under her, pulled the fur rug around her and curled up in the corner and tried to sleep.

Pretended to sleep, really. It should have been easier to make conversation with Edward, now that they were husband and wife, but somehow, it wasn't. All those lessons at school on the art of conversation—what use were they now?

As he read, she watched him from beneath her lashes. His eyes scanned each line, each page so swiftly, his long fingers turning the pages with calm deliberation. Such elegant masculine fingers.

His mouth was beautiful too; firm, cleanly cut lips. She recalled the taste of those lips. She would taste them again tonight.

She snuggled deeper into the furs.

He glanced up at her, turned a page and crossed his legs. For the journey he'd changed into buckskin breeches and boots. The soft chamois leather of his breeches clung to his thighs—horseman's thighs, long, lean and hard. She shivered, but not from cold.

She wasn't sure which she preferred him in—breeches and boots, or the severe black-and-white formal attire he'd worn for their wedding. Any way you dressed him, he was magnificent. And he was her husband.

A little thrill of excitement passed through her.

NED STARED AT THE PRINT AND TURNED THE PAGES blindly, taking in almost nothing of what he was reading. Pretending to read. He'd tried very hard to concentrate on his book, but it just wasn't possible, not with Lily curled up on the seat opposite, swathed in that fur rug, watching him surreptitiously.

He'd become aware of her subtle surveillance shortly after they'd passed out of London and were bowling smoothly along the Brighton road, her gaze like a light breath of warm air, almost a touch. It was damnably distracting.

She was so unselfconsciously sensual in everything she did, whether it was eating—he'd never forget the way she'd relished that pudding at the inn that time, licking every last morsel of sweetness off her spoon—or simply kicking off her shoes, tucking her small white-stockinged feet beneath her and curling up on the seat. Almost an invitation in itself. And all with the most innocent air.

Genuine innocence too. Though not for long. He forced his mind away from the night to come.

She sighed and shifted her position, a rustle of silk sliding over flesh. The way she snuggled into that wretched fur rug, evoking memories of her almost naked beneath that same rug—how could any man concentrate on a dry old book?

He should have given her a nice thick woolen blanket. There was nothing evocative or sensual about wool, especially next to the skin.

Though he supposed it depended on the skin. Hers was satin smooth and silky to the touch. Cool on the surface, and warm beneath.

Her eyes appeared closed, her lashes a delicate sweep of darkness fluttering against creamy skin. He crossed his legs and closed his eyes briefly as a blush rose softly on her cheeks. She wasn't asleep.

Arousal swirled through him and he stared out the window, willing himself savagely under control. This was neither the time nor the place. When he took her he intended to be restrained, disciplined, fully in control of himself, his appetites firmly leashed.

Not only because she was a virgin and deserved his consideration, but also because he didn't want to raise expectations in her breast. There was a light in her eyes when she looked at him sometimes that made him . . . wary. Unsettled.

She needed to learn that despite their first encounter— the real one, not her brother's wedding—he was nobody's hero. It was dangerous—worse, foolhardy—for anyone to place their happiness in his hands. He always let people down, those who loved him most of all.

Eventually she did fall asleep; he could tell by the way her body softened and her breathing became deep and even. In sleep she was as sensual as ever.

She had hopes of him, he could tell. He would set her straight tonight. That was what a honeymoon was for—to get things settled, establish the rules, clarify the expectations. Limit them.

He watched her sleeping, her chest rising and falling. She was so young and vulnerable. But also strong, he reminded himself.

THE SUN HUNG LOW IN THE SKY, AND AS THE CARRIAGE turned into a driveway between two tall stone pillars and rattled over a small bridge, Lily awoke, looking adorably mussed.

"Are we here?" She yawned and stretched, and looked out the window. "Oh, so this is Tremayne Park. What a pretty house. And the garden is charming." She tidied her hair—unsuccessfully; tawny curls sprang in all directions—crammed her hat over them and put her shoes back on. In the middle of pulling on her gloves, she started and turned a guilt-stricken face toward him. "Oh! I didn't even ask you about your friends. Quickly, Edward, tell me who we're staying with."

He laughed. "It's all right. My friend, Tremayne, is not here. He's gone to Paris for a couple of months. We have the place entirely to ourselves." He didn't add that Tremayne had taken his mistress with him. It occurred to him that he probably shouldn't have brought her here. Tremayne was far from respectable. It was a sign of how Galbraith's life was going to change, now he had the responsibility of a wife.

"Not quite to ourselves," Lily murmured as servants spilled from the house to meet them. The very respectable-looking butler; a neat, older woman who he presumed was the housekeeper; two footmen and a couple of maids emerged from the front door to greet them. Several grooms came running around the side.

Edward had arranged for his own valet and a maid for Lily to travel ahead with their luggage. They came out to welcome the newlyweds too.

After introductions, the housekeeper conducted them to a large suite of rooms, where hot water and Lily's maid awaited her. Ned was in the adjoining room. There was a connecting door between them.

He poked his head around it. "Everything to your satisfaction, Lily?" He jerked his head at the maid, who hastily made herself scarce.

Lily stood stiffly in front of the bed, as if hiding something from him, and said in a subdued voice, "Yes, thank you." She swallowed and, seeming to feel the need to say something else, added, "I can see the sea from my window— through the trees."

She was very pale. Was she ill? He strolled into the room, wondering what she was concealing on the bed. "Yes, the beach is quite close. I've ordered dinner for an hour's time. The dining room is on the floor below this. Do you want me to collect you, or will I send someone?"

"I'll find it."

He came closer and she stiffened. "Is something the matter?" he asked her.

"No." Her voice squeaked.

He sauntered toward the window and cast a quick glance at the bed. Ah. A very filmy nightgown lay draped on the bed, which had already been turned down.

Damn the convention that kept brides ignorant until their wedding night. He glanced at her again. Her skin was chalky pale and, now that he was looking, he could see she was trembling.

Did she expect him to pounce on her without warning? To rip her clothes off and have his wicked way with her? She might.

Surely her sister-in-law had explained it all to her. Though women were strangely inhibited about such things—why, he had never understood. Men weren't. Yet from what he gathered few women even knew what to expect from childbirth, even though the bearing of an heir was a woman's premier role in life.

Lily had been to boarding school, he recollected. Some girls' school in Bath. Hordes of schoolgirls had attended her brother's wedding, he remembered. No doubt those school friends of hers had filled her ears with lurid tales of gory wedding nights. Girls' schools were hotbeds of misinformation, the more dramatic the better, and the spinsters who ran them were no doubt just as ignorant. Or worse, men-haters. No doubt she'd been taught that all men were ravening beasts who couldn't control their carnal appetites.

One of his flirts had told him that on her wedding night she'd expected to be practically disemboweled. "The reality was such a letdown," she'd told him, laughing.

That was another reason for such secrecy and misinformation; it suited many men to have their brides ignorant. If a bride had no expectation of pleasure, the men's skills were not called into question. Ned had no patience with it.

In his experience women whose husbands didn't satisfy them wandered. And brides who were mishandled often became reluctant bedfellows. He wasn't having his own bride seek her pleasure elsewhere. Nor did he want her reluctantly enduring his attentions for the sake of heirs and duty.

Dammit, he'd planned to go out for a good hard ride before dinner, exercise some of the tension out of his body so that he'd be in absolute control tonight.

But he couldn't leave her here like this, trembling bravely before him, imagining God knew what, and letting her anxieties multiply.

He indicated the flimsy peach-and-lace confection spread out suggestively on the bed. "You won't be needing that until much later this evening," he said casually. "Come and look at this view."

She swallowed convulsively and came toward him. He slipped an arm around her waist and drew her closer. He pointed. "Over there is Brighton. We'll go there tomorrow or the next day. You will want to see the royal pavilion, of course—it has to be seen to be believed—it's still being added to. The prince regent has—well, you'll see. As well there's shopping. Brighton may be small, but it has many elegant and fashionable shops. I think you'll enjoy the lanes too." As he gestured and pointed with one hand, he soothed and stroked with the other, as if unaware.

"The lanes?"

"A delightful rabbit warren of shopping delights. You'll want to return with some small gifts for your family, I presume."

"Yes, yes, I would."

"It's very warm in here. Let me help you unbutton your pelisse." Without waiting for her reply, he turned her toward him and began undoing the buttons that ran down the front of her pelisse.

"Oh, but you don't need—" She caught her breath as his knuckles brushed across her breasts. Her nipples rose. He pretended not to notice and kept undoing buttons.

He kept talking, distracting her from his roaming hands. "Have you ever been dipped in the sea? It's supposed to be very healthful, though if you ask me, it looks rather grim— some of those female dippers look like wrestlers to me." He brushed his hands over her breasts again. "Do you swim at all? I could teach you when the weather warms up a bit."

"Swim? No, I d-don't." She shivered, but this time he didn't think it was nerves.

"Now, let's get this off you." He slipped the pelisse off her shoulders and tossed it on a nearby chair. "We might ride to the beach tomorrow if the weather is fine. My friend Tremayne keeps a fine stable and he said we were to ride as often as we want." Tremayne, of course, had laced the offer with double entendres. "Did you bring your riding habit with you?"

"Ye—er, I think so." She looked vaguely around, but he turned her around to look out the window.

"Can you see that slight hill over there?" She craned her neck to see where he was indicating, and he began to unhook her gown.

"What are you—"

"Making you more comfortable." He planted a warm

kiss on her velvet-soft nape, and she sighed and arched against him. He slipped his hands around her and stroked her breasts through the fabric of her dress. There were innumerable layers between his hands and her softness, but he could feel the hard aroused points of her nipples. He scratched them gently and felt her shiver.

He nuzzled her neck, nibbling on her skin, and she murmured her pleasure and leaned back against him. His fingers flew, unhooking her dress rapidly. It fell apart, revealing the lovely line of her back, and the nasty tight bindings of her corset.

How he hated corsets. Women didn't need them. How women could bear to be laced in, their lovely soft flesh tortured and pushed into some stupid unnatural shape . . .

He started on the hooks of her corset.

"Oh, but I'll need that," she said.

"What for?"

"If we're going riding before dinner."

"We are, but trust me, you'll be better off without it." He attacked her corset, undoing hooks, tugging free the laces. It too fell open, and he slipped it off her and tossed it unheeding across the room. Vile thing.

Her smooth white skin was creased with red lines from where the blasted thing had bitten into her. He ran his tongue along each crease, warming, soothing, sucking, the taste of her entering his blood.

"Edward." She sagged against him, gripping the windowsill to support herself.

Now all she wore was a chemise—a delicate, flimsy thing, through which her skin glowed—and her stockings. No drawers? God give him strength.

He gave silent thanks for her girls'-school upbringing that taught that only fast girls wore drawers. He ran his hand down over her hips, caressing the lush curves of her backside through the soft fabric. And moaned.

He was as hard as a rock. He breathed deeply, fighting for control.

Slowly he turned her around to face him. Oh, lord, the chemise hid nothing, caressed her ripe curves in a pretense of modesty that flaunted her beauty, even as it teasingly veiled it.

Creamy gossamer, cut low at the neck, a generous, tantalizing scoop barely covering a gorgeous pair of breasts, clinging to the rosy hard points of her nipples.

He groaned, wanting to rip it off her, to fling her back on the bed and plunge into her, into that warm place hidden beneath the shadowy dark smudge at the apex of her thighs. And to bury his face in those breasts.

Steady, Ned.

Her eyes devoured him, luminous with questions, her mouth ripe, plum-dark and satiny. He cupped her face between his hands and brushed his mouth over hers, once, twice, inhaling her breath, her sweetness. He would have moved back then, but she twined her arms around his neck and drew him closer as she opened her mouth to receive him, taste him.

His blood surged, pumping hard and hot through a body rigid and shaking with unfulfilled desire. His control was slipping. He had to leash it.

He slipped his fingers through her hair, sending pins flying. The scent of her hair, sweet as a summer night, blurred his awareness as her soft curls tumbled around them.

He ravished her mouth with deep, deliberate kisses, struggling to maintain a semblance of restraint, while she unraveled him with kisses that were eager and innocent and luscious.

He slid his hands over her buttocks, around her hips, sliding ever upward until he reached her breasts. He caressed them, their weight sweet and ripe in his hands. She gasped as he trailed his knuckles over her aching hard nipples. She shuddered under the featherlight touch, thrusting herself against him. "Again," she gasped, "again," her words fuel to his flame.

He bent and took a rosy nipple in his mouth, laving it with his tongue, teasing and sucking. She gripped his hair in damp frantic fingers, holding him to her, half collapsed against him. In one swift movement he gripped the hem of the chemise and pulled it up over her head. He dropped it on the floor and stared at her, this lush, ripe beauty, his bride. Her hands came up to cover herself in a move as old as Venus—and as enticing.

"No, don't," he rasped, catching her hands. "Don't hide from me. You're beautiful."

Her face quivered with some emotion. He swept her up in his arms and in three steps had her on the bed. He stood back, feasting his eyes on her, breathing like a drowning man.

She moistened her lips and gazed up at him, her eyes huge and liquid. She held her arms out to him; her thighs trembled, then parted a little, and he could wait no longer.

He ripped open his breeches, parted her legs and entered her with one slow thrust. She arched beneath him and stiffened, and he fought for the last shred of control, holding himself still while her untried body struggled to adjust to him.

Her eyes were squeezed shut, her face contorted in a grimace that cut him to the soul.

Cursing himself, barely able to think for the battle he was waging to slow his body, to hold back until she was ready, he slipped his hand between them and caressed her gently, seeking the little nubbin he ought to have attended to much earlier.

Her stiffness gradually softened. His fingers stroked and teased, and he felt her gasp and quiver in response. Faint shudders began deep within her and he could hold back no more. He began to move, thrusting deep and hard, again and again as the primeval rhythm took hold. The waves swallowed him and he was lost.

The last thing he remembered was his shout as he climaxed, and collapsed on top of her, oblivious.

Chapter Fifteen

❧

The desire of the man is for the woman,
but the desire of the woman is for the desire of the man.
—MADAME DE STAËL

SLOWLY NED CAME TO HIMSELF. HE HAD NO IDEA HOW
much time had passed. Lily lay still and silent under him,
breathing softly, her eyes closed. He was still deeply em-
bedded in her. He carefully withdrew and rolled off her.
And realized to his mortification that he was still fully
clothed, still wearing his boots and coat, with only his
breeches undone and his manhood shamefully exposed.

And that she lay, naked, but for her white silk stockings.
Looking wholly enticing—and he should not be thinking
such a thing, not when he'd just ravished her like a brute.

But she was flushed and rosy, all curves and female lus-
ciousness, and those white stockings that ended halfway up
her plump thighs framed a sweet temptation.

Her eyes fluttered open and he averted his gaze. He sat up,
turned away and buttoned his breeches. "Are you all right?"
His back was still turned. He wasn't ready to face her.

"Hmm? Oh, yes, thank you." She sounded vague, ab-
stracted.

He rose and walked across to where the cord hung down
for the servants' bell. He pulled it and, bracing himself,
turned to face her. She was sitting up in bed, her knees bent
and the covers pulled up around her. A froth of lace and
peach silk peeped out. She must have pulled her nightgown
on in the few seconds he'd had his back turned.

Her arms were locked around her knees and her chin rested on them. She was watching him, her expression thoughtful.

"What are you thinking?"

She blinked, as if he'd woken her. "Oh, nothing much. Just . . . thinking."

"About what?" As if he didn't know. But he needed to get it out in the open. Find out just how much damage he'd done. He'd been so taken up with his own pleasure, he couldn't even recall what he'd done—if anything—to ensure hers. Unforgivable carelessness with any virgin, let alone his bride.

"About . . ." A blush crept over her skin. "I didn't know—well, I suppose you can't really, until—" She broke off and took a steadying breath. "It's nothing, really, just—"

"I fear I was a bit hasty," he began stiffly.

But she wasn't listening. "It was . . . extraordinary."

Extraordinary good or extraordinary bad? Ned wanted to ask, but he'd never been the kind of coxcomb who elicited—let alone demanded—praise from his lovers.

If a man couldn't tell whether he'd satisfied a woman . . . He'd never had any difficulty knowing before. But today . . .

He swallowed. Time to be a man. "We're going to be doing this often, and if you are to, to enjoy it, you need to tell me how you feel about what we do. We'll get it right, eventually." The women he'd lain with in the past had no hesitation in telling him what they preferred. He didn't see why his wife couldn't learn do the same.

"Oh." Her face flamed and she pressed her palms against her cheeks as if to cool them. "Very well, I'll try." She thought for a minute, and her brow furrowed. "It's hard to know, you see—being my first time—and how to explain— I don't even know what words to use—sorry." She broke off and took a deep steadying breath. "Aunt Agatha warned me it was an unpleasantness to be endured—but Emm—she's my sister-in-law—said though it might hurt the first time— it did, but not very much—she said with practice it could be bliss."

"And?" He had to know which it was.

She hesitated and gave him a half-embarrassed, half-troubled look. "I'm not quite sure—somewhere in between? As I said, it was extraordinary. Like nothing I'd ever felt or imagined . . ."

He had no idea what to say. He had no words, no excuses. He couldn't believe they were even having this conversation, but he supposed he deserved it. It wasn't even as if she were trying to make him squirm—though he was.

A low rumble sounded from beneath the bedclothes, and she blushed and placed a hand over her stomach. "I'm sorry, that was me. I'm fearfully hungry. I suppose I should get dressed for dinner."

"Don't bother, I've rung for a servant," he said brusquely. "We'll eat up here." He wanted to finish the conversation, find out just how badly he'd messed up. And where on that wretched scale of hers he rated.

"In bed?" She brightened. "How lovely. Is that normal for a wedding night?"

He shrugged. Nothing about his wedding night was normal. Luckily at that moment the butler arrived, offering a temporary reprieve. Ned ordered dinner to be brought up, with champagne. And a glass of brandy to be brought to his room at once. He badly needed a drink.

"The food will be here in about fifteen minutes. I'll have a wash in my room and let you, er, take care of things here." First rule of soldiering: retreat, regroup and try again.

He stepped into his own room and shut the connecting door to give her privacy. He picked up the pitcher and poured some water into the basin. The water wasn't even lukewarm. He was about to ring for hot water and his valet, then hesitated.

Her water would be cold too, but he was reluctant to interrupt her private female ablutions to ask her. If she wanted hot water she could ring for her maid—though fifteen minutes to dinner wasn't enough time for a bath. Blast it, he could do without a shave, and if she wanted a bath, she could order one after dinner.

The everyday intimacies of married life. He supposed he would get used to it.

Why was it so different from the day-to-day intimacies he'd shared with lovers in the past? He didn't know, but somehow with a bride—with *this* bride—with *Lily*—it was different. Old habits, old understandings no longer fit. Marriage, Lily, it was all new territory.

He washed quickly, combed his hair, then paced about the room. The brandy arrived—a decanter as well as a glass—and he drank the whole glass down in two gulps and poured himself another. Lord, he'd needed that.

She probably needed one as well.

Though once again, she'd seemed to take it all in her stride without a fuss. He was sure other bridegrooms—the ones who'd bungled things as he had—he *never* lost control!—had to deal with tears and recriminations, or stiff, martyred silences. What had that aunt of hers told her? *An unpleasantness to be endured.*

He'd probably ensured that, pouncing on her like an eager boy. But Lily seemed quite philosophical. He was certain she wasn't trying to disconcert or tease him—she wasn't that sophisticated. She was simply trying to be candid.

But lord, to be on a wretched sliding scale somewhere between bliss and *endurance vile*! He snorted at the inadvertent pun. But it wasn't the least bit funny.

He prided himself on his skills in the bedroom. Never before, not since he was an awkward youth, had he left a woman less than thoroughly satisfied.

And now, to fall short of his usual standard, on his wedding night, with his innocent new bride—it was mortifying. He wanted to take her back to bed and show her how it was supposed to be.

Only she was bound to be sore. He had a feeling he'd been unwontedly rough. He'd utterly lost control. He couldn't recall the last time that had happened.

She hadn't complained—but that was Lily; she wasn't the type to whine. In any case, she'd been a virgin. *He* was the expert here, the one who was supposed to induct her into the pleasures of the bedchamber.

Somewhere between endurance vile and bliss. A vast gulf between the two.

Next time they lay together, he'd take it slowly and bring her to—forget bliss!—he'd show her the meaning of ecstasy. And in the meantime . . .

THE MINUTE EDWARD CLOSED THE DOOR BEHIND HIM, Lily slipped out of bed. She found a large jug of water behind a screen in the corner of the room, cold now, of course. She quickly washed her face and sponged the rest of her body, especially between her legs, which was a bit sticky.

She pressed the wet cloth against her heated skin, enjoying the cooling sensation. She was a woman now, a wife. Emm's explanations of what to expect on her wedding night had been a little vague and unclear, and Lily could see why now. Who could find words to describe . . . that?

She tried to recall that almost-feeling. As if she'd quivered on the brink of . . . something. And then lost it.

Had she done something wrong? The trouble was she couldn't think of anything she'd actually done. As well to expect a gale-tossed leaf to remember the journey it had taken.

But she could tell Edward hadn't been quite happy about it.

Imperfect or not, the experience had been . . . breathtaking. She'd had the physical procedure of the act explained to her, but she hadn't been in any way prepared for how it would make her *feel*.

She shivered deliciously in remembrance. It had been blissful at the start . . . those kisses and caresses, and the way he'd removed her clothing, piece by piece, as if unwrapping a very special gift.

The touch of his hands . . . of his mouth . . . She'd felt like a candle, ignited, melting.

And when he'd slid into her—it had hurt a little, of course, but she'd expected that—but oh, the way it had made her feel. Strange and raw and yet somehow, right. The intense *intimacy* of it was a little overwhelming. Then when he'd started to move inside her . . . her body responding without her volition, shuddering and gripping him, in a way she'd never imagined . . . And that buildup of almost unbearable intensity . . .

As if they were caught in a storm—she'd clung onto him for dear life, giving herself up to the rhythm and the power—and oh, if that wasn't glory, it was close. Then that sound he'd made at the end, primeval and masculine—possessive?—before he collapsed on top of her. She had held him tight—her husband—feeling his ragged breathing slow, his big, beautiful, powerful body, relaxed and satiated, stroking him through his jacket.

What might it be like if they were both unclothed, lying skin to skin? Another delicious ripple of sensation passed through her at the thought. She smiled to herself. She knew now what those inner shudders meant.

Emm had said it would get better with practice. Lily couldn't imagine how, but she was eager to try.

Poor Aunt Agatha, with her *unpleasantness to be endured*. Three husbands and it seemed as though none of them had made her feel the way Lily had felt after one time with Edward.

A sound outside startled her. Oh, heavens, she'd been dreaming for goodness knew how long. Dinner would be here any second and she didn't want strange and unknown servants to catch her in her beautiful but flimsy nightdress. She put on the bed jacket that went with the nightdress, but a glance in the looking glass showed her that it was just as delightfully improper and failed entirely to protect her modesty.

She looked in the wardrobe and found a pretty Chinese-style silk wrapper. She slipped it on and was searching for slippers when a knock sounded on the connecting door.

"Are you ready? They're here with the food." Edward's hair was damp and combed carelessly back. It curled a little at the end. He wore a robe, a long green brocade banyan, embroidered with glints of silver thread that brought out the color of his eyes in his somber, tanned face. He looked magnificent, like some exotic eastern potentate, with glittering, frosted emerald eyes.

At his command, the door opened and in came two footmen carrying trays ladened with covered dishes. The butler followed with a silver tray on which rested glasses and a champagne bottle, gently fizzing. They moved a side table close to the bed and set out everything on it, then, at a silent signal from Edward, the servants withdrew.

"They're very well trained," she said when they'd left. They hadn't so much as glanced in her direction. "They must have wondered—well, you can imagine what they must be thinking. But they didn't look in the least bit shocked."

"I never worry about what servants might think." Edward picked up the silver covers one by one and inspected the contents. "In any case these fellows are accustomed to much more scandalous goings-on when Tremayne is in residence."

Really? Lily wanted to ask for further details, but the food smelled wonderful. Her stomach rumbled again. So embarrassing.

"What would you like first?" he asked her.

She hurried over to inspect their dinner—it was a feast. Everything looked delicious.

A juicy capon roasted to golden perfection rested on a bed of lacy greens, carrots glistened with honey and a hint of nutmeg and delicate spears of asparagus came with a bowl of herbed buttery sauce, for dipping. There were tiny crispy tartlets containing scallops and mushrooms in a creamy pink sauce, potatoes sliced in layers and oozing butter, and fresh rolls, still warm from the oven. Lastly there was a sherry trifle in a crystal dish, a bowl of jewel-like berries in syrup and a dish of thick country cream.

"Everything," she said, and immediately wanted to bite her tongue. She always seemed to be stuffing herself in front of him. She could almost feel Aunt Agatha's lorgnette boring a hole in her.

But Edward only laughed. "A woman after my own heart. I'm starving too." He picked up one of the little tartlets and popped it into his mouth whole.

"How ungallant!" Laughing, she reached over, grabbed one herself and nibbled on it. "Mmm, that's delicious."

"Hop into bed and I'll serve you."

Lily slipped into bed. Dinner in bed; how delightfully decadent.

He set up a bed table, then poured the champagne and sat on the bed, the bed table between them. He raised his glass. "But first, a toast to my lovely wife."

"To my magnificent husband, and to a very happy marriage," she responded, clinking her glass against his.

He raised an eyebrow, and she wondered whether she'd been too effusive; her emotions were spilling over.

But he didn't comment, just drank and then began to carve the capon. "White meat or dark?"

"Dark, please. It's juicier."

"I prefer breasts," he said, his eyes on her. "They're more delicate and tender."

Lily felt herself blushing. He was flirting with her. She'd never been much good at that. But all things improved with practice. Which reminded her . . .

She took a large gulp of her champagne and said, "About before—"

"Don't worry about it. Here"—he handed her a laden plate—"eat it while it's hot."

"But I need to know, did I do something wrong? I mean before, when we—"

"You did nothing wrong. Eat your dinner." He served himself.

"But I think perhaps I—"

"Don't talk. Eat."

The food looked and smelled glorious and she'd hardly eaten anything all day, so Lily, recalling she'd promised him obedience, ate.

For a while there was only the clink of cutlery against china and the sounds of two people enjoying their food. But after a while, Lily realized he'd stopped eating.

She looked up guiltily and found her husband watching her with an intent expression. "You enjoy your asparagus, don't you?"

Flushing, she used her napkin to wipe her mouth. "Sorry, but it *is* correct to eat it with one's fingers."

"Don't be sorry, I know. And you must never hide your

pleasure from me." Without waiting for her answer, he picked up a spear of asparagus, dipped the end in the rich, buttery sauce and offered it to her. "Open up."

She parted her lips and he slipped the delicate morsel between them, tilting it so the sauce ran into her mouth, feeding her the tender shoot in slow increments. Without taking his eyes off her, he took another spear, dipped it in sauce and fed it to her, inch by slow inch.

The atmosphere hummed with a strange tension. She was embarrassingly aware of the little sounds she made as she ate. And achingly aware of his fingers, brushing her lips as she nibbled the asparagus to the end.

Why wasn't he eating? Didn't he like asparagus? Some people didn't.

"Enough?" he said when he'd fed her three more juicy spears, and she nodded. She lifted her napkin to blot her mouth, but in a surprise move he caught her hand in his, leaned forward and brushed his mouth over hers, letting his tongue linger, cleaning the sauce from her lips.

Sensations shivered through her, pooling in her middle.

He sat back, seemingly unaffected by an almost-kiss that had her practically dissolving into the bedclothes. "Now, ready for some sweet dishes? Trifle, or berries—no, don't tell me—both!" His smile erased any sting she might have found in the comment.

He piled a bowl with rich creamy trifle and added berries and a large dollop of cream. Heavens, if this was the way he was going to feed her she was going to be enormous by the time they got back to London. But he presented her with a spoonful of the delicious combination, saying, "Open," with such a look in his eyes that any willpower she might have had evaporated. She opened her mouth and again let him feed her, mouthful by mouthful, like a baby.

Only no baby ever felt the way Lily felt as he slipped each slow, luscious spoonful between her lips, his wintergreen eyes dark and burning into her.

She finished the bowl, and as the last spoonful slipped down, he asked, "Enough?"

"Mmm, more than enough. That was delicious." She

sighed and leaned back against the pillows. "That was the most perfect feast," she managed to say, and felt quite proud of herself for being able to speak even though her mind— and body—was halfway to mush.

He rose and rang for the servants, who must have been waiting outside, for they appeared immediately, swiftly removing all remnants of the feast. Lily watched sleepily from the bed, feeling full, perfectly replete and content.

Once they were alone again, Edward moved to the bed and looked down at her with an expression she could not read.

"Would you like to go for a walk?" she asked. She needed to do some exercise to wake herself up. It was only just after dusk.

"No. We haven't had dessert yet."

"Dessert? You mean pudding? But I just—" She broke off. He was undoing the fastenings of his banyan.

Her mouth dried as little by little the banyan slipped open, revealing smooth, firm, masculine skin. He was naked underneath. Had she realized that earlier, she would never have been able to eat a mouthful.

He tossed the banyan aside and stood there, stark naked, apparently unconcerned and unembarrassed, letting her look her fill. And look she did. She couldn't drag her eyes off him.

He was sleek and smoothly muscular—not like a stevedore or a farm laborer, which were the only men she'd ever seen even halfway unclothed—but lean and hard, a masculine kind of beauty, leashed power and grace. A broad, firm, flat chest, lightly sprinkled with dark hair, narrow hips and long muscular legs—horseman's legs.

Like a marble statue she'd seen once, only she couldn't imagine a fig leaf big enough to cover *that*. He was warm, and alive—and he was her husband.

Taking her hand, he drew her from the bed and undid the fastenings of her wrapper, murmuring, "A pretty thing, but we don't need it now." He slipped it off her shoulders, and smiled when he saw what she was wearing underneath. His eyes devoured her. "My compliments to whoever came up with this delightful little piece of nonsense." His voice was deep and slightly husky.

"It's from Miss Chance of the . . . H-House of . . . the House . . ." Words became gasps as he caressed her through the layers of silk and lace, the friction delicious against her skin. With one tug, the bow of the ribbon tie holding the front together unraveled and the bed jacket slid down her arms.

His eyes darkened, burning into her, as with one swift movement he whisked the frail nightgown over her head and tossed it aside. He drew her by the waist, his hands big and warm, and pulled her against him, skin to skin, her softness molding deliciously against his hard angled planes.

His hands slipped over her hips, caressingly, and cupped her bottom, lifting her so she was pressed against his hard, thrusting manhood. He stood, rocking her silently against him. Was this how he'd take her? Standing up? The heat of his body soaked into hers.

He released her with a sigh, cupped her breasts, then bent to kiss them, one by one. She shivered, barely able to stand as hot spears of pleasure spiked through her. She ought to do something, caress him back, but she could only stand—barely stand, her legs were like jelly—and hang on to him, while he lavished pleasure on her. Pleasure? She was unraveling.

His mouth wrought exquisite, delicious havoc as he tasted, teased, plundered . . . and teased again. He feathered kisses along her jawline, her eyelids, sucked gently on her earlobe, sending shivers through her whole body. His long, clever fingers stroked, and pinched and tantalized just to the edge . . . of what? . . . and then moved on, arousing her to a fever of blind, aching need.

She clung to him dizzily, her blood pounding, her whole awareness narrowed to each place on her body he touched. Her breath came in ragged gasps.

And then somehow they were on the bed, and he was nibbling at her breasts, her full and aching breasts, unbearably sensitive, laving them with his tongue, nibbling, as she trembled and shivered beneath him in uncontrollable pleasure. He sucked hard and a spear of pleasure-pain arced through her, and she shrieked as her body spasmed beneath him and almost came off the bed.

By the time her wits returned he was moving down her body, kissing her soft belly, nibbling at the tender skin. She was frenzied, burning, aching with need. She tugged at his shoulders, his hair, wanting him back at her breasts, to do that thing again. But he was relentless, his mouth moving lower as he kissed her thighs, and stroked the backs of her knees. Her legs quivered in expectation and fell apart.

"Now," she muttered. She knew what she wanted now.

He pressed her legs further apart and she readied herself for the surge of his possession. He was more than ready for it, she knew, his member huge, hard and so hot against her skin.

And then she felt his mouth on her, between her legs, moist and hot and . . . unbelievable.

"What are you doing?" she gasped, craning her head to stare down at him, lying between her legs. He looked up at her over the soft swell of her stomach and grinned.

"Having dessert."

Chapter Sixteen

❦

License my roaving hands, and let them go,
Behind, before, above, between, below.
—JOHN DONNE

LILY CAME SLOWLY AND SLEEPILY AWAKE THE NEXT
morning. She lay, her eyes closed against the chinks of
bright sunlight coming through the gaps in the curtains,
gathering her thoughts. She stretched sleepily, languidly.
She felt wonderful, as if her whole body wanted to smile.

She was smiling, she realized, though there was nobody
else there.

She was married. She was alone in bed.

When had he left? Last night, after . . . *dessert*. She
smiled again to herself. Bliss. Glory.

But only for her. She'd lain boneless, replete, satiated in
every way, and waited for him to enter her, to take her as
he'd taken her earlier.

Instead he'd slipped out of bed, picked up his robe,
kissed her on the nose and murmured, "Sleep well." And
left.

She remembered watching him in the firelight, walking
naked to his own room. His back was straight, the slope of
his shoulders and the line of his spine beautiful, his backside firm, taut, shapely. He'd closed the door.

She'd felt cold then, without him. She felt cold now.

He'd kissed her on the *nose*. The nose! Like a child. And
he hadn't taken her in the way a man was supposed to take
a woman—not if he wanted heirs. An heir was his main

reason for marrying—scandal aside. He owed it to his family name and title.

His body had wanted it; she remembered that proud hard shaft, velvety skinned with heat beneath. She must have done something wrong that first time. And now he was reluctant to repeat the experience.

But what he'd done to her—calling it *dessert*—would he call it that if he didn't enjoy it? She thought he had, but then he didn't follow through.

And he'd left her to sleep alone. Her brother and Emm always slept in the same bed.

It was all very confusing. But they were married; she had a lifetime to work it—work him—out.

NED KNOCKED SOFTLY, WONDERING WHETHER SHE WAS awake yet. He opened the connecting door and found Lily sitting bolt upright in bed, hugging her knees, the covers huddled around her. "Yes? I mean, good morning." She looked a little apprehensive.

He didn't blame her. If she realized how eminently beddable she looked, all soft and flushed and sleepy, with tawny curls clustering around her face and bare shoulders—well, he wasn't going to pounce on her. Not this morning, at any rate.

"Did you sleep well?" He was dressed for riding in buckskins and high polished riding boots. He'd shaved, which he wouldn't normally do before a ride, but he was a married man now and the decencies had to be preserved. His hair was still damp.

"Yes, thank you, very well."

"I wondered whether you felt like a ride."

Her eyes widened. She glanced at the window, where the sun was peeping in through the curtains. It was a glorious morning. "Now?" she asked.

"Yes, before breakfast."

It was as if the sun rose in her eyes. She glowed. "Yes, please." She flung back the bedclothes and sat there, rosy and naked, a creamy mermaid in a welter of sheets. She made no move to get up, no move to dress herself. She simply sat in her bed, wearing nothing but a smile and an expectant look.

He moved to stand behind a chair. His body had reacted predictably to the sight of her naked loveliness. "Do you want me to ring for your maid?" he asked stiffly.

"No, of course not." After a moment her smile faded and became a look of puzzlement. "I thought you wanted 'a ride.'"

"I do. You don't have to come if you don't want to. I just thought, seeing it's a beautiful morning, we should make the most of it. It could very well be raining by the afternoon."

"Oh." A blush suffused her whole upper body. It was fascinating. He tried not to stare. "You mean a ride?" She pulled the covers back over herself.

"That's what I said."

"On horses?"

"What else would I be wanting to ride?" He tried not to let the sarcasm show.

The blush intensified. "Nothing. I just thought . . . with your boots . . ."

"My boots?"

"Nothing, it's nothing." Avoiding his gaze she said in a low, hurried voice, "Thank you, yes, I would love to go for a ride, and if you would please ring for a maid, I'll put on my habit and be with you in a trice. I'll meet you downstairs, shall I?"

He didn't move. He stared at her, and his lips twitched in the beginning of a smile. "You thought *a ride* meant—?" He arched a brow suggestively. "Because I came to your bedchamber *in my boots*?"

"Y—no, I don't know what I was thinking. I was half asleep. Now, please ring for my m—" She was adorably flustered.

His smile grew. "You did. You thought I wanted to f— have marital relations with you in my boots, didn't you?"

"Well, you did yesterday," she said defensively. "How

am I to know what you mean when you say and do such strange things?"

"Strange things?" He prowled slowly toward her.

Her face was flaming by now. "Well, you called what you did last night *dessert*."

"And it was delicious. Am I to take it that you wouldn't object if I took you again this morning—boots and all?"

She looked up at him, earnest and very sweet. "Of course I wouldn't mind. It was very nice yesterday, though I don't think the housekeeper would be very happy about you wearing boots in bed—" She squeaked as he pounced on her.

"*Nice*, was it?" He edged her knees apart.

"V-very nice."

"Pah. I'll show you something better than *nice*." And he did.

A MISTAKE. THAT WAS WHAT IT HAD BEEN. A DAMNABLE, stupid mistake. A complete lack of self-discipline. Ned glanced sideways at the woman alongside him. They'd been for a fine gallop and now had slowed to a walk, giving their mounts some breathing space. Lily was glowing, and not from the exercise. At least, not this particular exercise.

His plans to apologize to her for his actions the day before—coming at her like an animal in his boots, not even bothering to disrobe—kept falling awry. He'd meant to do it last night over dinner, and then she'd started eating that blasted asparagus. All thoughts of an apology—in fact, all logical thought—had been driven from his mind.

And then *dessert*. He groaned.

So after that fiasco—pleasurable as it was—he'd been determined to get the apology over and done with this morning.

Instead he'd pounced on her again, fully clothed and in his boots, because instead of being appalled at his ungentlemanly behavior, she'd said she liked it. Liked it! He ground his teeth together.

And because of all that—damn him for a randy, unrestrained fool—it was as if someone had lit a candle inside her. She couldn't stop smiling, seemed to be bubbling over with it, finding delight in everything—the horses, the estate, lambs, flowers, birds—but the smiles that spilled out of her told him what was really going on.

She was making him out—again—to be some kind of hero.

Misplaced romantic expectations—they had to stop. If she kept going this way—no, he had to stop it, now, before any more damage was done.

He was nobody's hero, and the sooner she learned that, the better it would be for her.

He glanced at her, lit up with the afterglow of a vigorous round of bedsport, and imagining it to be some kind of romantic nonsense. He hated to do this to her, but it was kinder to crush those unrealistic expectations now, before they could develop any further. Better a small disappointment now than a big one later.

"You're new to this," he began.

She turned her head. "This?"

"Bedsport—sexual congress between a man and a woman—you're not used to it yet."

"No, but I do enj—"

"That's not what I mean, though I'm glad you didn't find it distasteful."

"Not at all, in fact—"

"But it's just bedsport," he said bluntly. "These feelings you're experiencing at the moment? It's the act that creates them. It's common to mistake those feelings for love, especially when one is new to sexual congress. But it's not." He gave her a steady look. "It's just bedsport. So don't fool yourself into imagining it's anything more."

There was a long silence. They rode on. Clouds were starting to build up. The breeze freshened, whipping the waves in the distance.

"You mean all the women you've lain with feel like"—she gestured vaguely—"this?"

"No, the women I lay with in the past were all very experienced. They knew it meant nothing, just pleasure." And how cynical was that? But it was true.

"I see." Her happy glow faded. "So you're telling me that lo—what I feel is just the result of . . . what we did in bed?"

"Yes." He felt like a brute, but it had to be done, for her own sake. "I know it sounds hard, but don't make yourself miserable crying for the moon. The best basis for marriage is liking and respect—friendship. If we can achieve friendship between us, that will be enough."

"Friendship. I see. And what if . . ." She hesitated, then lifted her chin and decided to say it anyway. "What if I want more than that?"

Ned knew what she was saying. This was the girl, after all, who'd told him she wanted to marry for love. But life wasn't what you thought it was at eighteen. He'd learned that the hard way. He'd rather die than put her through what he had.

"Then you'll be courting disappointment," he said in a hard voice. She didn't realize it, but he was letting her down gently.

She gave him a long, thoughtful look, then turned her horse around and headed at a fast canter back in the direction of the house. He didn't follow. She looked a bit upset, but that was understandable.

He watched her disappearing over the hill. He'd done the right thing. So why did he feel so . . . wretched?

Better to have lowered expectations early on, than to dream of glory and be shattered.

LILY URGED HER HORSE FASTER. THE BREEZE, CRISP AND cold and smelling of salt, was bracing, invigorating. But it didn't cool her anger.

She hate-hate-*hated* the term *bedsport*—it was nothing of the sort! What they did with her husband—in or out of the bed—"riding" or "dessert" or whatever silly name he wanted to call it—was not *sport*! It was part of the blessed sacrament of marriage.

And she *hated* hearing about the women he'd lain with

in the past—even if she had been the one to bring them up. Lesson learned. She'd never do that again.

So he didn't want her to have *feelings*. Such a ridiculous, manlike thing to say. As if she had any choice in the matter.

But if he didn't like her having feelings, she'd just have to keep them to herself.

And if he thought friendship was enough, well, fine—he could think what he wanted! It wasn't enough for her.

Maybe she was being unrealistic in hoping he would come to love her, but better to aim for the moon than not even *try*. Why wouldn't he try? Why try instead to crush all possibilities—on the very first day of their honeymoon? And after such a beautiful start.

She was so angry she could spit!

Did he really not believe in love? How could he not? There was evidence of love all around them. The whole world operated on love. Oh, she wasn't a fool—she knew there was hate and violence and terrible things—and people—in the world, but what held families together, what gave people hope, and strength, what nourished children— and adults—was love, an endless well of it.

It was almost as if he were somehow afraid of it. But that was ridiculous. Everybody wanted to be loved, didn't they?

Everyone except her husband, apparently.

It was a puzzle. It wasn't as if he couldn't love. She was sure he loved his grandfather, and that his grandfather loved him. The other day he'd told her about the time he'd almost married a woman his grandfather had chosen for him, just because he thought it would please the old man, who he thought at the time was dying.

"I didn't even like the woman. I was dreading it. Luckily for me, she cried off just before the wedding."

"But why didn't you call it off yourself?" she'd asked him. "What if she hadn't changed her mind? You'd be stuck with a wife you disliked."

"I know, but a man—a gentleman—once betrothed, cannot, in honor, back out of it. If he did, it would be an utter disgrace."

"I know, but I've never understood why."

"A gentleman's word is what separates us from the rabble," he explained. That was why cheating at cards was regarded as such a heinous act, because it was a breach of honor. A man caught cheating at cards was ruined socially forever.

The same rules didn't, apparently, hold true for women. Lily thought that was wrong. How peculiar the masculine world was, where a man could beat his wife or be unfaithful or neglect his children and still be regarded as a gentleman, but cheat at cards or break a betrothal and he became a social pariah, *persona non grata*.

More sobering was the thought that Edward had been prepared to marry a woman he didn't even like. What did that say about her own marriage? She didn't want to think about it.

Arriving back at Tremayne Park, she handed her horse over to a stable lad and, as soon as she entered the house, ordered hot water for a bath.

She undressed and took out the tiny sliver of soap that was left from the piece Edward had given her at the inn so long ago. It was almost finished. She would have to get some more. She loved using Edward's soap.

Lily sank into the hot water and smoothed the rich lather over her body. The scent, so clean and fresh and distinctive, calmed her.

It was early days yet in their marriage. It had taken Cal quite a while to realize he loved Emm, and then it was only because Emm had been shot. Lily had been there when it happened, had seen the horror on Cal's face when Emm collapsed, bleeding. Lily had witnessed her brother's stunned realization that he cared for his wife more than he'd known.

Over and over he'd told the unconscious Emm he loved her, admitted to Lily that he'd never told her before, didn't even realize it himself—until Emm was shot.

She hoped it wouldn't come to that with her and Edward.

Maybe, as a rake, Edward was simply uncomfortable with the idea of love. It was no wonder, really. All those cynical, experienced women of his, who called it *bedsport*, and to whom it meant nothing. It meant something to her.

But if talk of love disturbed him, she would not talk of it. Her feelings were her own business. She would be patient, give him time.

You couldn't make someone love you, no matter how desperately you wanted them to. And if you pushed too hard, it could make people withdraw further. She'd seen that with girls at school—poor Sylvia, for one—trying too hard to be popular and failing dismally.

She'd gone into this marriage—this *arranged* marriage—blindly, with hope in her heart. She had no excuse. Nobody had deceived her, not Edward, not her family.

If her heart yearned for love and was disappointed, she had only herself to blame. And if friendship was what her husband wanted from her—if it was *all* he wanted—there were worse things than friendship.

Besides, friendship *could* turn into love. She would not give up on him yet.

EDWARD WROTE A LOT OF LETTERS. EACH DAY HE SAT down and dealt with a small pile of correspondence. Lily had never seen anyone write so many letters.

"Who do you write all these letters to?" she asked him one rainy afternoon.

"A variety of people." He kept writing.

Of course. She should have known better than to ask.

He glanced up. "Don't you have letters to write?"

She stiffened. "What do you mean?"

"Most women I know are always scribbling off notes and letters to their friends." He frowned. "Come to think of it, you haven't received a single letter since we've been here."

A chill ran down Lily's backbone. "I—I didn't know where we were going, so how could I tell anyone where to write?"

"You could write to them now and tell them."

"I know, but there isn't anyone I want to write to."

He looked at her in astonishment. "You don't want to write to your sisters or aunts or any friends?"

She shook her head. "I'd rather wait. It's more entertaining to talk to them in person."

"I'm amazed. I don't think I've ever met a woman who wasn't forever dashing off a note to this friend or that, or writing down secret thoughts in a diary." He glanced at the writing desk, all set up with a freshly trimmed pen, a stoppered bottle of the best ink, and a neat pile of perfectly trimmed writing paper. "You don't have wedding letters to write—thank-you letters?"

Her mind went blank. Everyone knew the bride always wrote the thank-yous. But then it came to her. "I do, of course, but I left my address book at home. I'll do them when we get back to London. Besides, I'm not in the mood," she added, thinking he'd suggest she write the dratted letters now and post them when they returned to London.

"So you're not in the mood for writing letters—what about reading?" His voice was deep, almost accusative.

She stiffened, thinking her secret had been discovered. "N-no."

He put his pen down, rose and prowled toward her with a menacing expression. "Then I think, young lady, you need to be banished to your bed where you will contemplate the sin of idleness." He tossed her over his shoulder and carried her, shrieking and laughing, up to her bed.

It wasn't the sin of idleness she contemplated, either; he kept her very busy until dinnertime. Which they ate, again, in bed.

FRIENDS BY DAY, LOVERS BY NIGHT—OR WHENEVER THE mood struck. It was more difficult than Lily expected, keeping her feelings in check. They wanted to spill from her, to bubble up like a fountain. But all he wanted from her was friendship.

He made love to her almost every night. And if not at night, then he came to her in the morning. That was Lily's favorite, coming slowly awake to the feel of Edward's mouth and hands caressing her, feeling ripples of pleasure coil through her.

And then his possession, sometimes slow and dreamy, as sweet a thing as Lily had ever experienced, sometimes swift and fast and . . . glorious.

Of course it engendered emotion, and she refused to deny it. If he wanted to, he could, but Lily knew what she felt. She learned not to speak of it, for anytime she so much as hinted at an emotion, he withdrew, like the sea anemone he'd shown her in a rock pool, closing up at the slightest touch.

She was loving the seaside in all its variations. Most mornings they rode down to the beach before breakfast, long, leisurely rides together, sometimes racing—he nearly always won—sometimes just walking the horses quietly. And occasionally talking.

At least Lily talked. Getting information out of Edward was like talking to an oyster. He was a hard man to know. It was as if he'd built walls around certain aspects of his life and placed *Keep Out* signs all over them. Even with the things he was prepared to talk about, any details or feelings were sparse; he stuck to a few bare facts and left her to fill in the gaps.

"My father and I didn't get on," he'd told her one time. "Never did. I went to live with Grandpapa when I was six. The old man raised me."

"And your father and mother?"

"Dead." That was it—his life in a nutshell. With no embellishments. It was quite frustrating.

She knew better than to probe him about his wartime experiences—his grandfather had warned her about that—but even on the subject of his years with his grandfather and the things he'd done as a child, up came that wall with its big *Keep Out* signs.

Questions she thought would be harmless, about boyhood mischief, or playing Robin Hood that he'd once mentioned, made him clam right up, as chatty as a doorpost. He'd change the subject, or make some excuse, remembering something he needed to be doing.

It was a mystery. She had her own secrets and that kept her cautious, but she kept trying.

"How old were you when you went away to school?" she

asked him one morning as they walked their horses in the shallow waves. Up to now, the conversation on his side had been a series of one-word answers.

"Twelve."

"Did you like it or hate it?"

He shrugged. "Neither."

"Didn't you resent being sent away?" She'd had an impression that he'd enjoyed living with his grandfather.

"Not really. I didn't want to go, but schooling is necessary for boys. I was lucky. Most boys are sent away much younger."

With a little smile she edged her horse closer, reached out and placed a hand on his forehead.

He jerked his head back. "What are you doing?"

"That was four sentences in a row. I thought you might be delirious."

His mouth twitched. "You little—"

"Catch me if you can!" Laughing, she urged her horse into a gallop. The sand was firm and they flew across it, her horse's hooves splashing in the shallows. She could hear his horse coming up fast behind her. "First one past that stump is the winner," she called back, and pointed to a tree stump lying high up on the sand past the tide line. It was low and smooth, about two feet high.

She raced toward it and readied herself for the jump. But at the last instant her horse balked, and Lily found herself flying through the air.

She landed with a thud. And lay still. Unmoving.

"Lily!" Ned, just seconds behind her, flung himself off his horse and knelt down in the sand beside her. Her eyes were closed. She lay still and pale, not breathing.

"Lily, oh, God—" He grabbed her hand.

Her eyes flew open and she dragged in a long ragged breath. "Winded," she gasped, and Ned's own heart began to beat again. She gasped painfully for air and he could do nothing to help her.

She was alive, that was all he knew.

"Where are you hurt?" He ran his hands feverishly over her body.

"Not hurt, winded," she wheezed. She sat up, still gulping in air.

Ned sat back on his heels and watched her. His heart was thudding crazily. He'd thought he'd lost her, thought she'd killed herself.

"That was a stupid thing to do. Never do that again!"

She shrugged. "Most horses refuse a jump at some stage."

"You shouldn't be jumping at all!"

She frowned. "Why not?" Her breathing was smoother now. His pulse was still wildly erratic.

"It's too dangerous."

She looked at the fallen stump. "It's barely two feet high. My first pony could have jumped it in his sleep."

"I don't care." Ned drew in a slow, deep breath, seeking to present a calmer, more controlled appearance. "You are not to jump again."

"Because I fell? I'm not hurt."

He stood and put out a hand to pull her to her feet. She picked up the skirt of her habit, walked across to where her horse was calmly cropping grass and gathered the trailing reins. "What do you think you're doing?" he snapped.

She looked surprised. "Getting back on, of course. Will you give me a boost, please?"

"No, you'll ride back with me."

She gave him a puzzled look. "Are you angry with me?"

"No." Ned didn't know—or want to consider—what he was feeling. All he knew was that for a few appalling seconds he'd thought she was dead. "But you're not riding that wretched beast again."

"He's all right. It's the first time he's balked. You should always get back on a horse after you've taken a toss."

"I don't care." He collected the reins of her gelding, mounted his own horse and rode to the stump. "Up!"

She gave him a long thoughtful look, and for a moment he thought she was about to be stubborn, but then she gave a shrug and capitulated. She climbed onto the stump and gave him her hand. "On the count of three." He swung her up in front of him so that she was sitting more or less across him, in his lap.

They rode in silence. She was sitting bolt upright. He drew her back against him, and when her body softened against him and she laid her cheek against his chest, something inside him settled.

Ned tried to think of something to talk about—other than what had just happened—and he recalled that they'd been talking about school. Before she'd almost killed herself.

"When were you sent away to school?" he asked her.

"It was after Mama died. Papa sent us—Rose and me—off to Bath, to Miss Mallard's school there—the place where Cal and Emm's wedding breakfast was held."

She continued talking. Ned wasn't really listening. He'd had a shock. He'd thought he was immune, could keep himself separate and independent.

He glanced down at the woman in his arms. His wife. Her hair blew about in the breeze. Without thinking he stroked it back off her face. And kept it there, cupping her head protectively.

What had he done?

His horse ambled along. Birds squabbled in the hedgerow. Overhead, a hawk circled.

"Are you happy?" he found himself asking. He hadn't intended to ask such a thing. He held his breath, waiting for her answer.

She turned her head and gave him a smile he could not doubt. "Very happy."

He rode on in silence, his heart full of things he had no words for, things he did not want to feel but could not help.

WHEN THEY RETURNED TO TREMAYNE PARK, THERE WAS a letter waiting for Edward. He broke open the seal and scanned the letter. His face turned grim.

"What's the matter?"

"I have to go to London."

"When? Now?"

He nodded.

"Very well, I'll start packing at once." She hurried toward the stairs.

"No, you stay here. You don't need to come."

She turned around and stared down at him. "To London? Of course I do. I'm not staying here without you." She met his gaze. "There's no point arguing, Edward. I'm not staying here without you."

He stared at her a moment, then made an impatient gesture. "Very well, if you insist on coming, we'll leave in the morning." He disappeared for the rest of the day.

She questioned him over dinner, and all he would say was that it was nothing, just business, men's business, and was she sure she didn't want to stay here?

She was adamant that she didn't. What was a honeymoon without the groom?

He came to her that night, and made love to her with slow, intense deliberation, lavishing every part of her body with the most exquisite attention. She wasn't sure whether it was a benediction or a farewell. Whichever it was, her climax—climaxes—came with tears because of the power of the feelings he'd engendered.

He dried her tears tenderly. And made love to her again. And for the first time ever he slept the night in her bed, curled around her body like a big protective watchdog, warm and strong. And in his sleep he gathered her to him, holding her against him, skin to skin, so tenderly Lily felt like weeping.

Something had changed that morning at the beach, when her horse had thrown her. Something was different in her husband, she was sure of it. She could feel it.

"Trust your instincts," Aunt Dottie had told her.

She did, and she didn't want this, this honeymoon, this magical private time together, to stop. Especially not now, when they seemed on the brink of something wonderful . . .

Shortly after dawn he woke her, and two hours later they were on their way to London.

Chapter Seventeen

❧

I speak what appears to me the general opinion;
and where an opinion is general, it is usually correct.
—JANE AUSTEN, *MANSFIELD PARK*

THE CARRIAGE PULLED UP OUTSIDE THE VERY GRAND
Pulteney Hotel. "Why are we here?" Lily asked.

"It's where we'll be living for the next few weeks."

"In a hotel? I assumed we'd be living in Galbraith
House."

"We will, but it hasn't been used for years." He grimaced. "I inspected it before the wedding and realized it
needed a complete refurbishment. They'll still be working
on it—I was hoping it would be ready by the time we'd
finished our honeymoon, but since we came home early . . ."
He frowned at her expression. "Didn't I mention it?"

"No, you didn't."

He shrugged. "I didn't think you'd be interested in the
details. There was water damage, so the whole job was big-
ger than I'd imagined. They've had to fix the roof, replace
a good deal of plumbing—I ordered some more modern
installations while they were at it—and once all the repairs
are done, they'll need to replaster a number of rooms. And
then there are the furnishings and decoration to arrange—
the old furniture is completely out of date, and much of the
wallpaper is water damaged and stained."

"I see."

He shrugged, his mind clearly elsewhere. "That's why I
thought you'd prefer to stay at Tremayne Park. But no harm

done, we'll live here until the house is ready. Now, if you'll pardon me, my dear—"

"Who is arranging the new wallpaper and furnishings?"

He frowned. "I left the running of things in the hands of my man of business, Atkins. He'll hire someone." He paused. "Why? Do you wish to be involved? I thought you'd find it tedious."

Lily laughed. "Tedious? Setting up my own home and making it just as I would like it? Choosing wallpaper and curtains and furniture and rugs? I would love it."

He blinked. "Really? You could be bothered with all that nonsense?"

"Truly I could imagine nothing better."

"Then do whatever you'd like." He took a sheet of the hotel notepaper and scribbled a note. "I'll have this sent to Atkins and tell him he's to work under your orders. And now . . ." He picked up his hat and walked toward the door.

"Wait," Lily said. "Isn't there anything you want to tell me before you leave?"

He looked wary. "What sort of thing?"

"Any furniture you want to keep, rooms you have a particular fondness for, anything you don't want changed?"

He snorted. "I haven't lived in that house since I was six. As far as I'm concerned you could toss everything out and start new—in fact, that's what I'd prefer. Whatever you do will be fine by me. Now, I really must go."

Lily was stunned by his apparent indifference. But he'd given her *carte blanche* to arrange his house—her new home, and she couldn't wait to see it.

Leaving Edward's valet and her maid to see to the luggage and unpacking, Lily went immediately to Ashendon House, her old family home.

Cal and Emm were out, but Rose and George, and even Finn the lugubrious wolfhound, gave her a rapturous welcome.

"You're back early," Rose said once the initial greetings were over. "Has something happened? Has that man—"

Lily cut her off. "There's nothing wrong, Rose. I'm very happy."

"She looks well—even glowing," George observed.

Lily laughed. "I don't know about glowing, but I am well, and very happy."

Rose looked skeptical. "Then why are you back early from your honeymoon?"

"Oh, some business Edward had to attend to," she said airily. She wished she knew what he was doing, but she had business of her own to see to now. "I have two reasons for coming straight here," she said. "The first is, of course, to see you both—I missed you so much."

Rose exchanged glances with George. "And the second?"

Lily decided to ignore their suspicions. They'd soon realize that Edward was good to her. It might not be the love match she wanted, but she was happy enough.

"Edward is having Galbraith House refurbished. He arranged for the physical repairs to be done while we were away, and they're not quite finished, but that's not important. The thing is, he's given me permission to make all the decisions about the decoration and furnishings. I have a free hand with everything: wallpaper, lighting, floor coverings, curtains, furniture—everything!"

George frowned. "And you're happy about this? Sounds like a lot of work."

"It'll be fun, George," Rose said.

George gave her a doubtful look. "I'll take your word for it."

Lily glanced out the window. "As a matter of fact, I thought I might go around to Galbraith House this afternoon while it's still light, and see how it's all going and get some ideas. Do you two want to come with me?"

"ALL THIS IS FRIGHTFULLY OLD-FASHIONED," ROSE declared. "Thank goodness Galbraith is allowing you to order new furniture."

"What *is* this stuff?" George wandered around, examining the furniture they'd found under dust sheets. "I've never seen anything like it. A sofa with crocodile legs, animal feet on everything, people who are half man, half beast . . ."

"It's the Egyptian style," Rose explained. "It was all the rage when we were children." She pointed. "That's a sphinx, some of them are gods, I think."

"And this table and those chairs are dogs," George observed, stroking the head. "Aren't they beautiful?"

"Edward told me to throw everything out."

"You can't throw these dogs out," George objected, her hands going around them protectively.

"You can have them if you want," Lily said. "We're going to have to buy everything new." The prospect was delightful. "But first we must decide how to dress the walls—the head builder said they'd be ready to paper them in a few days."

They wandered through the various rooms, making suggestions and discussing possibilities. Rose wrote them all down in a little notebook. The light started to fade, and Lily suddenly remembered there was a place she wanted to see. "I need to see the nursery."

Rose and George immediately stared at her middle. "Isn't it too soon to tell?" George asked.

Lily laughed. "Not that, silly. Edward lived here until he was six. I want to see the part of the house he lived in as a little boy."

She hurried upstairs in search of the nursery. The others followed. They found it eventually in the attic, a big, bare, dusty room, with two small bedchambers off it, one for Edward and one for his nurse, Lily assumed.

Not a very appealing place for a child, she thought. Gloomy gray paint, and no pictures or any decoration on the walls. Gas hadn't been installed this high up, so the only light was coming from the slanted windows in the roof. No fireplace.

That window . . . She glanced around. George and Rose were poking through a low row of cupboards. A few toys, a small wooden sword—just one—and a moth-eaten toy dog. Remnants of a lonely childhood.

With some difficulty Lily forced open one of the windows, stood on her tiptoes and gazed out, thinking of the small dreamy boy who'd stood on a chair, gazing out over the rooftops and chimneys, as he explored mysterious imaginary lands half hidden in the swirling smog.

It wasn't mysterious, it was depressing. And this was no place to bring up a child, Lily decided.

"Come on, it's getting dark and there's nothing here," Rose said.

George looked at Lily. "Still think this is going to be fun?"

Lily smiled. "I can't wait."

LILY'S LIFE IN LONDON SOON SETTLED INTO A FAMILIAR routine—riding in the morning with either Edward or her family, morning calls in the afternoon, walks in the park and parties, routs, concerts and balls at night—the season was in full swing.

The only difference was that now she was a married woman and it was her husband who usually escorted her, not her brother or sister-in-law. And that they were living in a hotel, which she could not get used to. It was very comfortable and luxurious, and anything she wanted was instantly provided, but it didn't feel homey. The only thing she liked about the hotel was that the only suite that had been available to them was a one-bedroom suite, with one big, very comfortable bed.

Because of it, she and Edward slept together every night. He made love to her, then curled his big hard body around her and went to sleep. It was bliss, sleeping in his arms. And often he'd wake in the morning and make love to her again.

Most days she dropped in at Galbraith House to see the progress of the work. She and Rose had a lovely time visiting furniture showrooms, getting samples of wallpaper, examining rugs and so on. It was all most exciting. Sometimes George went with them, and sometimes Emm.

She talked to Edward about it, but it was clear he wasn't really interested, that he listened only to please her. Which was nice, but not very encouraging. The house was coming together, and she wanted to share her progress with him.

Edward was increasingly preoccupied. He was away most days and even spent some nights at his club. Because of having to conduct his business, he said. Lily was coming to hate his business, whatever it was.

Do not expect your husband to live in your pocket, as your brother, Ashendon, does with Emmaline. It is unfashionable and quite unseemly. It seemed Aunt Agatha was right.

Still, when he did come in at night, he made love to her so beautifully, there was really nothing for her to feel upset about, she told herself. It was a fact of life: Men's business was outside the home and women's arena was the domestic, and the sooner she got used to it the better.

IN THE PARK ONE DAY, WALKING WITH ROSE AND GEORGE in Hyde Park, Lily heard someone calling her. "Lily! I say, Lady Lily!"

She turned and saw Sylvia Gorrie hurrying toward her, waving. Her heart sank. She didn't really want to talk to Sylvia.

"Oh, lord, it's that dratted Sylvia Gorrie," Rose muttered. "Can't stand the woman. Her tongue runs on wheels, and none of it interesting. Want me to get rid of her, Lily?" Rose always could at school. But Lily always felt sorry for Sylvia. She tried so hard, yet never seemed to have any friends.

"No, I'll talk to her." She couldn't spend the rest of her life avoiding Sylvia, just because Sylvia's cousin had abducted her. People weren't responsible for the actions of their relatives.

Rose shook her head. "Too soft for your own good. Very well, when you're finished, George and I will be over there with the Peplowes."

Sylvia came rushing up. "Lady Lily—oh, I must call you Mrs. Galbraith now, must I not? A bit of a comedown, isn't it, losing your title?"

"No, not at—"

"Well, we're both 'Mrs.' now." Sylvia linked her arm through Lily's and began to walk. "Congratulations on your wedding, by the way. I was there, in the church, watching. Very pretty dress."

"Were you there? I'm sorry, I didn't notice."

Sylvia pursed her lips. "Oh, I'm easily overlooked. You weren't sick at all, were you? Those silly rumors about you running off with my cousin were obviously a ruse—so it was Galbraith all the time?"

"No, it wasn't—"

"I don't envy you, you know. He's handsome enough, but I wouldn't want a rake for a husband."

"He's not a r—"

Sylvia, oblivious as always, rattled on. "No, my husband isn't much, but at least I don't have to share him with a mistress. You're holding up quite well, though, I must say."

A mistress? "What do you mean?"

Sylvia gasped, then turned a distressed face to Lily. "You mean you didn't know? I'm sorry, just forget I said anything. It was a mistake, a misunderstanding. Take no notice—"

"But what did you—?"

"Look, isn't that the former Sally Destry over there, the countess of something now, I forget what. Such a spotty, insignificant little thing she was at school."

Lily wasn't to be distracted. "Are you saying my husband has a mistress?"

Sylvia waved to Sally, who didn't notice. "Quite the fashionable lady is La Destry now. Too grand for her old friends."

"Sylvia!"

Sylvia dropped her arm. "Look, I'm sorry I mentioned it. I assumed you knew. Put it out of your mind. There's nothing you can do about it anyway—men will be men, the horrid beasts."

"But why do you think so?"

Sylvia made an airy gesture. "How does one learn anything? *On-dits.* But rumor is often wrong, as you and I have good cause to know, and I'm sure this one must be too. After all, you're so recently married. He can't be bored with you yet, can he?" She linked her arm through Lily's again. "Now, let's just walk and chat and forget about it. I wish I'd never said anything, but you know me, my silly tongue runs away with me at times. My husband is always complaining of it."

They walked on. Lily thought about what Sylvia had suggested. It wasn't true. She didn't believe it. Edward wasn't bored with her. He came to her bed almost every night.

Almost. But that didn't mean anything—certainly not that he had a mistress. No, Sylvia had it wrong—again.

Lily had had enough of rumors and counter-rumors. She would clear one thing up at least. She glanced around to see who was nearby, and saw they were well out of earshot of the other fashionable strollers. She stopped, withdrew her arm and turned to face Sylvia.

"You're wrong about that, and about other things, as well. Your cousin *did* abduct me." Lily hated that the whole thing had been hushed up. She wanted—no, needed—to tell Sylvia the truth.

Sylvia blinked. "I beg your pardon—*what* did you just say?"

"On the night of the Mainwaring rout your cousin abducted me." Lily waited a moment for it to sink in. "He tricked me—that note wasn't from Rose at all—he drugged me, and he tied me up and imprisoned me under a seat in his coach." Sylvia stared, her expression horrified, her mouth opening and shutting silently.

"Your cousin's plan was to take me to Gretna Green and force a marriage on me—I presume for the sake of my inheritance. He must have learned about that from you."

Something flickered in Sylvia's eyes and Lily froze. She said slowly, "You knew he did, didn't you? You helped him."

Sylvia shook her head frantically. "I didn't know, I promise you." She gave a guilty grimace. "I might have told him about your inheritance—I don't remember. But he could have learned it from anyone. After all, it was no secret when we were at school. But I did *not* help him. I had no idea what he was planning. He tricked me, just as he tricked you."

Lily wasn't convinced. "He knew about my reading difficulties."

Sylvia hung her head. "Yes, that was me—but how was I to know what he would do with a tiny piece of information I innocently let drop? I told him all sorts of things about all sorts of people—he was interested in all my friends, and kept asking me questions, and . . . and I was flattered. Yes, what of it? He's a handsome man and I'm a married woman, but not many people like to listen to my chatter. My husband certainly doesn't. He calls me a silly gabble-tongue. But I'm sure Victor meant no harm."

"He *drugged* me, Sylvia. He tied me up and gagged me—I almost suffocated—and he shoved me in a compartment under his carriage seat and kept me there for hours and hours. I thought I was going to *die*."

There was a long silence. Sylvia's eyes narrowed as she considered what Lily had told her. Then she tossed her head. "I don't believe you. Victor is a gentleman; he would never treat a lady so."

"But he did!"

"No. I might believe that he kidnapped you—he must have been utterly desperate, poor boy—but he wouldn't do anything so, so brutal." She made a distasteful gesture. "Or so sordid."

"Well, he did. I'll spare you some of the truly sordid aspects, but I'll tell you this—he hit me across the face. Hard."

Sylvia snorted. "Rubbish!"

"He did. Hard enough that the bruise was visible for days. My family kept me indoors for nearly a week after I got home, because of that bruise."

Sylvia stamped her foot. "I don't believe you! Why would you say such vile things—oh, of course." Her mouth twisted spitefully. "You're angry because I told you about your husband's mistress."

Lily struggled to control her temper. "I don't believe my husband has a mistress. I think you're mistaken, or else you made it up—I don't care which. But your cousin *did* drug me, he *did* abduct me and lock me away in a horrid box and when I tried to escape, he *did* hit me. Hard."

"You're a horrid liar, Lily Rutherford, and I refuse to listen to any more of your lies." Sylvia stormed off.

Lily was shaking a little when she rejoined the others. She hated arguments but she was glad she'd confronted Sylvia at last. She felt lighter for having spoken the truth and, strangely, for having unleashed a little bit of temper.

She still wasn't convinced that Sylvia was as wholly innocent as she claimed, but she had been genuinely shocked—and upset—by Lily's reports of Nixon's brutality.

That was something. Sylvia's cousin was an evil brute and she needed to know it.

She thought about what Sylvia had told her about Edward. A mistress? She didn't believe it, but why would Sylvia say such a thing if she hadn't heard a rumor? And where would such a rumor come from?

"Everything all right?" Rose asked.

"Fine."

"You look a bit upset."

Lily made a dismissive gesture. "Oh, it's just Sylvia. She can be quite annoying at times."

Rose laughed. "And you're only just noticing?"

Lily smiled. Rose was right, Sylvia was not worth listening to. As for her stupid suggestion about Edward and a mistress, Lily would not even give it the dignity of consideration.

LILY ATTENDED A BALL WITH EDWARD THAT NIGHT. SHE heard no sly innuendos, noticed no significant glances, heard no whispered *on-dits* concerning her husband or herself. She hated herself for even thinking about such things, and silently cursed Sylvia for planting the seeds of poison in her mind.

Recalling Emm's advice—*take your happiness where you find it*—she put the horrid idea from her mind and set herself to enjoying the ball.

"You're in a good mood tonight," Edward said as he twirled her around the floor. He only ever danced the waltz with her. He rarely danced with anyone else—Rose and George and Emm if they were present, even Aunt Agatha, once—but he made it clear he was not looking for partners, that Lily was all he wanted.

He was a beautiful dancer too, and Lily knew she was the envy of many.

"I'm happy, that's all," she said.

"I'm enormously relieved."

"Relieved?" It was an odd thing to say. She tilted her head and gave him a quizzical look.

He gave a hunted glance around the crowded room. "As long as you're happy, I'm safe from being gutted with a rusty blade." His eyes glinted with roguish humor.

"What?"

"It's true. Your demure little niece threatened me with that, the day we became betrothed."

"George did?" She spluttered with laughter. "She can be a bit outrageous, but I'm sure she didn't mean it."

"I'm not so sure. Your sister threatened me too." He added darkly, "The innocent-looking ones are the worst."

They finished the dance laughing. It was the supper dance, and Lily began to make her way to the supper room. He detained her with a hand on her arm and a slow-burning smile. "Do you want to stay? Or shall we go home?"

His magnetic, half-hooded glance, light touch and lazy smile were an invitation she couldn't resist. "Home, please."

SYLVIA CALLED ON LILY AT THE HOTEL THE VERY NEXT day and was directed upstairs by a helpful, if misguided, staff member. Having no choice but to accept her visitor, Lily showed her to the sitting room that was part of their hotel suite. The sooner Lily was in her own home, the happier she'd be. With a butler who'd tell unwanted visitors she was not at home.

Sylvia's eyes were on stalks as she entered the lush apartment. "I must say, you've done very well for yourself, Lily. This place is positively—"

"What do you want, Sylvia?"

"Oh, sorry." She settled herself in a chair and folded her hands in her lap. "I've been thinking over what you told me yesterday and though I find it impossible to believe my cousin could do such a thing, treat you with such cruel incivility—"

"Sylvia, I don't want to talk about it any—"

She held up a hand. "No, let me finish—please. It *is* impossible for me to believe, but I know you wouldn't lie to me, Lily, not about such an important thing, and so I *must* believe it. I'm so very sorry I doubted you, and if I was rude—"

"You were."

"Well, that's why I'm here. To apologize." She eyed Lily anxiously. "I really am truly sorry, Lily." From the bag she was carrying she produced a large, flat box, wrapped in paper emblazoned with the name of a well-known shop. She offered it to Lily, and when Lily didn't take it, Sylvia put it on a side table.

Lily recognized the wrapping. Sweetmeats, the finest you could buy. She sighed. She really didn't want to make things up with Sylvia. She felt sorry for her, but she'd never much liked her. And there was a limit to how much she'd put up with.

But she hated to be cruel.

The silence stretched, and Sylvia's lower lip began to quiver. She stretched out a hand in appeal. "Please say you forgive me, Lily. You're my only friend—my only true friend—in London, and I could cut out my tongue for the things I said to you yesterday." She produced a handkerchief and dabbed at her eyes. She scrunched it up. Tears glistened on her lashes.

Where was Rose when you needed her? She wouldn't care about a few tears. But Lily wasn't her sister, and she couldn't stay angry for very long. She said with obvious reluctance, "Very well, I forgive you, Sylvia."

"Oh, thank you, thank you, dear Lily." Sylvia jumped up and embraced her. "So are we friends again?"

Lily nodded.

"Then you must let me take you out to tea."

"No, I don't think that's nec—"

"Oh, but I insist. To show you there are no hard feelings."

She really was the limit. Lily was the one entitled to the hard feelings. But if she did this—it was just a tea, after all—it would be worth it to get Sylvia off her back. "Very well. When?"

"Tomorrow afternoon? Now, where—oh, I know!—there's a new tea shop just opened and it has the most divine cakes. Now, we'll need to go in a carriage, and"—she gave Lily an apologetic look—"I'm afraid my husband won't let me have the carriage, so perhaps you could pick me up in yours, and I'll direct your driver. Will that be all right?"

"Yes, fine," Lily said wearily. Already she was regretting it.

Sylvia stood. "Lovely. Then I'll see you at two. Don't be late now."

THE TEA SHOP WAS VERY PRETTY, SITUATED IN A STREET OF elegant shops, opposite a large hotel called the Excelsior. It was a convenient location for people who'd been shopping to stop for tea and cakes and other refreshments. With gleaming tiled floors in a checkerboard pattern, a large, elegant bay window facing into the street and charming wrought-iron tables and chairs, it looked very appealing. If their cakes lived up to the rest of the place, she was sure the new business would succeed.

They ordered tea and cakes, which came quickly and were delicious. They drank, ate cakes and chatted. Lily was in the middle of telling Sylvia a story about the refurbishment of Galbraith House—every day a fresh discovery—when she realized that Sylvia wasn't listening. She was staring over Lily's shoulder at something out in the street.

"I don't believe it," Sylvia muttered as if to herself.

Lily, her back to the window, turned curiously.

"No, no, don't look!" Sylvia exclaimed, putting out her hand to stop Lily. "It's nothing, really nothing. Sorry, Lily, I was distracted for a minute. Tell me, what did the workmen do to the screen again?" She leaned forward with a look of interest so patently false, Lily couldn't stop herself. She turned and looked out the window.

There was nothing of note, just a few people walking along the street. "What is it?"

"Nothing, no one. Turn away, Lily. I don't want you to be cross with me again. Here, have a cake."

But Lily's curiosity was well and truly hooked. She turned and examined the people in the street again. Most were hurrying along purposefully, in twos or threes. The only single person was a plump, very pretty young woman in a crimson coat, lingering on the other side of the road. She seemed to be waiting for someone.

"I didn't know she'd be there, I promise you, Lily." Sylvia moaned.

"Who is she?"

"Your husband's—the one they say is your husband's—oh, no!" She didn't finish the sentence. She didn't have to.

Edward was walking briskly along the road, approaching the hotel from the opposite direction. As he neared the hotel entrance, the young woman brightened and began to walk toward him.

As Lily watched she said something to Edward and held out her hand. In dull disbelief, she saw her husband take the woman's hand. She swayed toward him, and he slipped his arm around her waist and escorted her tenderly up the steps and into the hotel.

The door closed behind them. In the tea shop there was a long silence.

Eventually Sylvia spoke. "I swear I didn't know—"

"I don't believe you." Lily made a weary gesture. "Just go, Sylvia. Get out. You've shown me what you wanted me to see, so please, just go—and don't bother trying to talk to me again."

Sylvia stood. "You're angry with me when you should be angry with him. I had to show you. He meets her here every week. So that's what your precious husband is worth." The vitriol and smug satisfaction in her voice were horribly blatant.

Lily said with quiet, hard-won dignity, "I don't know why you hate me, Sylvia, but I can see now that you do. Rose was right about you. You don't care about me or my marriage—you brought me here to see me hurt and humiliated. Leave, please. I don't ever want to see or speak to you again."

Sylvia flounced out. Lily called for another pot of tea and sat there, watching the hotel entrance opposite. Her brain was numb. The tea turned cold. Edward didn't come out.

Lily paid the bill and summoned the carriage. What to do now?

Chapter Eighteen

❧

Angry people are not always wise.
—JANE AUSTEN, *PRIDE AND PREJUDICE*

WALTON DROVE LILY AROUND THE PARK A FEW TIMES while she thought about what to do. She needed to talk to someone—but who?

She couldn't tell Rose and George about what had just happened. They'd been against her marrying Edward, and they'd be vigorous in their condemnation, both of Edward and of Lily's choice in marrying him.

And Rose would say that she'd said all along that Sylvia was a nasty cow—and then George would remind them that cows were lovely creatures and then—Lily stopped on a hiccup. She was close to tears.

But she would not cry, she would not. She didn't know for sure that Edward was keeping a mistress. The scene she'd observed was damning, to be sure, but she didn't *know*.

The truth was she didn't *want* to know. She wanted never to have gone to that horrid tea shop, never to have looked out that window. If she hadn't seen what she'd seen, she wouldn't be hurting so badly.

She wanted to go to her sister, to have Rose put her arms around her as she had when Lily was a little girl, and tell her everything would be all right. But she couldn't. She wasn't a little girl anymore, she was a married woman. A woman who'd married against everyone's advice. And who was trying to stand on her own two feet.

Besides, Rose and George would be on her side no matter what. Lily didn't need their partisan support, she needed to talk to someone more impartial, more experienced.

Emm? No, she didn't want to distress Emm, especially now with the baby coming. Emm and Cal might have made a convenient marriage, but they were very much in love now. It was what Lily had hoped would happen to her and Edward.

She shivered. She'd tumbled so easily in love with him. She'd hoped he would do the same.

But he'd been forced into marriage with her, punished for rescuing her. And his pleasure in their marriage was all about *bedsport*.

If she was hurting now, it was her own fault. It wasn't as if she hadn't been warned. He'd told her over and over that it wasn't a love match and that she wasn't to expect anything more than friendship.

She could love him with all her heart, but it would make no difference; you couldn't make someone love you if they didn't.

The question was how did an inconvenient convenient wife go on? How did she hold her head up in society, when it seemed half of society knew her husband of a few weeks had taken a mistress?

Who could advise her? She needed someone who'd be honest with her, someone who had experience with this kind of thing.

The answer jumped out at her. Aunt Agatha. She'd had three husbands, and married none of them for love. She'd know what Lily should do.

"SO THAT'S THE SITUATION, AUNT AGATHA. WHAT I should do?" Lily was seated in Aunt Agatha's private sitting room, a glass of sherry in her hand. She'd just finished explaining.

There was a long silence. Aunt Agatha gave her a thoughtful look, sipped her sherry then pursed her lips. "I'm disappointed, but I can't say I'm surprised. If you had—"

"Please don't tell me it's my fault for being too plump or too stupid or too young—criticizing me for things I can't change is not going to help!"

Aunt Agatha raised her brows. Lily eyed her defiantly and gulped her sherry. It was nasty stuff. "Besides, my being plump isn't the problem. I've seen his mistress and she's as plump as me."

"As plump as *I*. Does your husband know about your little problem?" She tapped the book she'd been reading and set aside when Lily arrived.

"No, I've kept that a secret from him." And she still felt torn in two about that.

"Good, so it's not that, then."

"No. And there's no point in offering me advice about winning him back," Lily said. You couldn't win back what you'd never had. "I just want to know how to bear it. You've had three husbands. Did any of them have mistresses?"

"Yes, of course, all three of them." She twirled her lorgnette thoughtfully. "In some ways it was a relief."

A relief? Lily couldn't imagine that, but then she recalled that Aunt Agatha hadn't enjoyed the marriage bed.

That was the hardest thing of all to think about. Up to now the best part of her marriage had been what passed between them in bed, but if Edward had sought the services of a mistress, it meant Lily had failed in that area as well. It was very disheartening. She took another sip of sherry.

"But wasn't it humiliating?" It was strange to be sitting here with her formidable aunt, talking like this, woman to woman, but also comforting. She felt closer to Aunt Agatha than she ever had in her life.

The old lady shrugged. "One learns to deal with such things."

Lily set down her glass and leaned forward. "How, Aunt Agatha? Tell me what I must do."

"Accept it. Ignore it. Act as if it isn't true."

"I'm not even sure it *is* true," Lily admitted. "It's just a rumor—from an unreliable source."

Aunt Agatha snorted. "And the evidence of your own

eyes. Face facts, gel, men are feckless creatures. It's their nature to stray. Now, do you want my advice or not?"

"Yes, Aunt Agatha," she said humbly.

"To begin with, a lady simply does not acknowledge the existence of such persons as mistresses. Banish the creature from your mind and go on with your life. Behave exactly as normal, and don't breathe a word of your suspicions to anyone—not to your sister-in-law, not to that whisky-frisky argumentative sister of yours, nor to Georgiana. All they will offer you is sympathy and a barrage of useless suggestions. Sympathy in these cases is poisonous—it will only encourage you toward self-pity and lachrymosity, which is revolting to behold."

There was a well of deeply buried pain beneath the brisk advice. Who had offered Aunt Agatha sympathy? And would anyone ever know the cause?

"Your only possible choice is to stiffen your spine and get on with your life. Say not a word to your husband. On no account must you let him know that you are aware of the situation—not by word, deed or implication. It will do you no good—a leopard doesn't change his spots—and it will only cause him to feel defensive and uncomfortable, and make him feel further justified in his infidelity. So, not a word to your husband, do you understand?"

"Yes, Aunt Agatha."

EDWARD SENT A MESSAGE TO SAY HE WOULD SLEEP AT HIS club again that night. Lily dined as arranged with Emm and Cal and Rose and George, and afterward attended the theater with them. Edward had been invited, of course, but she had to make his excuses, the ones that he'd given her the day before—that he was busy attending to his affairs. That important "men's business" excuse he'd used so often.

She didn't put it like that, of course. She simply smiled and said Edward was caught up in something and sent his apologies.

But she had a very good idea now what he meant by "men's business."

She slept badly—she'd become so used to having him sleeping in the bed that when he wasn't there, she missed him. She supposed when they finally moved into Galbraith House he would revert to having his own bedchamber. It was a bleak prospect.

She rode out with Cal and Rose and George in the morning and when she returned, she found Edward home, changing his shirt. She glanced at his valet and, copying Edward's tactics with her maid, jerked her head at him. He glanced at his master and made a discreet exit, leaving them alone.

Edward picked up a neckcloth. "Something you wanted, Lily?" He sounded quite unworried.

"Where did you sleep last night?" she found herself asking.

He gave her a quizzical look via reflection in his looking glass. "At my club—I told you."

Aunt Agatha's advice was all very well, but Lily was fed up with pretending all was well when it wasn't. And she wasn't going be plagued by questions any longer. "You have a mistress, don't you?"

"A mistress?" He gave her a quizzical look in the mirror. "Whatever gave you that idea?"

"People are saying you have one."

He frowned and swung around to face her. "You're serious?"

She nodded.

"Well, whoever these people are, they're wrong. I don't have a mistress. The idea is preposterous." He snorted. "When could I possibly fit one in?" He saw her expression and added, "I have no interest in a mistress. Why would I when I have you?"

She said nothing, just folded her arms defensively. He was so plausible. Was this what her future was going to be like? Lies and pretense?

"Lily? You can't possibly believe this nonsense." He moved to take her in his arms.

She fended him off and stepped back. "I saw you with her yesterday."

"What? Who? What are you talking about?"

"You went into a hotel with her—the Excelsior Hotel. I was having tea with—with someone in the tea rooms opposite. I *saw* you, Edward."

He frowned. "I did go into the Excelsior Hotel yesterday, to meet a fellow that didn't show up. There wasn't any woman involved."

"I saw you go in together. You had your arm around her." She recalled the solicitous, almost protective way he'd placed his hand in the small of the woman's back, and the way she'd leaned against him. A spurt of anger went through her.

He looked astonished, and a bit offended. "I did nothing of the—oh, yes, you're right, I remember now. There was a woman." His eyes narrowed. "She was increasing and felt faint. She asked for my arm to help her mount the stairs, told me her husband was inside. Naturally I assisted her, as any gentleman would." He added stiffly, clearly resentful of her accusation, "But I'd never seen her before in my life."

Lily bit her lip. It was credible. It could also be a clever lie.

The longer she remained silent, the darker his expression grew. "You don't believe me?"

Her face crumpled. "Oh, Edward, I want to, I truly want to." Hot tears prickled behind her eyes.

"I gave you my word before we were married that I'd never lie to you."

She shook her head. "You took that promise back."

"No, *you* took it back," he said with quiet emphasis. "I gave you my word of honor that day. I meant it then and I mean it now."

He put a lot of store in his word of honor, she remembered. He'd also promised that after they were married he'd be faithful to her.

"You really don't have a mistress?" she whispered.

"No, I don't."

"Promise?"

He said in a hard voice, "I gave you *my word*." He was

so obviously offended by the suggestion that she believed him.

The relief was enormous. Tears rolled down her cheek. She dashed them away. "I'm so sorry, Edward. I didn't want to believe it, but I was *told*, you see. Told that lots of people knew. And then—then I saw you with that woman and, and . . ."

He pulled out a handkerchief and dried her cheeks. "Hush now. Even if I hadn't given you my word, I have neither the time nor the energy to keep a mistress—and certainly not the inclination. I'm married to this irresistible young lady, you see . . ."

He drew her against him, tilted her face up and lowered his mouth to hers. As always, one thing led to another and he took her to bed and made love to her, slow, tender and a little bittersweet.

She loved him. She ached to tell him, but she couldn't, not now, after their first quarrel. It would be the worst time in the world for that—even if he wanted it, which he'd made it clear he didn't.

She'd taken a risk, accusing him of infidelity. She didn't regret it, though, because it had cleared the air. More or less. She lay quietly, enjoying the sensation of being snuggled close to her big warm husband.

"Go to sleep if you like," he said, sitting up. "I have to go out."

He slipped out of bed and started to dress.

"Where are you going?"

"Out."

She made an irritated sound, and he turned. "What?"

"You're always so secretive."

"What do you mean?

"This, this 'business' of yours that I'm not allowed to know about, and why do you have to sleep the night in your club so often?" She gave him a half-embarrassed look. "It gave credence to the rumors about you having a mistress."

He didn't answer. He was tying his neckcloth. But when he finished he said, "I stay away from you for several nights a week in order to spare you."

"Spare me from what? I don't mind if you come in late, or drunk, or smelling of cigars."

"From my attentions." She gave him a puzzled look, so he went on. "In the hotel we have only one bed. Since we've been living here, I've made love to you every single night I've slept here. And then—because I awake and find you in my bed, I make love to you again in the morning."

"Yes, what of it?" He said it as if it were a problem. She didn't find it so. Quite the contrary.

"It occurred to me that it might be too much for you— my intemperate desire. Morning and night and then morning again." He made a rueful gesture. "And at other times, like now."

She couldn't believe it. Hadn't she made it clear how she felt? "Edward, I am *thrilled* whenever we make love— however often, whatever time. Surely you know that? The nights you've stayed at your club, only a few minutes' walk away, I thought you didn't want me." She took a deep breath and added, "And when I thought you'd taken a mistress I thought it was because I hadn't pleased you in bed."

He stared down at her with a look of amazement. "How could you possibly think that?" He gave a harsh laugh. "A fine pair we make: me thinking I was pestering you too much, and you imagining you didn't please me enough. For the record, madam, let it be known that you drive me wild with desire, and everything you do pleases me enormously."

"Truly?"

"Are you doubting my word again?"

"No, of course not. Then what is this secret business you're always going away on?"

"Exactly what I said—business. I suppose I should have explained earlier, since it affects you." He sat on the bed again. "You know I am my grandfather's heir."

She nodded.

"You have probably assumed that my income comes from the family estate, but it doesn't. I decided years ago that I would earn a living for myself, separately—nothing to do with the estate. I own—personally own—several manufactories. I have interests in two mines, a canal company and I have recently become part owner of a ship. All that takes time. I won't take a penny from my grandfather."

"But why? I thought you loved your grandfather."

"I do, but I cannot justify taking money from an estate that I never visit. And when my grandfather dies, I won't be running it—I intend to put in a manager."

"But why? I don't understand. If you care for your grandfather, why wouldn't you—?"

"Just leave it, will you?" he said brusquely, and stood up. "Just accept that's how it is."

"Very well." It was very strange, though, and she wanted to know more. But it would keep. She'd pushed him far enough today.

She watched him dressing, and thought again about Sylvia and the whole incident. She thought about the choice of tea shop, and where they'd each been seated. And the coincidence of Edward and that woman meeting like that. It couldn't possibly have been accidental.

She sat up abruptly. "Edward! She planned the whole thing."

He picked up his coat "Who did? What?"

"Sylvia—Nixon's cousin. She's been oh-so-innocent and misunderstood about the whole thing, but she's shown her hand too clearly now with this mistress nonsense." She gave him an excited look. "Sylvia cajoled me into meeting her for tea. She chose the place and the time. As for that woman, I'm certain she arranged for her to come and accost you in front of that hotel." She broke off, frowning. "Oh, but how did she know you'd be there?"

"That fellow I went to meet never showed. I'd received a note that if I wanted to know Nixon's whereabouts I should come to the Excelsior at two fifteen precisely and bring twenty pounds."

"Nixon?"

He gave her a rueful smile. "Another thing I've kept secret from you. I've been trying to track down Nixon. By all accounts the villain is still in England. I have several men on the job, but most of the investigating I'm doing myself."

"But why on earth keep that a secret from me?"

He gave her a curious look and said slowly, "I thought it might upset you, having it all stirred up again. I thought you'd probably want to forget all about it, block it from your mind."

"Not at all. I would love Nixon to be caught and punished." She beamed up at him. "I think it's wonderful that you're trying to hunt him down. I think it's utterly heroic."

He stiffened and glanced away. "Don't call me that." He stood up. "I have to go. I'll see you tonight."

Puzzled and a little disturbed, she watched him leave. What had just happened?

LILY TOLD ROSE AND GEORGE WHAT SYLVIA HAD DONE, the mischief she'd tried to make between Lily and her husband.

"More than mischief," George commented. "It's a vicious little plot. What did you ever do to her to make her hate you like that, Lily?"

"Nothing," Lily and Rose said in chorus.

"Lily has been a perfect saint toward her," Rose declared. "I'd understand if she was trying to get back at me—I never liked her and never tried to hide it. Nobody liked Sylvia at school, but Lily was always nice to her. And Sylvia took advantage."

"No need to go into all that," Lily said quickly. "That's all in the past. The main thing is that I never want to speak to her again, and I wanted you both to know. And to help me if she tries anything again."

"The woman sounds cracked in the head," George said. "Now, what are we going to do this morning?"

"I'm going to see how the refurbishments are coming along," Lily said. "Anyone want to come with me?"

They all three went, and enjoyed themselves hotly debating the merits of various kinds of wall coverings: painted papers, silk or brocade. But apart from the excitement of choosing designs and colors, Lily was a little downhearted. According to the man in charge, it would be at least another two weeks before they could even think of moving in.

* * *

DAMMIT! NED HAD REVEALED MORE THAN HE MEANT TO. It was harder than he'd expected, being married and keeping himself to himself.

The trouble was, his wife had this way about her, a way of causing him to lower his barriers without realizing it—until it was too late.

Worse, it seemed that he needed to take his own advice about the effect of bedsport on one's . . . emotions. Ironic, that. It was because there was only one bed in the damned hotel, of course. Never before had he had such continuous access to a warm and willing female. It played havoc with his . . . equilibrium.

Still—he glanced at the letter he was holding—the solution was in his hand. Nixon had been spotted—reliably spotted by one of his own men, not another wild-goose chase—in Southampton. And this time Ned was going after the wretch himself. He wanted the man dealt with once and for all.

Lily needed that peace of mind.

He broke the news to her that evening as they were dressing to go to the theater. "I have to go away for a week or so. Maybe longer."

"Can you do this up for me, please? The catch is quite tricky." He bent over the necklace fastening—a fiddly little thing—and almost dropped it, startled, when she said, "I'll come with you."

He was shocked. "You can't. I'm sorry, but it's not possible. Not—" He was going to say *convenient* but that wouldn't go down too well. "It's business. Very dull. I need to be able to concentrate and if you came . . ."

"I would distract you?"

"Yes." It was true, but he didn't mean it as the compliment she was taking it for, if the little smile on her face was any indication. He would have stressed the danger element, except he didn't want her to worry.

Marriage was full of traps. The thing to do was to issue statements, not give anyone—meaning his wife—the opportunity to *discuss* things.

"So I'll be leaving first thing in the morning," he said in a brisk voice. End of conversation.

She eyed him thoughtfully in the looking glass, twirling a dusky curl around her fingers. "And what am I to do while you're away?"

"Do? The usual things, I suppose. Ride in the park, go visiting with your Rutherford relatives, attend balls, harry builders—that sort of thing. Are you ready?"

She picked up a lacy shawl and handed it to him. "Living here, in the hotel?"

"Of course. You told me the house won't be ready for a couple of weeks." He arranged the shawl around her shoulders.

She considered that. "I don't want to stay here on my own."

"Stay with your family at Ashendon House, then. I'm sure they'll be delighted to have you back."

She didn't look too delighted at the idea. She stood back for him to open the door for her. "I'll think about it."

Later that evening, as he was handing her down from the carriage, she said, "I've thought about it. I think I'll go and visit Aunt Dottie, in Bath."

"Fine. Excellent. If that's what you want."

"LILY, MY DEAR GIRL, WHATEVER ARE YOU DOING HERE?" The carriage had pulled up outside Aunt Dottie's house, and Lily had jumped down to ring the bell herself. To her surprise, instead of hugging her and dragging her inside, Aunt Dottie was peeking past Logan, her butler, regarding Lily with a look of horror.

"I've come to visit you, Aunt Dottie."

"Oh, dear—I wish I'd known! Why didn't you write to say you were com—oh, of course, I'm sorry, my dear, I wasn't thinking." Aunt Dottie's hands fluttered with distress, waving Lily back into the street. "But you cannot stay here, my love! You simply cannot!"

"But why, Aunt Dottie? What's the problem?"

"Chicken pox," the old lady declared tragically. "Two of

the housemaids and the youngest footman are stricken already, and the scullery maid started throwing out spots this morning. I suspect the butcher's boy," she added darkly. "But you cannot stay even for a minute—it can be horridly disfiguring, and you never had it that time Rose was so ill with it, did you?"

"No, I didn't."

"So you mustn't risk it. You must go away at once—oh, how dreadful to have to be so uncivil to a most beloved niece—I would have loved to have you stay. I've missed you girls so much—but I must *shun* you, my love, positively shun you, for your own good. Tell her, Logan dear." She appealed to the tall, silver-haired butler standing by her elbow.

"Your aunt is right," Logan said. "She's been all about-end with it, but can I convince her to stay elsewhere and let me deal with it?" He gave the old lady a fond look. "Stubborn as a mule she is and always has been."

"Quite right," Aunt Dottie said. "And I have no intention of changing."

Lily smiled. Her brother, Cal, strongly disapproved of Logan's informal manner toward their aunt, but Aunt Dottie insisted that she and Logan had known each other since she was fifteen, and to pretend otherwise was ridiculous. Nothing would convince her that a groom turned butler should not be treated as an old friend.

"Now go, Lily dearest, go. The longer you are here, the more chance of you catching the horrid thing." Her aunt made shooing motions at her, then clapped her hands to her cheeks in sudden realization. "Oh! But where will you go? And why isn't your husband with you? You haven't lost him, have you?"

Lily laughed. "No, Aunt Dottie, Edward's away on business, and don't worry, I'll spend the night at York House." It was the finest of Bath's hotels. "I'm a married woman now, you know, and have a great deal more freedom."

"That's all right then, dear. I suppose you'll have to go back to London tomorrow—such an inconvenience. I could wring the neck of that wretched butcher's boy. Give my love to everyone when you see them again. Now go, go. Flee and be healthy!"

Lily climbed back into the traveling chaise. Walton, the coachman, opened the little communication hatch in the roof of the carriage. "Where to now, ma'am?"

Lily thought for a minute. She didn't want to go back to London. She didn't want to live at the Pulteney without Edward, and staying with her family was out of the question while they still disapproved of Edward. Then an idea came to her. "You know where Shields, Lord Galbraith's estate, is, don't you, Walton?"

"Aye, in Hereford," he said cautiously.

"Good. We'll go there tomorrow, then." Edward's grandfather had issued her an open invitation, after all.

Besides, how could she resist an opportunity to learn more about her husband's childhood home, the estate he had not visited in more than ten years, and for which he refused to take responsibility?

Chapter Nineteen

❧

Teach me to feel another's woe,
To hide the fault I see,
That mercy I to others show,
That mercy show to me.
—ALEXANDER POPE, "THE UNIVERSAL PRAYER"

SOMEHOW LILY HAD EXPECTED SHIELDS TO BE SINISTER-looking, or grim, run-down and depressing, but as the carriage bowled up the tree-lined driveway, she saw that, on the contrary, everything looked to be in apple-pie order.

Shields was an ancient house, built in gray stone in the Gothic manner, but far from being sinister, it looked beautiful, open and welcoming, with gleaming many-paned Gothic windows. Crimson roses rambled over the gray stone, and the garden around the house was a riot of colorful spring flowers.

The setting too was lovely. To one side rolling fields of crops stretched green and gold to the horizon, and away behind the house, she could see the forest Edward had mentioned so long ago, one of the few things she knew about his childhood and his home. It looked ancient, the trees huge and gnarled, their branches spread magnificently, a thousand shades of green, shady and mysterious. A wonderful playground for an imaginative boy.

As the carriage pulled up, grooms ran up to tend the horses, and an elderly butler came carefully down the steps.

"May I help you, madam?" he said politely.

For a moment Lily didn't know what to say. She'd come all this way unannounced, if not uninvited. "I'm Mrs. Galbraith," she said. "Mrs. Edward Galbraith."

His face lit up. "Mr. Edward's wife," he breathed. "We didn't know, I mean, welcome, Mrs. Galbraith, welcome. Is, er . . ." He peered behind her, and she knew who he was hoping to see.

"I've come alone," she said gently. "My husband isn't with me."

"Oh." He made a valiant effort to hide his disappointment, mustered a bright smile and led her into the house. "Lord Galbraith will be delighted to see you, Mrs. Galbraith. He's in the library. I am Fenchurch, the butler. Would you care to refresh yourself before I take you to him?"

She didn't need to use the necessary but decided it would be politic to wash and tidy herself, so the butler could warn Lord Galbraith of his unexpected visitor and give the old man a few minutes to recover from the surprise—and perhaps his disappointment that she'd come alone—before he had to receive her.

She washed in a guest room, then came downstairs.

"My dear, dear girl." Edward's grandfather came toward her, wreathed in smiles. She was about to curtsey—she hadn't given thought to how she should greet him—but he said quickly, "None of that formal nonsense, young Lily, you're my granddaughter now and I'll have a hug and a kiss from you, thank you very much." He gave her a warm hug and grinned delightedly when she stood on tiptoe to kiss his leathery old cheek.

His likeness to Edward was uncanny. Lily felt as though she knew him, even though they'd only met a couple of times.

"Now, come into the warm, my dear child. Fenchurch will bring you tea and cakes—or would you prefer a glass of wine?" He escorted her into the library, a large room lined from floor to ceiling with shelves, filled with leather-bound tomes of every imaginable size. She'd never seen so many books in her life. A fire burned brightly in the hearth, making it very cozy.

"Now, sit ye down, child, and tell me what that silly chub of a grandson of mine has done to drive you all the way down here. He's not following, is he?" he added with ill-concealed hopefulness.

"No, I'm sorry, he's not. He doesn't even know I'm here." She explained the circumstances that had brought her to Shields.

Over an early dinner they talked, and Lord Galbraith showed her over the house, telling her some of its history, and in particular the bits that related most to Edward, or Ned as his grandfather called him.

He showed her Ned's old rooms, which had remained more or less unchanged since he ran off and joined the army. "The boy was mad for a pair of colors," his grandfather explained, "but his father and I—his father was still alive then, but the two of them clashed like stags whenever they met. But Ned was the heir, you see, the only heir, so of course we could not let him go off and get himself shot to pieces in the war."

He shook his head, remembering. "But he was ripe for adventure, and champing at the bit to get out into the world and prove himself a man. Lads of that age think they're men when they're just hey-go-mad boys, that's the tragedy of it." He heaved a sigh.

Lily sat quietly, listening, fascinated.

"So what must the wretched young tearaway do but run off and join up as a common soldier, along with half the lads in the village; one of those dashed recruiting sergeants— unscrupulous villains they are—came along banging his drum and got the lot of 'em all fired up, and off they went to take the king's shilling."

"How old was he then?"

"Not quite eighteen, the young fool. Of course we couldn't have the Galbraith heir serving with the common riffraff, so we bought him a commission—should have been the cavalry, but the stiff-necked young idiot refused to leave the fellows who'd joined up with him, so he became a lieutenant in the infantry. The infantry!" He snorted. "When he could ride almost before he could walk! More wine, my dear?"

"No, thank you. Tell me the rest."

"The rest? There is no rest. The boy never came home again. You probably know as much as I do about his military career—we read the newspapers, didn't we? Gleaned what shreds of information we could find. Of course he wrote, but the wartime letters were the barrenest things you've ever read. No details, just 'Dear Grandpapa, I am well and in need of socks,' or 'Wishing for some good red meat,' or some nonsense like that. Nothing to tell a man what the lad was feeling or doing. The letters are better now, of course."

Lily frowned. "He still writes to you?"

The old man nodded. "Always has, man and boy, a letter every week. Some as brief as a letter can be, barely deserving to be called a note, others long and well worth the reading." He smiled at her. "Hasn't he ever written to you?"

"No."

"I don't suppose he's had any need to, with you right there at hand. Tomorrow I'll show you some of the more interesting of his letters. I've kept them all, you know." His eyes, green like Edward's, only a little faded, twinkled. "There are a few I think you'll find particularly interesting."

Lily forced a smile. "I look forward to it."

THE NEXT MORNING DAWNED BRIGHT AND SUNNY, AND over breakfast Lord Galbraith declared his intention to take Lily on a tour of the estate while the weather held. "Horseback all right with you, young Lily? I seem to remember you're a fine little horsewoman. Ned and I saw you riding in the park with your sisters on the morning of your wedding—oh, no, we can't have seen you, can we?" He grinned roguishly. "Bad luck for the groom to see the bride before the wedding. I recall it now—your sisters were kidnapping a complete stranger."

She laughed, drizzling honey on her toast. "I suppose Edward told you. It's silly, I know. Rose got it wrong—the groom isn't supposed to see the bride *in her wedding dress*—but who was I to argue with superstition?" She crunched down on her toast.

He laughed. "Especially since you were being kidnapped at the time." He wiped his mouth and set his table napkin aside. "So, my dear, how do you feel about riding around the estate with an old man this fine morning?"

"An old man? Oh, dear"—she feigned dismay—"I thought I'd be riding with you."

"Minx." He chuckled delightedly. "Eat up. We need to get going while the weather is smiling on us.

Lily finished her tea and stood up. "I'll just run upstairs and put on my habit." She would have ridden out in the rain, the wind and the cold. Anything was better than having to read letters.

The tour took all day. Lord Galbraith was clearly as proud as Punch of his estate, but it wasn't long before Lily realized his true purpose was to show her off to the people of the estate, his tenants.

At every small cottage or hamlet, and for every person they came across, he would stop and introduce her. "Lily my dear, this is Mr. Tarrant"—or Norton or Bellamy or Weston or Toomer or Cole—"who's one of my tenant farmers. Tarrant, this is my boy's charming bride, the future Lady Galbraith." His pride and open delight in her was visible. And very touching.

What invariably followed was an eager inquiry—some delicate, others blunt—about Edward's whereabouts and, when it was clear he was not expected, their disappointment was palpable.

Lord Galbraith would then ask about every member of the family, and at the end of each conversation Lily was usually given an invitation to drop in on "the wife" whenever she was passing, and exhorted to "send our regards to the young master."

Several times they were invited into a farmhouse or cottage to meet a wife where they would be urged to drink a glass of milk, or have some tea and a bit of cake or take some other refreshment.

Lily loved every moment of it. She loved learning about people, getting to know them, hearing their tales of this and that. The warmth of their welcome almost overwhelmed her, even though she was under no illusions as to why. She left each place with messages for "the young master" ring-ing in her ear, and her saddlebags crammed with small gifts—preserves, homemade cheese, biscuits, and several mysterious bunches of herbs she suspected were intended to help her to conceive.

As the day passed, her mystification grew. It was clear her husband was loved and greatly missed here; she could see it in the face of every person she met, in the warm inquiries after his health and well-being, in their clear delight at the news of his marriage and their occasionally embarrassingly specific hopes for children to follow.

So many people had said words to the effect of *Time the young master came home, where he belongs.*

She didn't understand it. When Edward had told her he was never going back to Shields, that he wouldn't take any income from the estate and that when his grandfather passed on he would hire a manager to run the place, she'd imagined that something dreadful had happened here, that his childhood had been ghastly, that he'd been brutally treated, or that he was resented or hated for some reason. Even that he'd fallen in love with some village maiden and had his heart broken.

Instead he was loved, and not only by his grandfather.

"Why is Edward so reluctant to come here?" she asked Lord Galbraith as they rode slowly home. The sun was setting over the western hills, a glorious display of red and gold and pink, gilding the rooftops of the gracious old house and giving the ancient gray stonework a rosy glow. How could Edward reject such a beautiful home?

"Oh, my dear, if only I knew," he said sorrowfully. "I've asked myself that question a hundred—a thousand—times over the years. I've tried and tried to get him to talk about it." He darted her a hopeful glance. "I don't suppose he's said anything to you?"

She shook her head. "No, only that he doesn't come here. Never why, though of course I've asked."

The old man sighed heavily.

"Did anything happen—anything bad, I mean—before he went away to join the army?"

"Nothing that I can discover. As far as I know he was—

the whole pack of them—were excited as boys—well, they *were* boys. Silly, heedless, careless, joyful boys, off to follow the drum."

"He didn't have a broken heart perhaps? Some girl who decided she preferred someone else?" Though she couldn't imagine any girl rejecting Edward.

"No, he wasn't much interested in girls at that age. That all came later."

"He didn't leave any enemies behind?"

The old man snorted. "You saw them today, girl—did it look as though any one of them had a bad word to say about my lad?"

"I thought they all loved him." There was a lump in her throat as she said it.

"They did. They do. We all do." There was a world of pain in the choked old voice.

The horses walked slowly on. In the sky, gold and scarlet faded to pink and gray. The trees filled with birds, all chattering madly as they prepared for the night. Lily pretended not to notice the tears in the old man's eyes.

OVER DINNER SHE PROMPTED THE OLD MAN TO TELL HER more tales of Edward's boyhood, and he happily regaled her with tales of his wild, merry, loving boy. It was not the Edward she knew.

"But you must have heard that story before," he said after finishing one tale.

She shook her head. "He never mentions the past at all. And if I bring it up—"

"You mean about the war?"

"No, not just the war. If I ask him anything about his past, he just gets this look in his eyes . . ."

"Like ice over a window, so you can't see in or out. And then he changes the subject and starts talking about some wholly inconsequential thing," Lord Galbraith finished for her.

"Exactly." At least she wasn't the only one that Edward

shut out. "Every time he does it, I feel . . ." She swallowed, unable to go on.

"Like a little piece of your heart has been cut away?" he suggested gently.

Unable to speak for the surge of emotion that had swamped her at his words, Lily nodded.

There was a long silence, broken only by the sound of the wind outside and the coals of the fire settling gently in the grate.

"You love that boy of mine, don't you?"

Her face crumpled as she whispered, "With all my heart."

"Does he know how you feel?"

She shook her head. "He doesn't want my love. He made it very clear before we were married."

"And since then?"

"He made it even clearer."

"Young idiot." After a moment the old man tapped his fingers decisively on the table. "I'm not so sure. I think he's fonder of you than you realize. Let me show you some of those letters I mentioned before."

It was the last thing she wanted. Lily thought briefly about claiming to be tired after the long day, but it would only put off the moment. The old man was determined to show them to her. She might as well get it over with.

Again they retreated to the library; it was clearly Lord Galbraith's favorite room in the house. Something of an irony in that, Lily thought. A room filled from floor to ceiling with books.

He seated her close to the fire, poured her a glass of some pinky-gold liquid and set it on a table at her elbow. Then he brought out a large wooden inlaid box. "Now"— he shuffled through the stack of letters inside—"ah, here it is. The first letter he wrote from your honeymoon—or would you rather read some of his wartime ones first? I promise you, they're very sparse and uninformative."

She shook her head. "It doesn't matter." And that was the truth. Feeling in need of a little liquid courage, she took a large sip from the glass he'd given her and choked. "Wh—what is that?"

"Eh? Oh, peach brandy. Gift from a tenant. Don't you like it? I can get you something else."

"No, it's just—I didn't expect it to be so . . ."

"Sweet? Yes, horrible, but ladies usually like sweet drinks. Can I get you something else?" He hovered.

The word Lily had been thinking of was *strong*, but she didn't say so. "No, it's fine, thank you. I was just surprised." Now that it was down, it left a lovely warm feeling in the pit of her stomach.

"Good. Now, here's the first letter." He handed it to her and sat back, watching her eagerly. "See what he says about you?"

Lily unfolded the letter and pretended to read it.

"What do you think about that, eh?" he asked when, after what she judged would be a suitable interval, she handed it back.

"Very nice."

He blinked and the eager look faded. "Try this one." He passed her another, and sat there watching her as again she pretended to read it.

The fire crackled and hissed gently in the hearth. The silence of the great walls of books pressed heavily on her. Her throat burned from the drink she'd just swallowed; it threatened to come back up.

It was always unbearable when she tried to read, especially with someone watching, but this was somehow worse. Deceiving this dear old man after the lovely day they'd just had.

Just tell him. Confess. Get it over with. But she couldn't.

"Very interesting." She refolded the letter and handed it back, hating herself for being such a coward.

He didn't comment, just handed her another, saying, "You'll like this one."

She wanted to throw it in the fire. Smiling, she unfolded it and stared blindly at the unintelligible writing for as long as she could bear it.

She passed it back to him and said, "Lord Galbraith, I

think I'd like to retire now. I have a headache starting, and—"

"You didn't read a single one of those letters, did you?"

The silence in the room stretched. Lily said nothing. She
simply hung her head, drowning in waves of shame.

"You can't read, can you?"

She forced herself to admit it. "No," she whispered.

"There, there, girlie, no need to cry."

Was she crying? She hadn't noticed. She took the handkerchief he pressed into her hand and scrubbed at her face,
wanting to run, to hide, to just disappear.

"Does Ned know?"

She shook her head.

"Don't look like that, my dear—there are worse things
in life than not being able to read. I take it it's not a problem
with your eyes—" He broke off disgusted. "Well, of course
it's not your eyes—been out with you all day, haven't I?
Eyes like a hawk. Pretty too."

Lily forced herself to speak. "I suppose you think I'm
lazy, or stupid—"

"I think nothing of the kind!" The old man harrumphed.
"Clever little thing you are—observant, and with intelli-
gent things to say. And not a lazy bone in your body—saw
that when I dragged you all over the estate today, making
you talk to dashed near every person on it. And did you for
one minute let on how tired or bored you were—?"

"Oh, but I wasn't, I—"

"No, you straightened your spine and sat through it all
smiling, didn't you? Every slow-top on the estate jawing
your ear off with trivial rubbish, but did you show it?" He
snorted. "You're no shirker, my girl. Proud to have you in
the family. Ned couldn't have made a better choice."

At that, Lily's tears flowed afresh.

"Now, now, don't take on. It's nothing to cry over. Perfectly sure you've done your damnedest—forgive my language, my dear—done your best to learn, and if you can't,
well it's some dashed fault in the Creator, that's all it is.
One of God's mysteries and not for us to question it. Look
at me."

Surprised, she did, dabbing at her eyes.

"Can't for the life of me tell the difference between red socks and green ones—between red and green anything. Both colors look the same to me. But"—he flung up his hands in a gesture of cheery hopelessness—"does it matter? No, it does not."

"There's a big difference between not being able to read and not being able to distinguish red socks from green," she objected.

"Pooh! Ask me—ask anyone!—if they'd rather have a scholarly girl in the family or one with a warm and loving heart, and you *know* what they'll all choose. I know what matters to me, and it's not a piffling thing like reading."

She choked on a half laugh. "Says the man who owns the biggest library I've ever seen."

"Don't suppose you've seen many. Why would you want to? Yes, I like books; other people like cats. Who's to say who's right? The important thing to me right now is that you're going to make me very happy."

Lily looked up at him through tear-blurred eyes. "How?" It came out on a wobble.

"Two reasons." He ticked them off on his fingers as he spoke. "First, you're going to make my grandson very happy. Second, you're going to make me a great-grandfather."

"How do you know?" All these expectations. Lily was fed up with them, fed up with living with the likelihood of failure always looming. "I was forced on your grandson and he's still getting used to it. I don't think he's very happy. I can't really tell."

"If he's not, he's a fool, and my grandson is no fool."

Lily left that one untouched. "As for making you a great-grandfather, what if I don't have babies? My only two aunts are barren—well, one of them never married so I suppose she doesn't count—and anyway, people die in childbirth all the time."

He chuckled. "Cheery little creature, aren't you? Shall I order my blacks now?"

She gave a half laugh, half sob.

"That's better." He refilled her glass. "Now, sit back,

drink up, and I'll read some of my grandson's letters to you. I think you'll find them enlightening." He pulled out a letter and read, "'Lily made me laugh today. Such a clever observer of people, but she hasn't a nasty bone in her body. Some of the fine ladies of the ton could take lessons from her.'"

Did Edward really think that of her? She couldn't help but smile.

"And here, where he says this: 'Every day in some small way, my wife surprises and delights me.'"

Lily felt herself blushing with pleasure. Or perhaps it was the peach brandy.

He pulled out another letter and read, "'We ride out together most mornings. Lily is a first-rate horsewoman, as you observed—' Ah yes, this is the one about when you fell off your horse."

"When it refused a jump," Lily corrected him.

He chuckled. "Indeed, and that's just what he said. But this is the bit that'll interest you—he wrote it later that evening, after you were asleep. 'I thought I'd lost her, Grandfather, she was so still and pale. My heart simply stopped. Then when she finally moved—words cannot express what I felt then. In such a short time, my wife has become so dear to me.'"

Lord Galbraith refolded the letter and put it aside saying, "There you are, my dear. If that boy isn't in l— Oh, good grief, you're not crying again, are you? If ever I've seen such a girl for waterworks."

But the old man was smiling as he passed her his handkerchief again. "Take no notice of me, dear girl, you just have a good cry, let it all out and you'll feel better for it." He cleared his throat. "Learned that from my dear wife. Cried for all kinds of incomprehensible reasons. Wonderful woman." After a long pause he added softly, "You'd have loved her, Lily. More to the point, she'd have loved you. As do I."

Lily managed a misty smile.

Chapter Twenty

Happy the man whose wish and
care a few paternal acres bound,
content to breathe his native air in his own ground.
—ALEXANDER POPE, "ODE ON SOLITUDE"

OVER THE NEXT WEEK, LORD GALBRAITH TOOK LILY ALL
over the estate and the surrounding area. She met everyone,
from tenants to the leading members of local society. She
was entertained by stories of the Galbraith family, the tales
of Ralf de Corbeau who built the original manor in the
thirteenth century and how Nicholas Galbraith came south
from Scotland in the sixteenth century to marry a de Corbeau lass, the last of her line.

The portrait gallery was full of their pictures, these men
and women whose blood had slowly distilled down the ages
to the old man beside her and the young one whom her
heart craved.

Lord Galbraith, who turned out to have something of a
mischievous nature—or perhaps it was just kindness—
took pleasure in pointing out the many ancestors who
couldn't, in fact *refused* to learn to read, deeming it a rub-
bishy skill needed only by clerks and clergy, unimportant
people like that.

His scurrilous tales made her laugh and laugh, but entertaining and charming as the old man was, Lily was missing her husband. She wanted to hear these old family
stories from him—she was sure he would know them. She
wanted to learn about the estate from him, to have him in-

troduce her to former playmates and show her his secret boyhood places.

Everywhere she went there were reminders of the boy he had been, and people were eager to tell her about the boy they remembered—and missed.

The more she learned about him, the harder it was to reconcile the mischievous, merry, adventurous boy everyone talked about with the reserved man who was kind and careful and kept himself to himself. Except in bed.

How could a man who wrote so regularly to his grandfather—warm and entertaining letters too—how could he stay away for so long, when he must know, surely, that his grandfather desperately missed him? How could he refuse to come home? It would break his grandfather's heart if he ever learned of Edward's plan to hire a manager. In the short time she'd known him, Lily had grown to love the old gentleman. And she ached for the loneliness he so gallantly tried to hide. She understood it only too well.

"It's a letter from Ned." Lord Galbraith came to breakfast, waving it. "Eat while I read it to you." He broke open the seal and glanced at the letter, then frowned. "It's very short." He scanned quickly. "He's very worried about you, Lily. Frantic, in fact."

"Me? Why?"

"He says he's lost you—suspects you might have been kidnapped again."

"But I told him—" She broke off, her hand going to her mouth. "I told him I was going to Aunt Dottie's."

Lord Galbraith nodded. "He said he'd been to Bath—"

"Bath? But he was going to Southampton."

"Well, I don't know why he changed his plans, but he went to Bath. He says your aunt told him she'd sent you back to London. But when he returned to London, you weren't there, and nobody knew where you were."

Lily pushed her eggs away, her appetite gone. "Oh, dear, I hadn't planned to stay so long. I thought I'd come for just a few days and be back in London before him." She put her napkin aside and rose. "I'll go and pack at once. Can you send a message to my coachman that we leave for London immediately?"

"No."

Lily paused, and turned. There was a strange, almost arrested look on his face. "What do you mean, 'no'? You said Edward was worried. I must—"

"I wrote to him a couple of days ago, told him you were with me, said how much I was enjoying your visit. He'll have that letter by now. Sit down and finish your eggs."

She sat reluctantly, as much for good manners as anything else. "Very well, but I must leave as soon as possible."

"No. I want you to stay here. Please." There was a peculiar intensity in the old man's expression.

"But I can't. This was only meant to be a short vis—"

"I've been trying for more than ten years to get that boy to come here." He picked up the letter and showed it to her. "Look at that writing, all loops and scrawls—an absolute disgrace of a hand."

"I don't understand."

He looked up, his eyes gleaming. "His writing is normally neat, precise, every *i* dotted and every *t* crossed. This is the worst scrawl I've seen from him since he first picked up a pen." He laughed. "Don't you see, girl, he's half out of his mind with worry."

"About me? But that's terrible."

"No, it's wonderful." He poured himself another coffee and explained. "For years that boy has been writing to me, and oh, the letters are entertaining enough, but there's never any, any *feeling* in them. Nothing ever worries him, nothing excites him; he's never frightened or angry or delirious with joy. Have some toast." He pushed the toast rack toward her. Lily had not the slightest interest in toast.

"Ned went through years of war, and all he could write about was socks, or a tasty meal, or send an account of some foreign place that read like a damned guidebook. And we *know* that all the time he was risking his life like a madman, courting danger at every turn. Remember what his commanding officer told me? That Ned *didn't much care whether he lived or died.*

"And then came that letter about you falling off your horse, and now"—he patted the letter happily—"now he's half off his head with worry—about you."

"I don't understand," Lily said. "Are you happy because he's worried?"

"I'm happy because he's feeling *something* at last." He reached out and took her hand. "So I want you to stay here. As bait."

"Bait?"

"I haven't been able to get the boy to come home, not for years, but I have a feeling he might come for you. I hope so anyway. I believe he cares for you more than you realize—more than the young fool himself realizes." His faded old eyes gleamed with hope. "He'll only realize he loves you if he's provoked out of this, this slough of despond he's been in for years, where nothing touches him. Because he won't let it."

How often had Lily thought the same, that Edward didn't want to feel?

He sat back and gave her a challenging look. "Well, girl, don't you want to find out?"

Oh, but she did. "But what if he doesn't come?"

He spread his hands in a helpless gesture. "Then we're no worse off, are we?"

Lily bit her lip. It was one thing to live in hope that her husband might care for her, might even love her one day, but quite another to have those hopes shattered.

Still, she needed to know, one way or the other. She ached to know.

Lord Galbraith must have seen something in her eyes, for he leaned forward with a hopeful expression. "I'll write to Ned at once, tell him he must come here to collect you, that I won't let you leave otherwise."

"I'm not so spineless," Lily objected. "If I wanted to leave, I would."

"If he's angry at being forced to come here, he'll blame me, not you. Better to blame me, I think." He patted her hand. "So will you do it, my dear? For an old man?"

She swallowed. There was no choice, really. And wasn't it worth the risk? If there was the smallest hope of Edward loving her . . .

"Very well, I'll do it." For a young man as well as an old one. Whether he came because he loved her or to free her from his grandfather's custody, Lily believed with every instinct she owned that Edward needed to come home, to his grandfather, to Shields, and to the people who loved him.

Which included Lily, who loved him quite desperately.

THREE NIGHTS LATER EDWARD ARRIVED. IT WAS DUSK. Lily saw the hired carriage bowling down the drive and knew who it would be. She flew down the stairs and out the front door to greet him.

He looked tired and scruffy and unshaven—Edward was never scruffy. He leapt from the carriage, swept her into his arms and held her hard against him for an endless, shattering moment. His body was trembling.

As was hers. She'd never dreamed of such a greeting from her normally so controlled husband. She clung to him fiercely, not wanting the moment to end.

Eventually he released her, letting her slide slowly down his body until her feet touched ground again. He cupped her face in his hands. His eyes, winter-green and glittering with emotion, bore into her. "Never, *never* do that to me again." And he kissed her, a long, hard, shattering, possessive kiss.

"I thought you were taken, lost to me, dead," he said. She could barely stand. He kissed her again. Kisses that were hard. Tender. Desperate. Kisses that wrenched her heart right out of her body.

"I'm so sorry, Edward, I didn't mean to—"

But she couldn't finish because he pulled her hard against him, as if he'd never let her go. "Why," he murmured against her skin. "Why flee? And why here, of all places?"

"I wasn't fleeing." She planted kisses wherever she could

reach him. "It was just, there was chicken pox at Aunt Dottie's . . . and I didn't want to go back to London, not if you weren't there."

He kissed her again, and when she had breath to go on, she added, "And I wanted to see the place where you grew up. And since your grandfather had invited me—"

He stiffened, and Lily realized he was looking over her shoulder. She glanced back. Lord Galbraith stood at the top of the steps leading to the house. "You!" Edward's voice grated. "You had to trick her into coming here—"

"No!" She pulled on his arm to get his attention. "Don't blame your grandfather. He had no idea I was coming. It was an impulse on my part. Please don't be angry with him."

Edward gave her a long glance, then nodded wearily. He walked toward the old man, his expression stony. "Grandfather," he said tersely, and held out his hand.

Lord Galbraith ignored it. Half blind with tears, the old man embraced his grandson. "My boy, my dear, dear boy, you've come home at last." His voice was choked.

Edward stood stiffly in his embrace, his eyes blank and shuttered as if the contact were somehow painful. Enduring it. He said nothing, but his throat was working.

Lily's eyes filled.

After a moment, Edward gently released himself from the old man's embrace and stepped back. Lord Galbraith pulled out a large white handkerchief and blew into it loudly. "Well, come in, come in, no need to stand about in the wind," he muttered.

Lily started toward the house, but Edward caught her hand and stopped her. "We'll be in in a minute, Grandfather."

Lord Galbraith's gaze dropped to where their hands were joined. "I'm sure you two have a lot to talk about, but Lily's not dressed for the outdoors." He turned and stumped away. Edward glanced at Lily's dress and followed.

He led her to the library—it would always be the library for Galbraith men, she realized glumly. Once inside, he drew her close.

"I was beside myself with worry—why didn't you write

or leave a note? I can't tell you how I felt—" He broke off, his gaze somber. "Yes. I can. I've been a coward for so long—"

"You're not a coward."

"I am." He took a deep breath. "I love you, Lily. I think I loved you from the first, only I was too cowardly to admit it."

"No." Lily pressed her hands against his chest and stepped back. It was time. She was done with evasions and pretense. "Don't say any more. First I need to tell you something, a terrible secret I've been keeping from you all this time."

He paled. His grip tightened. "What? What is it?"

She held him off. "I didn't write to you"—she swallowed—"because . . . because . . ." She closed her eyes, unable to face the intensity of his gaze, and forced the words out in a rush. "I didn't write to you because I can't write. Or read. It's some defect in me, nobody knows why. I just can't."

She waited. The silence stretched. She could feel his heart beating under her palms.

The waiting was unbearable. She opened her eyes a crack.

"And?" he said.

She opened her eyes all the way. "And what?"

"The terrible thing?"

"That's it."

He stared down at her. "You're not ill, or dying?"

"No."

He pulled her hard against him. "Thank God! I thought it was something terrible. That there was something really wrong with you."

"There is. Don't you understand? I can't read or write."

He finally seemed to take it in. He frowned. "You can't read or write?"

"No." She felt like an egg about to be smashed, all smooth, brittle shell outside, a mess of yolk and white within.

"Not a word?"

"Not a w-word." Her voice trembled as she said it.

"Why didn't you tell me?"

"Why do you think, you silly young chub?" His grandfather stood in the doorway. His voice was gruff. "Think what she must have been through all these years, what people have said to her—think of the number of fools there are in this world and then try not to add yourself to their number."

Edward's arm tightened around her, but there was a smile in his voice when he said, "I don't need you or anyone to tell me what to think of my wife, Grandfather. She's a treasure." He turned to her, his voice deepening. "She's *my* treasure, whose value to me is above rubies and pearls— and letters."

Lily's sight blurred at the tender sincerity in his voice.

He cupped her face in his hands. "You stopped me from saying this before, so I'll say it now. I love you, Lily Rutherford Galbraith, with all my heart. It doesn't matter to me what you can or can't do. Don't ever think it does. Whatever life throws at us, we'll manage it together." It was a vow, and Edward Galbraith never broke his vows.

"Oh, Edward."

The old man beamed. "She's a grand girl, Ned, you couldn't have done better."

"I know it. Now, Grandfather, are you going to give me a drink or not?"

LILY SAT BESIDE HER HUSBAND ON THE LEATHER SOFA, HIS arm around her, her head on his shoulder as he and his grandfather talked. She wasn't really listening. Her heart and mind were too full.

He loved her. Edward Galbraith loved her. He'd said it, and he'd demonstrated it. He loved her despite her flaws.

She couldn't quite believe it; her dream had come true. But . . . she realized slowly, something wasn't quite right. She was practically boneless with relief and happiness, but although Edward was acting relaxed, his muscles were still tense and hard.

Underneath the nonchalant attitude, he was wound up as tight as a spring.

The door opened and she felt him stiffen. A servant entered with a tray of refreshments and after a swift glance at the man's face, he ignored him.

The same thing happened when they went upstairs to wash before dinner. Lord Galbraith had sent a man to attend his grandson. Edward had objected, but his grandfather waved the objections off.

Edward went upstairs, wary as a feral cat. But when he saw the manservant, the tension left him. It was the same at dinner. Each new servant who appeared received a hard, appraising glance, then her husband relaxed.

He seemed almost frightened, but surely that couldn't be right.

SHE TACKLED HIM ABOUT IT THAT NIGHT, AFTER THEY'D retreated to her bedroom. He was prowling back and forth. If he'd been a cat he'd be lashing his tail.

"You're imagining things. What on earth would I be frightened of, here in my grandfather's house?"

"Then what is the problem?"

"Nothing. It's just this place. I don't want to be here. I can't stand it."

"But why? I don't understand."

He made an impatient gesture. "It doesn't matter."

"It does matter, Edward, can't you see—?"

"I *said*, it doesn't matter." It wasn't like him to snap. He sighed. "I'm sorry. Let's not quarrel. Come to bed. First thing in the morning we leave this place and I take you home."

No, they wouldn't, Lily thought, but she wasn't going to argue. She hadn't had her husband in bed with her for ages, and he'd told her today that he loved her. She wasn't going to spoil things by arguing. Tomorrow would be soon enough for that.

Tonight she had things to say for herself. She dropped her wrapper on a chair. She was naked underneath. She slipped into bed.

"I didn't tell you this afternoon," she began. "I didn't get time."

In the process of ripping off his clothes, he froze. "What? Another secret?"

She nodded. "I love you too. I think it started when—oof!"

He lay on top of her, naked, his eyes glittering in the lamplight. "What did you say?"

She wound her arms around him. "Only that I love you, Edward Galbraith, with all my heart and soul and body."

His heat soaked into her and he kissed her like a man starved. "You waited all this time to tell me? God, but I've missed you." His fingers slid between her thighs, and finding her slick and hot and more than ready, he plunged into her, taking her fast and hard, driving into her with a smooth, relentless rhythm that built rapidly into a crescendo of such power that she shot straight over the top. She screamed and spasmed around him and he let out a triumphant shout as they shattered together.

Afterward, murmuring soft words of love, he lavished kisses all over her body. "Tell me again."

"I love you."

Between kisses they talked, but soon the caresses grew more and more feverish and they made love again. And again she shattered into a million pieces.

She waited then, for him to slip out of the bed—there were plenty of beds here, and he'd been given his own room, adjoining hers. But he made no move to leave her. Cautiously, not wanting to disturb him, she snuggled up against him, cuddling up against his chest. He grunted, half asleep, and wrapped a hard arm around her waist, pulling her closer, curving his body possessively around her as his breathing slowed and he slipped into heavy, exhausted sleep.

Lily kissed him softly, breathing in the scent of his skin, and followed him into oblivion. They were home. He just didn't know it yet.

WHERE WAS LILY? NED HAD TOLD HER THEY WERE LEAVing immediately after breakfast. It was almost ten, and where was she? He'd looked in her bedchamber and found a maidservant making up the bed—not anyone he recognized, and she didn't seem to know him, thank God. "Leave that and pack Mrs. Galbraith's things," he told her.

He couldn't wait to get away. There was an itch between his shoulder blades, as if everywhere he went there were snipers lurking in the shadows. He needed to grab Lily and go. But where the hell was she?

He found her, of all places, in the kitchen, packing food into a large wicker basket. "What are you doing here?" he said irritably.

"Packing food into a basket."

"I can see that." He supposed it was common sense to take food for the journey. "Hurry along, then, will you? Walton will be bringing the coach around in a few minutes. I told a maid to pack your things."

"There was no need." She continued flitting around the kitchen, collecting things for the wretched basket. She picked up a large jar of pickled onions and put it in the basket.

"There was every need. You hadn't even started packing. I don't like pickled onions, by the way."

She gave him a quick smile. "I know. There's plenty of time for me to pack." She didn't remove the jar of onions.

"There isn't. I told you last night that we would leave first thing this morning."

"Yes, you did." She wrapped two large wedges of cheese and added them to the basket. "You didn't ask me whether it suited me or not."

Whether it suited her or not? Blasted female pride. He mustn't order, he must *ask*. "If it suits you, my dear, I wish to leave this morning." His voice dripped with ironic courtesy. She was driving him wild, and not the way she had in bed last night.

It was this blasted place. He needed to get away.

"I know"—she gave him a blithe smile—"but I'm not ready to leave yet."

He blinked at her in stupefaction. "You're not ready to leave?" The itch between his shoulder blades deepened.

"No, not yet." She folded a cloth and tucked it over the contents of the basket. "There's a ruined abbey with a mineral spring—well, of course you must know of it. Twice now your grandfather and I planned to visit it, but our plans had to be canceled. I want to see it before I leave."

"Well, you can't!" he snapped. "We're leaving in fifteen minutes. If you're not in the carriage I'll leave without you." It was a bluff. He wasn't going anywhere without her. He'd missed her damnably in the past few weeks and then, when he thought she'd been taken . . . the nameless terror he'd felt . . .

He wasn't going to let her out of his sight.

She didn't turn a hair. "Very well, my dear, you go ahead. I'm going to visit the ruined abbey. It's a lovely day—really, we have been blessed with the weather, but it cannot last."

"I don't care about the weather," he began in exasperation.

"No, but a picnic is so much more comfortable when it's fine. The local women tell me the water from the spring is sure to guarantee an heir." She gave him a bland, sweet smile. "You can come with me. If we both drink it, we will surely double our chances."

He glared at her in baffled outrage. Where was the demure and obedient little creature he'd married, so eager to please? Was this what happened when you told a woman you loved her?

Didn't she realize he *had* to get away?

"No, dammit, I'm not going anywhere except back to London—today—and you're coming with me."

"Take this, will you?" She handed him the covered basket. "And this. It's sunny at the moment, but it might get chilly later." She draped a cloak over his arm.

"Lily, did you not hear me? I—"

But she'd whisked herself out the kitchen door and was gone. He followed her into the yard, where a horse stood patiently harnessed to a light gig—and stopped.

A groom stood holding the reins. Another waited to help Lily climb into the gig. They both gave him curious glances. They must know who he was. Word spread fast in a place like this. His skin prickled, but he didn't recognize either of them. They were both very young. The knots in his stomach eased.

"Pass me the basket, will you, Edward, please?"

He passed her the basket and the cloak and stood fuming quietly while she stowed everything carefully away. "There's no need for you to come with me after all, Bobby," she told the youngest groom. "My husband will escort me today." She smiled tranquilly down at him.

The grooms waited expectantly. The first one offered him the reins. The young one hesitated, then stepped forward as if maybe Ned was too old to climb into a damned gig without assistance.

Swearing silently and savagely Ned climbed into the gig, accepted the reins and drove out of the yard. The itch between his shoulder blades burned like acid.

Chapter Twenty-one

❧

"And in the lowest deep a lower deep
still threatening to devour me opens wide."
—JOHN MILTON

THEY TROTTED BRISKLY ALONG, SAYING NOTHING. SHE must know he was furious. Right now, though, he was feeling more sick than furious. It was like going into battle— worse. He knew what he was facing in battle. The knots in his stomach tightened.

They came to a fork in the lane. "Turn left here," she said.

He ignored her. "The ruins are to the right."

"Yes, but I need to drop a few things off on the way." She reached across and pulled on the reins and the horse turned left.

"What the—" He swallowed, forcing himself to calm. "Where are you dropping these things?" He knew, he damned well knew. He knew every house, every cottage on the estate, and he knew exactly where they were going.

He wanted to leap out of the gig and flee into the forest, his sanctuary of old.

But that was haunted too.

"Just Mrs. Prewett, and old Mr. Iles. I promised them both some of our home cheese from the Shields dairy. Old Mr. Iles told me how much he loves cheese with pickled onions. His daughter won't pickle onions for him, says it's too much trouble and she doesn't like the smell." She gave him a mischievous smile. "See, the pickled onions weren't for either of us."

He swallowed. She had no idea what she'd done.

Prewett. Could she have chosen anyone worse? And *Iles*. His mouth was dry, his throat constricted. The horse trotted inexorably on.

They turned a corner and he let out the breath he'd been holding as the first cottage came into view, stone, slate-roofed, smaller than he remembered. The garden was neat as a pin. Mrs. Prewett always did love her garden.

"Why are we stopping?" Lily asked. "The cottage is over there."

Fifty yards away and he couldn't go an inch closer. He hadn't even realized he'd tightened the reins. His breathing came raggedly, rapid and shallow. "You go. I, I'll go for a bit of a walk."

"What is it, Edward? You've gone very pale. Are you ill?"

His every instinct screamed at him to run. But it was too late. He could only wait, frozen and hollow, a butterfly staked on a pin, as fate in the shape of Mr. and Mrs. Prewitt opened the cottage gate and with loud cries came running toward him.

Mr. Prewitt reached the gig first. "Master Ned, you've come back at last. Welcome home, lad—oh, mustn't call you that now. Look at how tall and fine you've grown."

Like an automaton, Ned climbed down from the gig and held out a stiff hand. Mr. Prewitt wrung it, saying, "Come inside the house, let me look at you. Such a fine, tall man you've become, the image of his grandfather, isn't he, Martha?" He pressed his lips together. "It's that good to see you, lad. I never thought—" His voice broke. He pulled out a large handkerchief and blew into it noisily.

Mrs. Prewitt made no attempt to hide her emotions. Her face streaming with tears, she hugged him as if he were still a boy and, accepting no excuses, propelled him into the front parlor, saying, "I didn't bake my spiced currant biscuits this morning for nothing, my lad—his favorites, they are, Mrs. Galbraith. The minute I heard you were back, I knew you'd come to us."

She wiped tears away with her apron. "Never a day when he wasn't in and out of my kitchen, Mrs. Galbraith.

Him and our Luke. Like twins, they were, always up to mischief." She hurried off to the kitchen to make tea.

Ned sat stiffly. He'd hardly ever been in this room. It was for visitors, and he'd never been a visitor in this house. He and Luke . . . it was always the kitchen, and then away to the forest.

"So it's all London for you now, is it, Ned, lad? Country living lost its appeal?"

"Edward." Lily nudged him.

He blinked.

"Mr. Prewitt thinks you're bored with the country now."

"No." His voice sounded rusty. He cleared his throat. "It's just . . . I've been . . . busy." It was the least convincing lie Lily had ever heard.

Mrs. Prewitt entered carrying the tea tray and banished the awkward silence with the pouring of tea and the offering of biscuits. Lily brought out the cheese, and Mrs. Prewitt exclaimed over it with pleasure.

Edward drank his tea and ate a biscuit. Lily and Mrs. Prewitt talked about the ingredients, Mrs. Prewitt assuming Lily would want to bake them for her husband.

He sat there like a stranger, gray-faced and stiff, as if he were the stranger here, not Lily.

The Prewitts related stories of Edward and their boy, Luke, who'd been killed in the war, recalling boyhood adventures, and laughing over the mischief the two boys had gotten up to. "Right terrors, they were," Mr. Prewitt said proudly.

It was because Edward was here, Lily knew. They'd never mentioned their son before. But it was all for Edward, she saw; their eyes kept flickering back to him with every tale.

Edward sat like a statue, still and grave and stiff and cold.

The tea was finished, the biscuits eaten, and a short silence fell. Lily prepared to take her leave, but Mr. Prewitt reached out suddenly and placed a hand on Edward's knee. Edward jumped as if stung.

"That letter you wrote us."

Edward swallowed convulsively and met Mr. Prewitt's gaze. "Yes?" he croaked.

"It was such a comfort, knowing you were with our boy when he died." He took a deep, shaky breath. "And to know that he died bravely—a hero, you said—"

"And that he didn't suffer," Mrs. Prewitt added.

A quiver passed across Edward's face. His jaw tightened. He didn't speak.

Wiping tears away with the corner of her apron, Mrs. Prewitt rose and handed her husband a carved box. "Read it, Prewitt. Mrs. Galbraith should learn the kind of man her husband is."

Mr. Prewitt unfolded the letter. It was paper thin, worn and faded from many rereadings. As Mr. Prewitt began to read, Lily glanced at her husband. His face was stark and he stared at the floor. A nerve twitched in his jaw, almost the only evidence that he was alive.

The letter described how Luke had been killed, shot through the heart saving a fellow soldier. He died a hero. The whole regiment had mourned him, and when they buried him the buglers had played a tribute as the sun had set over his grave. And Ned had lost the best friend he ever had.

The letter was warm and deeply personal and gave comfort, even as it broke unimaginably painful news. By the time Mr. Prewitt finished, they were all damp-eyed, except for the author of the letter, Lily's husband, who sat grave and silent, dry-eyed and stiff.

Afterward there was a long silence. Then he stood abruptly. "I have to go." He stalked from the cottage, leaving Lily to say the good-byes.

"Don't fret, my dear," Mrs. Prewitt said comfortably. "Took it hard, he did. Always has. Expects more of himself than is humanly possible."

Lily nodded. She was starting to see that. "Thank you."

The Prewitts showed her out. Edward was sitting like a ghost in the gig. "You have a good man there, missus."

"I know."

Mrs. Prewitt pressed a wrapped bundle of Edward's favorite biscuits into her hands. "Take good care of him."

Lily gave her a misty smile. "I will."

* * *

"ILES NEXT, IS IT?" HE SAID AFTER A FEW MOMENTS. HIS voice was shaking.

Lily had a thousand questions, but she could see that her husband was in no state to answer them. He was hanging on by a thread.

Mr. Iles came hurrying out of his cottage before the gig had even stopped. His face worked wordlessly as he wrung Edward's hand and drew him inside. His daughter had clearly been primed; the kettle was already singing on the hob and slices of fruitcake and some little tarts set out on the table.

"Never thought I'd see you again, my boy," the old man said in a strangled voice. "Waited and waited for you to come home, I did . . . Your granfer too, I'll be bound." His eyes devoured Edward. "Silly to say you've growed— course you have—but it's our Seth I'm thinkin' of now. He'd be just under your height, I reckon, but a bit broader in the shoulders—well, we Ileses have always had strong backs. Woodchoppers, we are, Mrs. Galbraith," he added to Lily. "Always have been, always will be."

He gazed again at Edward, his eyes blurry with unshed tears. "He was a fine boy, wasn't he, our Seth?"

"The finest," Edward croaked. Tea arrived and he buried his nose in the cup.

Lily took charge of the conversation, encouraging Mr. Iles to talk about his son, all the mischief he and young Ned and the Prewitt lad and the rest had wrought on the people of the estate. "Proper young divils they were, and your lad the leader." The old man chuckled.

Lily felt rather than saw Edward wince.

"Never minded nobody. Ah, but they were fine lads all the same. I miss him, you know, more than you'd think."

Edward swallowed.

"That letter of yourn," Mr. Iles continued. "Grand letter, it was. I get 'un to read it to me whenever I feel a bit low." He jerked his head at his daughter, who sat at the edge of the room saying nothing. "Can't read, me," he explained to Lily. "Never went to school."

She nodded.

"Read 'em a bit, Sukey," Mr. Iles said, and his daughter went to the mantelpiece and took down a battered piece of paper.

Edward made a strangled sound in his throat. Lily slipped her hand into his. He clung to it tightly, but his face didn't move.

Sukey read the letter. Mr. Iles moved his lips silently as she read; he knew Edward's letter by heart. Lily held on to her husband's hand, and tried not to cry as she heard how Seth had been killed, defending a widow and three little girls from a vicious pack of deserters. They'd buried him near their cottage. The little girls planted flowers on his grave.

When it was finished, Mr. Iles wiped his eyes. "Brings me a deal of comfort, that, knowing he died saving that woman and her girls. I wonder, sometimes, about the flowers those little girls planted over him. Do you remember what they—"

"Poppies," Edward said. "Poppies. Red poppies."

"Ah, that's grand, then. Seth always did like a bit of color. Sukey, what say we plant a few poppies out the front there? For our Seth."

"Whatever you say, Dad."

Lily gave Mr. Iles the cheese and pickled onions, with the compliments of Shields, and they took their leave. They turned the gig around and were heading to the abbey—Lily was glad now she'd put a bottle of wine in the picnic basket—when Edward groaned.

A couple was standing at the divide in the road, obviously waiting. Edward pulled the horse to a halt and got down. "Mr. and Mrs. Bryant." He shook hands with Mr. Bryant and suffered himself to be hugged by Mrs. Bryant. His face was ash pale, grim but resigned.

"Heard you were home but weren't sure how long you were stayin'," Mr. Bryant said. "The missus here said you'd be sure to call on the Prewitts and she were right, as usual."

He glanced fondly at his wife, who hadn't spoken except to greet Edward.

She didn't say much, but she couldn't stop touching Edward, his arms, his shoulders, and once or twice his cheek, stroking him like a cat.

Like a long-lost son.

Lily waited in the gig, watching and listening. The conversation went much as the two previous, only this time it was about a boy called Peter. Another quick, honorable death, another tragic story, another memory to treasure.

Eventually, to Ned's relief, Mr. and Mrs. Bryant took their leave. "Now, don't be a stranger, lad. It does our hearts good to see you home again, so tall and hale, and with such a bonny sweet bride."

Thank God he'd had Lily with him today; he'd never have coped otherwise.

Though it was her fault he was here in the first place.

And it was a moot point whether he'd coped or not.

He settled himself in the gig and took up the reins. In a last farewell, Mr. Bryant reached up and laid a warm hand on Ned's arm. "Thanks again for taking such good care of our Peter—"

It was more than he could stand. "I didn't take care of him! I got him killed! I got them all killed." The words burst from him.

There was a short, shocked silence. The horse moved restlessly. Mr. Bryant's honest country face crinkled in distress. "Nay, lad, don't take on like that. You weren't responsible. T'was *war* that got our Peter killed—war that killed all those lads. You were just one of the lucky ones."

Lucky? Bitterness flooded him.

He said heavily, "It was my idea to join up, my fault they all came with me." He was their leader—he always had been, ever since he was Robin and they his merry men. His dead men.

They'd followed him to the grand adventure and they'd all been killed.

Bryant snorted. "If you think that, you've forgotten what it was like. You—all of you lads—were mad for adventure, mad for the army. I was the same at that age. Most lads can't wait to get a potshot at the enemy. They never think it might be them who gets shot."

"But if I hadn't taken them with me—"

"Whisht, lad, if not with you, some recruiting sergeant would have snapped them up—the country was thick with them back then. Mad to go, was our Peter, and no blame to anyone else."

His brown eyes were kind and compassionate, and he tapped Ned firmly on the knee. "You mind what I say now. You took care of our lads the best you could, and when the worst happened—" He broke off and cleared his throat. "To know you were with Peter when he died, and that it was quick and clean . . ."

Every word was a lash. "He was a good friend," Ned managed.

"Aye, and you were a good friend to him, to him and the other lads of the estate. I'm proud of my lad, and I'm proud of you—of all of them. Friends you were, from the time you could run, and friends you remained unto death."

Ned fought to keep his face from crumpling. *Breathe*, he told himself. *Don't fall apart.*

"Merrick Hird told us what you did for him and all the other lads."

Ned stiffened. "Merrick Hird? But he's dead."

Bryant chuckled. "Don't tell Merrick that. He'll be sore put out to hear it. Came home with one leg less, but he's alive and kicking still."

"Oh, God." He wanted to throw up. The last he'd seen of Merrick he was lying on the ground, on a makeshift stretcher in a welter of blood, nursing a bloody stump and swearing a blue streak. He knew then Merrick was done for. Men died like flies after the surgeon's knives.

"You go and see Merrick," Bryant recommended. "He'll be right glad to see you. He's living in the factor's cottage now."

"The factor's cottage?" he repeated incredulously. Wild Merrick Hird in the factor's cottage?

"Aye, a grand jest, ain't it? He's been your grandad's

factor for, oh, years now. Always was a clever lad, Merrick. Took losing a leg to make him slow down and start using his brain. Got a wife and kiddies and all. And a fine peg leg. You go along and see him." He patted Ned's knee again. "And don't you fret no more, you hear me, boy?"

Unable to say a word, Ned flicked the reins and they drove on. He drove until they reached the abbey, Lily silent beside him, still holding tight to his arm.

The abbey was set in a cool green clearing, a remnant of ancient, mossy stones that had witnessed miracles and violence over the ages and now was simply offering peace.

They sat in the gig, not moving. "Oh, God, Lily, oh, God." He pulled her against him, buried his face against her neck and just held her, shuddering and wretched until eventually it passed.

"Luke died in agony, both his legs shot off. Seth was gut-shot, the slowest, most horrible death you can think of. And Peter, Peter took two days to die. I lied, I lied to them all."

She stroked his cheek. "You gave them comfort."

"And it *was* my fault." And then he confessed, there in that ancient holy place, witnessed only by the birds and the wild things and his wife, his blessed, loving wife, he told her what he'd never told anyone, the guilt he'd carried for years.

He told her how in one of their first engagements, first their major, then the captain, then the lieutenant had been killed. "And so it was up to me, Lily—I was next in command. And it was—" He tried to describe it: the deafening boom of the cannons, the incessant rattle of gunfire, men and horses screaming, blood and sinew, smoke and confusion— they couldn't even see the enemy, but they could hear them yelling, closing in.

"I froze, Lily. I didn't know what to do. I just stood there in that hell on earth and . . . I froze."

"You were how old?"

"Eighteen, but what does that matter? I—"

"And how long did you freeze for?"

"I don't know. It seemed like forever."

"And then what happened?"

He stared at her. She was so calm. "We fought."

"You gave orders?"

"Yes."

"The men obeyed them?"

"Yes, of course."

"And who won?"

"It was just a battle."

"Did you win?"

"Our side did, yes. But the casualties were horrific."

She smoothed his hair back from his forehead. "You can't help that. You did your duty."

He jerked his head away from her. "You don't understand. I *froze*, Lily, and men *died* because of it! Because of me."

"Nonsense. I have to agree with Mr. Bryant. It was *war* that got those men killed. You were an inexperienced eighteen-year-old boy, thrust into a command you weren't ready for, and so what if you froze for a minute or two—anyone would. And do you honestly think that slight delay would have made any real difference?"

His jaw dropped.

She kissed him softly. "Mrs. Prewitt told me you've always expected more of yourself than is humanly possible, and I see now she was right. Think about it, my darling; imagine any other eighteen-year-old boy thrust into the situation you faced. I doubt one in a hundred would collect himself—"

"I *froze*!"

"—would collect himself after a few minutes and go on to give orders and win a battle."

"I didn't win—"

"Your side did. Don't quibble."

He stared at her and thought about what she'd said. It sounded so . . . reasonable when she said it. And yet for years he'd flayed himself with guilt, reliving those moments of sheer, frozen panic . . . Blaming himself for his friends'—and other men's—deaths. The nightmares had gone on for years.

Looking back now, eighteen seemed so young.

"You thought everyone here would blame you, didn't you? That's why you never came home."

He didn't answer.

"You thought that because you couldn't forgive yourself, nobody else could. Edward, my love, there is nothing *to* forgive. You did the best you could, and that's all that anyone can do." She let that sink in and added, "Those other boys made their own choices, and it's arrogance to blame yourself. I expect it's being the heir. Actually I think you did more than anyone could expect."

She kissed him again. "And if you didn't notice, my love, those people we met today, they were glad you survived, as if a part of their sons lives on in you, because of the childhood you shared with them. They love you, Edward, and so do I."

He sat stunned by the picture she had painted. And the gift she had given him. Forgiveness, hope, love. He began to breathe again.

She picked up the basket. "Now, help me down, and let's have this picnic. I want to explore the ruins and drink some of that water from the spring—and you're going to drink some too. Never mind about heirs, it's supposed to be very healing."

He jumped down and lifted her and the basket to the ground. Removing the basket from her grasp, he cupped her face in his hands and kissed her.

"Forgive me?" she said. "For making you stay?"

He kissed her again. "There is nothing to forgive." He took her hand and led her across the green sward to a place on the edge of the ruins where spring water bubbled up beneath a grotto of rough piled-up stones. It was a shrine. Moss and ferns grew in the cracks, and there were offerings of various kinds—fresh flowers, small clay objects, fruit—placed on an ancient slab of stone worn smooth by centuries of water.

He drew her against him. "This place is said to be the heart of Shields, the source of all our prosperity and our very well-being. It was here long before the Romans, was a place of worship for pagans long before the Christians built a church over it and, as you see, has survived long after Henry the Eighth destroyed the abbey. It's where the estate gets its name. Most people think it's named after the kind of shield used in war, but it's really this spring, which is supposed to shield its people from harm."

"It's a beautiful story, but I think there has been plenty of harm done to people here over the years."

"Perhaps, but we eventually bounce back."

"The spring is lovely, but, Edward, you are the heart of this estate. The people here and your grandfather need you."

"I know, I see that now. This place may be the heart of Shields, Lily, but you are my heart. The day I found you, running for your life, stinking of excrement—"

"Not excrement!"

"I'm sorry, but it was definitely excrement," he said firmly. "Don't interrupt, I'm making a romantic declaration here."

"Your idea of romantic declarations needs work."

"Then you will have to teach me." He gazed down into her eyes, shining and full of love and trust and compassion. How did he ever get so lucky as to find this woman, this beautiful loving, splendid woman? His voice was husky as he said, "I said it before, but I need to say it again. I love you, Lily Rutherford Galbraith, with all my heart and soul."

"And your body?"

"Definitely my body."

"Show me," she said.

And he did.

Chapter Twenty-two

❧

Forgiveness to the injured does belong,
For they ne'er pardon, who have done the wrong.
—JOHN DRYDEN

LILY AND EDWARD SPENT ANOTHER WEEK AT SHIELDS BEfore returning to London. They left, promising to return in a month when Lord Galbraith would give a grand ball to celebrate his grandson's marriage and long-awaited return to Shields.

Lily traveled curled up against her husband while he read aloud to her from a book his grandfather had selected for them. It was probably a very interesting book, but Lily's heart and mind were too full for her to concentrate. She let the deep rumble of his voice flow over her and thought about how her life had changed.

Her potential thimbleful of happiness was now a constantly flowing wellspring of joy. Edward loved her. He reminded her of it daily, in all kinds of delicious ways. He was incapable of doing anything halfheartedly, she was learning. He still expected more of himself than any man should, and she couldn't see that changing.

He still hadn't fully forgiven himself, nor could he quite believe that the parents of the friends who'd fallen in battle didn't hold him personally responsible. But he did accept that they cared for him and drew comfort from his visits, where they talked about their sons.

Such wounds as he'd carried, buried deep within him,

didn't heal overnight. But Lily had confidence that they would in time.

He'd gone to visit Merrick Hird one evening and ended up staying very late, drinking and talking. He crawled into bed with her in the wee small hours, reeking of beer and cigar smoke, and just held her. Not making love, just holding her as if she were something precious and necessary.

She'd slept in his arms all night.

He never told her what he and Merrick had talked about that night, and she didn't ask. She could see that something had eased within him, and that was enough.

How glad she was that he'd come to Shields. And that she'd made him stay. If she'd realized what was to come, she might not have had the courage. *Trust your own instincts*, Aunt Dottie had told her. *Listen only to your heart.*

If Aunt Dottie's maidservants hadn't come down with the chickenpox, Lily might never have gone to Shields. And if Edward hadn't . . .

"Edward, why did you go looking for me in Bath?"

He looked up from his book, half closing it with a finger in his place. "Because that's where you said you were going."

"Yes, but why go to Bath? You were going, I forget where, on business."

"Southampton, but he wasn't there, and then I got a message to say he'd been seen in Bath. So I went to Bath. Are you interested in this book or not?"

"Not. Who wasn't there?"

"Nixon."

She sat up and looked at him. "You were hunting Nixon? In Bath? What was he doing in Bath?"

Edward shrugged. "Sniffing around for an heiress, I presume, but by the time I got there, Nixon had already left. I gather he had no luck, for I didn't hear of any girl going missing." He set the book aside.

"No, keep reading it," she said.

"I thought you weren't interested in it."

"I'm not, but I love listening to your voice. You have a beautiful voice." And while he was reading she could watch him all she liked without either of them being self-conscious.

He snorted, but the tips of his ears turned red. He resumed reading to her.

Lily snuggled down again and pulled the rug around her. Life was good.

LILY CALLED IN AT ASHENDON HOUSE EARLY THE NEXT morning. On learning that Lady Rose and Lady Georgiana were still abed, she'd hurried straight upstairs, eager to see them.

Rose sat up in bed, frowning. "You look different. What has that man done to you?"

"Everything possible," Lily said with a giggle. "Oh, Rose, he *loves* me! You knew, of course, that I've been achingly in love with him for ages, and now—he loves me!" She twirled in a little pirouette and then plumped down on the bed.

"So you're happy, then, little sister?" Rose asked.

"You need to ask?" George said scornfully. "Just look at her. She's glowing. So come on, Lily, tell all. Marriage isn't horrible, I take it."

"It's blisssssful." Lily gave a big, happy sigh. "Now, hurry up, the builders say the house will be ready at two, and there's something I want to do before that. And I want you two to come with me."

"Galbraith too busy to escort you?"

"He doesn't know I'm doing it." Lily blushed. "You might think it's silly too, but it's important to me, and I want you with me. So hurry up and get dressed."

"WHY WESTMINSTER CATHEDRAL?" ROSE ASKED. IT WAS a fine morning, so they'd decided to walk. "St. George's is a lot closer."

"I don't think they do it there," Lily said.

"Do what? You still haven't explained what this is about."

"I want to light candles—like the Catholics do—for the boys who joined the army with Edward and were killed.

Don't look at me like that. I don't know why I want to do it; it just seems like a comforting sort of thing to do."

"Comforting for whom?"

"For them, those poor dead boys—to show that they're not forgotten—and for Edward, and perhaps, for me in a way too."

"But Galbraith won't know. Nor will the dead. The dead are dead."

"I told you you'd think it was silly. But I don't care, I want to do it. I don't know why we don't do it in our church—"

"Popish practice, can't be doing with it!" George said in a gruff, disapproving voice exactly like the vicar's, and they laughed.

"Here's Westminster Bridge. Nearly there now."

"Lily." Rose stopped abruptly. "Over there, isn't that Lavinia Fortescue-Brown?"

"Of the Surrey Fortescue-Browns?" Lily said laughingly. "In London? That girl! Has she run away from school again?"

"I think she might have." Rose was serious. She pointed to where a young girl stood with an older man, arguing.

"That's Nixon!" Lily hissed. "He's trying to abduct her." She ran toward them. George and Rose followed.

A traveling chaise rumbled over the cobbles and stopped next to Nixon and Lavinia. A door swung open, pushed from within. Nixon grabbed Lavinia and tried to shove her inside.

"Nixon! Don't you dare!" Lily screamed. "Stop! Abductor! Stop!"

Lavinia fought and kicked, screaming at the top of her lungs. Lily screamed too as she raced toward them.

Nixon kept trying to shove Lavinia into the carriage. Lily got there and whacked him over the head with her reticule. It was too light to do him much damage, but it distracted him enough to make him turn. "You!" he snarled.

"Release that girl!" She grabbed Lavinia's skirt.

"You interfering bitch!" Nixon swung her a backhander, but Lily saw it coming and ducked, still clinging to Lavinia's skirt.

With a loud yell George came flying through the air like a wild monkey, landing on top of Nixon, sending him sprawling on the cobblestones. She jumped up and kicked him, hard. He curled up in a ball, howling with pain and fury.

Rose grabbed the other half of Lavinia's skirt. "Pull, Lily!" They both pulled and suddenly Lavinia popped free, like a cork popping from a bottle. They fell back against the parapet of the bridge.

People, noticing the disturbance, were moving forward in curiosity and concern. The driver, seeing it, whipped the horses and the carriage rumbled away.

Lavinia, now safe, started weeping. Rose held her, murmuring reassurance. But where was Nixon? Lily spied him slinking into the crowd on Westminster Bridge. "Quick, he's getting away! Help! Someone stop that man! He's an evil child abductor!" she yelled. But nobody made a move.

A piercing whistle split the air, and in the sudden surprised silence, George yelled, at the top of her voice, "Ten quid for whoever brings me the man in the yellow waistcoat! That one there." She pointed.

At the chance of ten pounds, men emerged from the crowd: burly men, tattooed men, the kind of men nobody would want to meet on a public thoroughfare, let alone a dark alley. They prowled toward Nixon.

The crowd around him melted away until there was just Nixon, pressed against the parapet of Westminster Bridge, and a small group of hefty ruffians forming a ragged semicircle around him.

He produced a knife and brandished it. "Stay back!"

One brute snorted. A scarred thug spat. A third produced a much more wicked-looking knife. They moved closer. "Ten quid is ten quid," one of them said.

Nixon looked wildly around. There was no escape. He twisted around, and before anyone realized what he was about, he stood poised on the parapet. "There's always another way," he said. He turned and dived gracefully off the bridge.

They heard a thump and a splash and some shouting. Lily and George rushed to look down, pressing against the stone barrier, but all they could see was a barge passing under the bridge and men on it shouting as they peered into the water.

"Can you see him?" Lily shook her head.

"He can't have gotten away, not with all these people around, surely," George said.

A couple of rivermen rowed their boats out. They circled the area, probing the water with their long hooks while barge men shouted directions.

Lily glanced back to where Rose was comforting Lavinia. The girl was only fourteen. Lily shuddered, imagining what might have happened. Nixon needed to be caught and brought to trial.

There was a shout from the river. They all rushed to look. One of the rivermen had caught something. He hauled it up. A dripping body in a dirty yellow waistcoat.

"Still breathin'?" one of George's ragged gallants shouted.

The riverman gave him a thumbs-down and shook his head. "Hit the barge as it was comin' under the bridge," he yelled up. "Smashed his head in." He lifted Nixon's head by the hair and even from that distance they could see the bloody gash in his scalp.

George looked at Lily. "Brings new meaning to 'look before you leap,' doesn't it?"

Lily stared down at the thing that had been Nixon. He couldn't hurt anyone now. She felt shaky and a bit sick. Justice had been done, and by his own hand.

George fished about in her reticule, and, robbing Lily and Rose, managed to dig up seven half crowns. She gave a half crown to each man in her collection of thugs, and when one was inclined to argue, she said boldly, "You're lucky to get this much. You were supposed to catch him, not let him disappear into the Thames. But if you don't want my money—"

"I want it," he growled, and held out a dirty paw.

The show over, the crowd slowly dissipated. Lily turned to Lavinia. "What happened? What were you doing with Mr. Nixon?"

Lavinia started sobbing again and between sobs blurted

out an involved tale involving messages and secret assigna-
tions and declarations of love. Miss Mallard had learned of
Nixon's covert attentions, and because Lavinia's parents
lived abroad, she'd been sent to stay with her godmother in
London. But she'd managed to get a message to Nixon.
He'd followed her to London, but when he'd proposed a
runaway match, she'd changed her mind.

"You've had a lucky escape. He's a ruthless man and
was only after your money," Lily said severely. "Now, don't
cry. You're safe now. We'll take you home. Where does
your godmother live?"

Lavinia gave them the address. They hired a hackney
and, promising to come and see her the next day and bring
her to have tea with Emm, who was her former teacher,
they left her to deal with her very shocked godmother, who
had imagined her still in bed.

"Poor child," Lily said as they drove away.

"Little fool," George said. "She's fourteen. What's a
schoolgirl doing letting a grown man chase after her?"

Rose said nothing. She was very quiet.

Lily glanced out the window and saw where they were.
"Stop," she called to the driver. "Turn around, please."

"What are you doing?" Rose asked. "You surely don't
want to go back to light candles now, do you?"

"No, it's spoiled for today," Lily said. "But Sylvia lives
down that street. Turn right," she called to the cabbie.

"*Sylvia?*"

"Her cousin has just died. We saw it. We are implicated
in his death."

"No, he chose to—"

"It's all right, I don't feel in the slightest bit guilty about
it. To be honest, it's a neater ending than I'd hoped for. And
breaking the news to Sylvia will somehow finish it off for
me, once and for all."

Rose shrugged. "Go ahead, then."

But when they got to Sylvia's house they found her in the
street, supervising the loading of a large mound of luggage
onto an antiquated traveling coach.

They piled out of the hackney.

"What are you doing here?" Sylvia said rudely when she saw Lily. "I thought you said you never wanted to see or speak to me again."

"Sylvia, we've brought you some bad news. I think we should go inside."

"Do you indeed, Miss Bossy?" Sylvia said. "Well, I don't want to. I'm leaving that ghastly house and not coming back."

"You're returning to the country?"

"Lord, no!" Sylvia gave a brittle laugh. "If you must know, I'm leaving my husband. I'm going to live with Victor in Paris."

"Your cousin, Victor?"

"Who else? You didn't know, did you, Lily dear, that Victor and I are in love, and have been for ages. Yes, I helped him trick you, little dummy that you are. That inheritance of yours is wasted on you. Still, we've hatched another plan and Victor is even now securing our future income with another useless little heiress."

"If you mean he tried to abduct Lavinia Fortescue-Brown, he failed."

Sylvia gasped. "How did you know?"

"We saw it happen. And he didn't just fail, he was killed while trying to escape," Rose said. "He dived into the Thames and . . . died."

Sylvia looked from Rose to Lily and back. "I don't believe you. Victor can swim like a fish. I don't know how you found out about silly little Lavvy Fortescue-Brown—I suppose the wretched chit left someone a note—they always do"—she bared her teeth at Lily—"unless they can't." She laughed nastily. "You're too late to ruin my life again. Victor and his little pigeon will be halfway to the border by now."

"Ruin your life?" Lily was stunned by the accusation. "You're the one who tried to ruin my life. What did I ever do to you?"

Sylvia sneered. "Apart from having the fortune we needed? I hate you, Lily Rutherford—and you, Rose Rutherford." She looked at George. "And you, whoever you are.

But I especially hate you, Lily. At school nobody wanted to be friends with me—"

"Hard to understand why," George said.

"But they all loved you! Why? You're stupid and you're fat and you're not even pretty, but even so, everyone in that school loved you. And then you made me your friend, you—the dumbest girl in the school! So I would look stupid too!"

Lily was staggered. "You hate me because I tried to be friends with you?"

"Not only that. Because of you, I was expelled from Mallard's. Because of you, I was forced to marry a *miserly old man who I despise*!" She shouted the last bit to the upper stories of her house. A curtain twitched. The figure of a man stood behind it. Sylvia really was burning her boats.

"But I had *nothing* to do with you being expelled," Lily persisted.

"You did! I borrowed that tatty old painted locket of yours and someone found it in my drawer and claimed I'd stolen it."

"Along with a hoard of other people's jewelry that you just happened to have as well," Rose said.

Lily added, "That gold locket contained my only portrait of my mother. It was precious to me."

"All you girls had too much of everything. I had *nothing*!" Sylvia flashed.

"I think your coach is ready to leave," George interrupted. She stepped forward and opened the door.

Sylvia flounced into the coach. "Good-bye, Rutherfords, and good riddance. Think of me when you're rotting in London fogs and Victor and I are living it up in style in Paris."

"But Victor is—" Lily began.

"Leave it, little sister," Rose said. "She doesn't want to know, and to be honest, we'll all be better off if she's gone."

"But she conspired with her cousin to kidnap me. Lavinia too, I'm sure. She should be punished!" Lily started forward, with some vague idea of stopping Sylvia.

Rose held her arm. "She will be punished. Think about what she's doing. She's leaving everything behind her to meet up with a man who won't be there. She'll be alone in France, with no money, no support, and no friends. She can't ever come back to England—if she does, she'll be arrested, and I don't imagine her husband will lift a finger to help her."

Considering that, Lily almost felt sorry for Sylvia. Almost.

The laden old coach trundled away. Lily watched it go, still a little dazed by the savagery of Sylvia's attack and the hatred she'd nurtured for so long.

"Poisonous little flower, isn't she," George commented as the coach turned the corner and disappeared from sight. "I don't think even the French deserve her. Now, isn't it time for lunch? Violence and vitriol always give me an appetite."

LILY TOOK OUT THE KEY TO GALBRAITH HOUSE AND handed it to her husband. "I thought, for the first time . . ." She was dancing on her toes, excited to show him what she'd done with their new home, and a little bit nervous. What if he didn't like it? She knew he'd left here when he was a child, and that he'd never been very happy here, but men generally didn't like change.

He took the key from her and inserted it in the lock. The door opened soundlessly.

"If there's anything you don't—Edward, wh—?" She gave a squeak of surprise as he lifted her off her feet. It turned into a giggle. "What are you doing?"

"Carrying my bride across the threshold, of course." He kissed her, then set her back on her feet. "Tomorrow we'll finalize the staff."

"We? You mean both of us?"

"Yes, Atkins, my man of business, has prepared a list of suitable applicants and he's arranged for them to call here in the morning. Of course, if you don't want to help me choose . . ."

"I want to. Only . . ." She bit her lip.

"You're thinking of the list, and having to sort through character references."

She nodded.

"I'll be there, but in any case, the first staff member we'll decide on is your confidential secretary."

"A confidential secretary? For me?" It sounded rather intimidating. On the other hand, she couldn't go running to Emm and Rose for everything.

"Yes, I've arranged for her to come first thing in the morning."

"*Her?* You mean a *female* secretary?" She'd never heard of such a thing. Every secretary she knew of was male.

He nodded. "I thought you'd be more comfortable with a female. I learned of a lady—the widow of a soldier I knew—who has two little boys and a mother to support. She wouldn't live in, of course. Her mother would care for the children while she's at work." He looked down at Lily. "But if you don't like her, we'll find someone else."

"I'm sure she'll be perfect. It's a wonderful idea, Edward, thank you." Lily flung her arms around him and kissed him, moved by his thoughtfulness and sensitivity. It was the perfect solution to her problem, and it was just like Edward to present it in such a matter-of-fact way.

"Now, let's have a look at this house." He glanced around. "It looks—"

Lily put a hand over his mouth. "Don't say anything. Not until you've seen it all."

His mouth quirked with amusement, but he kept it shut. She led him through room after room, explaining all the changes she'd made. "Now that gas has been fitted throughout, you'll find it much lighter and more pleasant at night than when you were a child. Aren't the light fittings elegant? No, don't say anything."

She showed him the reception rooms and the library, the only room that was almost entirely unchanged. "I had all the books taken down and dusted, the shelves polished, the furniture repaired where necessary and the walls painted. Nothing else. Except for the gas lighting." She eyed him anxiously. Galbraith men loved their libraries.

He made a slow tour of the library, then turned to her with a smile. "It's perfect."

They went upstairs. "This is my bedroom." She threw open the door and stepped back. Edward admired the new cream silk wallpaper, the new curtains and the elegant new furniture—not nearly as heavy and oppressive as what had been there before. "I've replaced most of the furniture in the house," she admitted.

"I noticed all that ghastly Egyptian stuff has gone. It frightened me to death as a child. This is all very nice." He strolled toward the connecting door. "I suppose this is my room."

"Mmm."

He opened the door. Lily waited with bated breath as he examined every item in the room: the wardrobe, the tall chest of drawers, the cheval glass, the comfortable leather armchair, the elegant small table where he could write his endless letters . . .

He didn't say a thing, just nodded thoughtfully and with apparent approval.

She gave a surreptitious sigh of relief. He hadn't noticed. "And now I want to show you the upstairs." She took his arm and tugged him toward the door.

He didn't move. "There's something missing."

"Really?" she exclaimed in surprise. Hoping she wasn't overdoing it.

"Yes, really. A small matter of a missing bed."

Lily widened her eyes. "Good heavens, you're right. I didn't notice. The men must have forgotten. Or maybe it wasn't finished. Yes, that will be it. Your bed isn't yet finished."

He looked down at her, his eyes dancing with amusement. "I suppose until it arrives, I'll have to share your bed."

"Oh, dear." She tried to look concerned. "You won't mind, will you?"

He laughed. "You, Madam Wife, are a minx. I expect that missing bed of mine will turn up eventually."

She gave an innocent shrug. "In a year or two, at least." He kissed her and when she had breath to continue, she added, "Possibly more."

She showed him the rest of the house, but when they

came to the attic stairs, he paused. "I remember this place."
He glanced at her. "I was never very happy here.

"I've changed it quite a bit." She took his hand and led
him up the stairs.

He took two steps in and stopped. The gray walls were
now a soft yellow. The low line of cupboards was painted
blue, and the molded edging painted bright red. The book-
shelves were new. The floor had been varnished and waxed,
so the room smelled of beeswax instead of dust, and several
large, colorful fluffy rugs were scattered over it. In the corner was a French enamel stove.

He examined it curiously.

"Miss Chance, my dressmaker, has this kind of stove in
her shop. They keep her rooms lovely and warm, and are
clean and safe to use."

"This room was always so cold. And so bare and dull—
and grim. Now"—he glanced around with a smile—"I
could almost envy the children who will play here—our
children, God willing." He walked to the angled window in
the roof and pushed it open. He pulled a stool forward.
"Stand on this. I want to show you my childhood kingdom."

With one arm wrapped firmly around her waist, he
pointed out the silhouettes and rooftop lands he'd imagined, explaining what they'd been to a solitary small boy,
and where his imaginary friends and enemies—and several
monsters—had lived. She leaned against him, aching for
the lonely little boy he'd been.

He glanced at her and caught her blinking back tears.
He pulled her against him. "Don't weep for the past, my
love. Like the shabby, outworn furnishings of this place, it's
gone to dust. What you've done to this room"—he made a
sweeping gesture—"this whole house, is truly wonderful,
but it's nothing compared with how you've transformed
my life."

He linked both arms around her waist and looked down
at her. "You've given me back my home—and I'm not
talking about any building, but home in every sense of the
word. You restored me to my place and my people, opened
up my heart again and showed me the road to a future I

didn't dream was possible." His deep voice was ragged with emotion. His grip on her tightened.

"For the past decade and more, I've lived a kind of half-life. It was an existence, not a life, with no meaning and no purpose except not to feel, not to hope, and not to love." His expression was solemn, but his eyes blazed with a light that took her breath away. "You are my hope and my home. You're my future and my endless, eternal love. With all my heart, I thank you."

"Oh, Edward." Lily gave a happy sigh, wound her arms around his neck and lifted her face to receive his kiss.

Epilogue

❦

"I am the happiest creature in the world."
—JANE AUSTEN, *PRIDE AND PREJUDICE*

IT WAS THE FIRST BALL IN A GENERATION TO BE HELD AT Shields, and all the county was there, along with half the ton of London. Guests had been arriving all week, and from early afternoon carriages had been bowling down the tree-lined driveway.

Against all predictions, the day had dawned clear and sunny and had mellowed into a perfect spring evening, the air warm with the promise of summer and fragrant with the scent of a thousand blooms. And that of a roasting oxen, three sheep, dozens of loaves of bread and a bonfire.

It wasn't only the ton who'd come for the party. Old Lord Galbraith was determined to welcome his grandson and heir back to Shields after a ten-year absence—and the people of the estate were celebrating with him.

Much loved was the young master who'd grown up here along with their own lads. His sweet little bride was no less beloved, despite being a newcomer. They knew who was responsible for bringing their lad home.

The old house glowed with life and laughter, pretty dresses and sparkling jewels catching the light of hundreds of candles. Outside, blazing torches lined the driveway and entrance to the house, while the garden and the trees surrounding it glittered with hundreds of tiny lanterns, like fireflies or fairy lights in the velvety dark night.

A night for magic, everyone agreed.

In the flower-bedecked ballroom an orchestra played cotillions, country dances, Scotch reels and the Sir Roger de Coverley for the older generation, quadrilles and dashing waltzes for the younger ones.

Out the back behind the barn an enormous bonfire blazed, and a quartet of fiddlers played lively tunes while the estate workers, dressed in their best, danced and twirled and romped to their hearts' content.

Inside, champagne and other fine wines were served; outside beer and cider flowed, compliments of old Lord Galbraith, along with other less clearly defined brews brought by the villagers and passed around in flasks.

As the night went on, the distinction between workers and the gentry began to blur. Ned Galbraith and his pretty wife divided their time between the two groups, greeting villagers and gentry with equal pleasure, and soon others of the ton were venturing outside to dance by firelight—and some to slip into the shadows to taste more forbidden delights.

Ned watched the dancing, his arm around Lily's waist. They'd danced the last four dances and Lily was puffed. "It's a grand night," he said softly. "Grandfather is ready to burst with pleasure."

"Not just Grandfather, everyone's so happy that you've come home."

"You don't mind?"

"Mind what?"

"That we're going to make our principal home here."

"No, of course not, I love it here, Edward. Surely you knew that."

"But you put so much work into refurbishing the London house."

Lily laughed. "We'll use it, don't worry. I'll want to spend quite a bit of time in London, at least until my sister and George find husbands."

He chuckled and pointed to a slender figure crouched over a pen by the barn. She was flanked by a tall, shaggy Irish wolfhound who was sniffing the contents of the pen cautiously. "That might be some time. George is far more interested in those puppies than in any man here."

Lily smiled. "As long as she's happy, does it really matter whether she marries or not?"

His arm tightened around her. "I never wanted to marry, either, but my marriage has brought me more happiness than I ever imagined possible." He bent and kissed her. "And it began so unpromisingly."

"Oh? Did it?"

"Yes, there was a scandal, you see."

"How shocking."

"It was. And it created a most scandalous precedent."

She gave him a puzzled look. "How do you mean?"

"This bride of mine, she has the shocking habit of seducing me at every opportunity."

"How dreadful," she said demurely. "I wonder you can bear it."

"I can't. Do you see that?" He indicated a young couple disappearing into the shadows. "Making love under an oak tree on a warm evening in late spring is an ancient tradition in these parts. It's supposed to bring extreme good fortune."

She laughed, "To whom, pray?"

"To me, of course." He gave her a mock leer. "Can I interest you in an old Shields tradition, pretty lady?" And without waiting for her response he swept her up into his arms and carried her, laughing, into the darkness, to the cheers of those watching.

Lily wrapped her arms around his neck and kissed him, her heart full to bursting. She thought of what her father had said, all those years ago, that no man would want her. She might not deserve such happiness, but oh, Papa, she was going to seize it—and this beautiful, generous, loving man—with both hands. And never let go.

ABOUT THE AUTHOR

Anne Gracie is the award-winning author of the Chance Sisters Romances, which include *The Summer Bride*, *The Spring Bride*, *The Winter Bride* and *The Autumn Bride*, and the first book in the Marriage of Convenience Romance series, *Marry in Haste*. She spent her childhood and youth on the move. The gypsy life taught her that humor and love are universal languages and that favorite books can take you home, wherever you are. Anne started her first novel while backpacking solo around the world, writing by hand in notebooks. Since then, her books have been translated into more than sixteen languages, and include Japanese manga editions. As well as writing, Anne promotes adult literacy, flings balls for her dog, enjoys her tangled garden and keeps bees. Visit her online at annegracie.com.

Ready to find
your next great read?

Let us help.

Visit prh.com/nextread

Penguin
Random
House